Three women meet at a crossroads in their lives, each searching for new ways to grow—and find in each other the courage to take chances and embrace the future.

Roz is a woman of independent means who thought love was behind her, but when romance takes her by surprise, she won't allow anything to keep her from her second chance at happiness.

Second in a new trilogy from the #1 *New York Times* bestselling author.

Dear Reader:

When spring slides toward summer, and the flood of color from my azaleas has faded, the heavy heads of my peonies have given way to a dance of daylilies, my flower beds are approaching peak. I like mixed gardens, cottage gardens, shade gardens, herb gardens, sunny cutting gardens. I have nothing formal—formality wouldn't work for me, or my land. I live on a rocky hillside, with rough, uneven ground, but love finds a way. And I love flowers.

I have a long, long stream of raised beds behind my house, and more lining the land down my long front slope. They're a lot of work to maintain, and a great joy for me. In summer, I have purple floods of centaurea, feathery red heads of monarda, cheery yellow petals of coreopsis, pools of sage, and oceans of black-eyed Susans. The columbine and coralbells are done for the season, but there's always something new budding up or bursting out. Veronica, coneflowers, verbena, garden phlox, nasturtium. At a recent trip to a garden center, my son commented that I probably had everything in the place already.

Because I rarely see a plant I can resist, there's always something spilling or spearing or spreading.

So are the weeds I hunt out and destroy like a soldier on an endless mission.

In the shade, my astilbes are fanning their soft plumes, and my hostas are islands of soothing green. The deer love the hostas, and I love the deer. But that doesn't stop me from warding them off. I pour bags of dried blood and spray gallons of vile-smelling deer repellent annually. And have been known to run out of the house waving my arms like a madwoman if I spot a deer snacking on my dianthus or morning glories. I have dogs, but they don't seem to be interested in guarding my flowers against Bambi.

Take a walk in the garden. Pull a weed, smell a flower. See if it doesn't make you smile.

Number-one bestselling author Nora Roberts presents the second novel of her In the Garden trilogy, as three women must discover the secrets from the past contained within their historic home . . .

A Harper has always lived at Harper House, the centuries-old mansion just outside of Memphis. And for as long as anyone alive remembers, the ghostly Harper Bride has walked the halls, singing lullabies at night . . .

At forty-seven, Rosalind Harper is a woman whose experiences have made her strong enough to bend without breaking—and weather any storm. A widow with three grown sons, she survived a disastrous second marriage and built her In the Garden nursery from the ground up. Through the years, In the Garden has become more than just a thriving business—it is a symbol of hope and independence to Roz, and to the two women she shares it with. Newlywed Stella and new mother Hayley are the sisters of her heart, and together, the three of them are the future of In the Garden.

But now the future is under attack, and Roz knows they can't fight this battle alone. Hired to investigate Roz's Harper ancestors, Dr. Mitchell Carnegie finds himself just as intrigued with Roz herself. And as they begin to unravel the puzzle of the Harper Bride's identity, Roz is shocked to find herself falling for the fascinating genealogist. Now it is a desperate race to discover the truth before the unpredictable apparition lashes out at the one woman who can help her rest in peace . . .

"Roberts shines."
—*Publishers Weekly*

Turn the page for a complete list of titles by Nora Roberts and J. D. Robb from The Berkley Publishing Group . . .

NORA ROBERTS

BLACK ROSE

JOVE BOOKS, NEW YORK

THE BERKLEY PUBLISHING GROUP
Published by the Penguin Group
Penguin Group (USA) Inc.
375 Hudson Street, New York, New York 10014, USA
Penguin Group (Canada), 10 Alcorn Avenue, Toronto, Ontario M4V 3B2, Canada
(a division of Pearson Penguin Canada Inc.)
Penguin Books Ltd., 80 Strand, London WC2R 0RL, England
Penguin Group Ireland, 25 St. Stephen's Green, Dublin 2, Ireland (a division of Penguin Books Ltd.)
Penguin Group (Australia), 250 Camberwell Road, Camberwell, Victoria 3124, Australia
(a division of Pearson Australia Group Pty. Ltd.)
Penguin Books India Pvt. Ltd., 11 Community Centre, Panchsheel Park, New Delhi—110 017, India
Penguin Group (NZ), Cnr. Airborne and Rosedale Roads, Albany, Auckland 1310, New Zealand
(a division of Pearson New Zealand Ltd.)
Penguin Books (South Africa) (Pty.) Ltd., 24 Sturdee Avenue, Rosebank, Johannesburg 2196,
South Africa

Penguin Books Ltd., Registered Offices: 80 Strand, London WC2R 0RL, England

This is a work of fiction. Names, characters, places, and incidents either are the product of the author's imagination or are used fictitiously, and any resemblance to actual persons, living or dead, business establishments, events, or locales is entirely coincidental.

BLACK ROSE

A Jove Book / published by arrangement with the author.

PRINTING HISTORY
Jove mass-market edition / June 2005

Copyright © 2005 by Nora Roberts.
Excerpt from *Red Lily* © 2005 by Nora Roberts.
Cover design by Steven Ferlauto.
Cover illustration by Yuan Lee.

ISBN: 0-515-13865-7

JOVE®
Jove books are published by the Berkley Publishing Group,
a division of Penguin Group (USA) Inc.,
375 Hudson Street, New York, New York 10014.
JOVE is a registered trademark of Penguin Group (USA) Inc.
The "J" design is a trademark belonging to Penguin Group (USA) Inc.

PRINTED IN THE UNITED STATES OF AMERICA

10 9 8 7 6 5 4 3 2 1

For Stacie
It's wise for a mother to love the woman her son loves.
But it's a lovely gift to like the woman
who becomes your daughter.
Thanks for the gift.

A stock plant is grown purely to provide cutting material. It can be encouraged to produce the best type of growth for cuttings while plants that are grown for garden display can be left untouched.

AMERICAN HORTICULTURE SOCIETY
PLANT PROPAGATION

If you would know secrets, look for them in grief or pleasure.

GEORGE HERBERT

PROLOGUE

Memphis, Tennessee
December 1892

SHE DRESSED CAREFULLY, ATTENDING TO THE DETAILS
of her appearance as she hadn't done for months. Her personal maid had run off weeks before, and she had neither the wit nor the will to hire another. So she spent an hour with the curling rods herself—as she had in the years before she'd been kept so lavishly—meticulously coiling and arranging her freshly rinsed hair.

It had lost its bright gold luster over the long, bleary autumn, but she knew what lotions and potions would bring back its shine, what pots of paint to select to put false color in her cheeks, on her lips.

She knew all the tricks of the trade. How else could she have caught the eye of a man like Reginald Harper? How else had she seduced him into making her his mistress?

She would use them again, all of them, Amelia thought, to seduce him once more, and to urge him to do everything that must be done.

He hadn't come, in all this time, in all these months, he hadn't come to her. So she'd been forced to send notes to his businesses, begging him to come, only to be ignored.

Ignored after all she had done, all she had been, all she had lost.

What choice had she had but to send more notes, and to his home? To the grand Harper House where his pale wife reigned. Where a mistress could never walk.

Hadn't she given him all he could ask, all he could want? She'd traded her body for the comfort of this house, the convenience of servants, for the baubles, like the pearl drops she fixed on her ears now.

Small prices to pay for a man of his stature and wealth, and such had been the limits of her ambitions once. A man only, and what he could give her. But he'd given her more than either of them had bargained for. The loss of it was more than she could bear.

Why had he not come to comfort her? To grieve with her?

Had she complained, ever? Had she ever turned him from her bed? Or mentioned even once the other women he kept?

She had given him her youth, and her beauty. And, it seemed, her health.

And he would desert her now? Turn away from her *now*?

They said the baby had been dead at birth. Stillborn, they said. A stillborn girl child that had perished inside her. But . . . but . . .

Hadn't she felt it move? Felt it kick, and grow vital under her heart? In her heart. This child she hadn't wanted who had become her world. Her life. The son she grew inside her.

The son, the son, she thought now as her fingers plucked at the buttons of her gown, as her painted lips formed the words over and over.

She'd heard him cry. Yes, yes, she was sure of it. Sometimes she heard him cry still, in the night, crying for her to come and soothe him.

But when she went to the nursery, looked in the crib, it was empty. Like her womb was empty.

They said she was mad. Oh, she heard what servants she had left whispering, she saw the way they looked at her. But she wasn't mad.

Wasn't mad, wasn't mad, she told herself as she paced the bedroom she'd once treated like a palace of sensuality.

Now the linens were rarely changed, and the drapes always drawn tight to block out the city. And things went missing. Her servants were thieves. Oh, she knew they were thieves and scoundrels. And spies.

They watched her, and they whispered.

One night they would kill her in her bed. One night.

She couldn't sleep for the fear of it. Couldn't sleep for the cries of her son inside her head. Calling her. Calling her.

But she'd gone to the voodoo queen, she reminded herself. Gone to her for protection, and knowledge. She'd paid for both with the ruby bracelet Reginald had once given her. The stones shaped like bloody hearts against the icy glitter of diamonds.

She'd paid for the gris-gris she kept under her pillow, and in a silk bag over her heart. She'd paid, and dearly, for the raising spell. A spell that had failed.

Because her child lived. This was the knowledge the voodoo queen had given her, and it was worth more than ten thousand rubies.

Her child lived, he lived, and now he must be found. He must be brought back to her, where he belonged.

Reginald must find him, must pay whatever needed to be paid.

Careful, careful, she warned herself as she felt the scream beating at her throat. He would only believe her if she remained calm. He would only heed her if she were beautiful.

Beauty seduced men. With beauty and charm, a woman could have whatever she wanted.

She turned to the mirror and saw what she needed to see. Beauty, charm, grace. She didn't see that the red gown sagged at the breasts, bagged at the hips, and turned her pale skin a sallow yellow. The mirror reflected the tumbling tangle of curls, the overbright eyes, and the harshly rouged cheeks, but her eyes, Amelia's eyes, saw what she had once been.

Young and beautiful, desirable and sly.

So she went downstairs to wait for her lover, and under her breath, she sang.

"Lavender's blue, dilly, dilly. Lavender's green."

In the parlor a fire was burning, and the gaslight was lit. So the servants would be careful, too, she thought with a tight smile. They knew the master was expected, and the master held the purse strings.

No matter, she would tell Reginald they needed to go, all of them, and be replaced.

And she wanted a nursemaid hired for her son, for James, when he was returned to her. An Irish girl, she thought. They were cheerful around babies, she believed. She wanted a cheerful nursery for her James.

Though she eyed the whiskey on the sideboard, she poured a small glass of wine instead. And settled down to wait.

Her nerves began to fray as the hour grew late. She had a second glass of wine, then a third. And when she saw through the window his carriage pull up, she forgot to be careful and calm and flew to the door herself.

"Reginald. Reginald." Her grief and despair sprang out of her like snakes, hissing and coiling. She threw herself at him.

"Control yourself, Amelia." His hands closed over her bony shoulders, nudged her back. "What will the neighbors say?"

He shut the door quickly, then with one steely look had a hovering servant rushing forward to take his hat and walking stick.

"I don't care! Oh, why haven't you come sooner? I've needed you so. Did you get my letters? The servants, the servants lie. They didn't post them. I'm a prisoner here."

"Don't be ridiculous." A momentary disgust flickered over his face as he evaded her next attempt at an embrace. "We agreed you'd never attempt to contact me at my home, Amelia."

"You didn't come. I've been alone. I—"

"I've been occupied. Come now. Sit. Compose yourself."

Still, she clung to his arm as he led her into the parlor. "Reginald. The baby. The baby."

"Yes, yes." He disentangled himself, nudged her into a chair. "It's unfortunate," he said as he moved to the sideboard to pour himself a whiskey. "The doctor said there was nothing to be done, and you needed rest and quiet. I've heard you've been unwell."

"Lies. It's all a lie."

He turned to her, his gaze taking in her face, the ill-fitting gown. "I can see for myself you're not well, Amelia. I think perhaps some sea air. It would do you good." His smile was cool as he leaned back against the mantel. "How would you like an ocean crossing? I think it would be just the thing to calm your nerves and bring you back to health."

"I want my *child*. He's all I need."

"The child is gone."

"No, no, no." She sprang up to clutch at him again. "They stole him. He lives, Reginald. Our child lives. The doctor, the midwife, they planned it. I know it all now, I understand it all. You must go to the police, Reginald. They'll listen to you. You must pay whatever ransom they demand."

"This is madness, Amelia." He pried her hand from his lapel, then brushed at the creases her fingers had caused in the material. "I'll certainly not go to the police."

"Then I will. Tomorrow I'll go to the authorities."

The cold smile faded until his face was hard as stone. "You will do nothing of the kind. You will have a cruise to Europe, and ten thousand dollars to assist you in settling in England. They will be my parting gifts to you."

"Parting?" She groped for the arm of a chair, melted into it as her legs gave way. "You—you would leave me now?"

"There can be nothing more between us. I'll see to it that you're well set, and I believe you'll regain your health with a sea voyage. In London you're bound to find another protector."

"How can I go to London when my son—"

"You will go," he interrupted, then sipped his drink. "Or I will give you nothing. You have no son. You have nothing but what I deem to give you. This house and everything in it, the clothes on your back, the jewels you wear are mine. You'd be wise to remember how easily I can take it all away."

"Take it away," she whispered, and something in his face, something in her fractured mind gave her truth. "You want to get rid of me because . . . you know. It's you who've taken the baby."

He finished his drink as he studied her. Then set the empty glass on the mantel. "Do you think I'd allow a creature like you to raise my son?"

"My son!" She sprang up again, hands curled like claws.

The slap stopped her. In the two years he had been her protector, he had never raised a hand to her.

"Listen to me now, and carefully. I will not have my son known as a bastard, one born of a whore. He will be raised at Harper House, as my legitimate heir."

"Your wife—"

"Does what she is told. As will you, Amelia."

"I'll go to the police."

"And tell them what? The doctor and midwife who attended you will attest that you delivered a stillborn girl, while others will attest my wife delivered a healthy boy. Your reputation, Amelia, will not stand to mine, or theirs. Your own servants will swear to it, and to the fact that you've been ill, and behaving strangely."

"How can you do this?"

"I need a son. Do you think I selected you out of affection? You're young, healthy—or were. You were paid, and paid well for your services. You will be recompensed for this one."

"You won't keep him from me. He's mine."

"Nothing is yours but what I allow you. You would have rid yourself of him, had you been given the opportunity. You'll come nowhere near him, now or ever. You will make the crossing in three weeks. A deposit of ten thousand dollars will be put in your account. Until that time your bills will continue to come to me for payment. It's all you'll get."

"I'll kill you!" she shouted when he started out of the parlor.

At this, for the first time since he'd arrived, he looked amused. "You're pathetic. Whores generally are. Be assured of this, if you come near me or mine, Amelia, I will have you arrested, and put in an asylum for the criminally insane." He gestured for the servant to bring his hat and stick. "You wouldn't find it to your taste."

She screamed, tearing at her hair and her gown; she screamed until blood ran from her flesh from her own nails.

When her mind snapped, she walked up the stairs in her tattered gown, humming a lullaby.

ONE

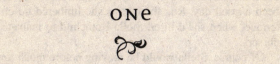

Harper House
December 2004

DAWN, THE AWAKENING PROMISE OF IT, WAS HER FA-
vorite time to run. The running itself was just something
that had to be done, three days a week, like any other chore
or responsibility. Rosalind Harper did what had to be done.

She ran for her health. A woman who'd just had—
she could hardly say "celebrated" at this stage of her life—
her forty-seventh birthday had to mind her health. She ran
to keep strong, as she desired and needed strength. And she
ran for vanity. Her body would never again be what it had
been at twenty, or even thirty, but, by God, it would be the
best body she could manage at forty-seven.

She had no husband, no lover, but she did have an image to uphold. She was a Harper, and Harpers had their
pride.

But, Jesus, maintenance was a bitch.

Wearing sweats against the dawn chill, she slipped out
of her bedroom by the terrace door. The house was sleeping
still. Her house that had been too empty was now occupied
again, and rarely completely quiet any longer.

There was David, her surrogate son, who kept her house in order, kept her entertained when she needed entertaining, and stayed out of her way when she needed solitude.

No one knew her moods quite like David.

And there was Stella, and her two precious boys. It had been a good day, Roz thought as she limbered up on the terrace, when she'd hired Stella Rothchild to manage her nursery.

Of course, Stella would be moving before much longer and taking those sweet boys with her. Still, once she was married to Logan—and wasn't that a fine match—they'd only be a few miles away.

Hayley would still be here, infusing the house with all that youth and energy. It had been another stroke of luck, and a vague and distant family connection, that had Hayley, then six-months pregnant, landing on her doorstep. In Hayley she had the daughter she'd secretly longed for, and the bonus of an honorary grandchild with the darling little Lily.

She hadn't realized how lonely she'd been, Roz thought, until those girls had come along to fill the void. With two of her own three sons moved away, the house had become too big, too quiet. And a part of her dreaded the day when Harper, her firstborn, her rock, would leave the guesthouse a stone's throw from the main.

But that was life. No one knew better than a gardener that life never stayed static. Cycles were necessary, for without them there was no bloom.

She took the stairs down at an easy jog, enjoying the way the early mists shrouded her winter gardens. Look how pretty her lambs ear was with its soft silvery foliage covered in dew. And the birds had yet to bother the bright fruit on her red chokeberry.

Walking to give her muscles time to warm, and to give herself the pleasure of the gardens, she skirted around the side of the house to the front.

She increased to a jog on the way down the drive, a tall, willowy woman with a short, careless cap of black hair. Her eyes, a honeyed whiskey brown, scanned the grounds—the towering magnolias, the delicate dogwoods, the placement of ornamental shrubs, the flood of pansies she'd planted only weeks before, and the beds that would wait a bit longer to break into bloom.

To her mind, there were no grounds in western Tennessee that could compete with Harper House. Just as there was no house that could compare with its dignified elegance.

Out of habit, she turned at the end of the drive, jogged in place to study it in the pearly mists.

It stood grandly, she thought, with its melding of Greek Revival and Gothic styles, the warm yellow stone mellow against the clean white trim. Its double staircase rose up to the balcony wrapping the second level, and served as a crown for the covered entryway on the ground level.

She loved the tall windows, the lacy woodwork on the rail of the third floor, the sheer space of it, and the heritage it stood for.

She had prized it, cared for it, worked for it, since it had come into her hands at her parents' death. She had raised her sons there, and when she'd lost her husband, she'd grieved there.

One day she would pass it to Harper as it had passed to her. And she thanked God for the absolute knowledge that he would tend it and love it just as she did.

What it had cost her was nothing compared with what it gave, even in this single moment, standing at the end of the drive, looking back through the morning mists.

But standing there wasn't going to get her three miles done. She headed west, keeping close to the side of the road, though there'd be little to no traffic this early.

To take her mind off the annoyance of exercise, she started reviewing her list of things to do that day.

She had some good seedlings going for annuals that should be ready to have their seed leaves removed. She needed to check all the seedlings for signs of damping off. Some of the older stock would be ready for pricking off.

And, she remembered, Stella had asked for more amaryllis, more forced-bulb planters, more wreaths and poinsettias for the holiday sales. Hayley could handle the wreaths. The girl had a good hand at crafting.

Then there were the field-grown Christmas trees and hollies to deal with. Thank God she could leave that end to Logan.

She had to check with Harper, to see if he had any more of the Christmas cacti he'd grafted ready to go. She wanted a couple for herself.

She juggled all the nursery business in her mind even as she passed In the Garden. It was tempting—it always was—to veer off the road onto that crushed-stone entryway, to take an indulgent solo tour of what she'd built from the ground up.

Stella had gone all out for the holidays, Roz noted with pleasure, grouping green, pink, white, and red poinsettias into a pool of seasonal color in the front of the low-slung house that served as the entrance to the retail space. She'd hung yet another wreath on the door, tiny white lights around it, and the small white pine she'd had dug from the field stood decorated on the front porch.

White-faced pansies, glossy hollies, hardy sage added more interest and would help ring up those holiday sales.

Resisting temptation, Roz continued down the road.

She had to carve out some time, if not today, then certainly later this week, to finish up her Christmas shopping. Or at least put a bigger dent in it. There were holiday parties to attend, and the one she'd decided to give. It had been awhile since she'd opened the house to entertain in a big way.

The divorce, she admitted, was at least partially to blame for that. She'd hardly felt like hosting parties when she'd felt stupid and stung and more than a bit mortified by her foolish, and mercifully brief, union to a liar and a cheat.

But it was time to put that aside now, she reminded herself, just as she'd put him aside. The fact that Bryce Clerk was back in Memphis made it only more important that she live her life, publically and privately, exactly as she chose.

At the mile-and-a-half mark, a point she judged by an old, lightning-struck hickory, she started back. The thin fog had dampened her hair, her sweatshirt, but her muscles felt warm and loose. It was a bitch, she mused, that everything they said about exercise was true.

She spotted a deer meandering across the road, her coat thickened for winter, her eyes on alert by the intrusion of a human.

You're beautiful, Roz thought, puffing a little on that last half mile. Now, stay the hell out of my gardens. Another note went in her file to give her gardens another treatment of repellant before the deer and her pals decided to come around for a snack.

Roz was just making the turn into the drive when she heard muffled footsteps, then saw the figure coming her way. Even with the mists she had no trouble identifying the other early riser.

They both stopped, jogged in place, and she grinned at her son.

"Up with the worms this morning."

"Thought I'd be up and out early enough to catch you." He scooped a hand through his dark hair. "All that celebrating for Thanksgiving, then your birthday, I figured I'd better work off the excess before Christmas hits."

"You never gain an ounce. It's annoying."

"Feel soft." He rolled his shoulders, then his eyes, whiskey brown like hers, and laughed. "Besides, I gotta keep up with my mama."

He looked like her. There was no denying she'd stamped herself on his face. But when he smiled, she saw his father. "That'll be the day, pal of mine. How far you going?"

"How far'd you?"

"Three miles."

He flashed a grin. "Then I'll do four." He gave her a light pat on the cheek as he passed.

"Should've told him five, just to get his goat." She chuckled, and slowing to a cool-down walk, started down the drive.

The house shimmered out of the mists. She thought: Thank God that's over for another day. And she circled around to go in as she'd left.

The house was still quiet, and lovely. And haunted.

She'd showered and changed for work, and had started down the central stairs that bisected the wings when she heard the first stirrings.

Stella's boys getting ready for school, Lily fussing for her breakfast. Good sounds, Roz thought. Busy, family sounds she'd missed.

Of course, she'd had the house full only a couple weeks earlier, with all her boys home for Thanksgiving and her birthday. Austin and Mason would be back for Christmas. A mother of grown sons couldn't ask for better.

God knew there'd been plenty of times when they were growing up that she'd yearned for some quiet. Just an hour of absolute peace where she had nothing more exciting to do than soak in a hot tub.

Then she'd had too much time on her hands, hadn't she? Too much quiet, too much empty space. So she'd ended up marrying some slick son of a bitch who'd helped himself to her money so he could impress the bimbos he'd cheated on her with.

Spilled milk, Roz reminded herself. And it wasn't constructive to dwell on it.

She walked into the kitchen where David was already whipping something in a bowl, and the seductive fragrance of fresh coffee filled the air.

"Morning, gorgeous. How's my best girl?"

"Up and at 'em anyway." She went to a cupboard for a mug. "How was the date last night?"

"Promising. He likes Grey Goose martinis and John Waters movies. We'll try for a second round this weekend. Sit yourself down. I'm making French toast."

"French toast?" It was a personal weakness. "Damn it, David, I just ran three miles to keep my ass from falling all the way to the back of my knees, then you hit me with French toast."

"You have a beautiful ass, and it's nowhere near the back of your knees."

"Yet," she muttered, but she sat. "I passed Harper at the end of the drive. He finds out what's on the menu, he'll be sniffing at the back door."

"I'm making plenty."

She sipped her coffee while he heated up the skillet.

He was movie-star handsome, only a year older than her own Harper, and one of the delights of her life. As a boy he'd run tame in her house, and now he all but ran it.

"David . . . I caught myself thinking about Bryce twice this morning. What do you think that means?"

"Means you need this French toast," he said while he soaked thick slices of bread in his magic batter. "And you've probably got yourself a case of the mid-holiday blues."

"I kicked him out right before Christmas. I guess that's it."

"And a merry one it was, with that bastard out in the cold. I wish it *had* been cold," he added. "Raining ice and frogs and pestilence."

"I'm going to ask you something I never did while it was going on. Why didn't you ever tell me how much you disliked him?"

"Probably the same reason you didn't tell me how much you disliked that out-of-work actor with the fake Brit accent I thought I was crazy about a few years back. I love you."

"It's a good reason."

He'd started a fire in the little kitchen hearth, so she angled her body toward it, sipped coffee, felt steady and solid.

"You know if you could just age twenty years and go straight, we could live with each other in sin. I think that would be just fine."

"Sugar-pie." He slid the bread into the skillet. "You're the only girl in the world who'd tempt me."

She smiled, and resting her elbow on the table, set her chin on her fist. "Sun's breaking through," she stated. "It's going to be a pretty day."

A PRETTY DAY IN EARLY DECEMBER MEANT A BUSY ONE for a garden center. Roz had so much to do she was grateful she hadn't resisted the breakfast David had heaped on her. She missed lunch.

In her propagation house she had a full table covered with seed trays. She'd already separated out specimens too young for pricking off. And now began the first transplanting with those she deemed ready.

She lined up her containers, the cell packs, the individual pots or peat cubes. It was one of her favorite tasks, even more than sowing, this placing of a strong seedling in the home it would occupy until planting time.

Until planting time, they were all hers.

And this year she was experimenting with her own potting soil. She'd been trying out recipes for more than two years now, and believed she'd found a winner, both for indoor and outdoor use. The outdoor recipe should serve very well for her greenhouse purposes.

From the bag she'd carefully mixed, she filled her containers, testing the moisture, and approved. With care she lifted out the young plants, holding them by their seed leaves. Transplanting, she made certain the soil line on the stem was at the same level it had been in the seed tray, then firmed the soil around the roots with experienced fingers.

She filled pot after pot, labeling as she went and humming absently to the Enya playing gently from the portable CD player she considered essential equipment in a greenhouse.

Using a weak fertilizer solution, she watered them.

Pleased with the progress, she moved through the back opening and into the perennial area. She checked the section—plants recently started from cuttings, those started more than a year before that would be ready for sale in a few months. She watered and tended, then moved to stock plants to take more cuttings. She had a tray of anemones begun when Stella stepped in.

"You've been busy." Stella, with her curling red hair bundled back in a tail, scanned the tables. "Really busy."

"And optimistic. We had a banner season, and I'm expecting we'll have another. If Nature doesn't screw around with us."

"I thought you might want to take a look at the new stock of wreaths. Hayley's worked on them all morning. I think she outdid herself."

"I'll take a look before I leave."

"I let her go early, I hope that's all right. She's still getting used to having Lily with a sitter, even if the sitter is a customer and only a half mile away."

"That's fine." She moved on to the catananche. "You know you don't have to check every little thing with me,

Stella. You've been managing this ship for nearly a year now."

"They were excuses to come back here."

Roz paused, her knife suspended above the plant roots, primed for cutting. "Is there a problem?"

"No. I've been wanting to ask, and I know this is your domain, but I wondered if, when things slow down a bit after the holidays, I can spend some time with the propagation. I'm missing it."

"All right."

Stella's bright blue eyes twinkled when she laughed. "I can see you're worried I'll try to change your routine, organize everything my way. I promise I won't. And I won't get in your way."

"You try, I'll just boot you out."

"Got that."

"Meanwhile, I've been wanting to talk to you. I need you to find me a supplier for good, inexpensive soil bags. One pound, five pound, ten, and twenty-five to start."

"For?" Stella asked as she pulled a notebook out of her back pocket.

"I'm going to start making and selling my own potting soil. I've got mixes I like for indoor and outdoor use, and I want to private-label it."

"That's a great idea. Good profit in that. And customers will like having Rosalind Harper's gardening secrets. There are some considerations, though."

"I thought of them. I'm not going to go hog-wild right off. We'll keep it small." With soil on her hands still, she plucked a bottle of water from a shelf. Then, absently wiping her hand on her shirt, twisted the cap. "I want the staff to learn how to bag, but the recipe's my secret. I'll give you and Harper the ingredients and the amounts, but it doesn't go out to the general staff. For right now we'll set up the procedure in the main storage shed. It takes off, we'll build one for it."

"Government regulations—"

"I've studied on that. We won't be using any pesticides, and I'm keeping the nutrient content to below the regulatory levels." Noting Stella continued to scribble on her pad, Roz took a long drink. "I've applied for the license to manufacture and sell."

"You didn't mention it."

"Don't get your feelings hurt." Roz set the bottle aside, dipped a cutting in rooting medium. "I wasn't sure I'd go on and do the thing, but I wanted the red tape out of the way. It's kind of a pet project of mine I've been playing with for a while now. But I've grown some specimens in these mixes, and so far I like what I see. I got some more going now, and if I keep liking it, we're going for it. So I want an idea how much the bags are going to run us, and the printing. I want classy. I thought you could fiddle around with some logos and such. You're good at that. In the Garden needs to be prominent."

"No question."

"And you know what I'd really like?" She paused for a minute, seeing it in her head. "I'd like brown bags. Something that looks like burlap. Old-fashioned, if you follow me. So we're saying, this is good old-fashioned dirt, southern soil, and I'm thinking I want cottage garden flowers on the bag. Simple flowers."

"That says, this is simple to use, and it'll make your garden simple to grow. I'll get on it."

"I can count on you, can't I, to work out the costs, profits, marketing angles with me?"

"I'm your girl."

"I know you are. I'm going to finish up these cuttings, then take off early myself if nothing's up. I want to get some shopping in."

"Roz, it's already nearly five."

"Five? It can't be five." She held up an arm, turned her

wrist, and frowned at her watch. "Well, shit. Time got away from me again. Tell you what, I'm going to take off at noon tomorrow. If I don't, you hunt me down and push me out."

"No problem. I'd better get back. See you back at the house."

WHEN SHE DID GET HOME, IT WAS TO DISCOVER THE Christmas lights were glinting from the eaves, the wreaths shimmered on all the doors, and candles stood shining in all the windows. The entrance was flanked by two minia-ture pines wrapped in tiny white lights.

She had only to step inside to be surrounded by the holiday.

In the foyer, red ribbon and twinkling lights coiled up the twin banisters, with white poinsettias in Christmas-red pots under the newel posts.

Her great-grandmother's silver bowl was polished to a beam and filled with glossy red apples.

In the parlor a ten-foot Norway spruce—certainly from her own field—ruled the front windows. The mantel held the wooden Santas she'd collected since she'd been pregnant with Harper, with fresh greenery dripping from the ends.

Stella's two sons sat cross-legged on the floor beneath the tree, staring up at it with enormous eyes.

"Isn't it great?" Hayley bounced dark-haired Lily on her hip. "Isn't it awesome?"

"David must've worked like a dog."

"We helped!" The boys jumped up.

"After school we got to help with the lights and every-thing," the youngest, Luke, told her. "And pretty soon we get to help make cookies, and decorate them and everything."

"We even got a tree upstairs." Gavin looked back at the spruce. "It's not as big as this one, 'cause it's for upstairs. We helped David take it up, and we get to decorate it *ourselves.*" Knowing who was the boss of the house, Gavin looked at her for confirmation. "He said."

"Then it must be true."

"He's cooking up some sort of trim-the-tree buffet in the kitchen." Stella walked over to look at the tree from Roz's perspective. "Apparently, we're having a party. He's already given Logan and Harper orders to be here by seven."

"Then I guess I'd better get myself dressed for a party. Hand over that baby first." She reached out, took Lily from Hayley and nuzzled. "Tree that size, it'll take all of us to dress it up. What do you think of your first Christmas tree, little girl?"

"She's already tried to belly-scoot over to it when I put her on the floor. I can't wait to see what she does when she sees it all decked out."

"Then I'd better get a move on." Roz gave Lily a kiss, handed her back. "It's a bit warm yet, but I think we ought to have a fire. And somebody tell David to ice down some champagne. I'll be down shortly."

It had been too long since there were children in the house for Christmas, Roz thought as she hurried upstairs. And damn if having them there didn't make her feel like a kid herself.

two

ROZ TOOK HER HOLIDAY MOOD SHOPPING. THE NUR-
sery could get along without her for half a day. The fact
was, the way Stella managed it, the nursery could get along
without her for a week. If she had the urge, she could take
herself off on her first real vacation in—how long had it
been? Three years, she realized.

But she didn't have the urge.

Home was where she was happiest, so why go to all the
trouble of packing, endure the stress of traveling, just to
end up somewhere else?

She'd taken the boys on a trip every year when they were
growing up. Disney World, the Grand Canyon, Washington,
D.C., Bar Harbor, and so on. Little tastes of the country,
sometimes chosen at whim, sometimes with great planning.

Then they'd taken that three-week vacation in Europe.
Hadn't that been a time?

It had been hard, sometimes frantic, sometimes hysterical, herding three active boys around, but oh, it had been
worth it.

She could remember how Austin had loved the whale-watch cruise in Maine, how Mason had insisted on ordering snails in Paris, and Harper had managed to get himself lost in Adventureland.

She wouldn't trade those memories for anything. And she'd seen a nice chunk of the world herself.

Instead of a vacation, she could concentrate on other things. Maybe it was time to start thinking about adding a little florist shop onto the nursery. Fresh-cut flowers and arrangements. Local delivery. Of course, it would mean another building, more supplies, more employees. But it was something to think about for a year or two down the road.

She'd have to go over some figures, see if the business could handle the outlay.

She'd sunk a great deal of her personal resources into the nursery to get it off the ground. But she'd been ready to gamble. Her priorities had been, always, that her children were safe, secure, and well provided for. And that Harper House remain tended, protected, and in the family.

She'd accomplished that. Though there'd been times it had taken a lot of creative juggling and had caused the occasional sleepless night. Perhaps money hadn't been the terrifying issue for her that it often was for single parents, but it had been an issue.

In the Garden hadn't just been a whim, as some thought. She'd needed fresh income and had bargained, gambled, and finagled to get it.

It didn't matter to Roz if people thought she was rich as Croesus or poor as a church mouse. The fact was she was neither, but she'd built a good life for herself and her children with the resources she'd had at hand.

Now, if she wanted to go just a little crazy playing Santa, she'd earned it.

She burned up the mall, indulging herself to the point that she needed to make two trips out to her car with bags.

Seeing no reason to stop there, she headed to Wal-Mart, intending to plow through the toy department.

As usual, the minute she stepped through the doors she thought of a dozen other things she could probably use. Her basket was half loaded, and she'd stopped in the aisles to exchange greetings with four people she knew before she made it to the toy department.

Five minutes later she was wondering if she'd need a second cart. Struggling to balance a couple of enormous boxes on top of the mound of other purchases, she turned a corner.

And rapped smartly into another cart.

"Sorry. I can't seem to . . . oh. Hi."

It had been weeks since she'd seen Dr. Mitchell Carnegie, the genealogist she'd hired—more or less. There had been a few brief phone conversations, some businesslike e-mails, but only a scatter of face-to-face contacts since the night he'd come to dinner. And had ended up seeing the Harper Bride ghost.

She considered him an interesting man and gave him top marks for not hightailing it after the experience they'd all shared the previous spring.

He had, in her opinion, the credentials she needed, along with the spine and the open mind. Best of all he'd yet to bore her in their discussions of family lineage and the steps necessary to identifying a dead woman.

Just now it looked as if he hadn't shaved in the past few days, so there was a dark stubble toughening his face. His bottle-green eyes appeared both tired and harassed. His hair badly needed a trim.

He was dressed much like the first time she'd met him, in old jeans and rolled-up shirtsleeves. Unlike hers, his basket was empty.

"Help me," he said in the tone of a man dangling from a cliff by a sweaty grip on a shaky limb.

"I'm sorry?"

"Six-year-old girl. Birthday. Desperation."

"Oh." Deciding she liked that warm bourbon voice, even with panic sharpening it, Roz pursed her lips. "What's the connection?"

"Niece. Sister's surprise late baby. She had the decency to have two boys before. I can handle boys."

"Well, is she a girly girl?"

He made a sound, as if the limb had started to crack.

"All right, all right." Roz waved a hand and, abandoning her own cart, turned down the aisle. "You could've saved yourself some stress by just asking her mother."

"My sister's pissed at me because I forgot *her* birthday last month."

"I see."

"Look, I forgot everything last month, including my own name a couple of times. I told you I was finishing some revisions on the book. I was on deadline. For God's sake, she's forty-three. One. Or possibly two." Obviously at wit's end, he scrubbed his hands over his face. "Doesn't your breed stop having birthdays at forty?"

"We may stop counting, Dr. Carnegie, but that doesn't mean we don't expect an appropriate gift on the occasion."

"Loud and clear," he responded, watching her peruse the shelves. "And since you're back to calling me Dr. Carnegie, I'd hazard a guess you're on her side. I sent flowers," he added in an aggrieved tone that had her lips twitching. "Okay, late, but I sent them. Two dozen roses, but does she cut me a break?"

He jammed his hands into his back pockets and scowled at Malibu Barbie. "I couldn't get back to Charlotte for Thanksgiving. Does that make me a demon from hell?"

"It sounds like your sister loves you very much."

"She'll be planning my immediate demise if I don't get this gift today, and have it FedExed tomorrow."

She picked up a doll, set it down again. "Then I assume your niece's birthday is tomorrow, and you waited until the eleventh hour to rush out and find something for her."

He said nothing for a moment, then laid a hand on her shoulder so that she looked over, and up at him. "Rosalind, do you want me to die?"

"I'm afraid I wouldn't feel responsible. But we'll find something, then you can get it wrapped up and shoot it off."

"Wrapped. God almighty, it has to be wrapped?"

"Of course it has to be wrapped. And you have to buy a nice card, something pretty and age-appropriate. Hmm. I like this." She tapped a huge box.

"What is it?"

"It's a house-building toy. See, it has all these modular pieces so you can design and redesign your own doll house, with furnishings. It comes with dolls, and a little dog. Fun, and educational. You hit on two levels."

"Great. Good. Wonderful. I owe you my life."

"Aren't you a little out of your milieu?" she asked when he took the box off the shelf. "You live right in the city. Plenty of shops right there."

"That's the problem. Too many of them. And the malls? They're like a labyrinth of retail hell. I have mall fear. So I thought, hey, Wal-Mart. At least everything's all under one roof. I can get the kid taken care of and get . . . what the hell was it? Laundry soap. Yeah, I need laundry soap and something else, that I wrote down . . ." He dug in his pocket, pulled out a PDA. "Here."

"Well, I'll let you get to it then. Don't forget the wrapping paper, ribbon, a big bow, and a pretty card."

"Hold on, hold on." With the stylus he added the other items. "Bow. You can just buy them ready-made and slap it on, right?"

"That will do, yes. Good luck."

"No. Wait, wait." He shoved the PDA back in his pocket, shifted the box. His green eyes seemed calmer now and focused on her. "I was going to get in touch with you anyway. Are you finished in here?"

"Not quite."

"Good. Let me grab what I need, then I'll meet you at the checkout. I'll help you haul your load out to your car, then take you to lunch."

"It's nearly four. A little late for lunch."

"Oh." He looked absently at his watch to confirm the time. "I think time must warp in places like this so you could actually spend the rest of your natural life wandering aimlessly without realizing it. Anyway. A drink then. I'd really like to have a conversation about the project."

"All right. There's a little place called Rosa's right across the way. I'll meet you there in a half hour."

BUT HE WAS WAITING AT THE CHECKOUT. PATIENTLY, from all appearances. Then insisted on helping her load her bags in her car. He took one look at what was already stacked in the back of her Durango and said, "Holy Mother of God."

"I don't shop often, so when I do I make it count."

"I'll say."

"There are less than three weeks left till Christmas."

"I'll have to ask you to shut up." He hefted the last bag inside. "My car's that way." He gestured vaguely toward their left. "I'll meet you."

"Fine. Thanks for the help."

The way he wandered off made her think he wasn't entirely sure just where he'd parked. She thought he should've plugged the location into that little personal data thingy he had in his pocket. The idea made her chuckle as she drove over to the restaurant.

She didn't mind a certain amount of absentmindedness. To her it simply indicated the person probably had a lot in his head, and it took a little longer to find just what he was after. She'd hadn't hired him out of the blue, after all. She'd researched Mitchell Carnegie and had read or skimmed some of his books. He was good at what he did, he was local, and though he was pricey, he hadn't balked—overmuch—about the prospect of researching and identifying a ghost.

She parked, then walked into the lounge area. Her first thought was to order a glass of iced tea, or some coffee. Then she decided, the hell with that. She deserved a nice glass of wine after such a successful shopping expedition.

While she waited for Mitch, she called the nursery on her cell phone to let them know she wouldn't be back in, unless she was needed.

"Everything's fine here," Hayley told her. "You must be buying out the stores."

"I did. Then I happened to run into Dr. Carnegie at Wal-Mart—"

"Dr. Hottie? How come I never run into hunks at Wal-Mart?"

"Your day will come, I'm sure. In any case, we're going to have a drink here and discuss, I assume, our little project."

"Cool. You ought to spin it out over dinner, Roz."

"It's not a date." But she did pull out her lipstick and slide a little pale coral on her lips. "It's an impromptu meeting. If anything comes up, you can give me a call. I should be heading home within the hour anyway."

"Don't worry about a thing. And, hey, you've both got to eat sometime, somewhere, so why not—"

"Here he comes now, so we'll get started. I'll fill everyone in later. Bye now."

Mitch slipped into the booth across from her. "This was handy, wasn't it? What would you like?"

She ordered a glass of wine, and he coffee, black. Then he flipped open the bar menu and added antipasto. "You've got to need some sustenance after a shopping safari like that. How've you been?"

"Very well, thanks. How about you?"

"Good, now that the book's out of my hair."

"I never asked you what it was about."

"A history and study of Charles-Pierre Baudelaire." He waited a beat, noted her questioning lift of brows. "Nineteenth-century poet. Wild man of Paris—druggie, very controversial, with a life full of drama. He was found guilty of blasphemy and obscenity, squandered his inheritance, translated Poe, wrote dark, intense poetry, and, long after his death from a sexually transmitted disease, is looked on by many to be the poet of modern civilization—and others as being one sick bastard."

She smiled. "And which camp do you pitch your tent in?"

"He was brilliant, and twisted. And believe me, you don't want to get me started, so I'll just say he was a fascinating and frustrating subject to write about."

"Are you happy with the work you did?"

"I am. Happier yet," he said as their drinks were served, "not to be living with Baudelaire day and night."

"It's like that, isn't it, like living with a ghost."

"Nice segue." He toasted her with his coffee. "Let me say, first, I appreciate your patience. I'd hoped to have this book wrapped up weeks ago, but one thing led to another."

"You warned me at the start you wouldn't be available for some time."

"Hadn't expected it to be quite this much time. And I've given quite a bit of thought to your situation. Hard not to after that experience last spring."

"It was a more personal introduction to the Harper Bride than I'd planned."

"You've said she's been . . . subdued," he decided, "since then."

"She still sings to the boys and to Lily. But none of us has seen her since that night. And to be frank, it hasn't been patience so much as being swamped myself. Work, home, a wedding coming up, a new baby in the house. And after that night, it seemed like all of us needed a little break."

"I'd like to get started now, really started, if that works for you."

"I suppose it was fate that we ran into each other like this, because I've been thinking the same thing. What will you need?"

"Everything you've got. Hard data, records, journals, letters, family stories. Nothing's too obscure. I appreciate the family photos you had copied for me. It just helps me immerse, you could say, if I have photos, and letters or diaries written in the hands of the people I'm researching."

"No problem. I'll be happy to load you up with more."

"Some of what I've managed so far—between bouts with Baudelaire—is what we'll call a straight job. Starting to chart the basic family tree, getting a feel for the people and the line. Those are the first steps."

"And at the end of the day, something I'll enjoy having."

"I wonder if there's a place I could work in your house. I'd do the bulk in my apartment, but it might be helpful if I had some space on site. The house plays a vital part in the research, and the results."

"That wouldn't be a problem."

"For the Amelia portion of the project, I'd like a list of names. Anyone who's had any sort of contact with her I'll need to interview."

"All right."

"And the written permission we talked about before, for me to access family records, birth, marriage, death certificates, that sort of thing."

"You'll have it."

"And permission to use the research, and what I pull out of it, in a book."

She nodded. "I'd want manuscript approval."

He smiled at her, charmingly. "You won't get it."

"Well, really—"

"I'll be happy to provide you with a copy, when and if, but you won't have approval." He picked up a short, thick breadstick from the wide glass on the table and offered it to her. "What I find, I find; what I write, I write. And *if* I write a book, sell it, you owe me nothing for the work."

She leaned back, drew air deep. His casual good looks, that somewhat shaggy peat-moss brown hair, the charming smile, the ancient high-tops, all disguised a clever and stubborn man.

It was a shame, she supposed, that she respected stubborn, clever men. "And if you don't?"

"We go back to the original terms we discussed at our first meeting. The first thirty hours are gratis, and after that it's fifty an hour plus expenses. We can have a contract drawn up, spelling it all out."

"I think that would be wise."

When the appetizer was served, Roz declined a second glass of wine, absently selected an olive from the plate. "Won't you need permission from anyone you interview as well, if you decide to publish?"

"I'll take care of that. I want to ask, why haven't you done this before? You've lived in that house your whole life and never dug down to identify a ghost who lives there with you. And, let me add, even after my experience, it's hard to believe that sentence just came out of my mouth."

"I don't know exactly. Maybe I was too busy, or too used to her. But I've started to wonder if I wasn't just, well, inoculated. The family never bothered about her. I can give you all sorts of details on my ancestors, strange little family anecdotes, odd bits of history, but when it came to her, no-body seemed to know anything, or care enough to find out. Myself included."

"Now you do."

"The more I thought about what I didn't know, the more, yes, I wanted to find out. And after I saw her again, for myself, that night last June, I need to find out."

"You saw her when you were a child," he prompted.

"Yes. She would come into my room, sing her lullaby. I was never afraid of her. Then, as happens with every child who grows up at Harper House, I stopped seeing her when I was about twelve."

"But you saw her again."

There was something in his eyes that made her think he was wishing for his notebook or a tape recorder. That inten-sity, the absolute focus that she found unexpectedly sexy.

"Yes. She came back when I was pregnant with each of my boys. But that was more of a sensation of her. As if she were close by, that she knew there was going to be another child in the house. There were other times, of course, but I imagine you want to talk about all that in a more formal setting."

"Not necessarily formal, but I'd like to tape the conversa-tions we have about her. I'm going to start off with some basic groundwork. *Amelia* was the name Stella said she saw written on the window glass. I'll check your family records for anyone named Amelia."

"I've already done that." She lifted a shoulder. "After all, if it was going to be that simple, I thought I might as well wrap it up. I found no one with that name—birth, death, marriage, at least, not in any of the records I have."

"I'll do another search, if it's all the same to you."

"Suit yourself. I expect you'll be thorough."

"Once I get started, Rosalind, I'm a bloodhound. You'll be good and sick of me by the end of this."

"And I'm a moody, difficult woman, Mitchell. So I'll say, same goes."

He grinned at her. "I'd forgotten just how beautiful you are."

"Really?"

Now he laughed. Her tone had been so blandly polite. "It shows what a hold Baudelaire had on me. I don't usually forget something like that. Then again, he didn't have complimentary things to say about beauty."

"No? What did he say?"

" 'With snow for flesh, with ice for heart, I sit on high, an unguessed sphinx begrudging acts that alter forms; I never laugh, I never weep.' "

"What a sad man he must have been."

"Complicated," Mitch said, "and inherently selfish. In any case, there's nothing icy about you."

"Obviously, you haven't talked with some of my suppliers." Or, she thought, her ex-husband. "I'll see about having that contract drawn up, and get you the written permissions you need. As far as work space, I'd think the library would work best for you. Whenever you need it, or want something, you can reach me at one of the numbers I've given you. I swear, we all have a hundred numbers these days. Failing that, you can speak with Harper, or David, with Stella or Hayley, for that matter."

"I'd like to set something up in the next few days."

"We'll be ready. I really should be getting home. I appreciate the drink."

"My pleasure. I owe you a lot more for helping me out with my niece."

"I think you're going to be a hero."

He laid some bills on the table, then rose to take her hand before she could slide out of the booth on her own. "Is anybody going to be home to help you haul in all that loot?"

"I've hauled around more than that on my own, but yes, David will be there."

He released her hand, but walked her out to her car. "I'll be in touch soon," he said when he opened the car door for her.

"I'll look forward to it. You'll have to let me know what you come up with for your sister for Christmas."

Pain covered his face. "Oh, hell, did you have to spoil it?"

Laughing, she shut the door, then rolled down the window. "They have some gorgeous cashmere sweaters at Dillard's. Any brother who sprang for one of those for Christmas would completely erase a forgotten birthday."

"Is that guaranteed? Like a female rule of law?"

"From a husband or lover, it better glitter, but from a brother, cashmere will do the trick. That's a promise."

"Dillard's."

"Dillard's," she repeated, and started the engine. "Bye."

"Bye."

She pulled out, and as she drove away glanced in the rearview mirror to see him standing there, rocking on his heels with his hands in his pockets.

Hayley was right. He was hot.

ONCE SHE GOT HOME, SHE PULLED THE FIRST LOAD out, carried it in the house and directly up the stairs to her wing. After a quick internal debate, she piled bags into her sitting room, then went down for more.

She could hear Stella's boys in the kitchen, regaling David with the details of their day. Better that she got everything inside by herself, upstairs and hidden away before anyone knew she was home.

When she was finished, she stood in the middle of the room, and stared.

Why, she'd gone crazy, obviously. Now that she saw everything all piled up, she understood why Mitch had goggled. She could, easily, open her own store with what she'd bought in one mad afternoon.

How the hell was she going to wrap all of this?

Later, she decided after dragging both hands through her hair. She'd just worry about that major detail later. Right now she was going to call her lawyer, at home—the benefit of knowing him since high school—and get the contract done.

And because they'd gone to high school together, the conversation took twice as long as it might have. By the time she'd finished, put some semblance of order back into her sitting room, then headed downstairs, the house was settled down again.

Hayley, she knew, would be up with Lily. Stella would be with her boys. And David, she discovered, when she found the note on the kitchen counter, was off to the gym.

She nibbled on the potpie he'd left for her, then took a quiet walk around her gardens. The lights were on in Harper's cottage. David would have called him to let him know he'd made potpie—one of Harper's favorites. If the boy wanted some, he knew where to find it.

She slipped back inside, then poured herself another glass of wine with the idea of enjoying it in a long, hot bath.

But when she went back upstairs, she caught a movement in her sitting room. Her whole body tightened as she went to the door, then loosened again when she saw Stella.

"You got my juices up," Roz said.

It was Stella who jolted and spun around with a hand to her heart. "God! You'd think we'd all stop jumping by now. I thought you'd be in here. I came by to see if you'd like to go over the weekly report, and saw this." She swept a hand toward the bags and boxes lining the wall. "Roz, did you just buy the mall?"

"Not quite, but I gave it a good run. And because I did, I'm not much in the mood for the weekly report. What I want is this wine and a long, hot bath."

"Obviously well deserved. We can do it tomorrow. Ah, if you need help wrapping some of this—"

"Sold."

"Just tap me any evening after the kids are in bed. Ah, Hayley mentioned you were having drinks with Mitch Carnegie."

"Yeah. We ran into each other, as it seems everyone in Tennessee does eventually, at Wal-Mart. He's finished his book and appears to be raring to go on our project. He's going to want to interview you, and Hayley among others. That's not going to be a problem, is it?"

"No. I'm raring, too. I'll let you get started on that bath. See you in the morning."

" 'Night."

Roz went into her bedroom, closed the door. In the adjoining bath she ran water and scent and froth, then lit candles. For once she wouldn't use this personal time to soak and read gardening or business literature. She'd just lie back and veg.

As an afterthought, she decided to give herself a facial.

In the soft, flickering light, she slipped into the perfumed water. Let out a low, lengthy sigh. She sipped wine, set it on the ledge, then sank nearly to the chin.

Why, she wondered, didn't she do this more often?

She lifted a hand out of the froth, examined it—long, narrow, rough as a brick. Studied her nails. Short, unpainted. Why bother painting them when they'd be digging in dirt all day?

They were good, strong, competent hands. And they looked it. She didn't mind that, or the fact there were no rings on her fingers to sparkle them up.

But she smiled as she raised her feet out. Her toenails now, they were her little foolishness. This week she'd painted them a metallic purple. Most days they'd be buried in work socks and boots, but she knew she had sexy toes. It was just one of those silly things that helped her remember she was female.

Her breasts weren't as perky as they'd once been. She could be grateful they were small, and the sagging hadn't gotten too bad. Yet.

While she didn't worry too much about the state of her hands—they were, after all, tools for her—she was careful about her skin. She couldn't stop all the lines, but she pampered it whenever she could.

She wasn't willing to let her hair go to salt-and-pepper, so she took care of that, too. Just because she was being dragged toward fifty didn't mean she couldn't dig her heels in and try to slow down the damage time insisted on inflicting.

She had been beautiful once. When she'd been a young bride, fresh and innocent and radiantly happy. God, she looked at those pictures now and it was almost like looking at a stranger.

Who had that sweet young girl been?

Nearly thirty years, she thought. And it had gone by in the snap of a finger.

How long had it been since a man had looked at her and told her she was beautiful? Bryce had, certainly, but he'd told her all manner of lies.

But Mitch had said it almost offhand, casually. It made it easier to believe he'd meant it.

And why did she care?

Men. She shook her head and sipped more wine. Why was she thinking of men?

Because, she realized with a half laugh, she had no one to share those sexy toes with. No one to touch her as she liked to be touched, to thrill her. To hold her in the night.

She'd done without those things, and was content. But every now and again, she missed having someone. And maybe she was missing it now, she admitted, because she'd spent an hour talking with an attractive man.

When the water turned tepid, she got out. She was humming as she dried off, creamed her skin, performed her nightly ritual with her moisturizer. Wrapped in her robe, she started into her bedroom.

She felt the chill even before she saw the figure standing in front of her terrace doors.

Not Stella, not this time. The Harper Bride stood in her simple gray gown, her bright hair in a crown of curls.

Roz had to swallow once, then she spoke easily. "It's been some time since you've come to see me. I know I'm not pregnant, so that can't be it. Amelia? Is that your name?"

There was no answer, nor had she expected one. But the Bride smiled, just a brief shadow of a smile, then faded away.

"Well." Standing, Roz rubbed the warmth back into her arms. "I guess I'll assume that's your way of letting me know you approve that we're getting back to work."

She went back to the sitting room and took a calendar she'd begun keeping over the last winter out of her desk. She noted down the sighting on the day's date.

Dr. Carnegie, she assumed, would be pleased she was keeping a record.

three

❧

HE'D NEVER BEEN MUCH OF A GARDENER. THEN AGAIN, he'd lived in apartments most of his life. Still, he liked the look of plants and flowers, and had an admiration for those who knew what to do with them.

Rosalind Harper obviously knew what to do with them.

He'd seen some of the gardens on her estate this past June. But even their graceful beauty had paled next to his encounter with the Harper Bride. He'd always believed in the spirit of a person. Why else would he be so drawn to histories, to genealogies, to all those roots and branches of family trees? He believed that spirit could, and did, have influence and impact for generations, potentially centuries.

But he'd never believed in the tangibility, the physical presence of that spirit.

He knew better now.

It was difficult for someone with Mitch's academic bent to rationalize, then absorb, something as fanciful as ghosts.

But he'd felt and he'd seen. He'd experienced, and there was no denying facts.

So now he was caught up. He could admit it. With his book finally put to bed, he could pour his energies and his time, his skills, into identifying the spirit that had—purportedly—walked the halls of Harper House for more than a century.

A few legalities to get out of the way, then he could dive in.

He turned into the parking area of In the Garden.

Interesting, he thought, that a place that certainly had its prime in spring and summer could look so attractive, so welcoming as December clicked away.

The sky was heavy with clouds that would surely bring a cold, ugly rain before it was done. Still there were things growing. He had no clue what they were, but they looked appealing. Rusty red bushes, lush evergreens with fat berries, silvery green leaves, brightly painted pansies. At least he recognized a pansy when he saw one.

There were industrious-looking piles of material—material he assumed one would need for gardening or landscaping. Long tables on the side that held plants he assumed could handle the chill, a small forest of trees and shrubs.

The low-slung building was fronted with a porch. He saw poinsettias and a small, trim Christmas tree strung with lights.

There were other cars in the lot. He watched a couple of men load a tree with a huge burlapped ball into the back of a truck. And a woman wheel out a red wagon loaded with poinsettias and shopping bags.

He walked up the ramp, crossed the porch to go inside.

There were a lot of wares, he noted. More than he'd expected. Pots, decorative garden stakes, tabletop trees already decorated, books, seeds, tools. Some were put together in gift baskets. Clever idea.

Forgetting his intention of seeking Roz out immediately, he began to wander. When one of the staff asked if he needed help, he just smiled, shook his head, and continued to browse around.

A lot went into putting a place like this together, Mitch mused as he studied shelves of soil additives, time released fertilizer pellets, herbal pest repellents. Time, labor, know-how, and, he thought, courage.

This was no hobby or little enterprise indulged in by a southern aristocrat. This was serious business. Another layer to the woman, he supposed, and he hadn't begun to get to the center of her.

Beautiful, enigmatic Rosalind Harper. What man wouldn't want the chance to peel off those layers and know who she really was?

As it was, he owed his sister and niece a big, sloppy thanks for sending him scrambling out to shop. Running into Roz, seeing her with her shopping cart, having an hour alone with her was the most intriguing personal time he'd had in months.

Hardly a surprise he was hoping for more, and that he'd made this trip to her garden center mainly to study yet another side of her.

He wandered through wide glass doors and found an exotic mass of houseplants. There were tabletop and garden fountains as well, and baskets of ferny and viney things hanging from hooks or standing on pedestals.

Through another set of doors was a kind of greenhouse, with dozens of long wooden tables. Most were empty, but some held plants. The pansies he recognized, and others he didn't. Though, he noted, they were labeled and billed to be winter hardy.

He was debating whether to continue on or go back and ask for Roz when her son Harper came in from the outside.

"Hi. Need some help?" As he walked toward Mitch, recognition crossed his face. "Oh, hey, Dr. Carnegie."

"Mitch. Nice to see you again, Harper," he said as they shook hands.

"You, too. That was some game against Little Rock last week."

"It was. Were you there?"

"Missed the first quarter, but the second half rocked. Josh ruled."

Pride in his son beamed through him. "He had a good game. Missouri this week. I'll have to catch that one on ESPN."

"Same here. You see your son, tell him I said that three-pointer in the last five minutes was a thing of beauty."

"I'll do that."

"You looking for something, or someone?"

"Someone. Your mother, actually." You have her eyes, he thought. Her mouth, her coloring. "I was taking a little tour before I hunted her up." As he looked around, Mitch slipped his hands in his pockets. "This is a hell of a place you've got here."

"Keeps us busy. I just left her in the propagation house. I'll take you back."

"Appreciate it. I guess I didn't think this kind of business would have so much going on this late in the year."

"Always something going on when you're dealing with gardening and landscaping." Mirroring Mitch's stance, Harper scanned the area. "Holiday stuff's big now, and we're working on getting plants ready for March."

When they stepped outside, Mitch stopped, hooked his thumbs in his jacket pockets. Low, long greenhouses spread, separated into two areas by a wide space where more tables stood under a screened shelter. Even now he could see a field where someone worked a machine to dig up a pine—or a spruce, or a fir. How could you tell the difference?

He caught a glimpse of a little pond, and a small stream, then the woods that shielded the business from the main house, and the main house from the business.

"I've got to say, wow. I didn't expect anything this expansive."

"Mom doesn't do things halfway. We started a little smaller, added on two more greenhouses and an additional space in the retail area a couple years ago."

More than a business, Mitch realized. This was a life. "It must take an incredible amount of work."

"It does. You've gotta love it."

"Do you?"

"Yeah. That's my castle over there." Harper gestured. "Grafting house. Mostly, I deal with grafting and propagation. But I get pulled out for other things, like the Christmas tree end this time of year. In fact, I was grabbing ten before I head out to the field when I ran into you."

As the rain began to fall, Harper nodded toward one of the greenhouses. "That's the propagation area. Since we've got Stella, Mom spends most of her time in there."

"Then I can find her from here. Why don't you go on, catch what you've got left of your break."

"Better get right out in the field." As the rain fell, Harper pulled the bill of his cap lower on his head. "Get those trees up before the rain scares the customers away. Just go ahead in. See you later."

Harper set off at a jog, and had made the turn toward the field when Hayley rushed up to him from the opposite direction. "Wait! Harper, wait a minute."

He stopped, lifting the bill a bit to get a better look at her. She was wearing a short red denim jacket over jeans, and one of the In the Garden caps Stella had ordered for employees.

"Jesus, Hayley, get inside. This rain's going to cut loose big-time any minute."

"Was that Dr. Carnegie?"

"Yeah. He was looking for the boss."

"You took him to the propagation house?" Her voice pitched up over the increasing drum of rain. "Are you just stupid?"

"What? He's looking for Mom, she's in the propagation house. I just left her there five minutes ago."

"So you just take him there, say go right in?" She made wild gestures with both hands. "Without letting her *know*?"

"Know what?"

"That he's here, for God's sake. And now he's going in, and she's all dirty and sweaty, with no makeup on and in her grubbiest clothes. You couldn't stall him for five damn minutes to give her some warning?"

"About what? She looks like she always does. What's the damn difference?"

"If you don't know, you are stupid. And it's too late now. One of these days, Harper Ashby, you're going to have use of the single brain men pass around among them."

"What the hell," he grumbled after she'd given him a punch on the arm and dashed inside again.

MITCH DUCKED INTO THE PROPAGATION HOUSE OUT of the rain. If he'd thought the houseplant section seemed exotic, it was nothing compared to this. The place seemed alive with plants in various stages of growth. The humid warmth was almost tropical, and with the rain pattering it seemed he'd walked into some sort of fantasy cave.

The air was pungent with green and brown—plants and soil. Music twined along with the scents. Not classical, he noted. Not quite New Age. Something oddly and appealingly between.

He saw tables and tools, buckets and bags. Shallow black containers holding delicate growing things.

And he saw Roz at the far end, on the side. Her back was to him as she worked.

She had a gorgeous neck. It was an odd thought, and, he admitted, probably a foolish one. But again, facts were facts. She wore her hair short and straight and to his mind, the style showed off that long, lovely neck perfectly.

Then again, all of her was rather long and lovely. Arms, legs, torso. At the moment that intriguing body was camouflaged in baggy pants and a shapeless sweatshirt she'd pushed up at the sleeves. But he remembered, very well, that willowy figure.

Just as he remembered, even before she heard his approach and turned, that her eyes were long as well. Long lidded and in a fascinating shade of deep, deep amber.

"I'm sorry. I'm interrupting."

"That's all right. I didn't expect to see you here."

"I got the paperwork, and thought I'd ride out and let you know it's signed, sealed, and on its way back to your lawyer. Plus, it gave me a chance to see your place. I'm impressed. Even though I don't know squat about gardening, I'm majorly impressed."

"Thank you."

He glanced down at her worktable. There were pots, some empty yet, some filled with soil and small green leaves. "What's going on here?"

"I'm potting up some seedlings. Celosia—cockscomb."

"I have no idea what that is."

"I'm sure you've seen them." She brushed a hand absently over her cheek, transferring a smudge of soil. "In bloom they're like small feather dusters in bold colors. Red's very popular."

"Okay. And you put them in these little pots because?"

"Because they don't like their roots disturbed after they're established. I pot them young, then they'll be blooming for our spring customers, and only have to tolerate that last transplanting. And I don't imagine you're all that interested."

"Didn't think I would be. But this is like a whole new world. What's this here?"

She raised her eyebrows. "All right, then. That's matthiola, also called gillyflower or stock. It's very fragrant. Those there with the yellowish green leaves? They'll be double-flowered cultivars. These will flower for spring. Customers prefer to buy in bloom, so I plan my propagation to give them plenty of blooms to choose from. This section is for annuals. I do perennials back there."

"Is it a gift, or years of study? How do you come to know what to do, how to recognize the . . . cockscomb from the gillyflower at this stage?"

"It's both, and a love of it with considerable hands-on experience thrown in. I've been gardening since I was a child. I remember my grandmother—on the Harper side— putting her hands over mine to show me how to press the soil around a plant. What I remember best about her is in the gardens at Harper House."

"Elizabeth McKinnon Harper, wife to Reginald Harper, Jr."

"You have a good memory."

"I've been skimming over some of the lists. What was she like?"

It made her feel soft, and a little sentimental, to be asked. "Kind, and patient, unless you riled her up. Then she was formidable. She went by Lizzie, or Lizzibeth. She always wore men's pants, and an old blue shirt and an odd straw hat. Southern women of a certain age always wear odd straw hats to garden. It's the code. She smelled of the eucalyptus and pennyroyal she'd make up into a bug repellant. I use her recipe for it still."

She picked up another pot. "I still miss her, and she's been gone nearly thirty years now. Fell asleep in her glider on a hot summer day in July. She'd been deadheading in the garden, and sat down to rest. She never woke up. I think that's a very pleasant way to pass."

"How old was she?"

"Well, she claimed to be seventy-six, but in fact, according to the records she was eighty-four. My daddy was a late baby for her, as I was for him. I broke that Harper family tradition by having my children young."

"Did she ever talk to you about the Harper Bride?"

"She did." As she spoke, Roz continued with her potting. "Of course, she was a McKinnon by birth and wasn't raised in the house. But she claimed to have seen the Bride when she'd come to live here, when my great-grandfather passed. My grandfather Harper grew up at Harper House, of course, and if we were right in dating Amelia, would have been a baby around the time she died. But he passed when I was about eight, and I don't recall him ever speaking of her."

"How about your parents, or other relatives?"

"Are we on the clock here, Doctor?"

"Sorry."

"No, I don't mind." She labeled the new potted plant, reached for another. "My daddy never said much, now that I think about it. Maybe it's a thing with the Harper men, or men in general. My mother was a dramatic sort of female, one who enjoyed the illusion of turmoil in her life. She claimed to have seen the Bride often, and with great stress. But then, Mama was always stressed about something."

"Did either she or your grandmother keep a journal, any sort of diary?"

"Yes, both of them. Another fine old tradition I haven't followed. My grandmother moved into the guesthouse when my father married and brought his own bride home. After she died, he cleaned out her things. I recall asking him about her journals, but he said they were gone. I don't know what became of them. As for my mother's, I have hers. You're welcome to them, but I doubt you'll find anything pertinent."

"Just the same. Aunts, uncles, cousins?"

"Oh, legions. My mother's sister, who married some British lord or earl—third marriage—a few years ago. She lives in Sussex, and we don't see each other often. She has children from her first two marriages, and they have children. My father was an only child. But his father had four sisters, older sisters—Reginald's daughters."

"Yeah, I've got their names on my list."

"I don't remember them at all. They each had children. Let's see, that would be my cousins Frank and Esther— both gone years now—and their children, of course. Ah, Lucerne, Bobby, and Miranda. Bobby was killed in World War II. Lucerne and Miranda are both gone now, too. But they all had children, and some of them have children now. Then there's Owen, Yancy, ah . . . Marylou. Marylou's still living, down in Biloxi where she suffers from dementia and is tended by her children, best they can. Yancy, I couldn't say. He ran off to join a carnival years back, and no one heard from him again. Owen's a fire-and-brimstone minister, last I heard, in Macon, Georgia. He wouldn't talk to you about ghosts, I can promise you."

"You never know."

She made a noncommittal sound as she worked. "And my cousin Clarise, who never married. She has managed to live to a ripe age. Too sour not to. She's living in a retirement village, other side of the city. She doesn't speak to me."

"Because?"

"You do ask questions."

"Part of the process."

"I'm not sure I remember exactly why she stopped speaking to me. I recall she didn't appreciate that my grandparents left everything to me and my daddy. But they were *my* grandparents, after all. My father's parents, while she was only a niece to them. She came to visit here when the boys were young. I believe that's when she cut me off, or we cut each other off, which is more accurate. She didn't care for my style of raising the boys, and I didn't care for her criticism of them, or me."

"Before the family rift, do you recall if she ever talked to you about the Bride?"

"I don't, no. Cousin Rissy's conversations mostly consisted of complaints or her own irritable observations. And I know damn well she pilfered things from the house. Little bits and pieces. I can't say I'm sorry we're not on speaking terms."

"Will she talk to me?"

Thoughtfully, Roz turned to him, studied his face. "She might, especially if she thinks I'd prefer she didn't. If you decide to go see the dried-up old bat, be sure you take her flowers, and chocolate. You spring for Godiva and she'll be very impressed with you. Then you turn on the charm. Be sure to call her Miss Harper, until she says otherwise. She uses the family name, and is very formal about everything. She'll ask about your people. If you happen to have any ancestors who fought in the War Between the States, be sure to mention it. Any Yankees in your tree, disavow them."

He had to laugh. "I get the type. I have a great-aunt who's on the same page."

She reached under the worktable to a cooler, took out two bottles of chilled water. "You look hot. I'm so used to it, I don't notice."

"Working in all this humidity every day must be what gives your skin that English rose look." Absently he reached out, flicked a finger over her cheek. When her brows shot up again, he eased back, just a step.

"Sorry. You had a little dirt . . ."

"Something else I'm used to."

"So . . ." He reminded himself to keep his hands otherwise occupied. "I guess from what I saw the other day, you're ready for Christmas."

"Near enough. You?"

"Not even close, though I owe you big—once again—for the gift for my sister."

"You went for the cashmere, then."

"Something the salesgirl called a twinset, and she said no woman could have too many of them."

"Absolutely true."

"Okay. So, I'm going to put some effort into the rest of it over the next few days. Get the tree out, fight with the lights."

"Get it out?" A look that might have been pity, might have been derision covered her face. "I assume that means you've got a fake tree."

His hands slid into his pockets, his smile spread slowly. "It's simplest. Apartment life."

"And from the state of that dieffenbachia, probably for the best."

"State of the what?"

"The plant you were slowly murdering. The one I took when I came to your place to meet you the first time."

"Oh. Oh, right." When she'd been wearing that lady suit, he thought, and those high heels that had made her legs look ten feet long. "How's it doing?"

"It's just fine now, and don't think I'll be giving it back."

"Maybe I could just visit it sometime."

"That could be arranged. We're having a holiday party at the house, a week from Saturday. Nine o'clock. You're welcome to come, if you like. And bring a guest, of course."

"I'd like that. Would you mind if I went over to the house now, took a look at the library? Get a ground floor started?"

·

"No, that'll be fine. I'll just call David and let him know you're coming."

"Good. I'll go on, then, and get out of your way. I appreciate the time."

"I've plenty of it."

He didn't see how. "I'll call you later, then. You have a strong place here, Rosalind."

"Yes, I do."

When he'd gone out, she set her tools aside to drink deeply from the water bottle. She wasn't a silly young girl who was flustered and giddy at the touch of a man's hand on her skin. But it had felt strange and oddly sweet, that careful brush of his fingers over her cheek, and that look in his eyes when he touched her.

English rose, she thought and let out a half laugh. Once, long ago, she might have appeared that fragile and dewy. She turned and studied one of her healthy stock plants. She was much more like that now, sturdy and strong.

And that, she thought as she got back to work, was just fine with her.

DESPITE THE STEADY RAIN, MITCH TOOK A WALK around the buildings, and gained even more respect for Roz and what she'd built. And built almost single-handedly, he thought. The Harper money may have given her a cushion, he decided, but it took more than funds to create all this.

It took guts and vision and hard work.

Had he actually made that lame, clichéd comment about her skin? English rose, he thought now and shook his head. Like she hadn't heard that one before.

In any case, it wasn't even particularly apt. She was no delicate English rose. More a black rose, he decided, long and slender and exotic. A little haughty, a lot sexy.

He'd learned a lot about her life, just from that conversation in her work space. A lot about her. She'd lost someone she'd loved very much—her grandmother—at a tender age. She hadn't been very close with her parents. And had lost them as well. Her relatives were far-flung, and it didn't appear she had close relations with any of them.

Other than her sons, she had no one.

And after her husband's death, she'd had only herself to depend on, only herself to turn to while she raised three boys.

But he'd detected no sense of pity, certainly no weakness in her.

Independent, direct, strong. But there was humor there, and a good heart. Hadn't she helped him out when he'd been floundering over a toy for a little girl? And hadn't she been amused by his dilemma?

Now that he'd begun to get a good sense of her, he only wanted to know more.

What was the deal with the second husband and the divorce, for instance? None of his business, of course, but he could justify the curiosity. The more he knew, the more he knew. And it wouldn't be difficult to find out. People just loved to talk.

All you had to do was ask the questions.

On impulse, he detoured back into the center. There were a few customers debating over the poinsettias and some sort of cactus-looking plant that was loaded with pink blossoms. Mitch had barely raked a hand through his wet hair when Hayley arrowed in his direction.

"Dr. Carnegie! What a nice surprise."

"Mitch. How are you, Hayley, and the baby?"

"We both couldn't be better. But look at you, you're soaked! Can I get you a towel?"

"No, I'm fine. I couldn't resist walking around, looking the place over."

"Oh." She beamed at him, all innocence. "Were you looking for Roz?"

"Found her. I'm about to head over to the house, get a sense of my work space there. But I thought maybe I'd pick up one of those tabletop trees. The ones that're already decorated."

"Aren't they sweet? Really nice for a small space, or an office."

"A lot nicer than the old artificial one I fight to put together every year."

"And they smell just like Christmas." She steered him over. "You see one you like?"

"Ah . . . this one's fine."

"I just love all the little red bows and those tiny Santas. I'll get you a box for it."

"Thanks. What are those?"

"Those are Christmas cacti. Aren't they beautiful? Harper grafts them. He's going to show me how one of these days. You know, you should have one. They're so celebrational. And they bloom for Christmas and Easter."

"I'm not good with plants."

"Why, you don't have to do much of anything for it." She set those big baby blue eyes on him. "You live in an apartment, don't you? If you take the tree, a Christmas cactus, a couple of poinsettias, you'll be all decorated for the holidays. You can have company over, and be set."

"I don't know how much attention Josh is going to pay to a cactus."

She smiled. "Maybe not, but you must have a date over for a holiday drink, right?"

"Ah . . . I've been pretty busy with the book."

"A handsome single man like you must have to beat the ladies off with a stick."

"Not lately. Um—"

"You should have a wreath for the door, too."

"A wreath." He began to feel slightly desperate as she took his arm.

"Let me show you what we've got. I made some of these myself. See this one here? Just smell that pine. What's Christmas without a wreath on the door?"

He knew when he was outgunned. "You're really good at this, aren't you?"

"You bet," she said with a laugh and selected a wreath. "This one goes so well with your tree."

She talked him into the wreath, three windowsill-size poinsettias, and the cactus. He looked bemused and a little dazed as she rang it all up and boxed his purchases.

And when he left, Hayley knew what she wanted to know.

She dashed into Stella's office.

"Mitch Carnegie's not seeing anybody."

"Was he recently blinded?"

"Come on, Stella, you know what I mean. He doesn't have a sweetie." She drew off her cap, raked her fingers through her oak-brown hair she was wearing long enough to pull back into a stubby tail.

"And he just spent a good half hour in the propagation house with Roz before he came in here to buy a tabletop tree. Harper sent him in there without even letting her know. Just go right on in while she's working and doesn't even have time to swipe on some lipstick."

"Just sent him in? What is Harper, stupid?"

"Exactly what I asked him—Harper, that is. Anyway, then he—Mitch—came in all wet because he'd been walking around the place checking it out. He's going over to the house for a while now."

"Hayley." Stella turned from her computer. "What are you cooking?"

"Just observing, that's all. He's not seeing anybody, she's not seeing anybody." She lifted her hands, pointing both index fingers, then wiggled them toward each other.

"Now they're both going to be seeing a lot of each other. And besides being a hottie, he's so cute. I talked him into buying a wreath, three mini poinsettias, and a Christmas cactus as well as the tree."

"Go, Hayley."

"But see, he didn't know how to say no, that was the cute part. If Roz doesn't go for him, I might myself. Okay, no." She laughed at Stella's bland stare. "He's old enough to be my daddy and blah blah blah, but he's just perfect for Roz. I'm telling you, I know this stuff. Wasn't I right about you and Logan?"

Stella sighed as she looked at the aquamarine he'd given her as an engagement ring. "I can't argue about that. And while I'm going to say, firmly, that observing's all we should do, I can't deny this may be a lot of fun to watch."

four

AS A RULE WHEN HE WAS WORKING, MITCH REMEM-
bered to clean his apartment when he ran out of places to
sit, or coffee cups. Between projects he was slightly better
at shoveling out, or at least rearranging the debris.

He hired cleaning services. In fact, he hired them routinely. They never lasted long, and the fault—he was willing to admit—was largely his.

He'd forget which day he'd scheduled them and, invariably, pick that day to run errands, do research, or meet his
kid for a quick game of Horse or one-on-one. There was
probably something Freudian about that, but he didn't want
to think too deeply about it.

Or he'd remember, and the team would come in, gog-
gle at the job facing them. And he'd never see them
again.

But a man had to—or at least should—make an effort
for the holidays. He spent an entire day hauling out, scrub-
bing down, and sweeping up, and was forced to admit that
if he were being paid to do the job, he'd quit, too.

Still, it was nice to have some order back in his apartment, to actually be able to see the surface of tables, the cushions of chairs. Though he didn't hold out much hope he'd keep them alive for the long-term, the plants Hayley had talked him into added a nice holiday touch.

And the little tree, well, that was ingenious. Now instead of dragging the box out of storage, fighting with parts, cursing the tangle of lights only to discover half of them didn't work anyway, all he had to do was set the cheerful tree on the Hepplewhite stand by his living room window and plug the sucker in.

He hung the wreath on the front door, set the blooming cactus on his coffee table, and the three little poinsettias on the top of the toilet tank. It worked for him.

By the time he'd showered, dragged on jeans and a shirt, his date for the evening was knocking at the door.

Barefoot, his hair still damp, Mitch crossed the living room to answer. And grinned at the only person he loved without reservation.

"Forget your key?"

"Wanted to make sure I had the right place." Joshua Carnegie tapped a finger on the greenery. "You've got a wreath on your door."

"It's Christmas."

"I heard a rumor about that." He walked in, and his eyes, the same sharp green shade as his father's, widened.

He was taller than Mitch by a full inch, but spread the height on the same lanky frame. His hair was dark, and it was shaggy. Not because he forgot haircuts like his father, but because he wanted it that way.

He wore a hooded gray sweatshirt and baggy jeans.

"Wow. You find a new cleaning service? Do they get combat pay?"

"No, haven't had a chance. Besides, I think I've ripped through all the cleaning services in western Tennessee."

"You cleaned up?" Lips pursed, Josh took a brief tour of the living room. "You've got a plant—with flowers on it."

"You're taking that with you."

"I am."

"I'll kill it. I've already heard it gasping. I can't be responsible."

"Sure." Josh pulled absently on his ear. "It'll jazz up the dorm. Hey. You got this little tree going on. And candles."

"It's Christmas," Mitch repeated, even as Josh leaned down to sniff the fat red candle.

"Smelly candles. Plus, if I'm not mistaken, you vacuumed." Eyes narrowed he looked back at his father. "You've got a woman."

"Not on me, no. More's the pity. Want a Coke?"

"Yeah." With a shake of his head, Josh started toward the bathroom. "Gotta use the john. We getting pizza?"

"Your choice."

"Pizza," Josh called out. "Pepperoni and sausage. Extra cheese."

"My arteries are clogging just hearing that," Mitch called out as he pulled two cans of Coke out of the refrigerator. From experience, he knew his son could steam through most of a pie on his own and still stay lean as a greyhound.

Oh, to be twenty again.

He speed-dialed the local pizza parlor, ordered a large for Josh, and a medium veggie-style for himself.

When he turned, he saw Josh leaning against the jamb, feet crossed at the ankles of his Nike Zooms. "You've got flowers in the john."

"Poinsettias. Christmas. Deal."

"You've got a woman. If you haven't bagged one, you've got one in the sights. So spill."

"No woman." He tossed one of the cans to Josh. "Just a clean apartment with a few holiday touches."

"We have ways of making you talk. Where'd you meet her? Is she a babe?"

"Not talking." Laughing, Mitch popped the can.

"I'll get it out of you."

"Nothing to get." Mitch walked by him into the living room. "Yet."

"Ah-ha!" Josh followed him in, plopped down on the couch, propped his feet on the coffee table.

"I repeat: Not talking. And that's a premature *ah-ha*. Anyway, I'm just feeling a little celebrational. Book's done, which means a check will be in the mail shortly. I'm starting on a new, interesting project—"

"Already? No decompressing?"

"I've had this one dangling awhile, and I want to get on it full steam. It's better than thinking about Christmas shopping."

"Why do you have to think about it? It's still a couple weeks away."

"Now, that's my boy." Mitch raised his Coke in toast. "So how are your mother and Keith?"

"Good. Fine." Josh took a long swallow from his can. "She's all jazzed up about the holidays. You know how it is."

"Yeah, I do." He gave Josh an easy slap on the knee. "It's not a problem, Josh. Your mom wants you home for the holidays. That's the way it should be."

"You could come. You know you could come."

"I know, and I appreciate it. But it'd be better if I just hang out here. We'll have our Christmas deal before you leave. It's important to her to have you there. She's entitled. It's important for you, too."

"I don't like thinking about you being alone."

"Just me and my cup of gruel." It was a sting, it always was. But it was one he'd earned.

"You could go to Grandma's."

"Please." Exaggerated pain covered Mitch's face, rang in his voice. "Why would you wish that on me?"

Josh smirked. "You could wear that reindeer sweater she got you a couple years ago."

"Sorry, but there's a nice homeless person who'll be sporting that this holiday season. When do you head out?"

"Twenty-third."

"We can do our thing the twenty-second if that works for you."

"Sure. I've just got to juggle Julie. She's either going to Ohio to her mother's, or L.A. to her father's. It's seriously messed up. They're both doing the full court press on her, laying on the guilt and obligation crap, and she's all, 'I don't want to see either one of them.' She's either crying or bitchy, or both."

"We parents can certainly screw up our children."

"You didn't." He took another drink, then turned the can around in his hands. "I don't want to get all Maury Povich or whatever, but I wanted to say that you guys never made me the rope in your personal tug-of-war. I've sort of been thinking about that, with all this shit Julie's going through. You and Mom, you never hung that trip on me. Never made me feel like I had to choose or ripped on each other around me. It sucks when people do. It sucks long."

"Yeah, it does."

"I remember, you know, before you guys split. It was rugged all around. But even then, neither of you used me as a hammer on the other. That's what's going on with Julie, and it makes me realize I was lucky. So I just wanted to say."

"That's a . . . That's a good thing to hear."

"Well, now that we've had this Hallmark moment, I'm getting another Coke. Pregame show should be coming on."

"I'm on that." Mitch picked up the remote. He wondered what stars had shone on him to give him the gift of such a son.

"Hey, man! Salt and vinegar chips!"

Hearing the bag rip, and the knock on the door, Mitch grinned, and rising, took out his wallet to pay for the pizza.

"I DON'T GET IT, STELLA. I JUST DON'T GET IT." Hayley paced Stella's room while the boys splashed away in the adjoining bath.

"The sexy black shoes that will kill my feet, or the more elegant pumps?"

When Stella stood, one of each pair on either foot, Hayley stopped pacing long enough to consider them. "Sexy."

"I was afraid of that. Well." Stella took them both off, replaced the rejected pair in her closet. Her outfit for the evening was laid out on the bed, the jewelry she'd already selected was in a tray on the dresser.

Now all she had to do was settle the boys down for the night, get dressed, deal with her hair, her makeup. Check the boys again, check the baby monitors. And . . . Hayley's pacing and muttering distracted her enough to have her turn.

"What? Why are you so nervous? Do you have a date going on for tonight's party I don't know about?"

"No. But it's dates I'm talking about. Why would Roz tell Mitch to bring a date? Now he probably will, because he'll think if he doesn't, he'll look like a loser. And they'll both miss a golden opportunity."

"I missed something." She hooked on her earrings, studied the results. "How do you know Roz told him to bring a date? How do you find this stuff out?"

"It's a gift of mine. Anyway, what's up with her? Here's this perfectly gorgeous and available man, and she invites him for tonight—points there. But then tells him he can bring somebody. Jeez."

"She'd have considered it the polite thing to do, I guess."

"You can't be polite in the dating wars, for God's sake." On a long huff, Hayley plopped down on the foot of the bed, then lifted her legs out to examine her own shoes. "You know, *date*'s from the Latin—or maybe it's Old English. Anyway, it comes from *data*—and it's a *female* part of speech. Female, Stella. We're supposed to take the controls."

Since she hadn't yet started her makeup, Stella was free to press her fingers to her eyes. "How? How do you know that kind of thing? Nobody knows that kind of thing."

"I was a bookseller for years, remember. I read a lot. I don't know why I retain the weird stuff. But anyway, it's a holiday party here—her house. And you know she'll look amazing. And now he'll show up with some woman and screw everything up."

"I don't actually think there's anything to screw up at this point."

Hayley tugged at her hair in frustration. "But there *could* be. I just know it. You watch, you just watch them tonight and see if you don't get the vibe."

"All right, I will. But now I've got to get the kids out of the tub and into bed. Then I have to get dressed, and strap on my sexy shoes with the single goal of driving Logan crazy."

"Want a hand? With the kids, not with driving Logan crazy. Lily's already sleeping."

"No, you'll get wet or wrinkled, and you look fantastic. I wish I could wear that shade of red. Talk about sexy."

Hayley looked down at the short siren-red slip dress. "You don't think it's too . . ."

"No, I think it's exactly."

"Well, I'll go down, see if I can give David a hand with the caterer and all. Then I can get his take on the outfit. He rules in fashion."

Roz was already downstairs, checking details and second-guessing herself. Maybe she should have opened the third-floor ballroom and held the party there. It was a gorgeous space, so elegant and graceful. But the main level, with its hive of smaller rooms, the fires burning, was warmer and more friendly somehow.

Space wasn't a problem, she assured herself as she checked the positioning of tables, chairs, lamps, candles. And she liked throwing open the rooms this way, knowing people would wander from here to there, admiring the home she loved.

It was a clear night, so they could spill onto the terraces, too. There were heaters if it got too chilly, and more tables, more seating, more candles and all those festive lights in the trees, the luminaries along the garden paths.

And you'd think, for heaven's sake, that it was the first party she'd given in her life.

Been awhile, though, since she'd held anything this expansive. Because of that, the attrition rate on her guest list had been very low. She was going to be packed.

Avoiding the caterers and extra staff bustling around, she slipped outside. Yes, the lights were lovely, and fun, she decided. And she liked the poinsettia tree she'd created out of dozens of white plants.

Harper House was designed for entertaining, she reminded herself. She'd been shirking her duty there, and denying herself, she supposed, the pleasure of socializing with people she enjoyed.

She turned when she heard the door open. David stepped out, holding two flutes of champagne.

"Hello, beautiful. Can I interest you in a glass of champagne?" .

"You can. Though I should be inside, helping with the madhouse."

"Under control." He tapped his glass to hers. "Another twenty minutes, and it'll be perfect. And look at us! Aren't we gorgeous?"

She laughed, slipped her hand into his. "You always are."

"And you, my treasure." Still holding her hand, he stepped back. "You just shimmer."

She'd chosen a gown of dull silver in a long, narrow column with an off-the-shoulder neckline that would showcase her great-grandmother's rubies.

She brushed her fingertips over the platinum necklace with its spectacular ruby drops. "I don't have many opportunities to wear the Harper rubies. This seemed the night for them."

"And a treat they are for the eyes plus they do amazing things for your collarbone. But I was talking about you, my incandescent beauty. Why don't we run away to Belize?"

Champagne and David, the perfect combination to make her feel bubbly and relaxed. "I thought it was going to be Rio."

"Not until Carnival. It's going to be a wonderful party, Roz. You just put all the other crap out of your mind."

"You read me, don't you?" She shook her head, staring into the gardens as she sipped champagne. "Last time I threw one of these holiday bashes, I walked upstairs into the bedroom to change my bracelet because the clasp was loose, and what do I find but my husband nibbling on one of our guests instead of the canapés."

She took a longer, deeper sip. "A singularly mortifying moment in my life."

"Hell with that. You handled it, didn't you? I still don't know how you managed to step back out, leave them there, to get through the rest of the party and wait until everyone was gone before you pitched the son of a bitch out on his ear."

His voice heated up on the rant, his fury for her lighting little fires. "You've got balls of steel, Roz. And I mean that in the best possible way."

"It was self-serving, not courageous or ballsy." She shrugged it off, or tried to. "Causing a scene with a house full of guests would only have been more humiliating."

"In your place, I'd've scratched both of them blind, then chased them out the door brandishing one of your great-great . . . however many greats-granddaddy's muskets."

She let out a little sigh, sipped again. "That would've been satisfying, and damn if I don't wish I'd thought of the musket after the guests had gone. Well, we didn't let him spoil that evening, and we won't let him spoil this one."

She polished off the champagne and turned to David with the determined look of a woman prepared for battle. "Let's get the rest of these candles lit, put some music on. I'm ready for a party."

YES, IT WAS GOOD TO OPEN THE HOUSE AGAIN. To have wine and music, good food, good friends. She listened to snippets of gossip, political debates, discussions on sports and the arts as she moved from group to group, from room to room.

She hooked her arm through her old friend Will Dooley's, who was also Stella's father, and Roz's landscaper, Logan Kitridge's future father-in-law. "You slipped by me."

"Just got here." He brushed his lips over her cheek. "Jo kept changing her shoes. She just went upstairs with Hayley. Said she had to peek at the baby."

"I'll find her. Lose your fiancée, Logan?"

"She's everywhere." He shrugged, sipped from his pilsner. "Woman can't rest until she's checked every detail personally. Nice party, Roz."

"Oh, you hate parties."

Now Logan grinned, a quick grin that added charm to his rugged looks. "A lot of people. But the food's first-rate, the beer's cold, and my date's the most beautiful woman in the world. Tough to complain. Don't tell her daddy, but I plan to lure her out to the gardens later to neck."

He winked at Will, then shifted his gaze. "Your Dr. Carnegie just came in. Seems to be looking for you—or somebody."

"Oh?" Roz glanced around, and those expressive eyebrows lifted. He'd worn a suit, stone gray, that flattered his lean build. He'd gotten a haircut since the last time she'd seen him, she noted, and was looking a little more *GQ* than professorial.

She could admit, to herself at least, that it was a treat to study him either way.

Still, he seemed slightly befuddled with the crowd, and shook his head when one of the efficient servers offered him a glass from a tray of champagne.

"Excuse me just a minute," she said to Will and Logan.

She started to wind her way through the room, and broke her stride when his gaze skimmed over, then locked on her face.

She felt a little bump under her heart, and a quickening of pulse she found both baffling and embarrassing.

He just hones in, she thought. Those eyes just zeroed right on in so she felt—anyone would feel—that she was the only person in the room. A good trick in a space jammed with people and noise, and just a little disconcerting.

But her expression was easy and friendly as she walked to him.

"I'm so glad you could come."

"When you throw a party, you mean it. I could see the lights from a mile away. You don't actually know all these people, do you?"

"Never seen them before in my life. What can I get you to drink?"

"Club soda, lime."

"There's a bar set up over here." To guide him, she laid a hand on his arm. "Let's get you fixed up."

"Thanks. Listen, I have something for you. A gift."

He dug into his pocket as they crossed to the bar, then offered her a small wrapped box.

"That's completely unnecessary, and awfully sweet."

"Just a thanks for bailing me out with the gift for my niece." He ordered his drink. "You look . . . *amazing* is the word that springs to mind, with *spectacular* coming right behind it."

"Thank you."

"From head." His gaze skimmed down to her silver-heeled sandals—and the ruby-red toenails. "To toe."

"My mama always said a woman wasn't groomed unless her toenails were painted. It's one of the few pieces of advice she gave me I agreed with. Should I open this now?"

He'd barely glanced at the rubies, though his amateur antiquer's eye judged them to be vintage. But the toes. The toes were terrific.

"What?"

"The gift." She smiled. It was hard not to be pleased, and a little bit smug, when a man was enraptured by your feet. "Should I open it now?"

"Oh, no, I wish you wouldn't. If you open it later, and you hate it, you'll have time to prepare a polite lie."

"Don't be silly. I'm opening it now."

She tugged off the ribbon, lifted the top. Inside was a miniature clock, framed in silver filigree. "It's lovely. It's really lovely."

"Antiquing's a hobby of mine. Makes sense, considering. I figured with this house, you'd enjoy old things. There's an inscription on the back. It got to me."

She turned it over and read.

L, Count the hours. N

"Lovely, and romantic. It's wonderful, Mitch, and certainly more than I deserve for picking out a toy."

"It made me think of you." When she lifted her head, he shook his. "That put a cynical look in your eye. But fact's fact. I saw it, thought of you."

"Does that happen often?"

"My thinking of you?"

"No, thinking of someone and buying her a charming gift."

"From time to time. Not in some time, actually. Does it happen often on your end?"

She smiled a little. "Not in some time. Thank you, very much. I want to put this upstairs. Why don't I introduce you to . . . oh, there's Stella. Nobody can steer you through a party better than our Stella."

"Mitch." Stella held out a hand for him. "It's good to see you again."

"And you. You're blooming," he said. "It must be love."

"I can confirm that."

"And how are your boys?"

"They're great, thanks. Conked out upstairs, and . . . oh." She broke off when she saw the little clock. "Isn't that sweet? So romantic and female."

"Lovely, isn't it?" Roz agreed. "It was a gift, for a very small favor."

"You wouldn't say small if you'd been on the receiving end of the phone call I got from my sister and my niece," Mitch told her. "I'm not only officially forgiven, I'm currently enjoying favorite-uncle status."

"Well then, obviously I deserve this. Stella, show Mitch around, will you? I just want to put this upstairs."

"Sure." And Stella noted the way Mitch's gaze followed Roz out of the room.

"One question before we make the rounds. Is she seeing anyone?"

"No, she's not."

He grinned as he took Stella's arm. "How about that?"

Roz mingled her way to the foyer, then started up-stairs. It reminded her that she'd walked up these stairs at another party, with the voices and the music and lights behind her. And she'd stepped into the end of a relation-ship.

She wasn't naive. She knew very well Mitch was asking her if she was interested in beginning a relationship, and was laying some groundwork so she would be. What was strange was that her answer wasn't a flat no. What was strange, Roz thought as she walked to her bedroom, was not knowing the answer.

She slipped into the room to set the romantic little clock on her dresser. She couldn't stop the smile as she traced the frame. A very thoughtful gift, she thought, and yes, her cynical side added that it was a very clever gift. Then again, a woman who'd been through two marriages was bound to have a healthy dose of cynicism.

A relationship with him might be interesting, even en-tertaining, and God knew she was due for some passion in her life. But it would also be complicated, possibly in-tense. And potentially sticky with the work she'd hired him to do.

She was allowing the man to write a book that involved her family history, and would certainly involve herself to some extent. Did she really want to become intimate with someone who could, if things burned out, slap her, and her family, in print?

Her experience with Bryce warned her that when things went bad, things got worse.

A lot to consider, she mused. Then she raised her eyes to the mirror.

She saw not only herself, her skin flushed, her eyes bright from her own thoughts, but the pale figure behind her.

Her breath caught, but she didn't jolt. She didn't spin around. She simply stood as she was, her eyes linked with Amelia's in the glass.

"Twice in so many weeks," she said calmly. "You, I imagine, would tell me to brush him off. You don't like men much, do you, Amelia? Boys, yes, children, but men are a different kettle. No one but a man puts that kind of anger in a woman. I know. Was it one of my blood who put that anger in you?"

There was no answer, none expected.

"Let me finish this one-sided conversation by saying I have to think for myself, decide for myself, just as I always have. If I let Mitchell into my life, into my bed, the consequences, and the pleasure, will be on me."

She took a slow breath. "But I'll make you one promise. Whatever I do, or don't, we won't stop looking for the answers for you. Not now that we've started."

Even as the figure began to fade, Roz felt something brush her hair, like a soft stroke of fingers that warmed even as it chilled.

She had to steady herself, pressing both hands to the top of the dresser. Then she meticulously freshened her lipstick, dabbed a bit more scent on her throat. And started back to the party.

She thought a ghostly caress would be enough of a shock for one night, but she had another, harder shock, as she reached the bottom of the stairs.

Bryce Clerk stood in her foyer.

The rage spewed through her, hot and horrid, and had a vision of herself flashing through her brain. Of leaping down the stairs, spitting out all the bitter insult and fury as she beat him senseless, and threw him out the door.

For an instant, that vision was so sharp, so clear, that the rest, the reality around her, blurred and vanished. She heard nothing but the pounding blood in her ears.

He beamed up at her as he helped a woman she knew from the garden club with her wrap. Roz clutched the newel post until control clamped down over temper and she was marginally sure her hand wouldn't bunch into a fist and fly out.

She took the last step. "Mandy," she said.

"Oh, Roz!" Amanda Overfield giggled, kissed both of Roz's cheeks in a couple of quick pecks. She was Harper's age, Roz knew, a silly, harmless, and wealthy young woman. Recently divorced herself, she'd only relocated in Memphis the previous summer. "Your house is just *gorgeous*. I know we're awfully late, but we got . . ." She giggled again, and set Roz's teeth on edge. "It doesn't matter. I'm so glad you asked me to come. I've been dying to see your home. Where are my manners? Let me introduce you to my date. Rosalind Harper, this is Bryce Clerk."

"We've met."

"Roz. You look spectacular, as always."

He started to lean down, as if to kiss her. She knew conversations nearby had died off, knew people were watching, listening. Waiting.

She spoke very softly. "Touch me, and I'll kick your balls right up into your throat."

"I'm an invited guest in your home." Bryce's voice was smooth, and lifted enough to reach interested ears. She watched him fix an expression of injured shock on his face. "Rudeness doesn't become you."

"I don't understand." Hands clasped together, Mandy looked from one to the other. "I don't understand."

"I'm sure you don't. Mandy, why don't you and your escort come out front with me a moment?"

She heard the vicious curse behind her, fought valiantly not to wince. She turned, and again kept her voice low. "Harper. Don't. Please."

When she shifted her body to block his, Harper's gaze snapped from Bryce to his mother. "Once and for all."

"I'm going to take care of it. Let me take care of it." She rubbed a hand over his arm, felt his muscles quivering. "Please."

"Not alone."

"Two minutes." She kissed his cheek, whispered in his ear. "He wants a scene. We won't give it to him. He gets nothing from us. Two minutes, baby."

She turned. "Mandy? Let's get a little air, all right?" She took the woman by the arm.

Bryce held his ground. "This is ungracious of you, Rosalind. You're embarrassing yourself, and your guests. I'd hoped we could be civil, at least."

"I suppose your hopes are dashed then."

She saw the change in his face as he looked over her shoulder. She followed his direction, noted that Mitch stood beside Harper now, and that Logan and David were both moving into the foyer. Their expressions were far less *civil*, she decided, than hers.

"Who's the asshole?" Mitch's question was barely a mutter, but Roz heard it, just as she heard Harper's answer.

"Bryce Clerk. The garbage she tossed out a few years ago."

Roz drew Mandy outside. Bryce was an idiot, she thought, and he might've enjoyed an altercation, a public one, with Harper. But he wouldn't take on several strong, angry men, even for the pleasure of embarrassing her in her own home.

She was proven right as he walked stiffly out the door behind her. Roz shut it.

"Mandy, this is my ex-husband. The one I found upstairs, at a similar party, with his hands all over the naked breasts of a mutual acquaintance."

"That's a damn lie. There was nothing—"

Her head whipped around. "You're free to tell Mandy your side of things, when you're not standing on my doorstep. You are not welcome here. You will never be welcome here. If you come onto my property again, I will call the police and have you arrested for trespassing. And you can bet your lying, cheating ass I will prosecute. Now you have one minute, and one minute only, to get in your car and get off my land."

She turned, smiled now into Mandy's shocked face. "Mandy, you're certainly welcome to come in, to stay. I'll arrange for you to be taken home later if you like."

"I think I should . . . I, ah, guess I should go."

"All right, then. I'll see you next month at the meeting. Merry Christmas."

She stepped back, but didn't open the door. "I believe you're down to about forty seconds now before I go inside and contact the police."

"Everyone in there knows what you are now," Bryce shot out at her as he pulled Mandy toward his car.

"I'm sure they do."

She waited until he'd gunned the engine, until he'd sped off.

Only then did she press a hand to her sick stomach, and squeeze her eyes shut until she could bank back the trembling rage and embarrassment.

She took two deep breaths, lifted her head high, then walked back into the house.

She smiled, brilliantly, then held out a hand for Harper's.

"Well," she said, giving his hand a squeeze as she scanned curious faces, "I could use a drink."

five

When the party was over, and the guests on their way home, Roz couldn't settle. She knew better than to go up to her rooms, where she would just pace and rehash and twist herself up over this personal humiliation.

Instead, she made herself a big mug of coffee and took it out on the patio to enjoy the cool and the solitude. With the heaters humming and the lights still twinkling, she sat down to sip, to enjoy and maybe to brood just a little.

Harper was angry with her, she knew. Angry because she'd held him off from physically ejecting Bryce from the house. He was still young enough—and bless his heart, he was a man on top of it—to believe that brute force could solve this particular problem. And he loved her enough to chain his temper down because she'd asked.

At least this time he'd managed to chain it down.

The single other time Bryce had attempted to enter Harper House without invitation, she'd been too shocked to hold Harper off. Or David, for that matter. Bryce had been thrown out on his cheating ass, and she was small enough to gain some satisfaction from the way her boy had hauled the man out. But what had it solved?

Bryce had accomplished then just what he'd accomplished this round. He'd upset her.

How long, she wondered, just how goddamn long was she supposed to pay for one stupid, reckless mistake?

When she heard the door open behind her, Roz tensed up. She didn't want to rehash this nasty little business with David or Harper, didn't want a man to pat her head and tell her not to worry.

She wanted to sit and brood alone.

"I don't know about you, but I could use some chocolate."

Surprised, Roz watched Stella set a tray on the table. "I thought you'd gone up to bed."

"I always like to decompress a little after a big party. Then there was the matter of these chocolate truffles, just sitting out there in the kitchen, calling my name."

She'd brewed tea, Roz noted, and remembered Stella wasn't one for late-night coffee. And she'd arranged the leftover truffles on a pretty plate.

"Hayley would be down, too, but Lily woke up. She must be cutting a tooth, because she's fussing. It's beautiful out here. Middle of December, and it's just so beautiful. Not even much of a bite to the air yet."

"Did you practice the small talk, decide you'd open with the weather?"

There had been a time when that aloof tone would have had Stella easing back. But those days were over. "I always figure the weather's a good starter, especially for a couple of gardeners. I was going to segue into how spectacular the poinsettias are this year, but I guess we'll skip that part."

She selected a truffle, bit in. "But the chocolate was just a natural, all around. God, whoever invented these should be canonized."

"Ask Hayley. If she doesn't know who made the first chocolate truffle, she'll find out." Since the chocolate was there, Roz couldn't come up with a good reason not to have one.

"I've been here nearly a year now," Stella began.

"Is this your way of leading up to asking for a raise?"

"No, but good idea. I've worked for you for nearly a year, lived in the same house with you. The second part is certainly longer than I intended."

"No point in moving somewhere else, then moving again when you and Logan get married."

"No, and I appreciate you understanding that, and making it easy for me not to shuffle my kids around. The fact is, even though I'm looking forward to getting married, and moving into Logan's place—especially now that I've been getting my hands on it—I'll miss being here. So will the boys."

"It's nice to hear."

"Even with everything that went on last spring, maybe in some ways because of it, I'm attached to this house. And to you."

"That's nice to hear, too. You have a sweet heart to go with that orderly mind of yours, Stella."

"Thanks." She sat back in her chair, cupping her tea in both hands. Her flower-blue eyes were directly on Roz's. "Living with and working for you for nearly a year, I know your mind and heart. At least as much as I can. One of the things I know is that despite your generosity, your hospitality, you're a very private woman. And I know I'm stepping into that private area when I say I'm sorry about what happened tonight. I'm sorry and I'm angry and just a little bit stunned that some asshole would walk into your home, uninvited and unwelcomed, for the purpose of embarrassing you."

When Roz said nothing, Stella took a long breath. "So,

if you're in the mood to eat truffles and trash the son of a bitch, I'd be happy to listen. If you'd rather sit out here alone, and let it fester, then I'll take my tea and half these chocolates upstairs."

For a moment, Roz just sat, sipping her coffee. Then she thought, what the hell, and had another chocolate. "You know, having lived here all my life, I have a number of friends, and a bevy, we could say, of acquaintances. But I haven't had what you might call close, important female friends. There's a reason for that—"

She lifted a finger, wagged it before Stella could speak. "The reason being my own preference to an extent, and that having its roots in being widowed young. So many of my social circle, in the female area, became just a little wary. Here I was, young, attractive, fairly well off—and available. Or so they assumed. In the other camp were those eager, just innately, to pair me up with a man. A friend, a brother, a cousin, whatever. I found both of those attitudes annoying. As a result, I got out of the habit of having close women friends. So I'm a little rusty. I consider you a friend, the best I have of the female persuasion."

"Since I feel the same about you, I wish you'd let me help you. Even if it's only to say really nasty things about that fucking Bryce Clerk and bring you chocolate."

"Why, Stella." Roz's voice was as creamy as the truffles. "I believe that's the first time in this entire year I've heard you say fuck."

Stella flushed a little, the curse of redheads. "I reserve it for special occasions."

"This is certainly that." Roz tipped her head back and studied the stars. "He didn't do it to embarrass me. That was just a side benefit."

"Then why? Did he think, could he actually be stupid enough to think you'd have let him come in and party?"

"He may have thought my need to maintain image would give him a pass, and if I had, just a little more grease to oil the gears of whatever moneymaking plots and plans he has going."

"If so, he couldn't know you very well to have underestimated you like that."

"He knows enough that he got exactly what he was after tonight. The young woman he had on his arm? She's very wealthy, and very silly. Chances are she'll feel some sympathy, even some outrage on his behalf over tonight."

"Then she's more than silly. She's bone stupid."

"Maybe, but he's an accomplished liar, and slick as a snake. I'm not silly or stupid, and I fell for it."

"You loved him, so—"

"Oh, honey, I didn't love him. Thank God for that." She shuddered at the thought of it. "I enjoyed the attention, the flattery, and initially at least, the romance and sex of it. Added to that I had a raging case of empty nest, so I was ripe for plucking. My own fault that I went and married him instead of sleeping with him until I got bored, or saw what was under that pretty exterior."

"I don't know if that makes it worse or better," Stella said after a moment.

"Neither do I, but it is what it is. In any case, he wanted to remind me he exists, that he can and does swim in the same social pond. He wanted, primarily, for me to be upset and to think about him. Mission accomplished. He has a need for attention, to have attention focused on him—for better or worse. The worst punishment I can give him is to ignore him, which I've done, fairly successfully, since he came back to Memphis. Tonight was a way, a very clever way, of shoving himself in my face, in my own home, in front of my guests."

"I wish I'd gotten there quicker. I was nearly at the other end of the house when I heard the rumbles. But I don't see how anyone could get any sort of satisfaction out of being turned away, in public, the way I heard you turned him away."

"You don't know Bryce. He'll dine off the incident for weeks. Center of attention, and he has a smooth way." Her short, unpainted nails tapped against her teacup. "Before he's done, he'll be the underdog. All he'd done was try to mend fences, to come by to wish me well, it being the holidays and all. And what had I done but rebuffed him, and humiliated his date—an invited guest."

She stopped a moment to suck back the fresh rage. "People will say: 'My goodness, how cold and hard, how ungracious and rude of her.'"

"Then people are idiots."

"Yes, indeed they are. Which is why I rarely socialize with them. And why I've been so particular in my friends. And why I'm very grateful to have one who would sit out here with me at this time of night, eating chocolate truffles while I feel sorry for myself."

She let out a long breath. "And damned if I don't feel better. Let's go on up. Get some sleep. We're going to have us a busy day tomorrow, with the gossip sniffers slinking in along with the regular customers."

SOME WOULD HAVE CALLED IT BURYING HERSELF IN work. Roz called it doing what needed to be done and enjoying every minute of it. She loved winter chores, loved closing herself in for hours, even days in a greenhouse and starting new life, nurturing it along. Her seedlings, and cuttings, sprouts started by layering or leaf buds. She loved the smell of rooting compound and damp, and watching the stages of progress.

There were pests and problems to guard against here, just as there were in life. When she caught signs of downy mildew or rusts, she snipped off the infected leaves, sprayed the plants. She checked air circulation, adjusted temperature.

Any cuttings that showed signs of rot or virus were systematically removed and discarded. She would not allow infection here, any more than she allowed it in her life.

It soothed her to work, and to remember that. She had cut Bryce off, discarded him, rid her life of *that* infection. Maybe not quite soon enough, maybe she hadn't been quite vigilant enough, so even now she was forced to guard and control.

But she was strong, and the life she'd built was strong enough to withstand these small, annoying invasions.

Thinking of that, she finished her list of tasks for the day, then sought out Harper.

She slipped into his grafting house, knowing he wouldn't hear her right away, not with Beethoven soaring for the plants, and whatever music he'd chosen for himself that day booming in his headset.

She took a moment, a moment that made her feel tender, to watch him work. Old sweatshirt, older jeans, grubby boots—he'd have been out in the field off and on that day, she realized.

He'd gotten a haircut recently, so all that glossy black fell in a sleeker, more ordered style. She wondered how long that would last? If she knew her boy—and she did—he'd forget about that little grooming task for weeks until he ended up grabbing a piece of raffia to tie his hair back while he worked.

He was so competent, so creative here. Each of her sons had his own talent, his own direction—she'd made sure of it—but only Harper had inherited her abiding love for gardening.

She moved down through the tables crowded with plants and tools and mediums to watch him skillfully graft a miniature rose.

When he'd finished the specimen, reached for the can of Coke that was always nearby, she moved into his line of vision.

She saw him focus on her as he sipped.

"Nice job," she said. "You don't often do roses."

"Experimenting with these. Thought we might be able to have a section for container-grown miniatures. Working on a climbing mini, and some ground-cover specimens. Want a Coke?"

"No, thanks." He was so much *her*, she thought. How many times had she heard that polite, cool tone come out of her own mouth when she was irritated. "I know you're upset with me, Harper."

"No point in me being upset."

"Point isn't, well, the point, is it?" She wanted to stroke his shoulders, rub her cheek to his. But he'd stiffen, just as she would if someone touched her before she was ready to be touched.

"You're angry with the way I handled things last night. With the way I wouldn't let you handle them."

"Your choice." He jerked a shoulder. "And I'm not mad at you. I'm disappointed in you, that's all."

If he'd taken his grafting knife and stabbed it into her heart, she'd have felt less pain, less shock. "Harper."

"Did you have to be so goddamn polite? Couldn't you have given him what he deserved right then and there instead of brushing me back and taking it outside?"

"What good would—"

"I don't give a *shit* about what good, Mama." The infamous Harper temper smoldered in his eyes. "He deserved to have his clock cleaned, right on the spot. You should've let me stand up for you. But it had to be your way, with me standing there doing nothing. So what is the damn point?"

She wanted to turn away, to take a moment to compose herself, but he deserved better. He deserved face-to-face. "There's no one in this world who can hurt me the way you can."

"I'm not trying to hurt you."

"No, you're not. You wouldn't. That's how I know just how angry you are. And how I can see where it comes from. Maybe I was wrong." She lifted her hands to rub them over her face. "I don't know, but it's the only way I know. I had to get him out of the house. I'm asking you to understand that I *had* to get him out of our house, quickly and before he'd smeared it all again."

She dropped her hands, and her face was naked with regret. "I brought him into our home, Harper. I did that, you didn't."

"That doesn't mean you're to blame, for Christ's sake, or that you have to handle something like that by yourself. If you can't depend on me to help you, to stand up for you—"

"Oh, God, Harper. Here you are, sitting in here thinking I don't need you when half the time I'm worried I need you too much for your own good. I don't know what I'd do without you, that's the God's truth. I don't want to fight with you over him." Now she pressed her fingers to her eyes. "He's nothing but a bully."

"And I'm not a little boy you have to protect from bullies anymore, Mama. I'm a man, and it's my job now to protect you. Whether you want it or not. And whether you damn well need it or not."

She dropped her hands again, nearly managed a smile this time. "I guess that's telling me."

"He comes to the door again, you won't stop me."

She drew a breath, then framed his face with her hands. "I know you're a man. It pains me sometimes, but I know you're a man with his own life, his own ways. I know you're a man, Harper, who'll stand beside me when I ask, even though you'd rather stand in front of me and fight the battle."

Though she knew she wasn't quite forgiven, she pressed a kiss to his forehead. "I'm going on home to work in the garden. Don't stay mad at me too long."

"Probably won't."

"There's some of that baked ham left over from the party. Plenty of side dishes, too, if you wanted to come by and forage for dinner."

"Might."

"All right, then. You know where to find me."

WITH GARDENS AS EXTENSIVE AS HERS, THERE WAS always some chore to do. Since she wanted work, Roz hauled mulch, checked her compost, worked with the cuttings and seedlings she grew for her personal use in the small greenhouse at home.

Then grabbing gloves and her loppers, she headed out to finish up some end-of-the-year pruning.

When Mitch found her, she was shoving small branches into a little chipper. It rattled hungrily as it chewed, with its dull red paint looking industrious.

As she did, he thought, in her dirt-brown and battered jacket, the black cap, thick gloves, and scarred boots. There were shaded glasses hiding her eyes, and he wondered if she wore them against the beam of sunlight, or as protection against flying wood chips.

He knew she couldn't hear him over the noise of the chipper, so took a moment just to watch her. And let himself meld the sparkling woman in rubies with the busy gardener in faded jeans.

Then there was the to-the-point woman in a business suit who'd first come to his apartment. Roz of the tropical greenhouse with a smudge of soil on her cheek. And the casual, friendly Roz who'd taken the time to help him select a child's toy.

Lots of angles to her, he decided, and likely more than he'd already seen. Strangely enough, he was attracted to every one of them.

With his thumbs hooked in his front pockets, he moved

into her line of vision. She glanced up from under the brim of the ballcap, then switched off the machine.

"You don't need to stop on my account," he told her. "It's the first time I've seen one of those things in action except in *Fargo*."

"This one isn't quite up to disposing of a body, but it does the job for garden chores."

She knew *Fargo*, he thought, ridiculously pleased. It was a sign they had some common ground. "Uh-huh." He peered down where most of a branch had gone inside. "So you just shove stuff in there, and chop, chop, chop."

"More or less."

"Then what do you do with what's left?"

"Enough branches and leaves and such, you get yourself a nice bag of mulch."

"Handy. Well, I didn't mean to interrupt, but David said you were out here. I thought I'd come by, get in a couple hours of research."

"That's fine. I didn't figure you'd have much time to spare on it until after the holidays."

"I've got time. I'm getting copies of official records, and I need to make some notes from your family Bible, that sort of thing. Get some order before I can dig down below the surface."

He brushed a good-sized wood chip from her shoulder and wished she'd take off the sunglasses. Her eyes just killed him.

"And I'd like to set up times for those interviews, for after the holidays."

"All right."

He stood, his hands in the pockets of his leather jacket. He was stalling, he knew, but she smelled so damn good. Just a hint of secret female under the woody scent. "Funny, I didn't think much went on in a garden this time of year."

"Something goes on every time of year."

"And I'm holding you up. Listen, I wanted to see if you were all right."

"I'm fine. Just fine."

"It'd be stupid for me to pretend I didn't hear murmurs about what was behind that scene last night. Or what would have been a scene if you hadn't handled things so . . . adroitly."

"Adroitly's how I prefer handling things, whenever possible."

"And if you're going to get your back up when a conversation between us touches on the personal, it's going to be tough to research your family history."

Because he was watching carefully, because he was learning to read her, he saw the annoyance flick over her face before she composed it. "Last night has nothing whatsoever to do with my family history."

"I disagree. It involves you, and this . . . thing going on in your house involves you."

She might kick him out as . . . adroitly as she had Bryce Clerk, but if so, it would be because he was honest and up-front.

"I'm going to pry, Roz. That's what you've hired me to do, and I won't always pry gently. If you want me to move forward with this, you'll have to get used to it."

"I fail to see what my regrettable and thankfully brief second marriage could have to do with the Harper Bride."

He didn't have to see her eyes clearly to know they'd chilled. He heard it in her voice. "Bride. Whether or not she was one, she's referred to as such through your family lore. When she . . . manifested herself," he decided, "last spring—in spades—you said she'd never bothered with you when you'd socialized with men, or when you'd married— as she had with Stella."

"Stella has small children. My children are grown."

"Doesn't make them less your children."

Her shoulders relaxed, then she bent to scoop up some smaller twigs and toss them in the mouth of the chipper. "No, of course, it doesn't."

"So, we can theorize that she didn't feel threatened by Bryce—and what the hell kind of name is that anyway? Stupid. Or that she considered your maternal duties done, and didn't care what you did regarding your sex life. Or that after a certain point, she stops showing herself to whoever's living in the house."

"It can't be three, as I've seen her recently."

"Since June?"

"Just a few days ago, and then again last night."

"Interesting. What were you doing, what was she doing? I should have my notebook."

"It was nothing. She was there, then she wasn't. I don't expect you to solve the puzzle of why she comes, or to whom. I want you to find out who she was."

"One puzzle's connected to the other. I really want some time to talk to you. And this is obviously not it. Maybe we can have dinner, next evening you're free."

"It's not necessary for you to buy me dinner to get an interview."

"It might be enjoyable to buy you dinner. If you have strong objections to mixing business and pleasure, I'm going to be sorry to wait to ask you out until I'm finished with this project."

"I don't date anymore, Mitch. I gave it up."

"The word *date* always makes me feel like I'm back in college. Or worse, high school." He took a chance and reached out to slide her glasses down her nose. Looked directly into her eyes. "We could just say that I'm interested in spending time with you on a social level."

"That says *date* to me." But she smiled before she scooted the glasses back in place. "Not that I don't appreciate it."

"We'll settle for an interview for now. I'm going to be in and out the next couple of weeks, so you can let me know when you've got time to sit down for an extended period. Otherwise, you can call me at home, and we'll set it up."

"That's fine."

"I'll go in, get some work done. Let you get back to yours."

When he started to walk away, she reached for the switch on the chipper.

"Roz? Any time you change your mind about dinner, you just let me know."

"I'll be sure to do that." She switched on the machine, pushed the branch in.

SHE WORKED UNTIL SHE LOST THE LIGHT, THEN STOWED her tools before climbing the steps to the second-floor terrace and her outside door.

She wanted an endless hot shower, soft clothes, then a cold glass of wine. No, she thought. A martini. One of David's amazing, icy martinis with the fancy olives he squirreled away. Then she'd make a sandwich out of that glorious leftover ham. Maybe she'd spend most of the evening playing with sketches and ideas for the florist expansion. Then there were the bag selections Stella had gotten for her, for the in-house potting soil.

Dates, she thought as she shed her clothes and turned on the shower. She didn't have time, certainly didn't have the inclination to date at this stage of her life. Even if the offer had come from a very attractive, intelligent, and intriguing man.

One who'd ask her out when she was covered with wood chips.

Why couldn't they just have sex and clear the air?

Because she wasn't built that way, she admitted. And wasn't that too damn bad. There had to be a little more . . . something before she stripped down, literally and figuratively, with a man.

She liked him, well enough, she thought as she tipped her head back and let the hot water beat on her face, her shoulders. She appreciated the way he'd reacted last spring when there'd been trouble, admired—now that she had the distance to look back—the way he'd leaped in without hesitation, without investment.

Some men would have run the other way, and would certainly have dismissed the idea of working for her, in a house haunted by what they now knew could be a dangerous spirit.

And well, she'd been charmed, really, at the way he'd been so flummoxed over buying a child's gift—and how much he'd wanted to find the right thing. It was a point in his favor.

If she were keeping score.

If she wanted to dip her toe in the dating pool again, it would probably be with someone like him. Someone she could have conversations with, someone who attracted and interested her.

And it didn't hurt that he was what Hayley termed a hottie.

Then again, look what happened last time.

It was a stupid woman who'd use anyone like Bryce as a yardstick. She *knew* that, so why couldn't she stop? The fact that she was doing it was a sort of victory for Bryce, wasn't it? If she could do nothing else about it, she could and would work on pushing him out of her thoughts.

Prick.

All right, she thought as she switched the water off again and reached for a towel. Maybe she'd consider—just consider—going out to dinner with Mitch. Just to prove to herself that she wasn't letting Bryce affect her life in any way.

A little dinner out, some conversation, a mix of business and pleasure. That wouldn't be so bad, when she drummed up the energy for it. She wouldn't mind seeing him on a personal level. In fact, it might help all around if she got to know him better.

She'd think about it.

After wrapping the towel around her body, she reached automatically for her lotion. And her hand froze inches from the bottle.

Written in the steam of the bathroom mirror were two words.

Men Lie!

SIX

ROZ PUT MEN, FAMILY GHOSTS, AND MESSAGES WRITTEN in steam out of her mind. Her sons were home.

The house was full of them, their voices, their energy, their debris. Once, the piles of shoes, the hats, the *things* they'd leave scattered around had driven her slightly crazy. Now she loved seeing the evidence of them. Once, she'd longed for an ordered, quiet house, and now reveled in the noise and confusion.

They'd be gone soon enough, back to the lives they were building. So she would treasure every minute of the two days she had her family under one roof again.

And wasn't it fun to see her sons with Stella's boys, or watch Harper lift a fussy Lily and cuddle her in his arms? It made up for finding herself at the head of this mixed generational train.

"I want to thank you for letting Logan stay tonight." Stella settled onto the sofa beside Roz.

"It's Christmas Eve. We generally have room at the inn."

"You know what I mean, and *I* know it's probably fussy

and anal and silly, but I really want our first Christmas in his—*our*—house to be when we're official."

"I think it's sweet and sentimental, and selfishly I'm glad everyone's here tonight." She watched Hayley scoop Lily up as the baby made a crawling beeline for the tree. "Glad to have children in the house tonight. Austin!" she called out as her middle son began to juggle three apples he'd plucked out of a bowl. "Not in the parlor."

"That tune's so familiar, I can add the music." A tall, narrow-hipped young man with his father's wavy blond hair, he winked at Gavin while giving the apples one more rotation. "Not in the parlor, Austin, not in the parlor," he sang, making Stella's sons roll with laughter before he tossed them each an apple, and took a bite out of the third.

"Here, Mama, have some wine." Her youngest, Mason, sat on the arm of the sofa and handed her a glass. There was a wicked twinkle in his blue eyes that warned Roz trouble was coming. "Austin, you know the parlor is sacred ground. You don't want to be juggling in here. Especially something like, say, shoes."

"You can juggle shoes!" Awestruck, Luke goggled at Austin.

"I can juggle anything. I have amazing talent and dexterity."

"But sadly, I wasn't able to talk him into running off and joining the circus when he was eight." Harper took Lily when she leaned away from Hayley and held out her chubby arms to him.

"Can you juggle mine?" Luke asked.

"Hand one over."

"Austin." Resigned, Roz sighed and sipped her wine. "You break anything, you're grounded."

"Why, another familiar tune. Let's see, I need a challenge. Logan, looks to me like that shoe's big enough to house a family of four. Let's have it."

"I give you my shoe, you get grounded, I get fired. Call me a coward, but I'll soon have two growing boys to feed." He reached down to poke Gavin in the ribs. "And they eat like pigs."

"Oink." Showing off, Gavin grabbed a cookie from a tray and stuffed it whole in his mouth. "Oink."

"Oh, go ahead, Logan." Roz waved a hand. "He won't be satisfied otherwise."

"Let's see, one more." His gaze scanned, landed on Hayley. "Look at those pretty, delicate feet. How about it, sweetheart?"

Hayley laughed. "They're about as delicate as banana boats." But she slipped her shoe off.

"Harper, move your grandmother's Baccarat there to safer ground," Roz ordered, "so your brother can show off."

"I prefer the term *perform*."

"I recall a performance that cost Mama a lamp," Harper commented as he moved heirlooms. "And got all three of us—and you, too, David, if memory serves—KP duty."

"In my salad days," Austin claimed. After giving the trio of varied footwear a few testing tosses, he began to juggle. "As you can see, I've sharpened my skills since that regrettable incident."

"Fortunate to have a fallback career," Mason told him. "You can take that act down to Beale Street."

The circling shoes had Lily giggling and bouncing on Harper's hip. For herself, Roz just held her breath until Austin took his bow.

He tossed a shoe back to a delighted Luke. "Can you teach me?"

"Me, too!" Gavin insisted.

"She's going to say 'not in the parlor,'" Austin announced even as Roz opened her mouth. "We'll work in a lesson tomorrow—outside—keep us all safe from Mama's wrath."

"She's the boss of everybody," Luke told him solemnly.

"No flies on you. Since nobody's seen fit to throw money, I'll have to settle for a beer."

He strolled over to hand Logan his shoe, then walked to Hayley. "All right, Cinderella, let's see if this fits."

He made a production out of slipping it back on her foot, then grinned at Harper over Hayley's head. "Shoe fits." He took her hand, kissed it. "We'll just have to get ourselves married when I get back from the kitchen."

"That's what they all say." But she gave him a flirting sweep with her eyes.

"Why don't you get me a beer while you're at it?" Mason asked.

"If I'm taking orders, what can I get everyone?"

After a scatter of requests, he looked over at Harper again. "Why don't you give me a hand fetching the supplies?"

"Sure." He passed Lily back to Hayley, and followed his brother out of the room.

"Can't miss this," Mason whispered to his mother, then strolled out behind them.

"PRETTY THING, ISN'T SHE, OUR COUSIN HAYLEY?" Austin commented.

"You've always had a keen knack for stating the obvious."

"Then I'll keep my streak going by saying I think she's soft on me."

"And an infallible way of misjudging women."

"Hold on," Mason told them. "I've got to find something to write on so I can keep score."

"She's got the prettiest mouth. Not that you'd notice, big brother, since it's not something growing out of a pot." He took out a beer, had a swig from the bottle even as Harper got out pilsners.

"And the only way you'd get your fat lips on hers is if she has a seizure and requires mouth-to-mouth."

"He shoots, he scores. By the way, I'm the doctor here," Mason reminded them. "She needs mouth-to-mouth, I'm first in line. We got any Fritos or anything around here?"

"Got ten bucks says different." In an old habit, Austin boosted himself up to sit on the counter. "Maybe you could babysit so I can see if our resident babe would like a little stroll around the gardens. Seeing as I haven't heard you call dibs."

"She's not the damn last piece of pie." With some heat, Harper grabbed the beer from his brother, took a long swallow. "What the hell's wrong with you talking about her that way? You ought to have a little more respect, and if you can't come up with it on you're own, you and I can take a little stroll outside so I can help you find it."

With a grin, Austin jabbed a finger at Mason. "Told ya. Can I call 'em or can I call 'em?"

"Yeah, he's hooked on her. What kind of kitchen is it that doesn't have any Fritos?"

"In the pantry, top shelf," Roz said from the doorway. "I'm surprised you'd think I'd forget your childish addiction to corn chips. Austin, have you finished messing with your brother's head for now?"

"I was really just getting started."

"You'll have to postpone that portion of your holiday entertainment." She glanced over, had to smile when she heard Mason's cheer as he located the bag of chips. "We have company, and it might be nice if we present the illusion that I raised three respectable and mature young men."

"That's pretty well shattered since he's already juggled," Harper grumbled.

"There's a point." She moved over to touch Harper's cheek, then Austin's before she turned to Mason. "You may not be respectable and mature, but by God, the three of you sure are handsome. I could've done worse. Now get those drinks together, Harper, and take them out to our guests. Austin, get your butt off my counter. This is a house, not the neighborhood bar. Mason, put those chips into a bowl, and stop dropping crumbs all over the floor."

"Yes'm," they said in unison, and made her laugh.

CHRISTMAS DAY WENT BY IN A BLUR. SHE TRIED TO imprint specific moments on her mind—Mason's sheer delight in the antique medical bag she'd found him, Harper and Austin squaring off over a foosball table. There was Lily's predictable fascination with boxes and wrapping rather than toys, and Hayley's joy in showing off a new pair of earrings.

She loved seeing Logan sitting cross-legged on the floor, showing Stella's boys—his boys now—the child-sized tools inside the toolboxes he'd made them.

She wanted to slow the clock down—just for this day, just this one day—but it sped by, from dawn and the excitement of opening gifts, to the candlelight and the lavish meal David prepared and served on her best china.

Before she knew it, the house was quiet once more.

She wandered down to take a last look at the tree, to sit alone in the parlor with her coffee and her memories of the day, and all the Christmases before.

Surprised when she heard footsteps, she looked over and saw her sons.

"I thought you'd all gone over to Harper's."

"We were waiting for you to come down," Harper told her.

"Come down?"

"You always come down Christmas night, after everyone's gone to bed."

She lifted her eyebrows at Mason. "I have no secrets in this house."

"Plenty of them," he disagreed. "Just not this one."

Austin came over, took her coffee, and replaced it with a glass of champagne.

"What's all this?"

"Little family toast," he told her. "But that comes after this one last gift we've got for you."

"Another? I'm going to have to add a room on the house to hold everything I got this morning."

"This is special. You've already got a place for it. Or did at one time."

"Well, don't keep me in suspense. What have y'all cooked up?"

Harper stepped back into the hall and brought in a large box wrapped in gold foil. He set it at her feet. "Why don't you open it and see?"

Curious, she set her glass aside and began to work on the wrap. "Don't tell Stella I'm tearing this off, she'd be horrified. Myself, I'm amazed the three of you got together and agreed on something, much less kept it quiet until tonight. Mason always blabs."

"Hey, I can keep a secret when I have to. You don't know about the time Austin took your car and—"

"Shut up." Austin punched his brother's shoulder. "There's no statute of limitations on that sort of crime." He smiled sweetly at Roz's narrowed look. "What you don't know, Mama, can't hurt this idiot."

"I suppose." But she wondered on it as she dug through the packing. And her heart simply stuttered as she drew out the antique dressing mirror.

"It was the closest we could come to the one we broke. Pattern's nearly the same, and the shape," Harper said.

"Queen Anne," Austin added, "circa 1700, with that gold and green lacquer on the slanted drawer. At least, it's the best our combined memories could match the one Mason broke."

"Hey! It was Harper's idea to use it as a treasure chest. It's not my fault I dropped it out of the damn tree. I was the baby."

"Oh, God. Oh, God, I was so mad, so mad, I nearly skinned y'all alive."

"We have painful recollection of that," Austin assured her.

"It was from your daddy's family." Voice thick, throat aching, she traced her fingers over the lacquered wood. "He gave it to me on our wedding day."

"We should've been skinned." Harper sat down beside her, rubbed her arm. "We know it's not the same, but—"

"No, no, no." Swamped with emotion, she turned her face to press it against his arm for a moment. "It's better. That you'd remember this, think of this. Do this."

"It made you cry," Mason murmured, and bent to rub his cheek over her hair. "It's the first time I remember seeing you cry. None of us ever forgot it, Mama."

She was struggling not to cry now as she embraced each one of her sons. "It's the most beautiful gift I've ever been given, and I'll treasure it more than anything I have. Every time I look at it, I'll think of the way you were then, the way you are now. I'm so proud of my boys. I always have been. Even when I wanted to skin you."

Austin picked up her glass, handed it to her, then passed around the other three flutes. "Harper gets the honors, as he's the oldest. But I want it on record that I thought it up."

"We all thought it up," Mason objected.

"I thought most of it up. Go on, Harper."

"I will, if you'll shut up for five seconds." He lifted his glass. "To our mama, for everything she's been to us, every-thing she's done for us, every single day."

"Oh. That's done it." The tears welled into her throat, spilled out of her eyes. "That's done it for sure."

"Go ahead and cry." Mason leaned over to kiss her damp cheek. "Makes a nice circle."

* * *

GETTING BACK TO BUSINESS AS USUAL HELPED FILL THE
little hole in her heart from kissing two of her sons goodbye.

It would be a slow week—the holiday week was,
routinely—so she took a page out of Stella's book and
shouldered in to organizing. She cleaned tools, scrubbed
down worktables, helped with inventory, and finally settled
on the style of potting-soil bag, and the design.

With some time to spare, she worked with Hayley to
pour a fresh supply of concrete planters and troughs.

"I can't believe Christmas is over." Squatting, Hayley
turned the mold as Roz poured. "All that anticipation and
prep, and it's over in a snap. Last year, my first after
my daddy died? Well, it was just awful, and the holidays
dragged and dragged."

"Grief tends to spin time out, and joy contracts it. I
don't know why that is."

"I remember just wanting it all to be over—so I wouldn't
keep hearing "Jingle Bells" every time I went to work, you
know? Being pregnant, and feeling alone, the house up for
sale. I spent most of Christmas packing things up, figuring
out what I was going to sell so I could leave Little Rock."

She sat back on her heels to sigh, happily. "And here,
just one year later, and everything was so bright and happy.
I know Lily didn't know what was going on, but it was so
much fun to watch her play with her toys, or mostly the
boxes."

"Nothing like a cardboard box to keep a baby entertained. It was special for me, for all of us, to have her, to be
able to share that first Christmas with her."

With the mold full, Hayley tidied the edges with a trowel.
"I know you love her, but, Roz, I just don't feel right about

you staying home New Year's Eve to sit with her while I go out to a party."

"I prefer staying home New Year's Eve. Lily gives me the perfect excuse. And I'm looking forward to having her to myself."

"You must've been invited to half a dozen parties."

"More." Roz straightened, pressed the small of her back. "I'm not interested. You go on out with David and celebrate with other young people. Wear your new earrings and dance. Lily and I will be just fine seeing the new year in together."

"David said he never could talk you into going to this party, even though it's been a tradition for years now." She picked up a bottle of water, drank casually. "He said Harper would probably drop by."

"I imagine so. They have a number of mutual friends." Amused, she patted Hayley's shoulder. "Let's get this next one done, then call it a day."

She was tired when she got home, but in that satisfied way of knowing she'd crossed several chores off her list. When she noticed Mitch's car in her drive, she was surprised to find herself considering going up to change before seeking him out in the library.

Which was, she reminded herself, both a waste of time and hardly her style. So she was wearing her work clothes when she walked into the library.

"Have everything you need?"

He looked up from the piles of books and papers on the library table. Stared at her through the lenses of his horn-rim reading glasses. "Huh?"

"I just got in. I thought I'd see if there was anything else you need."

"A couple dozen years to organize all of this, a new pair of eyes . . ." He lifted the pot on the desk with him. "More coffee."

"I can help with the last at least." She crossed over, mounted the steps to the second level.

"No, that's all right. My blood level's probably ninety percent caffeine at this point. What time is it?"

She noted the watch on his wrist, then looked at her own. "Ten after five."

"A.M. or P.M.?"

"Been at it that long?"

"Long enough to lose track, as usual." He rubbed the back of one shoulder, circled his neck. "You have some fascinating relatives, Rosalind. I've gathered up enough newspaper clippings on the Harpers, going back to the mid-nineteenth century so far, to fill a banker's box. Did you know, for instance, you have an ancestor who rode for the Pony Express in 1860, and in the 1880s traveled with Buffalo Bill's Wild West Show?"

"My great-great-uncle Jeremiah, who'd run off as a boy, it seems, to ride for the Pony Express. Fought Indians, scouted for the Army, took both a Comanche wife and, apparently, another in Kansas City—at more or less the same time. He was a trick rider in the Wild West Show, and was considered a black sheep by the stuffier members of the clan in his day."

"How about Lucybelle?"

"Ah . . ."

"Gotcha. Married Daniel C. Harper, 1858, left him two years later." The chair creaked as he leaned back. "She pops up again in San Francisco, in 1862, where she opened her own saloon and bawdy house."

"That one slipped by me."

"Well, Daniel C. claimed that he sent her to a clinic in New York, for her health, and that she died there of a wasting disease. Wishful thinking on his part, I assume. But with a little work and magic, I found our Lucybelle entertaining the rough-and-ready crowd in California, where she lived in apparent good health for another twenty-three years."

"You really love this stuff."

"I really do. Imagine Jeremiah, age fifteen, galloping over the plains to deliver the mail. Young, gutsy, skinny. They advertised for skinny boys so they didn't weigh down the horses."

"Really." She eased a hip on the corner of his desk.

"Bent over his mount, riding hell-for-leather, outrunning war parties, covered with dirt and sweat, or half frozen from the cold."

"And from your tone, you'd say having the time of his life."

"Had to be something, didn't it? Then there's Lucy-belle, former Memphis society wife, in a red dress with a derringer in her garter—"

"Aren't you the romantic one."

"Had to have a derringer in her garter while she's manning the bar or bilking miners at cards night after night."

"I wonder if their paths ever crossed."

"There you go," he said, pleased. "That's how you get caught up in all this. It's possible, you know. Jeremiah might've swung through the doors of that saloon, had a whiskey at the bar."

"And enjoyed the other servings on the menu, all while the more staid of the family fanned themselves on the veranda and complained about the war."

"There's a lot of staid, a lot of black sheep here. There was money and there was prestige."

He pushed some papers around, came up with a copy of another clipping. "And considerable charm."

She studied the photo of herself, on her engagement, a fresh and vibrant seventeen.

"I wasn't yet out of high school. Green as grass and mule stubborn. Nobody could talk me out of marrying John

Ashby the June after this picture was taken. God, don't I look ready for anything?"

"I've got clippings of your parents in here. You don't look like either of them."

"No. I was always told I resembled my grandfather Harper. He died when I was a child, but from the pictures I've seen, I favor him."

"Yeah, I've come across a few, and you do. Reginald Edward Harper, Jr, born . . . 1892, youngest child and only son of Reginald and Beatrice Harper." He read his notes. "Married, ah . . ."

"Elizabeth McKinnon. I remember her very well. It was she who gave me her love of gardening, and taught me about plants. My father claimed I was her favorite because I looked like my grandfather. Why don't I get you some tea, something herbal, to offset the coffee?"

"No, that's okay. I can't stay. I've got a date."

"Then I'll let you go."

"With my son," he added. "Pizza and ESPN. We try to fit one in every week."

"That's nice. For both of you."

"It is. Listen, I've got some other things to deal with and some legwork I'd like to get in. But I'll be back on Thursday afternoon, work through the evening, if that's all right with you."

"Thursday's New Year's Eve."

"Is it?" As if baffled, he looked down at his watch. "My days get turned around on me during holidays. I suppose you're having people over."

"Actually, no."

"Then, if you're going out, maybe you wouldn't mind if I worked."

"I'm not going out. I'm going to take care of the baby, Hayley's Lily. I'm scooting her out to a party, and Stella

and her boys are going to have a little family party of their
own at Logan's house."

"If you weren't asked to a dozen parties, and didn't
have twice that many men after you for a New Year's Eve
date, I'll eat those newspaper clippings."

"Your numbers might be somewhat exaggerated, but the
point is, I declined the parties, and the dates. I like staying
home."

"Am I going to be in your way if I work in here?"

She angled her head. "I imagine you were asked to your
share of parties, and that there were a number of women
eager to have you for their date."

"I stay in on New Year's. A tradition of mine."

"Then you won't be in my way. If the baby's not restless,
we can take part of the evening to start on that interview."

"Perfect."

"All right, then. I've been busy," she said after a moment. "The house full over Christmas, all my sons home.
And those are only part of the reason I haven't brought this
up before."

"Brought what up?"

"A couple of weeks ago, Amelia left me a message."

"A couple of *weeks* ago?"

"I said I'd been busy." Irritation edged into her voice.
"And besides that, I didn't want to think about it through the
holidays. I don't see my boys very often, and there were a
lot of things I wanted to get done before they got here."

He said nothing, simply dug out his tape recorder, pushed
it closer to her, switched it on. "Tell me."

Irritation deepened, digging a line between those dark,
expressive eyebrows. "She said: *Men lie.*"

"That's it?"

"Yes, that's it. She wrote it on a mirror."

"What mirror? Did you take a picture of it?"

"No, I didn't take a picture." And she could, privately, kick herself for that later. "I don't know what difference it makes what mirror. The bathroom mirror. I'd just gotten out of the shower. A hot one. The mirror was steamy, and the message was written on it through the steam."

"Written or printed?"

"Ah, printed, with an exclamation point at the end. Like this." She picked up one of his pens, demonstrated. "Since it wasn't threatening or earth-shattering information, I figured it could wait."

"Next time don't—figure it can wait. What had you been doing before you . . ." Don't think about her naked in the shower, he ordered himself. "Before you went up to shower?"

"As a matter of fact, I'd been out in the garden talking to you."

"To me."

"Yes, that day you came by and I was mulching up branches."

"Right after your holiday party," he said, making notes. "I asked you out to dinner."

"You mentioned something about—"

"No, no, I asked you out socially." In his excitement, he came around the table, sat on it so they were closer to eye level. "Next thing you know, she's telling you men lie. Fascinating. She was warning you away from me."

"Since I'm not heading in your direction, there's hardly any reason to warn me away."

"It doesn't seem to bother her that I'm working here." He took off his glasses, tossed them on the table. "I've been waiting, actually hoping for some sort of sighting or confrontation, something. But she hasn't bothered about me, so far. Then I make a personal overture, and she leaves you a message. She ever leave you one before?"

"No."

"Hmm." But he caught something flicker over her face. "What? You thought of something."

"Just that it might be a little odd. I saw her recently right after I'd taken a long, hot bath. Shower, bath. Strange."

Don't think of her naked in the tub. "What had you been doing before the bath?"

"Nothing. Some work, that's all."

"All right. What were you thinking while you were in the tub?"

"I don't see what that has to do with anything. It was the night that I did that insane bout of Christmas shopping. I was relaxing."

"You'd been with me that day, too."

"Your ego looks a little heavy, Mitch. Need any help with it?"

"Facts are facts. Anyway, she might have been interested, or upset, by what you were thinking. If she could get into Stella's dreams," he said when she started to brush that aside, "why couldn't she get into your waking thoughts?"

"I don't like that idea. I don't like it at all."

"Neither would I, but it's something to consider. I'm looking at this project from two ends, Roz. From what's happening now, and why, to what happened then, and why. Who and why and what. It's all of a piece. And that's the job you hired me to do. You have to let me know when something happens. And not a couple weeks after the fact."

"All right. Next time she wakes me up at three in the morning, I'll give you a call."

He smiled. "Don't like taking orders, do you? Much too used to giving them. That's all right. I can't blame you, so why don't I just ask, politely, if I could take a look at your bathroom."

"Not only does that seem downright silly at this point, but aren't you supposed to be meeting your son?"

"Josh? Why? Oh, hell, I forgot. I've got to go." He

glanced back at the table. "I'm going to just leave this—do me a favor and don't tidy it up."

"I'm not obsessed with tidy."

"Thank God." He grabbed his jacket, remembered his reading glasses. "I'll be back Thursday. Let me know if anything happens before then."

He hurried toward the door, then stopped and turned. "Rosalind, I have to say, you were a lovely bud at seventeen, but the full bloom? It's spectacular."

She gave a half laugh and leaned back on the table herself she was alone. Idly she studied her ancient boots, then her baggy work pants, currently smeared with dirt and streaks of drying concrete. She figured the flannel shirt she was wearing over a ragged tee was old enough to have a driver's license.

Men lie, she thought, but occasionally, it was nice to hear.

SEVEN

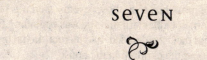

WITH THE NURSERY CLOSING EARLY FOR THE HOLIDAY, Roz earmarked the time to deal with her own houseplants. She had several that needed repotting or dividing, and a few she wanted to propagate for gifts.

With the weather crisp and clear outside, she settled into the humid warmth of her personal greenhouse. She worked with one of her favorites, an enormous African violet that had come from a plantlet her grandmother had given her more than thirty years before. As Norah Jones's bluesy voice surrounded her, she carefully selected a half dozen new leaves, taking them with their stalks for cuttings. For now, she used a stockpot, sliding the stems in around the edges. In a month they would have roots, and other plantlets would form. Then she would plant them individually in the pale green pots she'd set aside.

They'd be a gift for Stella, for her new house, her new life.

It pleased her to be able to pass this sentimental piece of her heritage along to a woman who'd understand, to someone Roz had come to love.

One day she'd do the same for her sons when they married, and give to them this living piece of her heritage. She would love the women they chose because they did. If she was lucky, she'd like the women they married.

Daughters-in-law, she mused. And grandchildren. It didn't seem quite possible that those events weren't far around her next corner. Odder still that she was beginning to yearn for them. And that, she decided, had its roots in having Stella and Hayley and the children in the house.

Still, she could wait. She accepted change, but that didn't mean she was in a hurry for it.

Right now her life was in pretty good order. Her business was flourishing, and that was not only a personal triumph, it was an intense relief.

She'd risked a great deal by starting In the Garden. But it was a risk she'd had to take—for herself, and for her heritage.

Harper House, and she would never give it up, cost a great deal to maintain. She was well aware there were people who believed she had money to burn, but while she certainly wasn't at the point where she needed to pinch every penny, she was hardly rolling in it.

She'd raised three children, clothed and fed them, educated them. Her legacy had allowed her to stay home with them rather than seek outside employment, and her own canniness with investments had added a cushion.

But three college educations and medical school for Mason hadn't come cheap. And when the house demanded new plumbing, new paint, a new roof, she was obliged to see it got what it needed.

Enough so that she'd discreetly sold some things over the years. Admittedly, paintings or jewelry she hadn't cared for, but it had still given her a little twinge of guilt to sell what had been given to her.

Sacrificing pieces to preserve the whole.

There'd come a time when she'd been confident her sons' futures were seen to, as best she could, and the house was secure. But money was needed nonetheless. It wasn't as if she hadn't considered finding a job—considered very briefly.

Mitch was right, she didn't care to take orders. But she was, without question, very adept at giving them. Play to your strengths, after all, she thought with a glimmer of a smile. That's just what she'd done.

It had been a choice between gathering her courage to start her own business, or swallowing her pride to work for someone else.

For Roz, it was no contest.

She'd piled a great deal of her eggs into that single basket, and the first two years had been touch and go. But it had grown. She and Harper had made it grow.

She'd taken a hit with the divorce. Stupid, stupid mistake. While Bryce had gotten very little out of the deal—and only what she'd permitted him to get—it had cost her dearly in pride and in money to shed herself of him.

But they'd weathered it. Her sons, her home, her business were thriving. So she could think, a little, of changes. Of expansions on both her business and personal fronts. Just as she could enjoy the successful present.

She moved from the African violets to her bromeliads, and by the time she'd finished dividing, she decided Stella was going to get one of these, too. Pleased, she worked another hour, then shifted to check the spring bulbs she was forcing. She'd have narcissus blooming in another week.

When she was satisfied, she carted everything she wanted in the house inside, arranging, as she preferred them, a forest of plants in the solarium, then placing other pots throughout the house.

Last, she carried a trio of bulbs in forcing bottles to the kitchen.

"And what have you brought me?" David asked.

"David, I despair of teaching you anything about horticulture. They're very obviously tulips." She arranged them on the windowsill beside the banquette. "They'll bloom in a few weeks."

"I despair of teaching you anything about the choices of stylish gardening wear. How long have you owned that shirt?"

"I have no idea. What are you doing in here?" She pulled open the refrigerator, took out the pitcher of cold tea that was always there. "Shouldn't you be starting your primping marathon for tonight's party?"

"I'm making you up a nice platter of cold cuts and sides, as you refuse to come out and play with us tonight. And as I treated myself to a few hours at the day spa today while you were grubbing in dirt, my primping has already started."

"You don't have to go to any trouble with platters, David. I can find the makings for a sandwich myself."

"Nicer this way, especially when you have company." He chuckled. "The professor's in the library, and I put a couple of bottles of champagne in to chill so the two of you can—let's say—pop a cork."

"David." She gave him a light cuff on the side of the head before she poured the tea. "I'm not popping anything with anyone. I'm minding the baby."

"Babies sleep. Roz, my treasure, he's *gorgeous*, in that sexily rumpled academic sort of way. Jump him. But for God's sake, change your clothes first. I set out your white cashmere sweater, and those black pants I talked you into—the ones with lots of lycra, and those fabulous Jimmy Choo's."

"I'm certainly not wearing white cashmere, skintight pants—which I'd never have bought if you hadn't hypnotized me or something—or a pair of five-inch heels when

I'm babysitting for a seven-month-old. It's not even a date."

"Don't you just love those horn-rims? What is it about a man in horn-rim glasses?"

She took an olive out of the bowl he'd filled. "You're certainly wound up tonight."

He covered the bowls and the tray he'd prepared with plastic. "There now. You're going to have yourself a nice New Year's Eve picnic with the horn-rimmed hunk."

"David, why in the world do you think I need a man?"

"My darling Roz, we *all* need a man."

SHE DID CHANGE, BUT BRUTALLY REJECTED DAVID'S choices in favor of a simple cotton shirt and jeans, and her favored wool socks in lieu of shoes. Still, she had enough vanity to do her makeup.

In the nursery, she listened patiently to all of Hayley's nervous-mother instructions, assured, and reassured, swore an oath she would call if there was any sort of a problem. And finally nudged the girl out and on her way.

She waited, watching from the window until she saw the car drive away. Then, grinning, she turned to where Lily gurgled in her bouncy chair.

"I've got you all to myself now. Come on up here to Aunt Roz, 'cause I've just got to eat you right up like a bowl of sugar."

In the library, Mitch pretended to read, took sketchy notes, and listened to the baby monitor that stood on a table on the lower level.

Every room had one, at least every room he'd been in, he thought. Since the experiences last spring, he thought that was a wise and basic precaution.

But he wasn't thinking of safety or precautions now. He

was simply charmed and amused, listening first to Hayley's anxiety-filled departure, and now Roz's verbal love affair with the baby.

He'd never heard that tone in her voice before, hadn't known it could soften like that, like fragrant wax under low heat. Nor had he expected her to dote, as she so obviously doted, on a child.

She talked nonsense, cooed, laughed, made the silly noises adults habitually made around babies and, from the sounds of Lily's response, made the baby as happy as the sitter.

It was another angle to a woman he'd seen as formidable, confident, a little aloof, and oddly direct. All those facets had already combined into a woman he found smoothly sexy. Now this . . . softness, he supposed, was a surprising icing on an already desirable cake.

He heard her laugh, a long, lovely roll, and gave up even the pretense of working.

He heard the music and banging of toys, the child's burbling and giggles, and the undiluted pleasure in the woman's voice. Later, he heard her singing as she rocked the baby to sleep.

Soon after, he heard her murmured words, her quiet sigh, then the monitor was silent.

He sighed himself, sorry the interlude was over. Then reaching for his coffeepot, found it empty. Again.

He carried it into the kitchen to brew another pot, and was just measuring out the coffee when Roz came in.

"Hi," he said. "Be out of your way in a minute. David said I should just make myself coffee whenever."

"Of course. I was about to make use of the cold cuts he put together earlier, if you'd like something to eat."

"I would, thanks. He mentioned there'd be makings when he showed me where I could find what I needed for coffee. And . . ." He widened his eyes as Roz took out the tray, the bowls. "I see he meant it."

"He's constantly afraid I'll starve to death if he doesn't leave me enough food for six people." She glanced over. "And?"

"Sorry?"

"You started to say something else? Regarding David?"

"Oh well, just that I think he was hitting on me."

She got long, fresh rolls from the bread drawer. "Not very hard, I'm sure."

"No, not hard. Just . . . charmingly actually."

"I hope you weren't offended."

"No, I was, well, sort of flattered, really. Considering the age difference."

"He likes the way you look in your glasses."

"In my . . . what?"

"Horn-rims. They just turn him to mush, apparently. You want me to just pile everything on here, or would you rather pick and choose?"

"Just pile, thanks. I appreciate it."

"It's no trouble as I'm making some for myself as it is." She looked up sharply, as a voice, Amelia's voice, began to sing through the monitor.

"It's a jolt, isn't it?" Mitch said. "Every time."

"She doesn't go into Lily's room every night, not like she did with the boys. She favors boys. I suppose she knows Hayley's out, and wants to . . ."

She trailed off, her fingers fumbling, as they rarely did, with the sandwiches as she recalled the monitor in the library. And her own session with Lily.

"I hadn't thought about the monitor where you were working, disturbing you."

"It didn't—you didn't—in the least."

"In any case, feel free to switch it off in there when

you're working. God knows we have them everywhere. Hayley went out and bought one that has video, too, for her room. Amazing the sorts of things they have now, to make life a bit easier for new mothers."

"You must've been a good one. It came through," he added, "when you were up there with her."

"I was. Am. It's my most important job." But her interlude with Lily had been private—or so she'd thought. Just how many times had she sang the hokeypokey along with Elmo?

Best not to think about it.

"Would you like to take this back in, eat while you work, or take a break, and eat in here?"

"In here, if it's all right with you."

"That'll be fine." She hesitated, then opened the refrigerator again, took out the champagne. "Seeing as it's New Year's Eve, I'm going to open this. We can have something a little more festive than coffee with our poor boys."

"Thanks, but I don't drink. Can't."

"Oh." She felt abominably slow and stupid. Hadn't she noticed herself that he never took alcohol? Couldn't she have used her brain to put two and two together before embarrassing a guest? "Coffee it is, then."

"Please." He stepped over to lay a hand on her arm before she replaced the bottle. "Open it, enjoy it. It doesn't bother me when other people have a drink. In fact, it's important to me that they're comfortable. That you're comfortable. Here, let me do it."

He took the bottle. "Don't worry, opening a bottle of champagne isn't backsliding."

"I certainly didn't mean to make *you* uncomfortable. I should've realized."

"Why? I'm not still wearing that sign that says Recovering Alcoholic around my neck, am I?"

She smiled a little, walked to the display cabinet for a flute. "No."

He released the cork, a quick, celebrational pop. "I started drinking when I was about fifteen. Sneaking a beer now and then, the way boys often do. Nothing major. I did love an ice-cold beer."

He set both their plates on the table, then poured his coffee while she arranged the rest of the simple meal. "Went through the drinking insanity in college, but again, plenty do the same. Never missed a class because of it, never caused me any trouble, really. My grades stayed up—enough I graduated with honors, top five percent of my class. I loved college nearly as much as I did an ice-cold beer. Am I going to bore you with this?"

"No," she said, her eyes on his. "You're not."

"All right." He took his first bite of the sandwich, nodded. "Miz Harper, you make a hell of a po'boy."

"I do."

"So I went to grad school, got my master's. Taught, got married, worked on my doctorate. Had myself a gorgeous baby boy. And I drank. I was . . . an amiable drunk, if you know what I mean. I was never confrontational, never abusive—physically, I mean, never picked fights. But I can't say I was ever completely sober from the time Josh was born—a bit before that to be honest, until I set the bottle down the last time."

He sampled David's potato salad. "I worked—taught, wrote, provided my family with a good living. Drinking never cost me a day's work, any more than it had cost me class time. But it cost me my wife and my son."

"I'm sorry, Mitch."

"No need to be. Sara, my ex, did everything she could do. She loved me, and she wanted the life I'd promised her. She stuck with me longer than many would have. She begged me to quit, and I'd promise or reassure, or fluff her off. Bills were paid, weren't they? We had a nice house, and we never missed a mortgage payment. I wasn't some stumbling-down, sprawled-in-the-gutter drunk, was I, for God's sake? I just had a few drinks to take the edge off. Of course, I started taking the edge off at ten in the morning, but I was entitled."

He paused, shook his head. "It's easy to delude yourself that you're entitled, that you're just fine when you're in a haze most of the time. Easy to ignore the fact that you're letting your wife and child down in a dozen ways, every single day. Forgetting dinner parties or birthdays, slipping out of bed—where you are useless to her in any case—to have just one more drink, dozing off when you're supposed to be watching your own baby. Just not being there, not completely there. Ever."

"It's a hard thing to go through, I imagine. For everyone involved."

"Harder for the ones you shipwreck with you, believe me. I wouldn't go to counseling with her, refused to attend meetings, to talk to anyone about what she saw as my problem. Even when she told me she was leaving me, when she packed her things, and Josh's things, and walked out. I barely noticed they were gone."

"That was tremendously brave of her."

"Yes, it was." His gaze sharpened on Roz's face. "Yes, it was, and I suppose a woman like you would understand just how brave it was. It took me another full year to hit the bottom, to look around at my life and see nothing. To realize I'd lost what was most precious, and that it was too late to ever get it back. I went to meetings."

"That takes courage, too."

"My first meeting?" He took another bite of his sandwich. "Scared to death. I sat in the back of the room, in the basement of this tiny church, and shook like a child."

"A lot of courage."

"I was sober for three months, ten days, and five hours when I reached for a bottle again. Fought my way out of that, and sobriety lasted eleven months, two days, and fifteen hours. She wouldn't come back to me, you see. She'd met someone else and she couldn't trust me. I used that as an excuse to drink, and I drank the next few months away, until I crawled back out of the hole."

He lifted his coffee. "That was fourteen years ago next March. March fifth. Sara forgave me. In addition to being brave, she's a generous woman, one who deserved better than what she got from me. Josh forgave me, and in the past fourteen years, I've been a good father. The best I know how to be."

"I think it takes a brave man, and a strong one to face his demons, and beat them back, and keep facing them every single day. And a generous one, a smart one who shoulders the blame rather than passing it on, even partially, to others."

"Not drinking doesn't make me a hero, Roz. It just makes me sober. Now if I could just kick the coffee habit."

"That makes two of us."

"Now that I've talked your ear off, I'm going to ask you to return the favor, and give that first interview when we've finished eating."

"All right. Am I going to be talking for the recorder?"

"Primarily, yeah, though I'll take some notes."

"Then maybe we could do that in the parlor, where it's a little more comfortable."

"Sounds like a plan."

She checked on Lily first, and took the first phone call from Hayley. While Mitch gathered whatever he needed from the library, she pulled the tray of fresh fruit—David never missed a trick—and the brie and cheddar, the crackers, he'd stocked.

Even as she wheeled it toward the parlor, Mitch came up behind her. "Let me get that."

"No, I've got it. But you could light the fire. A fire'd be

nice. It's cold tonight, but thank God, clear. I'd hate to worry about my chicks navigating slick roads on their way home to roost later."

"I thought the same thing about my own earlier. Never ends, does it?"

"No." She set out the food, the coffee, then sat on the couch, instinctively propped her feet on the table. She stared at her own feet, surprised. It was a habit, she knew, but one she didn't indulge in when she had guests. She glanced at Mitch's back as he crouched to light kindling.

She supposed it meant she was comfortable with him, and that was fine. Better than labeling him a guest as she'd be trusting him with her family.

"You're right, it's nice to have a fire."

He came back, set up his recorder, his notebook, then settled on the other end of the couch, shifting his body toward hers. "I'd like to start off with you telling me about the first time you remember seeing Amelia."

Straight to business, she thought. "I don't know that I remember a first time, not specifically. I'd have been young. Very. I remember her voice, the singing, and a kind of comforting presence. I thought—to the best of my memory, that is—that it was my mother. But my mother wasn't one to look in at night, and I never remember her singing to me. It wasn't her way. I remember her—Amelia—being there a few times when I was sick. A cold, a fever. It's more that she was there, and expected to be in a way, than a jolting first time."

"Who told you about her?"

"My father, my grandmother. My grandmother more, I suppose. The family would talk about her casually, in vague terms. She was both a point of pride—we have a ghost—and a slight embarrassment—we have a ghost. Depending on who was talking. My father believed she was one of the Harper Brides, while my grandmother maintained she was a servant or guest, someone who'd been misused somehow. Someone who had died here, but wasn't blood kin."

"Did your father, your grandmother, your mother, ever tell you about their specific experiences with her?"

"My mother would get palpitations if the subject was brought up. My mother was very fond of her palpitations."

Mitch grinned at the dry tone, watched her spread some brie. "I had a great-aunt like that. She had spells. Her day wasn't complete without at least one spell."

"Why some people delight in having conditions is more than I can understand. My mother did speak to me of her once or twice, in a sort of gloom-and-doom manner— something else she was fond of. Warning me that one day I'd inherit this burden, and hoping for my sake it didn't shatter my health, as it had hers."

"She was afraid of Amelia, then."

"No, no." Roz waved that away, nibbled on a cracker. "She enjoyed being long-suffering, and a kind of trembling martyr. Which sounds very unkind coming from her only child."

"Let's call it honest instead."

"Comes to the same. In any case, other times, it was bearing and birthing me that had ruined her health. And others, she'd been delicate since a bout of pneumonia as a child. Hardly matters."

"Actually, it's helpful. Bits and pieces, personal observations and memories are helpful, a start toward the big picture. What about your father?"

"My father was generally amused by the idea of a ghost and had fond memories of her from his own childhood. But then he'd be annoyed or embarrassed if she made an appearance and frightened a guest. My father was fiercely hospitable, and mortified on a deep, personal level if a guest in his home was inconvenienced."

"What sort of memories did he have?"

"The same you've heard before. It hardly varies. Her singing to him, visiting him in his room, a maternal presence until he was about twelve."

"No disturbances?"

"Not that he told me, but my grandmother said he sometimes had nightmares as a boy. Just one or two a year, where he claimed to see a woman in white, with her eyes bulging, and he could hear her screaming in his head. Sometimes she was in his room, sometimes she was outside, and so was he—in the dream."

"Dreams would be another common thread, then. Have you had any?"

"No, not . . ."

"What?"

"I always thought it was nerves. In the weeks before John and I were married, I had dreams. Of storms. Black skies and thunder, cold winds. A hole in the garden, like a grave, with dead flowers inside it." She shivered once. "Horrible. But they stopped after I was married. I dismissed them."

"And since?"

"No. Never. My grandmother saw her more than anyone, at least more than anyone would admit to. In the house, in the garden, in my father's room when he was a boy. She never told me anything frightening. But maybe she wouldn't have. Of all my family, that I recall, she was the most sympathetic toward Amelia. But to be honest, it wasn't the primary topic of conversation in the house. It was simply accepted, or ignored."

"Let's talk about that blood kin, then." He pulled his glasses out of his shirt pocket to read his notes. "The furthest back you know, personally, of sightings starts with your grandmother Elizabeth McKinnon Harper."

"That's not completely accurate. She told me my grandfather, her husband, had seen the Bride when he was a child."

"That's her telling you what she'd been told, not what she claimed to have seen and experienced herself. But speaking to that, can you recall being told of any experiences that happened in the generation previous to your grandparents?"

"Ah . . . she said her mother-in-law, that would be my great-grandmother Harper, refused to go into certain rooms."

"Which rooms?"

"Ah . . . lord, let me think. The nursery, which was on the third floor in those days. The master bedroom. She moved herself out of it at some point, I'm assuming. The kitchen. And she wouldn't set foot in the carriage house. From my grandmother's description of her, she wasn't a fanciful woman. It was always thought she'd seen the Bride. If there was another prior to that, I don't know about it. But there shouldn't be. We've dated her to the 1890s."

"You've dated her based on a dress and a hairstyle," he said as he scribbled. "That's not quite enough."

"It certainly seems sensible, logical."

He looked up, smiling, his eyes distracted behind his glasses. "It may be. You may be right, but I like a little more data before I call something a fact. What about your great-aunts? Reginald Jr.'s older sisters?"

"I couldn't say. I didn't know any of them, or don't remember them. And they weren't close with my grandmother, or my father. There was some attempt, on my grandmother's part, to cement some familial relations between their children and my father, as cousins. I'm still in contact with some of their children."

"Will any of them talk to me?"

"Some will, some won't. Some are dead. I'll give you names and numbers."

"All," he said. "Except the dead ones. I can be persuasive.

Again," he murmured as the singing came from the monitor across the room.

"Again. I want to go check on Lily."

"Do you mind if I come with you?"

"No. Come ahead." They started upstairs together. "Most likely it'll stop before we get there. That's the pattern."

"There were two nursemaids, three governesses, a housekeeper, an under-housekeeper, a total of twelve housemaids, a personal maid, three female kitchen staff between 1890 and 1895. I've dug up some of the names, but as ages aren't listed, I'm having to wade through a lot of records to try to pinpoint the right people. If and when, I'll start on death records, and tracking down descendants."

"You'll be busy."

"Gotta love the work. You're right. It's stopped."

But they continued down the hall to the nursery. "Cold still," Roz commented. "It doesn't last long, though." She moved to the crib, slid the blanket more neatly around the sleeping baby.

"Such a good baby," she said quietly. "Sleeps right through the night most of the time. None of mine did at this age. She's fine. We should leave her be."

She stepped out, leaving the door open. They were at the top of the stairs when the clock began to bong.

"Midnight?" Roz looked at her watch to be certain. "I didn't realize it was so late. Well, Happy New Year."

"Happy New Year." He took her hand before she could continue down the steps and, laying the other on her cheek, said, "Do you mind?"

"No, I don't mind."

His lips brushed hers, very lightly, a kind of civilized and polite gesture to commemorate the changing year. And somewhere in the east wing, Roz's wing, a door slammed shut like a gunshot.

Though her heart jumped, she managed to speak evenly. "Obviously, she doesn't approve."

"More like she's pissed off. And if she's going to be pissed off, we might as well give her a good reason."

He didn't ask this time, just slid the hand that lay on her cheek around to cup the back of her neck. And this time his mouth wasn't light, or polite, or civilized. There was a punch of heat, straight to her belly, as his mouth crushed down on hers, as his body pressed, hard against hers. She felt that sizzle zip through her blood, fast and reckless, and let herself ride on it for just one mad moment.

The door in the east wing slammed, again and again, and the clock continued to chime, madly now, well past the hour of twelve.

He'd known she'd taste like this, ripe and strong. More tang than sweetness. He'd wanted to feel those lips move against his as they were now, to discover just how that long, slender body fit to his. Now that he was, she settled inside him and made him want more.

But she eased back, her eyes open and direct. "Well. That ought to do it."

"It's a start."

"I think it'd be best to keep everything . . . calm for tonight. I really should tidy up the parlor, and settle down up here, with Lily."

"All right. I'll get my notes and head home."

In the parlor she loaded the cart while he gathered his things. "You're a difficult woman to read, Rosalind."

"I'm sure that's true."

"You know I want to stay, you know I want to take you to bed."

"Yes, I know." She looked over at him. "I don't take lovers . . . I was going to say just that. That I don't take lovers, but I'm going to say, instead, I don't take them rashly, or lightly. So if I decide to take you as a lover, or let you take me, it will be serious business, Mitchell. Very serious business. That's something both of us need to consider."

"Ever just jump off the ledge, Roz?"

"I've been known to. But, except for the regrettable and rare occasion, I like to make certain I'm going to land on my feet. If I wasn't interested, I'd tell you, flat out. I don't play games in this arena. Instead, I'm telling you that I am interested, enough to think about it. Enough to regret, a little, that I'm no longer young and foolish enough to act without thinking."

The phone rang. "That'll be Hayley again. I need to get that or she'll panic. Drive carefully."

She walked out to get the phone, and heard, as she assured Hayley the baby was fine, was sleeping like an angel, had been no trouble at all, the front door close behind him.

eight

A LITTLE DISTANCE, MITCH DECIDED, WAS IN ORDER. The woman was a paradox, and since there was no finite solution to a paradox, it was best accepted for what it was—instead of puzzling over it until blood leaked out of your ears.

So he'd try a little distance where he could funnel his energies into puzzles other than the enigmatic Rosalind Harper.

He had plenty of legwork, or, more accurately, butt work. A few hours on his computer and he could verify the births and deaths and marriages listed in the Harper family Bible. He'd already generated a chart of the family ancestry, using his on-line and his courthouse information.

Clients liked charts. Beyond that, they were tools for him, as the copies of family pictures were, as letters were. He pinned everything onto a huge board. Two in this case. One for his office in his apartment, and one in the library at Harper House.

Pictures, old photos, old letters, diaries, scribbled family recipes, all of those things brought the people alive for him. When they were alive for him, when he began to envision their daily routines, their habits, their flaws and grievances, they mattered to him more than any job or project could matter.

He could lose hours paging through Elizabeth Harper's gardening notes, or the baby book she'd kept on Roz's father. How else would he know the man who'd sired Roz had suffered from celiac at three months, or had taken his first steps ten months later?

It was the details, the small bits, that made the past full, and immediate.

And in the wedding photo of Elizabeth and Reginald Junior, he could see Rosalind in her grandfather. The dark hair, the long eyes, the strong facial bones.

What else had he passed to her, and through her to her children, this man she barely remembered?

Business acumen for one, Mitch concluded. From other details, those small bits, found in clippings, in household records, he gained a picture of a man who'd had a sharp skill for making money, who'd avoided the fate of many of his contemporaries in the stock market crash. A careful man, and one who'd preserved the family home and holdings.

Yet wasn't there a coolness about him? Mitch thought as he studied the photographs on his board. A remoteness that showed in his eyes. More than just the photographic style of the day.

Perhaps it came from being born wealthy—the only son on whose shoulders the responsibilities fell.

"What," Mitch wondered aloud, "did you know about Amelia? Did you ever meet her, in the flesh? Or was she already dead, already just a spirit in this house when your time came around?"

Someone knew her, he thought. Someone spoke to her, touched her, knew her face, her voice.

And someone who did lived or worked in Harper House.

Mitch moved to a search of the servants he had by full names.

It took time, and didn't include the myriad other possibilities. Amelia had been a guest, a servant whose name was not included—or had been expunged from family records—a relative's relative, a friend of the family.

He could speculate, of course, that if a guest, a friend, a distant relation had died in the house, the information would have trickled down, and her identity would be known.

Then again, that was speculation, and didn't factor in the possibility of scandal, and the tendency to hush such matters up.

Or the fact that she'd been no one important to the Harpers, had died in her sleep, and no one considered it worth discussing.

And it was just another paradox, he supposed as he leaned back from his work, that he, a rational, fairly logical-thinking man, was spending considerable time and effort to research and identify a ghost.

The trick was not to think of her that way, but to think of her as a living, breathing woman, a woman who had been born, lived a life, dressed, ate, laughed, cried, walked, and talked.

She had existed. She had a name. It was his job to find *who*, *what*, *when*. *Why* was just the bonus question.

He dug the sketch out of his file, studied the image Roz had created of a young, thin woman with a mass of curly hair and eyes full of misery. And this is how they'd dated her, he thought with a shake of his head. By a dress and a hairstyle.

Not that it wasn't a good sketch. He'd only seen Amelia once, and she hadn't looked calm and sad like this, but wild and mad.

The dress could have been ten, even twenty years old. Or brand-new. The hairstyle a personal choice or a fashion statement. It was impossible to pinpoint age or era on such, well, sketchy information.

And yet, from his research so far, he tended to think they were close to the mark.

The talk of dreams, the bits of information, the lore itself appeared to have its roots during Reginald Harper's reign.

Reginald Harper, he thought, kicking back in his chair to stare at the ceiling. Reginald Edward Harper, born 1851, the youngest of four children born to Charles Daniel Harper and Christabel Westley Harper. Second and only surviving son. Older brother, Nathanial died July 1864, at age eighteen, during the Battle of Bloody Bridge in Charlestown.

"Married Beatrice . . ." He rummaged through his notes again. Yes, there it is, 1880. Five children. Charlotte, born 1881, Edith Anne, 1883, Katherine, 1885, Victoria, 1886, and Reginald Junior, 1892."

Big gap between the last two kids, considering the pattern beforehand, he thought, and noted down possibilities of miscarriages and/or stillbirths.

Strong possibilities with the factors of unreliable birth control, and the natural assumption that Reginald would have wanted a son to continue the family name.

He scanned the family chart he'd generated for Beatrice. A sister, one brother, one sister-in-law. But neither female relation had died until well after the first reports of sightings and dreams, making them unlikely candidates. And neither had been named Amelia.

Of course, he hadn't found a servant by that name, either. Not yet.

But for now he circled back to Reginald Harper, head of the house during the most likely era.

Just who were you, Harper? Prosperous, well-heeled. Inherited the house, and the holdings, because the older brother ran off to be a solider, and died fighting for the Cause. Baby of the family on top of it.

Married well, accumulating more holdings through that marriage. Expanded and modernized the house, according to Roz's notes. Married well, lived well, and you weren't afraid to spend the dough. Still, there'd been a consistent turnover of housemaids and other female staff during his years at the helm.

Maybe Reginald liked to play with the help. Or his wife had been a tyrant.

Was the long wait for a son frustrating and annoying, or was he happy with his girls? It would be interesting to know.

There was no one alive to say.

Mitch went back to his computer and contented himself, for the moment, with facts.

SINCE SHE HAD SO MANY HOUSEPLANTS FROM THE DI-vision of her own, Roz rotated some into store stock, and at Stella's suggestion worked with her to use more in creating some dish gardens.

She enjoyed working with Stella, and that was rare. Primarily when she was potting or propagating, Roz preferred only the company of her plants and her music.

"Feels good to get my hands in the dirt," Stella commented as she selected a snake plant for her arrangement.

"I figure you'll be getting plenty of that soon enough dealing with your new gardens."

"Can't wait. I know I'm driving Logan crazy changing and redefining and tweaking the plan." She blew a stray curl out of her face and slid her gaze over to Roz. "Then again, *plan* isn't exactly the word for what he was doing with the landscape. It was more of a concept."

"Which you're refining."

"I think if I show him one more sketch he might make me eat it. This coleus is gorgeous."

"Focusing on the gardens helps keep down the nerves over the wedding."

Stella paused, hands in dirt. "Bull's-eye. Who'd think I'd be nervous? It's not the first time around for me, and we're keeping it small, simple. I've had months to plan, which hasn't made him all that happy, either. But we had to at least get the living room and the boys' rooms painted and furnished. You wouldn't believe some of the gorgeous pieces his mother gave him that he's had stuffed in a storage garage."

"This dracaena should work here. Nerves are expected, I'd think. A bride's still a bride, first time around or not."

"Were you nervous the second time? I know it turned out awful, but . . ."

"No, I wasn't." Her tone was flat. Not bitter, just empty. "Should've told me something. You're nervous because you're excited and you're happy, and because you're the type who'll worry over every detail. Worry especially when it's important."

"I just want everything to look special. Perfect. I must've been crazy, deciding to have the wedding outside in the backyard when the gardens weren't even finished. Now we only have until April to get it all done."

"And you will. You and Logan know what you're doing about the planting, about each other, about everything that matters."

"Remind me of that every now and again, would you?"

"Happy to. These look good." She stepped back, fisted her gloved hands on her hips. "You got prices worked up?"

"Thirty-four fifty. Forty-five ninety-five for the large size."

"Sounds good. Nice profit margin since the plants are mostly all divisions."

"And a good value for our customers since they're not going to see dish gardens this full or lush anywhere. I'll help you carry some in, then plug these into the inventory."

They loaded a flat cart, wheeled it into the main building. When Stella started to shift stock to rearrange, Roz nudged her aside.

"Go on, do the paperwork. If you start here fiddling with display, you'll be here an hour. You're just going to come back when I'm done and fool with it anyway."

"I was just thinking if we grouped some of the smaller ones over there, and used a couple of those tile-topped tables—"

"I'll figure it out, then you can come behind me and . . . refine it."

"If you put one of the larger ones on that wrought-iron patio table, and put one of the little brass lanterns with it, then set that sixteen-inch clay pot of bird of paradise beside it, it would be a strong display. And I'm going."

Amused, Roz shifted stock, arranged the new. And since she had to admit Stella was on target, as usual, set up the table as outlined.

"Why, Rosalind Harper, there you are!"

Because Roz's back was turned, she indulged herself in a single wince before schooling her face to more welcoming lines.

"Hey there, Cissy."

She allowed the standard greeting, a peck that stopped an inch from her cheek, then resigned herself to losing a quarter of an hour in chatter.

"Don't you look pretty," Roz said. "Is that a new suit?"

"This?" Cissy waved one of her French-manicured hands, dismissing the cherry-red suit. "Just yanked it out of my closet this morning. I swear, Roz, are you *ever* going to gain an ounce? Every time I see you, I feel obliged to sweat an extra twenty minutes on my exercise machine."

"You look wonderful, Cissy." Which was invariably true. One of the skills Cecilia Pratt had most honed was in turning herself out. Her hair was an attractive streaky blond worn in a ruler-straight swing that suited her round, youthful face with its winking dimples and walnut-brown eyes.

From the outfit, Roz assumed she'd just come from some lady lunch, or committee meeting, and had come by to sow and to harvest gossip.

Gossip was Cissy's other keen skill.

"I don't see how I could, I'm just worn *out*. The holidays just about did me in this year. Every time you turned around, there was another party. I don't think I've caught my breath since Thanksgiving. Now before you know it, it'll be the Spring Ball at the club. Tell me you're going this year, Roz. It's just not the same without you."

"Haven't thought about it."

"Well, do. Sit down here a minute and let's catch up. I swear I can't stay on my feet another *minute*." To prove it, she sat on the bench near the table display Roz had just completed. "Isn't this nice? It's just like sitting in a tropical garden somewhere. Hank and I are heading down to the Caymans next week for some sun. I need the break, let me tell you."

"Won't that be fun." Trapped by manners, Roz joined her on the bench.

"You ought to take yourself a nice tropical vacation, honey." Cissy patted Roz's hand. "Sun, blue water, handsome half-naked men. Just the ticket. You know I worry that you just chain yourself to this place. But you've got that girl from Up North managing things now. How's she working out for you, by the way?"

"Her name's Stella, Cissy, and she's worked for me for a year now. That should be a good indication it's working out just fine for both of us."

"That's good. You should take advantage of that and get away for a while."

"There's no place I want to go."

"Well, I'm going to bring you some brochures, that's

what I'm going to do. I don't know if I could get through the next day if I didn't know we'd be sitting on a beach sipping mai tais soon. You were smart to skip most of the parties, though I was sorry I didn't see you New Year's Eve at Jan and Quill's. Lovely gathering, really, though it didn't come *near* the one you put on. Flowers were on the skimpy side, and the food wasn't much more than mediocre. Not that I'd say so to Jan. Did you know she was going in for liposuction next week?"

"No, I didn't."

"Well, it's one of those ill-kept secrets." Cissy edged closer, her dimples doing a conspirator's wink. "Butt and thighs is what I hear. I just this minute came from lunch with her, and *she* says how she's going to be spending a week at a spa in Florida, when everybody knows she's going for the vacuum, then holing up in her house till she can get around again. And, bless her heart, since you could set a table for a family of four on the shelf of her ass, I'd say it'll be more than a week before she's walking straight again."

Despite herself, Roz laughed. "For God's sake, Cissy, her ass looks normal enough to me."

"Not compared to the new administrative assistant Quill's said to have his eye on. Twenty-eight years old, and you could set that table quite a bit higher on that one, as long as you don't mind eating off silicone."

"I hope that's not true, about Quill. I've always thought he and Jan were good together."

"Some men just lose all sense around a big pair of tits, no matter if God or man made them. Which brings me around to what I really came by to tell you. I'm just not quite sure how."

"I'm sure you'll find a way."

"It's just that I feel I must, I'm obliged . . . How long have we been friends, Rosalind?"

"I couldn't say." Since knowing someone since high school didn't make you friends, she thought.

"At our age, it's best not to count the years in any case. But since we've known each other longer than either of us cares to admit to, I feel like I have to let you know what's going around. But first I want to say, since I haven't had a minute to talk to you since . . . the *incident*, that I've never been so shocked or so *dumbfounded* as I was when that horrible Bryce Clerk walked into your house, just like he had a right to, the night of your party."

"It's all right, Cissy. He walked right back out again."

"And a good thing, too, as I don't know if I could've held myself back. I just don't know. I couldn't believe that Mandy. Of course, that girl hasn't got the sense God gave a retarded flea, but that's no excuse for not taking the time to find out who the man *was* before she came traipsing into your home on his arm."

She waved a hand. "I just can't speak of it."

"Then we won't. I really have to get back to work."

"But I haven't *told* you. My tongue just runs away from me when I'm upset. He was *there*, with that ridiculous, brainless girl again. He was there, Roz, at Jan and Quill's, big as life, like he didn't have a care in the world. Drinking champagne and dancing, smoking cigars out on the veranda. Talking about his *consulting* company. Just turned my stomach."

She held a hand to it, as if even now it threatened to revolt. "I know Jan said you'd sent your regrets, but I lived in horror that you'd change your mind and walk in any minute. I wasn't the only one, either."

"I'm sure." Very sure, Roz thought, that there'd been plenty of excited buzz, and half-hopeful glances toward the door. "Jan's entitled to have anyone she wants to in her own home."

"I certainly don't agree with that. It's a matter of loyalty, if not good taste. And I had lunch with her today to say just that."

As she spoke, she opened her purse and took out a compact to blot her nose. "Turns out Quill cleared the way for him. They're doing some business together, not that Jan seems to know a thing about that, the woman's just clueless when it comes to money matters. Not like you and me."

"Mmm" was the most polite response Roz could think of, as Cissy had never worked a day in her life.

"To her credit she was mortified while we talked about it over lunch. Mortified." Taking out a lipstick, she repainted her mouth to match her suit. "But there are some, and I admit I heard some of this at the party as well as here and there, there are some who feel some sympathy for the man. Who actually believed he was treated poorly, which just beats all, if you ask me. The worst of it is, the version that you physically assaulted him the night of the party, running him out when he attempted to make bygones, so to speak. That you threatened him and that silly girl even when they went out again. Of course, every time I hear it, I do what I can to straighten it out. I was there, after all."

Roz recognized the avid tone. Give me some fuel for this fire. And that she wouldn't do, no matter how angry, how vilified she felt. "People will say or think what they want to say or think. There's no point in me worrying about it."

"Well, some are saying and thinking that you didn't come to Jan's, or other get-togethers, because you knew *he* would be there, and sporting a woman nearly half your age."

"I'm surprised anyone would spend so much time concerned with speculating on how I might react to someone who is no longer a part of my reality. If you see Jan, be sure to tell her not to worry about it on my account."

Roz rose. "It was good to see you. I've just got to get back to work here."

"I want you to know I'll be thinking about you." Cissy got to her feet, gave Roz another air peck. "We've got to have lunch sometime soon, my treat."

"You and Hank have a good time in the Caymans."

"We will. I'm going to send you those brochures," she called over her shoulder as she walked out.

"You do that," Roz muttered.

She walked out the opposite way, furious with herself for being hurt and insulted. She knew better, knew it wasn't worth it, but still the score to her pride ached.

She started to turn into the propagation house, but veered off. In this mood she'd do more harm than good. Instead, she skirted around, headed into the woods that separated her private and personal domains, and took the long way home.

She didn't want to see anyone, speak to anyone, but there was David out in the yard, playing with Stella's boys and their dog.

The dog spotted her first, and with a few welcoming yips raced over to jump, and scrabble at her knees.

"Not now, Parker." She bent to scratch his ears. "Not a good time now."

"We're hunting buried treasure." Luke ran over. He wore a silly black beard hooked over his ears and hiding half his freckled face. "We have a map and everything."

"Treasure?"

"Uh-huh. I'm Blackbeard the pirate, and Gavin's Long John Silver. David's Captain Morgan. He says Captain Morgan can put a shine on a bad day. But I don't get it."

She smiled, ruffled the boy's hair as she had the dog's fur. She could use a belt of Captain Morgan herself, she decided. A double. "What's the treasure?"

"It's a surprise, but David—Captain Morgan says if we scallywags don't find it, we have to walk the plank."

She looked over at Gavin, who was hobbling around with a broomstick strapped to his leg. And David, sporting a black eyepatch and a big plumed hat he must have dug out of his costume party bag.

"Then you'd better go on back and find it."

"Don't you wanna play?"

"Not right now, sugar."

"Better find my pieces of eight," David said as he came over, "or I'll hang you from the highest yardarm."

With an un-piratelike squeal, Luke scrambled off to count off more paces from the map with his brother.

"What's wrong, honey?"

"Nothing." Roz shook her head. "Little headache, came home early. I hope to God you didn't actually bury something. I'd hate to fire you."

"New PlayStation game, up in the crook of the lowest branch of that sycamore."

"You're a treasure, Captain Morgan."

"One in a million. I know that face." He lifted a hand to it. "It'd pass most anybody, but not me. What's upset you, and what the hell are you doing walking all that way without a jacket?"

"I forgot it, and I do have a headache. Brought on by some foolishness Cissy Pratt was obliged to carry over to me."

"One of these days her flapping tongue's going to wrap around her own throat." He flipped up his eye patch. "And when she's in the funeral home, I'm going in and dressing her in an outdated, off-the-rack outfit from Wal-Mart. Polyester."

It brought on a half smile. "That's cruel."

"Come on inside. I'm going to fix us a batch of my infamous martinis. You can tell me all about it, then we'll trash the bitch."

"As entertaining as that sounds, I think what I need is a couple of aspirin and a twenty-minute nap. And we both know you can't disappoint those boys. Go on now, Captain." She kissed his cheek. "Shiver some timbers."

She went inside, directly upstairs. She took the self-prescribed aspirin, then stretched out on her bed.

How long, she wondered, how long was the albatross of

that joke of a marriage going to lay across her neck? How many times would it flap right up and slap her in the face?

So much for her superstitious hope that by letting the fifteen thousand dollars she'd discovered he'd nipped out of her account slide, she would have paid the debt, balanced the scales of the mistake.

Well, the money was gone, and no use regretting that foolish decision. The marriage had happened, and no point punishing herself for it.

Sooner or later he'd slip again, screw the wrong woman, bilk the wrong man, and he'd slither out of Memphis, out of her circle.

Eventually people would find something and someone else to talk about. They always did.

Imagine him being able to convince anyone that she'd attacked him—and in her own home. Then again, he did play the injured party well, and was the most accomplished liar she'd ever known.

She could not, and would not, defend herself on any level. Doing so would just feed the beast. She would do what she had always done. Remove herself, physically and emotionally, from the storm of talk.

She'd indulge in this brief sulk—she wasn't perfect, after all. Then she'd get back to her life, and live it as she'd always done.

Exactly as she chose.

She closed her eyes. She didn't expect to sleep, but she drifted a bit in that half-state she often found more soothing.

And while she drifted, she sat on the bench in her own shade garden, basking in the late-spring breeze, breathing in the perfumes it had floating on the air.

She could see the main house, and the colorful pots she'd planted and set herself on the terraces. And the carriage house, with its dance of lilies waiting to open wide.

She smelled the roses that climbed up the arbor in a

strong stream of golden sun. The white roses she'd planted herself, as a private tribute to John.

She rarely went to his grave, but often to the arbor.

She looked over beyond the rose garden, the cutting garden, the paths that gently wound through the flowers and shrubs and trees to the spot where Bryce had wanted to dig a swimming pool.

They'd argued over that, and had a blistering fight when she'd headed off the contractor he'd hired despite her.

The contractor had been told, she recalled, in no uncertain terms that if he so much as dipped a blade into her ground, she'd call the police to scrape up what she left of him.

With Bryce she'd been even less patient while reminding him the house and grounds were hers, the decisions made involving them hers.

He'd stormed out, hadn't he, after she'd scalded him. Only to slink back a few hours later, sheepish, apologetic, and with a tiny bouquet of wild violets.

Her mistake in accepting the apology, and the flowers.

Alone is better.

She shivered in the shade. "Maybe it is, maybe it isn't."

You did this alone. All of this. You made a mistake once, and look what it cost you. Still costs you. Don't make another.

"I won't make another. Whatever I do, it won't be a mistake."

Alone is better. The voice was more insistent now, and the cold deeper. *I'm alone.*

For an instant, only an instant, Roz thought she saw a woman in a muddy white dress, lying in an open grave. And for that instant, only that instant, she smelled the decay of death under the roses.

Then the woman's eyes opened, stared into hers, with a kind of mad hunger.

NINE

Roz came into the house out of a nasty, sleeting rain. She peeled out of her jacket, then sat on the bench in the foyer to drag off her boots. David strolled out, sat beside her, and handed her the cup of coffee he'd brought out of the kitchen.

"Dr. Delish is in the library."

"Yes, I saw his car." She drank coffee, holding the cup in both hands to warm them.

"Harper's with him. He snagged our boy for an interview. We had ours over lattes and applesauce cake earlier."

"Applesauce cake."

"I saved you a big slice. I know your weaknesses. They're saying we might get some snow out of this."

"So I heard."

"Stella and the boys are at Logan's. She's going to fix dinner over there, and the boys are hoping the snow comes through and they can stay the night."

"That's nice. I need a shower. A hot one."

He took the cup she passed back to him. "I thought you

might want to ask our handsome professor to stay to dinner. I'm making some hearty chicken and dumplings to
ward off the cold."

"Sounds good—the chicken—and Mitch is certainly
welcome to stay if he likes, and doesn't have other plans."

"He doesn't," David said confidently. "I've already
asked."

She chuckled at his broad grin. "Just who are you
matching him up with, David? You or me?"

"Well, being the utterly unselfish person I am—and seeing as the doctor is unfortunately and absolutely straight—
I'm going with you."

"Just a pitiful romantic, aren't you?"

She started up, and only rolled her eyes when he called
out: "Put something sexy on."

In the library, Harper nursed his after-work beer. It
didn't seem to him that he could tell Mitch much more
than he already knew, but he'd answered the questions,
filled in little gaps in the stories both his mother and David
had already related.

"I've got David's rundown of the night you saw her outside, in the gardens, when you were boys."

"The night we were camping out, David, my brothers,
and me." Harper nodded in acknowledgment. "Some night."

"According to David, you saw her first, woke him."

"Saw, heard, felt." Harper shrugged. "Hard to pin it
down, but yeah, I woke him up. Couldn't say what time
it was. Late. We'd stayed up eating ourselves half sick, and
spooking ourselves out with scary stories. Then I heard
her, I guess. Don't know how, exactly, I knew it was her. It
wasn't like the other times."

"What was different?"

"She wasn't singing. She was more . . . moaning, I
guess, or making these unintelligible sounds. More like
what you'd expect from a ghost on a hot, moonlit night

when you're a kid. So I looked out, and there she was. Only not like before, either."

Brave boy, Mitch thought, to look out instead of pulling the sleeping bag over his head. "What was it like?"

"She was in this white nightgown sort of thing. The way she was last spring when she was upstairs. Her hair was down, tangled and dirty. And I could see the moonlight going through her. Right through. Jesus." He took a deeper sip of beer.

"So I got David up, and Austin and Mason woke up, too. I wanted Austin to stay back with Mason, but there was no chance of that, so we all set out to follow her."

Mitch could imagine it very well. A pack of young boys, moonlight and lightning bugs and heavy summer heat. And a ghostly figure trailing through the gardens.

"She walked right over Mama's evening primrose, straight through the hollyhocks. Through them. I was too wound up to be scared. She kept making this noise, a kind of humming, or keening, I guess you could say. I think there were words mixed in there somewhere, but I couldn't make them out. She was going toward the carriage house. Seemed to me she was heading toward the carriage house anyway. And she turned, and she looked back. And her face . . ."

"What?"

"Like last spring again," he said, and let out a little breath. "She looked insane. Horror-movie insane. Wild and crazy. She was smiling, but it was horrible. And for a minute, when she looked at me and I looked back, it was so cold, I saw my own breath. Then she turned, kept walking, and I started after her."

"Started after her? An insane ghost? You had to be scared."

"Not so much, not that I realized anyway. I was caught up, I guess. Really fascinated. I had to *know*. But Mason started screaming. Then I was scared spitless. I thought somehow she'd gotten him, which was stupid since she was up ahead and he was behind me. Farther behind me, all of them, than I'd realized. So I went running back, and there was Mason on the ground with his foot bleeding. And Austin's running back to the tent for a T-shirt or something to wrap it 'cause we're not wearing anything but our jockeys. David and I were trying to carry him back when Mama came running out like the wrath of God."

He laughed then, eyes twinkling at Mitch. "You should've seen her. She's wearing these little cotton shorts and some skinny little T-shirt. Her hair was longer back then, and it's flying as she came hauling ass. And I see—the others didn't, but I see she's got my granddaddy's pistol. I tell you what, if it had been some ghost after us, or anything else, she'd have run it off. But when she saw what was what, more or less, she shoved the pistol in the waistband of those little shorts, around the back. She picked Mason up, told us all to get some clothes on. And we all piled into the car to take Mason into the ER for stitches."

"You never said you'd seen the gun." Roz stepped into the library.

"I didn't think you wanted the others to know."

She walked right to him, bent down, and kissed the top of his head. "Didn't want you to know, either. You always saw too much." She turned her cheek, left it on top of Harper's head as she looked at Mitch. "Am I interrupting?"

"No. You could sit down if you have a minute. I've gotten this story from two sources now, and wouldn't mind having your version."

"I can't add much. The boys wanted to sleep out. God knows why as it was hot as hell and buggy with it. But boys do like to pitch a tent. As I wanted to be able to keep an eye on things, and hear them, I closed off my room, and did without the air-conditioning so I could have my doors open to the outside."

"We were right in the yard," Harper objected. "How much trouble could we get in?"

"Plenty, and as events proved just that, it was wise of me to sweat through the night. Once they settled down, I drifted off to sleep myself. It was Mason screaming that woke me. I grabbed my daddy's pistol, which in those days I kept on the top shelf of my bedroom closet. Got the bullets out of my jewelry box and loaded it on the run. When I got there, Harper and David were carting Mason, and his little foot was bleeding. I had to tell them to hush, as they were all talking at once. Took the baby in, cleaned up his foot, and saw it was going to need stitches. I got the story on the way to the hospital."

Mitch nodded, then looked up from his notes. "When did you go to the carriage house?"

She smiled. "First light. It took me that long to get back, settle them all down."

"You take the gun?"

"I did, in case what they'd seen was more corporeal than they'd thought."

"I was old enough to go with you," Harper objected. "You shouldn't have gone out there alone."

She cocked her head at him. "I believe I was in charge. In any case, there was nothing to see, and I can't tell you if I felt anything, genuinely, or if I was still so worked up I thought I did."

"What did you think?"

"That it was cold, and it shouldn't have been. And I felt . . . it sounds melodramatic, but I felt death all around me. I went through the place top to bottom, and there was nothing there."

"When was the place converted?"

"Oh . . . hmm." She closed her eyes to think. "Around the turn of the twentieth century. Reginald Harper was known for wanting the latest things, and automobiles were one of them. He housed his car in the carriage house for a time, then he used the stables for them, and the carriage house became a kind of storage house, with the gardener living on the second floor. But it would've been later, more like the twenties, I think, before it was done up as a guest cottage by my grandfather."

"So it's unlikely she would have stayed there, or visited the gardener there, as those dates are after first sightings. What would've been kept in there while it was an actual carriage house?"

"Buggies, some tack, I suppose. Tools?"

"An odd place for her to go."

"I always wondered if she died there," Harper commented, "and figured she'd let me know once I moved in."

Mitch's attention sharpened on him. "Have you had any experiences there?"

"Nope. She doesn't have much to do with guys once they pass a certain age. Hey, it's snowing."

He popped up to go to the window. "Maybe it'll stick. You need me anymore?" he asked Mitch.

"Not right now, thanks for the time."

"No problem. Later."

Roz shook her head as he walked out. "He'll head right outside, try to scrape up enough for a snowball so he can throw it at David. Some things never change. Speaking of David, he's making chicken and dumplings if you'd like to stay, wait for this snow to peter out again."

"It's a foolish man who turns down chicken and dumplings. I've made some progress, if elimination is progress, the last week or so. I'm running out of candidates, those who're documented, in any case, for Amelia."

She wandered to his work board, studied the photos, the charts, the notes. "And when you run out of candidates who are documented?"

"I start looking outside the box. Off topic, how do you feel about basketball?"

"In what way?"

"In the going to a game sort of way. I scored an extra ticket to my son's game tomorrow night. They're playing Ole Miss. I was hoping I could talk you into going with me."

"To a basketball game?"

"Casual, lots of other people, a specific form of entertainment." He smiled at her easily, when she turned back. "Seemed like a good place to start. And you might be more inclined toward that sort of socializing than a quiet dinner for two. But if you prefer the latter, I find my calendar free the night after next."

"A basketball game might be interesting."

LILY SAT ON THE BOKHARA IN ROZ'S BEDROOM, banging the buttons of a toy phone with a plastic dog. Lily's mother had her head in the closet.

"Just try the eyeshadow, Roz." Hayley's voice was muffled as she pawed through clothing. "I knew it was the wrong color for me when I bought it, but I just couldn't stop myself. It'll look awesome on you, won't it, Stella?"

"It will."

"I've got enough makeup of my own for three women," Roz objected and tried to concentrate on using it. She wasn't entirely sure how her personal space had come to be invaded by females. She just wasn't used to females.

"Oh, my God! You *have* to wear these!"

Hayley pulled out the pants David had talked Roz into buying—and which, to date, had never been on her body again. "I certainly don't."

"Roz, are you kidding?" She waved them at Stella. "Look at these."

Stella did. "I couldn't get my hips in those with a crowbar."

"Sure you could, they stretch." Hayley demonstrated. "Besides, your hips are perfect, seeing as you have breasts. But these are too long for you. You know that sweater I got for Christmas, the red angora David gave me? It'd be fabulous with these pants."

"Then you take them," Roz suggested.

"No, you're wearing them. Watch the baby a minute, okay? I'll run and get the sweater."

"I'm not wearing your sweater. I have plenty of my own. And for heaven's sake, this is just a basketball game."

"No reason not to go looking like the complete babe you are."

"I'm wearing jeans."

Deflated, Hayley dropped onto the bed beside Stella. "She's a hardcase."

"Here, I'll use your eyeshadow. We'll consider it a compromise."

"Can I pick out your earrings?"

Roz shifted her gaze in the mirror until her eyes met Hayley's. "Will you stop nagging the skin off my back?"

"Deal." Hayley leaped up, and when Lily reached toward her, scooped the baby on the fly. Settling Lily on her hip, she began to go through Roz's everyday jewelry box one-handed. "What top are you wearing?"

"I don't know. Some sweater or other."

"The green cashmere," Stella told her. "The dark green mock turtle, and that great black leather coat? The knee-length."

Roz considered as she worked on her eyes. "Fine. That'll work."

"All right, then . . . these." Hayley held up silver spiral dangles. "Shoes?" she asked, turning to Stella.

"Those black leather half boots with the stubby heel."

"You get those, I'll get the sweater, and—"

"Girls," Roz interrupted. "Scoot. I can handle the rest of this myself." But she leaned over to kiss Lily's cheek. "Y'all go play somewhere else now."

"Come on, Hayley, before she decides to wear a sweat-shirt and gardening shoes just to spite us. She was right about the eyeshadow," Stella added as she pulled Hayley out.

Maybe so, Roz decided. It was an interesting shade of brown, with a hint of gold to jazz it up. She knew how to use it to her advantage. God knew she had plenty of prac-tice fixing herself up, and enough vanity to put effort into looking her best when looking her best was called for.

At the same time, there was a certain advantage to having other women, *younger* women in the household, she sup-posed, and she'd take their advice on the wardrobe.

Except for the pants.

She crossed to her dresser, opened the middle drawer where she kept her good sweaters. She did love those soft fabrics, she thought as she went through the folded gar-ments. The cashmeres and brushed cottons, the silks.

She took out the dark green, unfolded it.

The chill hit with a shock, a punishing little slap, that had her taking a step back. Then freezing as the sweater was ripped out of her hands. She watched with disbelief as it hit the opposite wall, then fell to the floor.

Her knees wanted to buckle, but she kept her feet and walked slowly across the room to pick it up.

There were jagged tears across the front, as if angry nails had raked through the material. Her breath streamed out in visible vapors as she fought to stay calm.

"Well, that was nasty, and small of you. Petty and mean. I was fond of this sweater. Very fond. But it won't make a damn bit of difference."

Angry now, she whirled around, waiting, hoping to see something, someone, to battle. "I've got more, and if you're thinking to repeat this performance on the rest of my clothes, I'll tell you now I'll walk out of here bare-assed naked before I give in to this kind of blackmail. So you go have your temper fit somewhere else."

Roz tossed the sweater onto her bed, marched back to her dresser. She grabbed a sweater at random, dragged it over her head. Her fingers trembled as much with rage as distress as she pulled on jeans.

"I make my own decisions," she ranted, "and always have. Keep this up, you just keep this up, and I'll sleep with him just to piss you off."

She finished dressing, shoved her feet into her boots, grabbed the leather coat, then had to order herself not to slam the door.

On the other side, she leaned back against it, breathed in and out until she was calm again. One thing for certain, she decided, she and Mitch wouldn't lack for things to talk about en route to the game.

Still she waited until they were on their way, with the lights of Harper House behind them. "There are a couple of things I need to tell you, then I think it'd be nice if both of us put business aside for a few hours."

"Something happen?"

"Yes. First, I had an irritating encounter at work one day recently with an acquaintance who has gold-medaled in the gossip Olympics for more than twenty consecutive years."

"Hell of a record."

"And she's proud of it. It dealt with my ex-husband, and isn't important of itself, but it upset me a bit, gave me what I call a temper headache, so I went home, took some aspirin, and decided to lie down for a few minutes. I wasn't asleep, just sort of hovering in that nice, cozy in-between—and in my head I was out in the garden, sitting on the bench in the shade, and it was late spring."

"How did you know it was spring?"

"Late spring, early June. I could tell by the plants, the flowers that were blooming. Then it got cold."

She told him the rest, careful with every detail.

"This is the first dream you've mentioned."

"It wasn't a dream. I wasn't asleep." She gave an impatient wave of her hand. "I know people say that all the time, when they *thought* they were awake. I was awake."

"All right. You should know."

"She took me there in my mind. I felt the cold, I smelled the flowers—the white roses on the arbor—I felt the air on my skin. All the while I was aware, in another part of myself, that I was still in my room, on the bed, with the headache pounding."

"Disconcerting."

"You're subtle," she replied. "Yes, it was disconcerting. Disorienting and upsetting. I don't like having anyone direct my thoughts. And the way she looked at me, when she opened her eyes in that grave, it was with a terrible kind of . . . love. She's never hurt me, and I've never felt that she would. Until tonight."

He pulled off the side of the road, braked hard, then turned to her. The calm she most usually saw in him, felt from him, was replaced by a percolating anger. "What do you mean? Did she attack you? For God's sake—"

"Not me, but a very nice cashmere sweater. It was a birthday gift, so I've only had it since November, and I'm still mad she ruined it."

"Tell me exactly what happened."

When she had, he sat back, tapped his fingers on the wheel. "She didn't want you coming out with me tonight."

"Apparently not, but that's too bad. Here I am."

He looked at her again. "Why?"

"I said I would, and I do what I say I will. Then you can add that she made me mad, and I don't back down, either.

And lastly, I wanted to explore whether or not I'm going to like your company on a purely social level."

"You shoot very straight."

"I do. It irritates some people."

"I'm not one of them. Sorry about the sweater."

"So am I."

"We could speculate—"

"We could," Roz interrupted. "But I'd just as soon not, right now. She didn't stop the evening, so I don't see why she should drive it, either. Why don't we talk about something else until it's time to get down to business again?"

"Sure. What would you like to talk about?"

"I could start by wondering out loud how long you intend to sit here beside the road, and how late that's going to make us to your son's game."

"Oh. Right." He pulled onto the road again. "How about if I start this conversation off by telling you I've got a new cleaning lady."

"Is that so?"

"She's a friend of a friend of a friend. Sort of. She's into feng shui, so she's rearranging everything in the place—career areas, and health areas, I dunno. And making me lists for things I have to buy, like a money frog for my prosperity corner—or something. And these Chinese coins. And she says I have to have a green plant. I think it's for the health area, I'm not sure, and I'm too afraid of her to ask. So I was wondering if I could possibly have that plant back you took from my place last spring."

"The one you were murdering."

"I didn't know I was murdering it. I didn't even know it was there."

"Benign neglect is still neglect."

"Hardass. How about I sign an oath to take better care of it? The fact is, she'll be the one taking care of it, at least every other week. And you could have visitation rights."

"I'll think about it."

THE AUDITORIUM WAS ALREADY PACKED WHEN THEY arrived, and humming with pregame excitement. They moved through the noise and color and excitement, scooting down the row to their seats while both teams practiced layups on the court.

"That's Josh there, number eight."

She watched the tall boy in his trimmed-in-blue white jersey lope forward and tap the ball off the backboard and into the net. "Nice form."

"He was the NBA's number-ten draft pick. He'll play for the Celtics next year. It's hard for me to believe it. I'm not going to brag all night, but I had to get that one in."

"He's going pro? The Celtics? Brag all you want. I would."

"I'll keep it to a minimum. In any case, Josh is point guard, that's the position that directs the team's offense from the point."

She listened, sipping the soft drink he'd bought her, as he ran through a primer of basketball terms and explanations.

At tip-off she watched the action, enjoyed the lightning movements on court, the echoing voices, the thunder of the ball on wood.

Now and again through the first quarter, Mitch would lean closer to explain a call, a strategy, or a play.

Until she got to her feet with the rest of the Memphis crowd to boo a blown call. "What, do those refs need eye surgery? We had established position, didn't we—does he need *three* feet planted on the ground? That was charging, for God's sake. All he was missing was a Visa card!"

When she sat again, with a disgusted huff, Mitch scratched his chin. "Okay, either I'm an exceptional teacher or you know basketball."

"I have three sons. I know basketball. I know football and baseball, and at one time I knew entirely too much about professional wrestling. But they mostly outgrew that one." She took her eyes from the game long enough to smile at him. "But you were having such a nice time educating the little lady, I didn't want to break your stride."

"Thanks. Want some nachos?"

"I wouldn't mind."

She enjoyed herself, and was amused at halftime when Josh zeroed in on his father in the crowd and grinned. More amused when the boy's gaze drifted to her, then back to his father before Josh executed an enthusiastic thumbs-up.

And when at game's end, the Memphis Tigers clipped Ole Miss's Rebels by three points, she decided the experience had nearly been worth one cashmere sweater.

"You want to wait around, congratulate your boy?"

"Not tonight. It'll be better than an hour before he gets out of the locker room, and through the groupies. I'd like you to meet him sometime, though."

"I'd be glad to. He's a pleasure to watch on the court, not just his style and skill—though he has plenty of both—but his enthusiasm. You can tell he loves the game."

"Has since he was a baby." Mitch slipped an arm around Roz's waist to help maneuver them both through the departing crowd.

"It'll be tough on you, him moving to Boston."

"He's always wanted it. Part of me wants to move up there with him, but sooner or later, you've got to let go."

"Nearly killed me when my two youngest moved away. They were five years old yesterday."

He dropped his arm, then took her hand as they crossed the parking lot. "Can I interest you in a postgame meal?"

"Not tonight. I need to get an early start in the morning. But thanks."

"Dinner tomorrow."

She slid a look up at him. "I should tell you getting me out of the house two nights running generally takes a team of wild horses. And I've got a garden club meeting tomorrow, which for personal reasons, I can't miss."

"The night after."

"I sense a campaign."

"How's it going?"

"It's not bad." Not bad at all, she thought, enjoying the bracing air, and the warmth of his hand over hers. "I'll tell you what, you can come to dinner night after next, but I'll warn you, I'll be cooking. David's night off."

"You cook?"

"Of course I cook. Not that I'm allowed to when David's in the house, but it happens I'm a very good cook."

"What time's dinner?"

She laughed. "Let's make it seven."

"I'll be there." When they reached his car, he walked her to her side, then turned her around, slid his arms around her, and drew her toward him. Laid his mouth on hers in a long, lazy kiss.

She curled her hands around his arms, held on to them, to him, and let herself float on the sensation—the warmth of his body, the cool of the air, the simmering demand just under the lazy tone of the kiss.

Then he eased back, his eyes on hers, and reached around to open her door. "I did that now because I figured if I waited until I walked you to your door, you'd be expecting it. I'm hoping to surprise you, at least now and again. I don't think it's the easiest thing to do."

"You've managed it a few times so far."

When she slid into the car, he closed the door. And thought he might have a few more surprises up his sleeve before they were done.

ten

HARPER COULD AND DID SPEND HOURS A DAY IN THE grafting house without being bored or missing the company of others. The plants he worked with were an endless fascination and satisfaction to him. Whether he was creating another standard or experimenting with a hybrid, he was doing the work he loved.

He enjoyed the outdoor work as well, the grafting and propagation he performed with the field stock. He'd already selected the trees he intended to graft and would need to spend part of the week collecting his scions, and pruning the maiden trees he'd grafted the year before.

His mother left these sort of decisions up to him. The what, the how, the when. It was, he knew, a strong level of trust and confidence from her to step back and let him run that end of the show.

Then again, she'd taught him not only the basics of the work, but had instilled in him a love for what grew.

They'd spent countless hours together in the garden and greenhouse when he was growing up. She'd taught his brothers as well, but their interests had veered off where his had centered. In Harper House, in the gardens, in the work.

His college years, his studies there, had only cemented for him what would be his life's work.

His responsibility to them—the house, the gardens, the work, and the woman who'd taught him—was absolute.

He considered it a bonus round that love and obligation so neatly united for him.

Tchaikovsky played for the plants, while through his headset his choice of classic was Barenaked Ladies. He checked his pots, making notations on his various clipboards.

He was especially pleased with the dahlias he'd grafted the previous spring at Logan's request. In a couple of weeks, he'd bring the overwintered tubers into growth, and in spring take cuttings. In the Garden should be able to offer a nice supply of Stella's Dream, the bold, deeply blue dahlia he'd created.

Interesting the way things worked, he thought. Through Logan and tidy Stella falling in love—and Logan showing his sentimental side over the blue dahlia Stella had dreamed of. Dreamed of, Harper thought, because of the Harper Bride.

It sort of circled around, didn't it, back to the house, and what grew there.

There would be no Stella's Dream without the Bride. And no Bride without Harper House. None of it, he supposed, without his mother's steady determination to keep the house and build the business.

Since he was facing the door, he saw it open. And watched Hayley walk in.

She wouldn't be here, either, without his mother. There would have been no beautiful, pregnant woman knocking on the door of Harper House last winter looking for work and a place to live.

When she smiled, his heart did that quick, automatic stutter, then settled back to normal again. She tapped the side of her head, and he pulled off his headset.

"Sorry to interrupt. Roz said you had some pots mature enough for me to rotate into the houseplant stock. Stella's looking to do a winter sale."

"Sure. You want me to bring them out?"

"That's okay. I got boxes and a flat cart outside the door."

"Let me check the inventory, adjust it first." He walked down to his computer station. "Want a Coke?"

"Love one, but I'm still watching my caffeine."

"Oh right." She was nursing Lily, a concept that made him feel sort of warm and twisty inside. "Ah, got some water in the cooler, too."

"That'd be good. When you've got time, can you show me some grafting? Stella said how you do most of it, at least the field work, about this time of year. I'd really like to do something, then, you know, follow it on through."

"Sure, if you want." He handed her a bottle of water. "You can try your hand on a willow. It was the first graft my mother showed me how to do, and they're the best to practice on."

"That'd be great. I thought one day, when I get a place for me and Lily, I could plant something I'd made myself."

He sat, ordered himself to concentrate on his inventory program. The scent of her, somehow essential female, fit so perfectly with the smell of earth and growth. "You've got plenty of room at the house."

"More than." She laughed, tried to read over his shoulder. "Been there a year, and still can't get used to all the space. I love living there, I do, and it's wonderful for Lily to have so many people around, and nobody, nobody could be more amazing than your mama. She's the most awesome person I know. But sooner or later, I need to, well, plant Lily and me somewhere of our own."

"You know Mama loves having you there or she'd've nudged you along by now."

"Boy, that's the truth. She really knows how to structure things, doesn't she? Sets them up to suit her. I don't mean that exactly the way it sounds. It's just that she's strong and smart, and doesn't seem to be afraid of anything or anyone. I admire that so much."

"You seem to have plenty of guts and brains of your own."

"Guts maybe, but I've started to realize a lot of that came from not knowing any better." Idly, she picked up a scrap of raffia, twisted it around her finger. "When I look back, I don't know how I worked up to setting out six-months pregnant. Not now that I have Lily and realize, well, everything. I'm going to owe Roz for the rest of my life."

"She wouldn't want that."

"That's one thing she's not going to have any choice about. My baby's got a good, loving home. I've got a job that I swear I like more every day. We've got friends, and family. We'd've done all right, I'd've made sure of it. But we wouldn't be where we are now, Lily and I, without Roz."

"Funny, I was thinking how most everything—the house, this place, even Logan and Stella wind around to my mother. Maybe even the Bride."

"Why the Bride?"

"If Mama had sold the place—and there had to be times it would've been easier to do that—maybe the Bride wouldn't still be there. Maybe it takes a Harper being in the house. I don't know." He shrugged, got up to select the plants he'd checked off his inventory. "It was just something I wondered about."

"Could be right. You wouldn't sell it, would you, when it comes to you?"

"No. Fact is, every time I think, maybe I should move out of the carriage house, get some place, I just can't do it. It's where I want to be, that's one thing. And the other is no matter how smart or strong my mother is, I feel it's better that I'm around. I think she'd be sad, and a little lonely, if you and Lily went somewhere else, especially since Stella and the boys'll be moving into Logan's in a couple months."

"Maybe, and I'm not planning on anything right away. But with her and Mitch dating, it could be she'll have all the company she wants."

"What?" He stopped dead, with a young, healthy ficus in his arms. "Dating? What do you mean dating? They're not dating."

"When two people go out two or three times, to basketball games, to dinner and what not, when the *she* in the pair cooks the *he* dinner herself, I tend to call it dating."

"They're working on this project. It's like . . . meetings."

She gave him the female smile he recognized. The one that categorized him as a pitifully out-of-touch male. "You don't generally adjourn a meeting with a long, hot kiss—at least I haven't been lucky enough to have a meeting like that for some time."

"Kiss? What—"

"I wasn't spying or anything," she said quickly. "I happened to be up with Lily one night, looked out the window when Mitch brought Roz home. Okay, I sort of looked out on purpose when I heard the car, just to see what was what. And if the liplock I witnessed is anything to go by, that's some serious dating."

He set the plant down again, with a thump. "Well, for Christ's sake."

She blinked. "Harper, you don't have any problem with Roz seeing a man like that. That'd be just silly."

"Last time she was seeing a man like that, she ended up married to the son of a bitch."

"She made a mistake," Hayley said, heating up. "And Mitch is nothing like that bastard Bryce Clerk."

"And we know this because?"

"Because we do."

"Not good enough."

"He certainly is good enough for her."

"That's not what I said. I said—"

"Just because he isn't rich, or doesn't have that fancy Harper blood running through him doesn't mean you should build a case against him." She drilled a finger straight into Harper's chest. "You ought to be ashamed of yourself, talking like some snob."

"I'm not saying that, don't be stupid."

"Don't you call me stupid."

"I didn't call you stupid. Jesus Christ."

"I don't even want to talk to you right now." She turned on her heel, stomped out.

"Fine. I don't want to talk to you, either," he shot back.

He stewed about it, worked himself up about the entire situation while he loaded and transported the plants himself.

Ready for battle, he searched out his mother.

She was in the field, checking on the nursery beds, and the roses he'd t-budded earlier in the season.

She wore a stone-gray hoodie, fingerless gloves, and a pair of boots so old and scarred they were no discernable color. She looked, Harper realized, more like a contemporary than his mother.

"Hayley find you?" she called out.

"Yeah, it's done."

"You know, I'm thinking of adding a mist propagation tent, and doing more palms. Honey, I've got to tell you, I'm excited at how these multiple trees you did are coming along. Our customers are going to have fun with these. I'm thinking of taking one of the nectarine and peach myself."

She studied one of the young trees Harper had grafted, then fan-trained on stakes. "This is lovely work, Harper, and that weeping pear over there—"

"Mama, are you sleeping with Mitch Carnegie?"

"What?" She turned fully to face him, and the pleased smile, the glint of pride in her eyes both froze away. "What did you ask me?"

"You heard what I asked. I'd like an answer."

"And why would I answer a question that you have no business asking?"

"I want to know how seriously you're involved with him. I have a right to know."

"You certainly do not."

"I kept my mouth shut about Clerk. That was my mistake. I'm not making it again. I'm looking after you whether you like it or not. So if you don't tell me, I'll go ask him."

"You'll do no such thing, Harper." She paced away, stood with her back to him. He knew her well enough to be sure she was battling back a spew of temper. They both had a dangerous one, and were both very careful with it. "When's the last time I quizzed you about who you see socially, or who you're intimate with?"

"When's the last time I married a fortune hunter?"

She whirled back, and the temper was so close to the surface now, he saw it burning out of her eyes. "Don't you throw that in my face. I don't like it."

"I don't like doing it. I don't care how mad you get, nobody's going to hurt you like that again while I'm around. Just how much do we know about him? From where I'm standing he's already crossing a line hitting on someone he's working for."

"You're so damn proper about the oddest things. How did I ever manage that?" She let out a long breath. "Let me ask you this. Have you ever known me to make the same mistake twice?"

"Not so far."

"Your confidence in me is overwhelming." She took off one of the gloves she wore, slapped it against her thigh. "I'll tell you this. He's an interesting and attractive man who I've enjoyed seeing a couple of times on a social level. He has a strong and loving relationship with his son, and since I pride myself on the same, that goes a long way with me. He's divorced, and maintains a cordial relationship with the mother of his son and her second husband. This is not always an easy feat. He's done nothing improper, even by your lofty standards."

"They're lofty when it comes to you."

"Oh, Harper. I'm not a paragon."

"Who wants you to be? What I want you to be is safe and happy."

"Honey." She stepped to him then, laid her hands on his cheeks, shook his head gently from side-to-side. "That's supposed to be my line to you. If I promise you, take a solemn oath, that I learned my lesson with Bryce, will you relax?"

"Only if you promise to tell me if he pushes where you don't want to be pushed."

"Listen to you. All right, then, I'll promise. Come on, let's take a look at the rest of this before we go in."

IT CERTAINLY GAVE ROZ A LOT TO THINK ABOUT. How could she know her firstborn so well, yet have been completely surprised by the altercation that afternoon?

Then again, did any mother ever consider her children would worry about her? There just wasn't enough room in the brain or heart for that possibility, when they were both so full of worry and concern for the child.

Added to that, it had come home fully, for the first time, just how much she'd let him down with Bryce. She'd hurt Harper as much, and maybe more, than she herself had been hurt.

Was that something you could make up to those you loved, or was it something that just had to heal over, like a wound?

Because she wanted quiet, she went into her room from the outside entrance, peeled off her outer gear.

She wandered into her sitting room, intending to put on

music and spend some time sketching just to wind down from the day. But she saw the neat piles of mail on her desk. David, as was his habit, had separated the personal correspondence—not much these days as she and most everyone she knew had slid into e-mail posts—business, and bills.

Because she believed in handling the bad news first, she sat and began to open the bills. The utilities on the house made her wince a bit, but that was the price to be paid for having so much space, and so many people using it.

She got out her checkbook, promising herself that soon—before next month—she would master the bill-paying business on-line. Of course, she promised the same every month. But this time she meant it. She'd have Stella show her the ropes, first chance.

She paid the electric, the gas, the phone, a credit card bill. Then frowned at another envelope from another credit card company. She nearly tossed it, assuming it was a so-licitation, then opened it, just to check.

Her eyes widened as she looked at the charges, the total. Over eight thousand dollars. Eight *thousand*? It was ridicu-lous, absurd.

She didn't have a card with this company, and certainly hadn't charged eight thousand dollars. Restaurants, electron-ics, the men's department at Dillard's.

Baffled, she picked up the phone to report the mistake, then spent the next half hour winding her way through tan-gled and sticky red tape.

The next call she made was to her lawyer.

Once the wheels were set in motion, she sat back, the sinking sensation in her stomach making her queasy. The card had been taken out in her name, with all her informa-tion—her address, her Social Security number, even her mother's maiden name. The other user on the card was listed as Ashby Harper.

Clever, she thought. Very clever.

He hadn't used his own name, and hadn't accumulated charges at his most usual haunts. By now, she had no doubt the card was destroyed. The last charge had been made three days before the end of the billing cycle.

Covered all the bases as usual—that bastard Bryce.

The money wouldn't have been the main thrust, she thought now. Not that he wouldn't enjoy the benefits of eight thousand and change. But the point would have been the trouble for her, the irritation, and most of all the *reminder* that he was still in her face. And there was little she could do about it.

It was doubtful the charges could be traced back to him, that it could be proved he'd defrauded the credit card company. It was she who would be forced to untangle the knots, spending the time, the effort, and paying any legal fees.

It was mean and small of him, and suited him perfectly.

And Harper, poor Harper, worried she'd make that kind of mistake again. Not in a million years.

To give herself more time to settle, she skipped dinner, then wrote long, detailed posts to her two younger sons before calling Harper.

Once she knew the children were in bed for the night, she asked Harper, David, along with Stella and Hayley to join her in the front parlor.

"I'm sorry," she began. "I know some of you might have plans for the night. I don't think this will take long."

"It's all right," Stella told her. "Something's the matter. Just tell us what it is."

"I've already taken steps to deal with it, but it's likely all of you will be asked, at least, to answer some questions. In going through my bills this evening, I came upon a credit card bill—a card I don't have, charges I didn't make. However, it was applied for and taken out with considerable personal information. The credit card company will, of course, follow this through. But as I was obliged to list all those who live in this house, I wanted you to be aware. I've no doubt the card was taken out by Bryce. He'd know the information, and it's just his style."

"You don't have to pay it," Hayley said quickly. "This kind of thing happened in the bookstore once where I used to work. You don't have to pay it."

"No, I won't pay it. It simply costs me time and energy, and upsets me—which would have been the motive. It also upsets the household, which he'd enjoy, I'm sure. I'm sorry for that." She looked at Harper. "I'm sorry."

"Don't say that again." He spoke very softly. "I don't want to hear you say you're sorry again, Mama. What about the police?"

"They may very well be involved. But I'm going to tell you what my lawyer told me. While the credit card company will follow through, it'll be very difficult to prove he's the one who used the card. He didn't use his name, and he didn't charge so much at any given time or place to raise an eyebrow. No one's going to remember he breezed into Dillard's and bought some shirts or a pair of shoes. This is the sort of thing he knows how to do quite well."

She had to get up, to move, so rose to add a log to the fire. "The best we can do is step back from it, as much as we can, and let it play out. Sooner or later, and I believe this, he'll do one of three things. He'll get bored with it, he'll find someone else to harass, or he'll go just a little too far and hang himself."

"I vote for Door Number Three," David put in.

"Your mouth, God's ear," Roz assured him, and made herself sit again. "I've written both Austin and Mason, because I want them, and all of you, to be on guard. He may very well choose to amuse himself by doing this same sort of thing to one or more of you."

At the thought of it, the tension in her shoulders increased until her muscles felt like iron rods under her skin. "And Stella, you and I should be particularly vigilant regarding any charges to the business."

"Don't worry. He won't get by us. Roz, I'm so sorry you have to deal with this. Anything I can do—anything any of us can do?"

"I'll let you know, I promise. All right." Roz got to her feet. "That's all, then. I'm going to go on up, get to some work I've put off."

"You haven't had any dinner," David reminded her. "Why don't I bring you something?"

"Not now. I'll get something later."

David stayed on his feet, watching her walk out. "Son of a bitch," he muttered when she was out of earshot. "Smarmy, sleazy, last-season Ferrogamo-wearing son of a bitch."

"Why don't you and I go pay him a visit?" Harper stayed in his chair. His voice was still soft, as it had been, but now it had an edge to it, a predatory edge.

"That's a damn good idea." Hayley sprang up, fists clenched at her sides. "Let's all go pay him a call. Right now."

"Stand down, Xena." David patted her shoulder. "While there's little more I can think of that would be more entertaining than breaking a few of his caps, it's not the answer."

"I hear four when you add two and two," Harper said. "I say it's the right answer."

"David's right," Stella pointed out. "It would upset and embarrass Roz, more than she's already upset and embarrassed."

"Then we won't tell her." Hayley threw out her arms. "We can't just *sit* here."

"I'm not," Harper said. "You are."

"Just a damn minute—"

"Hold on." Like a referee, David stepped between them. "Think, Harper, past your temper. We go take a few very deserved hits at Clerk, his bruises'll heal soon enough. And he'll have the satisfaction of knowing he got to her, that he upset her. That's the last thing she wants, and you and I know that. The most important weapon she has against him is indifference. She won't have that when she has to bail you out on assault charges."

"I'll tell you what else." Stella continued to sit, her hands gripped tight in her lap. "The more we make of it, the more upset she'll be. The best thing we can do for her is to take a page from her book. Treat it coolly, like business. And to remember, if it's hard for us to do that, how much harder it is for her."

"I hate it," Hayley raged. "I hate that you're right, and I wish you'd been right *after* we'd beat the hell out of him. It shows character, Harper, that you want to stand up for her. And it shows character, I guess, to know it's not the way."

MAYBE NOT, BUT HARPER COULDN'T QUITE ERASE THE picture of Bryce in a bloody pulp at his feet. It probably didn't hurt that he didn't know exactly where to find the man. Oh, he could find out, a few calls would do the trick. But those calls might trickle back to the source before he got there.

And in the end, he knew David was right.

But he couldn't just sit at home and stew. There was another matter he could deal with, and he didn't give a damn whether or not his mother liked it.

He was still spoiling for a fight when he knocked on Mitch's apartment door.

He half hoped he'd find Mitch with another woman. Then he could punch him in the mouth and defuse the sparking end of his temper.

But when Mitch answered, he appeared to be alone. Unless you counted the noise that Harper recognized as a televised basketball game.

"Hey. How's it going? Come on in."

"I want to talk to you."

"Sure. Wait." Mitch's attention had already swung back to the huge television screen that dominated one wall. "Less than a minute to halftime. We're down two. Damn it. Goddamn it, loose ball."

Despite himself, Harper found himself standing there, caught up in the action, calling out when number eight recovered the ball and, pivoting with a kind of magical grace, sent it sailing through the air.

"Three! That's three." Mitch punched Harper companionably in the arm. "And there's the buzzer. Want a drink?"

"Could use a beer."

"Don't have any, sorry. Coke?"

"Fine, thanks." He slipped his hands into his pockets as Mitch wandered off. Alone, he scanned the room, brow knitting over some coins dangling from red ribbons. "Hell of a TV," he said when Mitch came back with a can.

"Next to my son, my pride and joy. Have a seat."

"I'll get right to it. Where's this thing you've got going with my mother heading?"

Mitch sat, studied Harper as he lifted his own can. "I can't tell you, as a lot of it depends on her, and where she wants it to head. Obviously, since I'm not blind, deaf, or dead, I find her very attractive. I admire what she's done with her life, and enjoy her company."

"If any of that attraction has to do with her money or her position, you're going to want to step away, right now."

With apparent calm, Mitch picked up the remote, hit the mute button, then set it down again. "That's a very ugly thing to say."

"She had a very ugly time not that long ago."

"Which is why I'm not kicking you out of my home. Such as it is." He reached down below the insult and got a tenuous hold on patience. "Your mother doesn't need money or position to be attractive. She's one of the most beautiful and fascinating women I've ever known. I feel something for her, and I believe she feels something for me. I'm hoping we'll be able to explore those feelings."

"Your first marriage cracked up."

"It did. I cracked it." He turned the Coke can in his hand. "There's no beer in the fridge because I don't drink anymore, and haven't for fourteen years. I'm an alcoholic, and I destroyed my first marriage. All of which I've told your mother, in more detail than I'm willing to tell you. Because I thought she deserved to know before we took those initial steps into what I'm hoping is a relationship."

"I apologize for embarrassing you."

"You haven't. Pissed me off some."

"I'm not sorry about that. She's my mother, and you weren't there to see what she went through. What she's still dealing with."

"How do you mean, still?"

"She found out tonight he opened a credit card in her name—can't prove it, not yet anyway, but it was him. Charged on it, so she's got the hassle of closing it down, dealing with the legal end—and having to tell the rest of us about it."

Mitch set the drink aside, pushed out of the chair to pace a circle around the room. And it was the temper pumping off him that calmed Harper.

"I thought about hunting him down, beating the crap out of him."

"I'll hold your coat, then you can hold mine."

Another knot in Harper's belly loosened. It was exactly the sentiment he could respect. "David talked me out of it. David and Stella, actually. Mama would hate it. It's one of those things she'd find . . . unseemly—then there'd be the gossip that rolled out of it. So I came here to take a few punches at you instead. Work off some of the mad."

"Mission accomplished?"

"Seems like it."

"That's something." Mitch scooped both hands through his hair. "Is she okay? How's she handling it?"

"Like she handles everything. Straightforward, takes the steps. She deals. But she's churned up. More worried that he'll take the same sort of shot at me, or my brothers. Embarrassed, too," he added. "It's the kind of thing that embarrasses her."

Mitch's expression went grim. "He'd know that, wouldn't he? That'll be the perk, even more than whatever he charged on the bogus account."

"Yeah, you got that right. I want you to know, if you hurt her, any way, shape, or form, I'll make you pay for it. Seems fair to tell you up-front."

"Okay." Mitch came back to the chair, sat. "Let me lay this out so we understand each other. I'm forty-eight. I make a good living. Nothing spectacular, but I do fine. I like my work, I'm good at my work, and lucky for me it pays the bills and gives me enough to be comfortable."

As an afterthought, Mitch shoved the open bag of chips on the table in Harper's direction. "My ex-wife and her husband are good people, and between us—without much help from me for the first six years, we raised a hell of a young man. I'm proud of that. I've had two serious relationships since my divorce, and a few that weren't so serious. I care about your mother, I respect what she's accomplished, and I have no intention of causing her any sort of harm or unhappiness. If I do, I have a feeling she'll pay me back for it before you can get off the mark."

He paused, took a drink. "Is there anything else you want to know?"

"Just one thing right now." Harper picked up the bag, dug in. "Can I hang out and watch the rest of the game?"

eLeven

❧

With her hands on her hips, Roz studied her newly arranged In the Garden potting soil preparation area. It had taken two full days, eking out time between other chores and working with the precise-minded Stella to set it up.

In Roz's estimation it would have taken her half that time alone, but it wouldn't have been nearly as practical a work space. There were tubs of soil she'd already mixed herself, the worktables, the bag storage, the scale, scoops, bag sealer, stools.

Everything was arranged in assembly-line efficiency.

The outlay had been relatively little, which had pleased Stella, who had a head for profit as well as precision. With the simple design of the bags, some clever marketing, and what she knew to be an excellent product, Roz felt confident they'd do very well. Very well indeed.

Her mood was very bright when she turned to greet Harper as he came through the door of the work shed.

"What do you think of our new enterprise?" She held

out her arms. With a laugh, she picked up a five-pound bag she'd already filled and sealed and tossed it over to him.

"Good look," he said, turning the bag over. "No frills. It says this is serious dirt. Looks like something you'd see in a high-end garden boutique."

"Exactly, and we'll keep the price down initially, to get it moving. I'm having the bags overfilled by a couple ounces to give me a safety zone. I thought we'd put Ruby on the job, for a start anyway. Maybe see if Steve wants to take some part-time work. It won't be that labor intensive, or take that much time."

"It's smart business, Mama." He laid the bag down. "You've got a knack for it."

"I like to think so. We still mad at each other?"

"No, but we might be after I finish telling you I went into Memphis to see Mitch Carnegie."

Her face went blank; her voice turned cool. "Why would you do that, Harper?"

"One, I was pissed off. Two, David and Stella talked me out of hunting up Clerk and beating his face in. Third, I wanted to hear for myself what Mitch had to say about what's going on between you."

"I understand one perfectly. I appreciate two, on several levels. But I fail to comprehend why you would assume to interrogate a man I'm seeing. It's unpardonably rude and interfering. I don't run around snooping on the women you choose to see."

"It wasn't snooping, and I've never chosen to see a woman who stole from me or set out to interfere with my life or smear my reputation."

"You're young yet." Ice dripped from the words. "Do you think I'm the only woman foolish enough to get tangled up with an asshole?"

"No, I don't. But I don't much care about other women. You're my only mother."

"That doesn't give you the right to—"

"I love you."

"Don't use that weapon on me."

"I can't help it. It's all I've got."

She pressed her fingers to the center of her forehead, rubbed hard. "It would help if you added a little trust and respect to that love, Harper."

"I've got all the trust and respect in the world for you, Mama. It's the men I'm not so sure about. But if it helps any, I worked up plenty of trust and respect for Mitch last night. He might almost be worthy enough to court my mama."

"He's not courting me, for God's sake. Where do you get this sort of . . . We went to a college basketball game, we had dinner."

"I think he's stuck on you."

She stared, and this time lifted both hands to the sides of her head. "My head is reeling."

He walked to her, slid his arms around her, and drew her in. "I couldn't stand to see you get hurt again."

"Bryce only hurt my pride."

"That's a mortal wound for us Harpers. And he did more than that. I don't think Mitch will do the same, at least not deliberately."

"So, you approve."

He grinned when she tipped her head up to look at him. "That's a trick question, and my mama didn't raise any fools. I say yes, and you'll rip my butt reminding me you don't need my approval. So I'm just going to say I like him. I like him a lot."

"You're a slippery one, Harper Ashby. Tell you what." She patted his back, eased away. "You can give me a hand in here for a while. I want to do up twenty bags of each weight category."

"I thought you wanted Ruby to do that."

"Changed my mind. Doing some uncomplicated and

monotonous work ought to give you some time to reflect on the error of your ways."

"Talk about slippery."

"The day you can outwit me, my baby, is the day I see about moving myself into a home. Let's get started."

AFTER WORK SHE WENT STRAIGHT HOME, AND DIRECTLY upstairs to clean up. Wary now, she checked the mail on her desk, looked through the bills. She couldn't say she was relieved when she found nothing. It was like waiting for the other shoe to drop.

There had been a similar sort of harassment right after the divorce, then a nice period of peace. When, she assumed, he'd had some other woman on the string and was too involved to waste his time poking sticks at an ex-wife.

She'd handled it then; she'd handle it now.

As she was dressing the phone rang. When it hit the third ring, she assumed David was otherwise occupied and answered herself.

"Good evening. Is Rosalind Harper available?"

"This is she."

"Ms. Harper, this is Derek from the Carrington Gallery in New York. We're just following up to let you know the Vergano will be shipped to you tomorrow."

"I don't think that's a good idea, Derek, is it? I didn't order anything from your gallery."

"The Cristina Vergano, Ms. Harper. Your representative spoke with me personally only last week."

"I don't have a representative."

"Ms. Harper, I'm very confused. The charge has already been cleared to your account. Your representative indicated that you were very taken with the painting, and wished to have it shipped as soon as the showing was over. We've had considerable interest in this work, but as it was already sold—"

She rubbed hard at the back of her neck where the tension had settled. "It looks like we both have a problem, Derek. Let me give you some of the bad news." She explained briefly, caught herself pacing as she spoke, and as a fresh headache brewed. She noted down the credit card company and number.

"This is very upsetting."

"Yes," she agreed, "it certainly is. I'm sorry you and your gallery have been inconvenienced by this. Would you mind, just for curiosity's sake, telling me the name of the painting?"

"Vergano's a very powerful and dynamic artist. This oil on linen, custom framed by the artist, is from her Bitches collection. It's called *The Amazing Bitch*."

"Of course it is," Roz replied.

She went though the routine, calling the credit card company, and her lawyer, then writing to both to document the incident.

She took aspirin before going down to the kitchen and pouring herself a large glass of wine.

David's note sat propped on the counter.

Hot date. An exceptional lasagna's on warm in the oven. Hayley and the baby went over to Logan's with Stella and the boys. They're having a little painting party. More than enough lasagna for two. Dr. Studly's in the library. Just warm up the bread, toss the salad—in the fridge—and you're set. Buon appetito!

David

P.S. Appropriate CDs already loaded in the player. Now please *go up and put on those Jimmy Choo's.*

"Well." She noted David had set the kitchen nook with festive plates, fat candles, a bottle of San Pellegrino, pale green glasses. And it explained why a bottle of good Italian red was breathing on the counter.

"Lasagna's fine," she said aloud. "But I'm not putting on those shoes to eat it."

Content and comfortable in the thick gray socks she habitually wore around the house, she walked to the library.

He was sitting at the table, wearing his glasses and a Memphis Tigers sweatshirt. His fingers were moving quickly over the keyboard of his laptop. On the desk was a large bottle of water. David's doing, no doubt. He'd have nagged Mitch to rotate water with his habitual coffee.

He looked . . . studiously sexy, she decided, with his intellectual glasses and the mass of thick, disordered hair. That rich brown, with just a hint of chestnut.

There were good eyes behind those glasses, she thought. Not just the color, so deep, so unique, but good, direct eyes. A little intense, unnervingly intense, and she had to admit she found that exciting.

Even as she watched, he paused in his typing to scoop the fingers of one hand through his hair. And muttered to himself.

It was interesting to hear him mutter to himself, since she often caught herself doing the same.

It was interesting, too, to feel this long slow pull in her belly, and the little dance of lust up her spine. Wasn't it good to know those instinctive charges still had spark? And wasn't she curious to see what would happen if she took a chance, and lit the fuse?

Even as she thought it, books flew off the shelf, slammed into each other, then the walls, the floor. In the fireplace, flames leaped in hot reds, while the air shivered with cold.

"Jesus Christ."

Mitch shoved back from the table so fast his chair hit the floor. He managed to duck one book, then block another. As Roz rushed forward, everything stopped.

"You see that? Did you *see* that?" He bent, picked up a book, then dropped it on the table. It wasn't fear in that lovely, liquid drawl, she noted. It was fascination. "It's like ice."

"Temper tantrums." She picked up a book herself, and the cold nearly numbed her fingers.

"Impressive ones. I've been working in here since about three." Grinning like a boy, he checked his watch. "Nearly four hours. It's been quiet as, you'll excuse the expression, a tomb. Until now."

"I suppose I set her off, as I was about to ask if you'd like to have dinner. David left a meal."

Together they began to retrieve the rest of the books. "No question that she doesn't like the two of us together."

"Apparently not."

He set the last book on the shelf. "So . . . what's for dinner?"

She glanced over at him, smiled. And in that moment realized that beyond the lust, there wasn't anything about him she didn't like. "Lasagna, which David bills as exceptional. As I've sampled it in the past, I can vouch for his claim."

"Sounds great. God, you smell good. Sorry," he added when her eyebrows lifted. "Thinking out loud. Listen, I've been able to eliminate more names, and I've been transcribing the interviews we've done so far. I've got a file here for you."

"All right."

"I'm going to work on tracking down some of the descendants of staff, and what we'll call the outer branches of the family tree. But what I'm seeing as the oldest living relative is your cousin Clarise—and happily she's local. I'd like to talk to her."

"Good luck with that."

"She's still in the area, at the . . ."

"Riverbank Center. Yes, I know."

"She puts me a full generation closer to Amelia. It'd be simpler, I'd think, to approach her if you spoke to her first."

"I'm afraid Cousin Clarise and I aren't on speaking terms, or any sort of terms whatsoever."

"I know you said there was a rift, but wouldn't she be interested in what I'm doing with the family?"

"Possibly. But I can assure you, she wouldn't take my call if I made one."

"Look, I understand about family schisms, but in this case—"

"You don't understand Clarise Harper. She dropped her surname years ago, choosing to go legally by her first and middle names. That's how entrenched in the Harper name she is. She never married. My opinion being she never found anyone soft or stupid enough to take her on."

Frowning, he hitched a hip on the table. "Is this your way of telling me you don't want me contacting her, because—"

"I hired you to do a job, and don't intend to tell you how to go about it, so don't get your back up. I'm telling you she's chosen to banish me and mine from her plane of existence, which is just fine by me. The one good thing I can say about her is once she's made up her mind on something, she follows through."

"But you don't have any objection to me talking to her, involving her."

"None. Your best bet is to write her—very formally— and introduce yourself, being sure to use the doctor part, and any other impressive credentials you might have at hand. If you tell her you intend to do a family history on the Harpers, and play up how honored you would be to interview her, and so on, she might agree."

"This is the one you kicked out of the house, right?"

"In a manner of speaking. I don't recall telling you about that."

"I talk to people. She's not the one you chased off with a Weedwacker."

Amusement, very faint, ran over her face. "You are talking to people."

"Part of the job."

"I suppose. No, I didn't chase her with a Weedwacker. That was the gardeners. And it wasn't a Weedwacker, come to that. It was a fan rake, which was unlikely to do any serious damage. If I hadn't been so mad and thinking more clearly, I'd've grabbed the loppers those idiots had used on my mimosa trees. At least with those I could've given them a good jab in the ass as they skeddadled."

"Loppers. Would those be . . ." He made wide scissoring motions with both arms.

"Yes, that's right."

"Ouch. Back to your cousin. Why'd you give her the boot?"

"Because when I invited her, to my lasting regret, to a family barbecue here years ago, she called my sons disreputable brats and stated—she without chick or child—that if I were a proper mother I'd've taken a switch to them regularly. She then called Harper a born liar, as he was entertaining some of his young cousins with stories about the Bride, and told him to shut his mouth."

He angled his head. "And still she lives."

Temper had brought a flush to her cheeks, but his comment had a small smile curving her lips. "She was on shaky ground already as she constantly criticized my parenting, my housekeeping, my lifestyle, and occasionally my morals. But nobody stands on my ground and attacks my children. While I did consider murder, knowing my quarry, I was certain banishment from Harper House was a more painful punishment."

"As I believe I said before, you're a hardass. I like that."

"Good thing, 'cause that's not going to change at this

late date. In any case, on her way out the door, she cursed my name and said it was a black day when Harper House came into my grasping, incompetent hands."

"She sounds delightful. I'll write her tomorrow."

"Just don't mention you're working for me."

"It wouldn't be hard for her to find out."

"True enough, but the less you mention me the better. Anything else on your mind?"

"Other than wondering how you manage to work all day and still look amazing, no. Nothing that springs, anyway."

She waited another moment, nodded. "You're not going to mention it."

"What would it be?"

"The visit my son paid to you last night."

"Oh." Because she was watching his face, she caught the flicker of surprise that moved over it before he picked up the glasses he'd taken off and began to polish them with his sweatshirt. "He told you?"

"Yes. He was angry, so he acted rashly."

"Like grabbing a fan rake instead of loppers."

Her laugh snuck out. "Very like. We have, both of us, horrible tempers. Which is why we both make a concerted effort not to lose them. It doesn't always work. I'd like to apologize for his behavior."

"I can't accept."

There was distress, something he rarely saw from her, in her eyes. "Mitch, I know he overstepped, but he's young and—"

"You misunderstand. I can't accept an apology when there's no need for one. From either of you. He was looking out for you."

"I don't need, or want, looking out for."

"Maybe not, but that's not going to stop someone who loves you from trying. We discussed, came to understand each other, and that's all there was to it."

"And you're not going to elaborate on that."

"It was between him and me."

"You men do have your codes of honor."

"You weren't going to tell me about this latest harassment."

For an instant, she thought of the phone call from New York, then tucked it away again. "Nothing to tell. I'm dealing with it."

"What's happened since last night? You're good, so I must've caught you off guard. What else happened?"

"Just a minor irritation, one I've already handled. It's not important. More accurately, I won't let it be important. If I do, it makes me the victim, and he wins. I won't be his victim. That's one thing I never allowed myself to be, and I won't start now."

"Telling me, venting some of the stress, doesn't make you a victim, either."

"I'm not used to airing my problems. I'm not comfortable with it. But I appreciate the offer."

He took her hand, held it. "Consider it a standing one. For my next offer, *Chicago*'s coming to the Orpheum next week. Come with me, have a late supper with me after."

"I might. Are you courting me, Mitchell?"

His thumb grazed back and forth over her hand. "I like to think I'm romancing you, Rosalind."

"That's a pretty word, *romancing*. You've been careful not to pressure me into taking that romancing into intimacy."

"If I pressured you, it wouldn't be romance, or intimacy. Besides the fact, I imagine the door would hit me in the ass as you shoved me out of it."

Humor danced over her face. "That's astute. I think you're a clever man."

"I know I'm a besotted one."

"Another pretty word."

"I'll have to be careful with them. They're the sort of thing you'd distrust."

"Yes, a clever man. Well." She had a choice, and she made it. "Come upstairs."

For the second time that night, she watched surprise run over his face. Then he lifted her hand to his lips. "Would this be serious business?"

"It would. Very serious business."

"Then I'd love to."

She led him out of the room, and down the hall. "The house emptied out on me tonight. So it's just the two of us. Well, three." She looked up at him as they walked up the stairs. "Will that bother you?"

"The fact that she may be watching." He took a little breath. "I guess we'll find out. Did you—" He cut himself off, shook his head.

"What?"

"No, we'll save that."

"All right. I hope you don't mind putting off dinner a bit."

As an answer he turned to her, into her, backing her against a wall. Then laying his lips on hers.

It began warm and soft, then edged up to heat, and demand. She trembled, just once, a shiver of anticipation that spread through her system and reminded her what it was like to be poised on the brink.

He lifted his head, angled it. "You were saying?"

It made her laugh, and feel easy. Taking his hand, she drew him into her bedroom. Shut the door.

He took a moment, scanned the room with its lovely old four-poster and tall windows with the curtains drawn back to let in the night.

"It looks like you. The room," he explained, taking in the silvery green walls, the antiques, the clean lines and elegant details. "Beautiful and classy with a simple elegance that reflects an innate grace and sense of style."

"You make me wish I'd taken the time to fuss with myself a bit."

He looked at her then, the casual sweater, the comfortable trousers. "You are exactly right."

"Right or not, I'm what I am. I think a fire would be nice." She stepped toward it, but he laid a hand on her arm.

"I'll do it. You'd have a view of the back gardens from here," he began as he crouched in front of the fire.

And the terrace doors slashed open on a frigid gust of wind.

"Yes, I do." Calmly Roz crossed over, muscled the doors closed again. "Some mornings, when there's time, I like to take coffee out on the terrace."

He set the kindling to blaze, and his tone was as matter-of-fact as hers. "I can't think of many better ways to start the day."

She stepped to the bed to turn down the duvet. "Or end it. I often have a last glass of wine or cup of coffee out there before I go to bed. It helps smooth out any rough edges left over from the day." She reached over, turned out the lamp.

"Why not leave it on?"

She shook her head. "The firelight's enough, the first time. It's more flattering, and I'm vain enough to prefer that."

She stood where she was, waited for him to come to her. As he laid his hands on her shoulders, the bedroom door slammed open, and closed.

"I expect we might have more of that to contend with," she said.

"I don't care." His hands slid up to her face. "I don't care," he repeated and took her mouth with his.

She felt her pulse jump, what a glorious jolt. The sort that woke the whole system at once, brought it to quivering life. In answer, she lifted her arms to link them around his neck, changed the angle of the kiss to deepen it.

Clocks began to chime, insanely. In defiance as much as

need, she pressed her body to his. "I want you to touch me," she murmured against his mouth. "I want to be touched. By you. Your hands on me."

He eased her back on the bed, sank in with her. The weight of him made her sigh, the weight of a man, and what it meant. Then he touched, and she moaned.

He felt the heat from her. He'd known it was there, under that fascinating and cool veneer. Her skin was like velvet, warmed velvet, over her sides, her torso, the lovely curve of her breasts.

Slim, but not delicate, her body was tough and disciplined. Like her mind, he thought. And just as appealing.

She tasted of ripe, forbidden fruit and smelled of midnight gardens.

Her hands slid under his shirt, up his back. Hard, strong hands, an arousing contrast to the wand-slim body, the satiny skin.

She drew his shirt over his head, reared up enough to set her teeth on his bare shoulder. And the shock of it speared straight to his loins.

The terrace door flew open once more, and the wind burst through to slap over him. He simply reached down, hauled the duvet up. And burrowed under it with her.

She laughed, and found his mouth in the blanketing dark.

Tasting her, feasting on her, he tugged her sweater up and off. "Tell me if you're too cold."

"No. I couldn't be."

She was burning up from the inside out, and only wanted more. More of his hands, his mouth. She arched to him, demanding, exalting when those hands, that mouth claimed her breast. The thrill of it stabbed through her, the bliss of giving her body, of having it *used*.

They rolled together, tugging each other free of clothes, sliding together naked as flesh began to slick from heat and passion.

The blankets fell away, so firelight flickered over them. And if in some dim corner of her brain she heard someone weeping, she could feel only that steady rise of excitement. She could see only him, in the glow of the fire, rising over her.

She lifted to meet him, opened to take him. And sighed, sighed, when he slipped inside her.

He watched her now as she watched him, gazes and bodies locked. Then the movement, slow, intensely focused as her breath came short and ragged, as dark, deep pleasure flooded her, swept her away.

He watched her crest, the arch of her throat, the blur of her eyes, felt her fly over as she squeezed around him. He fought to hold on another moment, just another moment while she quaked under him, while her breath hitched, then released on a long, low moan. And her body went soft and limp in surrender.

He kissed her then, one last, desperate kiss before he plunged, and emptied.

THE DOORS WERE CLOSED AS THEY SHOULD BE. THE fire crackled and simmered. And the house was quiet, settled, and warm.

She was cocooned with him in the center of the bed, allowing herself to enjoy the bliss and the glow. With very little effort, she could have drifted straight off to sleep.

"Looks like she gave up," Mitch commented.

"Yes. For now, anyway."

"You were right about the fire. It's nice. Very nice."

Then he rolled so that she was under him again, and he could look down at her face. "Being with you," he began, then shook his head, touched his lips to hers. "Being with you."

"Yes." Smiling, she stroked her fingers through his hair. "That's very nice, too. I haven't wanted to be with anyone in a very long time. You know, you've got good arms, for a scholar." She gave his biceps a squeeze. "I like good arms. I don't like to think I'm shallow, but I have to say it's a pleasure being naked with a man who keeps in shape."

"I'll change that to a woman, then say the same. The first time I met you, I stood and watched you walk away. You've got one excellent ass, Ms. Harper."

"It happens I do." With a laugh, she gave his a light slap. "We'd better get dressed, go on down before everyone starts coming home."

"In a minute. It was your eyes that hooked me—hooked right through me."

"My eyes?"

"Oh yeah. I thought maybe it was because they're the color of good aged whiskey—and I did love a good whiskey. But that's not it. It's the way they look straight at me. Straight on. Fearless, and just a little regal."

"Please."

"Oh yeah, there's lady of the manor in there, and it beats the hell out of me why it's so sexy. Ought to be irritating, or intimidating at least. But for me, it's just . . . stimulating."

"If that's the case, I'm going to have to start wearing dark glasses so I don't get you heated up at inappropriate times."

"Won't matter a damn." He gave her a light kiss, then shifted. Took her hand. "This mattered. This was important. There isn't anyone else."

Her heart trembled a little, made her feel young and just a little foolish. "Yes, this mattered. This was important. There isn't anyone else."

"Serious business," he said, and drew her hand to his lips. "I'm going to start wanting you again, real soon."

She squeezed his hand. "We'll have to see what we can do about that."

twelve

ROZ FOLLOWED THE SCENT OF COFFEE, AND THE NOISE, into the kitchen. The dreary gray rain had canceled her morning run, so she'd channeled the energy into three miles on her treadmill. It was an alternative that usually bored her senseless, but today she'd found herself singing along with commercial jingles during the *Today* show breaks.

In the kitchen the baby was banging away on her high chair tray with the enthusiasm of a heavy metal drummer, and Stella's boys were whining over their cereal.

"Yes," Stella announced with the snap of motherly frustration in her voice, "you both have to wear your raincoats, because I'm mean and bossy and I want you to be miserable."

"We *hate* the raincoats," Gavin informed her.

"Really? That's not what you said when you begged me to buy them."

"That was before."

Perhaps in sympathy, perhaps for the fun of it, Lily stopped banging her teething rattle and threw it—along with her mangled Zwieback. The eagle-eyed Parker fielded the Zwieback before it hit the floor, and the rattle landed with a solid *plop* in Luke's bowl of Cap'n Crunch.

Milk fumed up and over the rim of the bowl, causing Lily to scream in delight. In a chain reaction, Parker let out a spate of ear-piercing barks and did canine flips while Gavin doubled over in hysterics.

Stella was quick, but for once Luke was quicker and had the rattle out of the bowl and tossed, dripping, into his brother's lap.

"Oh, for God's sake." Stella grabbed a napkin with one hand and held up the other to block Gavin's retaliation. "Don't even think about it."

"I'm sorry. I'm sorry." Hayley scooped up the bowl, more napkins as the boys shoved at each other.

A calm in the storm, David walked over with a damp rag. "We'll mop it up. Troublemaker," he said to Lily, who answered him with a huge, crumby grin.

Roz studied the chaos, and just beamed.

"Morning," she said and strolled in.

Heads turned.

"Roz?" Stella stared at her. "What are you doing here?"

"Since I live here, I thought I'd come in and get myself a cup of coffee." She bent down to brush a kiss over the top of Lily's head. "Hello, boys. That baby's got pretty good aim, doesn't she? Two-pointed it right in the goal."

The idea was so intriguing the boys stopped fighting. "Do it again, Lily!" Luke tugged on his mother's sleeve. "Give it back to her, Mom, so she can do it again."

"Not right now. You've got to finish up or you'll be late for school." She checked her watch and saw it was indeed just after eight, and a full hour after Roz was usually on her way out the door.

"My cereal's got baby spit in it now," Luke complained.

"You can have a muffin instead."

"Then I want a muffin." Gavin shoved his cereal aside. "If he can have a muffin, I can have a muffin, too."

"Fine, fine."

"I'll get them." Hayley gestured Stella back. "Least I can do."

"Mmm, don't they smell great?" Roz sniffed at the bowl filled with fresh apple muffins. She plucked one out for herself, then leaned back against the counter, her coffee in one hand, her muffin in the other. "Can't be a better way to start the day. And look at that rain. Nothing like a good all-day soaker."

After Hayley passed out muffins, she bent close to Stella's ear. "Somebody got her batteries charged."

Stella fought to swallow a snorting laugh. "We'll be out of your way in a minute."

"No rush." Roz bit into the muffin.

"You're usually gone, or finishing up before the invasion."

"Slept in a little today."

"That explains the bulletin I heard on the news this morning about hell freezing over." David didn't bother to hide the smirk as he brought the coffeepot over to top off Roz's mug.

"Aren't you full of sass this morning."

"I'm not the only one full of something. How'd the . . . lasagna go over?"

"Very well." She gave him a bland look over the rim of her cup, and wondered if she was wearing a sign: Recently Got Laid.

"You ought to have a nice big helping of it more often. Puts roses in your cheeks."

"I'll keep that in mind."

"I could use a nice hot dish of lasagna myself," Hayley commented. "Come on, baby doll, let's get you cleaned up." She took Lily out of the high chair.

"You guys go up and get your things—including rain-coats," Stella ordered. "It's almost time to go."

But she loitered another minute. "You want to ride over with me?" she asked Roz.

"I guess I will."

STELLA WAITED UNTIL THEY WERE STARTING DOWN the drive. By her calculations, swinging just a half a mile out of the way to drop Lily off at the babysitter's should give them enough time.

"We made a lot of progress on the painting last night. It's going to be nice to have the dining room finished and put together by the wedding. I'd really like to have a dinner party once we're set. David and all of us, Harper, my parents. Oh and Mitch, of course."

"That'd be nice."

"He's around so much—Mitch, I mean—these days, he feels like part of the household." At Roz's noncommittal *hmmm*, Stella glanced in the rearview mirror to see Hayley rolling her eyes and giving get-to-it hand signals.

"So . . . ah, did you and Mitch work on the project last night, or take advantage of the quiet house and just relax?"

"Stella, why don't you just ask me if I had sex with him instead of beating around the bush? Nothing I hate more than seeing a bush beat half to death."

"I was being subtle," Stella replied.

"No, you weren't."

"I told her she didn't have to lead up to everything," Hayley said from the back. "Besides, we know you had sex. You've got that recently waxed and lubed look."

"God."

"Of course, it's none of our business," Stella put in, shooting Hayley a hot look in the mirror.

"Of course it's not," Roz agreed easily.

"But we just wanted to find a way to say that we're happy if you're happy. That we think Mitch is a terrific guy, and we're here to support—"

"Jeez." Hayley leaned forward as much as her seat belt would allow. "What she's trying to say in her Stella way is: Score!"

"I am not. Exactly. I'm trying to say, with some delicacy—"

"Screw delicacy. Hey, just because people are a little older and all doesn't mean they don't want and deserve some touch the same as the next guy."

"Oh," Roz declared. "I repeat, God."

"You're beautiful and sexy," Hayley continued. "He's great looking and sexy. So, it seems to me that sex is . . . She really can't understand all this, right?" Biting her lip, she glanced at Lily, who was busy playing with her own fingers. "I read this theory on how babies absorb all the stimuli around them, including voices and words, and kind of file them away, and shoot, here we are."

She gathered the diaper bag, then jumped out of the car in the rain. After jogging around, she opened the door to release Lily's harness and drape a blanket over her head. "Don't say anything interesting while I'm gone. I mean it."

When she dashed off, Roz let out a long, heartfelt sigh. "Half the time that girl makes me feel old and creaky, and the other half she makes me feel about eighteen and grass green."

"I know exactly what you mean. And I know it sounds like we're pushing and prying into your private life, but it's because, well, it's just because we love you, that's all. And added to it, we were wondering when you and Mitch might take things up a level."

"Wondering, were you?"

Stella winced. "The subject might have come up in casual conversation. Once or twice."

"Why don't I let you know when and if I'd like to have a casual conversation on the subject?"

"Sure. Absolutely."

When Hayley ran back out, jerked open the door, Stella cleared her throat—loudly—and gave a quick shake of her head. As Hayley let out a disgusted sigh, Stella pulled away from the side of the road and spoke brightly.

"So, I've been working on ideas for displaying the potting soil."

HER LIFE DIDN'T CHANGE, ROZ REMINDED HERSELF, just because she'd gone to bed with a man she found attractive and appealing. Life went on, with its duties and obligations, its irritations and its pleasures.

As she headed for her garden club's monthly meeting, she wasn't sure which category her current destination landed in.

A Harper had been a member of the garden club since her grandmother's day. In fact, her grandmother had helped form it in 1928, and Harper House had held many of its early meetings.

As the owner of a garden center, she felt a double obligation to support the group and remain an active member. And there were some pleasures attached to it. She enjoyed talking with like-minded people about gardening and felt the club had worked hard to implement fund-raisers for beautification projects.

But then, there were plenty who just wanted to dress up, have lunch, and gossip.

She walked into the meeting room at the country club into that beehive hum of female voices. Square enameled pots exploding with forced narcissus sat festively on tables draped with spring-green linen. A podium stood in front of the room for the various committee chairs who'd give their reports or pitches.

She could only thank God she wasn't chairing anything currently.

When she stepped farther into the room, glances shot her way, and the hum of voices trailed off. And died.

Almost immediately they started up again, just a bit too loud, just a bit too bright. She let the cold shield slide over her, and continued to walk straight to a table.

"Aren't these flowers sweet." She looked directly at Jan Forrester as if she couldn't hear the whispers under the forced chatter. "A nice reminder spring's just around the corner. How are you, Jan?"

"Oh, fine, Roz. I'm just fine, how about you?"

"Couldn't be better. How's Quill doing?"

She flushed, deep and rosy. "Oh, you know Quill."

"I certainly do. You just give him my best, won't you?"

It was pride that had her walking the gauntlet, mingling with the crowd, speaking with more than a dozen people before she moved to the pots of coffee and tea. She opted for tea, cold, rather than her habitual coffee.

Her throat felt scalded.

"Roz, honey, don't you look fabulous." Cissy sidled up, smelling of Obsession and smiling like a hungry cat. "I swear, nobody wears clothes like you do. What color would you call that suit?"

Roz glanced down at the trim jacket and pants. "I have no idea."

"Apricot. That's just what it looks like, a nice ripe apricot. That little turnip-head Mandy's been flapping her foolish tongue as fast as she can," she said under her breath. "You and me need to have ourselves a *tête-à-tête*."

"That's all right, I've got the picture. Excuse me." She walked deliberately to Mandy and had the small pleasure of watching the woman's cheeks go white even as she stopped speaking in mid-sentence.

"Mandy, how are you? I haven't seen you since before Christmas. You didn't make last month's meeting."

"I was busy."

Roz took a slow sip of tea. "Life is a circus, isn't it?"

"You've been busy yourself." Mandy jerked up her chin. "If there's not one thing that needs doing, there's a half dozen."

"Maybe if you spent more time tending to your own business, you wouldn't have so much left over to make harassing phone calls or tell vicious lies."

All pretense of other conversation stopped, as if a switch had been thrown.

"You don't know me very well," Roz said in the same conversational tone, "or you'd know that I don't make any phone call that isn't necessary. I don't care to spend much time on the phone. And I don't lie. I just don't see the point in it when the truth usually serves best."

Mandy folded her arms, cocked a hip in an aggressive stance. "Everybody knows what you've been up to, but they're too afraid of you to say it to your face."

"But you're not—good for you—so you go right ahead and say what's on your mind. Or if you'd feel more comfortable, we can have this conversation in private."

"You'd like that, wouldn't you?"

"No, not any more than I like having it in public."

"Just because your family's gone back in Shelby County since God doesn't give you the right to lord it over everybody. My family's just as important as yours, and I've got as much money and prestige."

"Money and prestige don't buy good manners. You aren't showing any at the moment."

"You have nerve, talking to me about manners when you're doing everything you can to ruin Bryce's reputation, and mine."

"Bryce's reputation is of his own making. And as for

yours, honey, you haven't even been on my radar screen. You seem like a likable enough girl. I've got nothing against you."

"You've been telling people I was a cheap tramp, using my daddy's money to try to buy some class."

"And where'd you hear such a thing? Bryce, I imagine."

"Not only him." With her chin still lifted, red spots of color flagged in her cheeks, Mandy looked over at Jan.

"Jan?" Surprise softened Roz's voice, and regret flickered in her heart, just once as she saw the woman flush. "You know better. Shame on you."

"It was something I heard, from a reliable source," Jan said as she hunched her shoulders.

"A reliable source?" Roz didn't bother to temper the disgust in her voice. "And suddenly you're, what, an investigative reporter hunting up sources? You might've come and asked me. It would've been the simple and decent thing to do before spreading such nonsense any further."

"Everyone knows how mad you were when Bryce showed up at your house with Mandy. This isn't the place to discuss it."

"No, it isn't, but it's too late for that. At least this girl has the spine to say what she has to say straight to my face, which is more than you."

Dismissing Jan, Roz turned back to Mandy. "Mandy, did I seem mad when you arrived at my door with Bryce for my holiday party?"

"Of course you were mad. You turned us away, didn't you, when he was only trying to make peace with you."

"We can disagree on what he was trying to do. How did I seem mad? Did I shout and scream?"

"No, but—"

"Did I curse and push you physically out the door?"

"No, because you're cold-blooded, just like he says. Just like plenty others say when you're not around to hear. You waited until we were gone to go in and say awful things about us."

"Did I?" She turned, determined now to finish it out. "Most of you were there that night. Maybe someone here could refresh my memory, as I can't recall saying awful things."

"You did nothing of the sort." Mrs. Haggerty, one of Roz's oldest customers and a pillar in the gardening community, pushed her way through. "I'm as interested in juicy gossip as the next, and don't mind some enhancements to a story, but these are outright lies. Rosalind comported herself with absolute propriety under extremely difficult circumstances. And, young lady, she was kind to you, I saw that with my own eyes. When she came back inside, she said nothing whatsoever about you or that unfortunate bastard you've chosen to champion. If there's anyone here who can say different than that, let's hear it."

"She didn't say a word against you," Cissy put in, and gave a wicked smile. "Even when I did."

"He said you'd try to turn people against me."

"Why would I do that?" Roz said, wearily now. "But you'll have to believe what you have to believe. Personally, I'm not interested in speaking of this, or to you, any longer."

"I have as much right to be here as you."

"You certainly do." To end it, Roz turned away, walked to a table across the room, and sat down to finish her tea.

Ten humming seconds of silence followed, until Mandy burst into tears and ran from the room. A few women hustled after her after shooting glances at Roz.

"Lord," Roz said when Mrs. Haggerty sat down beside her, "she is young, isn't she?"

"Young's no excuse for being flat-out stupid. Rude, on top of it." She looked up with a nod as Cissy moved to join them. "Surprised at you."

"At me? Why?"

"For speaking straight for a refreshing change."

Cissy shrugged, sat. "I like ugly scenes, and I won't deny it. Sure does spice up a dull day. But I don't like Bryce Clerk. And sometimes speaking straight makes things more interesting anyway. Only thing better would've been seeing Roz give that bobble-headed fool Mandy a good smack. Not your style, though," she said to Roz.

Then she touched a hand to Roz, gently. "You want to leave, I'll go with you."

"No, but thanks. I'll stick it out."

SHE GOT THROUGH THE MEETING. IT WAS A MATTER of grit, and of duty. When she got home she changed, then slipped out the back to go in the gardens, to sit on her bench in the cool and study the little signs of coming spring.

Her bulbs were spearing up, the daffodils and hyacinths that would burst into bloom before too long. The crocus were already in flower. They came so soon, she thought, left so early.

She could see the tight buds on her azaleas, and the faint haze on the forsythia.

While she sat, the control she'd locked into place wavered, so she was allowed, finally, to shake inside. With rage, with insult, with temper, with hurt. She gave herself the gift of swimming in the sea of all those dark emotions while she sat, alone in the quiet.

While she sat, the fury peaked, then ebbed, until she could breathe clear again.

She'd done the right thing, she decided. Faced it down, though she'd hated doing so in public. Still it was always better to face a fight than it was to run from it.

Had he thought she would? she wondered. Had he

thought she'd break apart in public, run off in humiliation to lick her wounds?

She imagined he did. Bryce had never understood her.

John had, she thought, studying the arbor where his roses would ramble and bloom for her from spring into the summer, and well into fall. He had understood her, and he'd loved her. Or at least he'd understood and loved the girl she'd been.

Would he love the woman she'd become?

An odd thought, she decided, tipping her head back, closing her eyes. She might not be the woman she was if he'd lived.

He'd have left you. They all do. He'd have lied and cheated and broken you. Taken whores while you sat and waited. They all do.

I should know.

No, not John, she thought, squeezing her eyes tighter as that voice hissed in her head.

You're better off he died than if he'd lived long enough to ruin you. Like the other. Like the one you take to your bed now.

"How pitiful you are," Roz whispered, "to try to smear the memory, and the honor, of a good man."

"Roz." The hand on her shoulder made her jump. "Sorry," Mitch told her. "Talking in your sleep?"

"No." Didn't he feel the cold, or was it only inside her? Inside her along with the quivering belly. "I wasn't sleeping. Only thinking. How did you know I was out here?"

"David said he saw you through the window, heading out this way. Over an hour ago. It's a little chilly to sit out so long." He took her hand, rubbed it between his as he sat beside her. "Your hands are cold."

"They're all right."

"But you're not. You look sad."

She considered a moment, then reminded herself there

were things that couldn't be personal. He was working for her. "I am, I guess. I am a little sad. She was talking to me. In my head."

"Now?" His hands tightened on hers.

"Mmm. You interrupted our conversation, though it was the same old, same old 'men are deceivers' sort of thing on her side."

He scanned the gardens. "I doubt Shakespeare could have created a more determined ghost than your Amelia. I was hoping you'd come by the library, for several reasons. This is one."

He turned her face toward his, pressed his mouth to hers.

"Something's wrong," he stated. "Something more."

How could he see her so well? How could he see what she was able to hide from most? "No, just a mood." But she drew her hand from his. "Some female histrionics earlier. Men are so much less inclined to drama, aren't they?"

"Why don't you tell me about it?"

"It's not worth the breath."

He started to speak again, she could feel him check the instinct to press. Instead he tapped his shoulder. "Put your head here?"

"What?"

"Right here." To ensure she did, he wrapped an arm around her waist, drew her close to his side. "How about it?"

She left it there, smiled a little. "It's not bad."

"And the world didn't spin on its axis because you leaned on someone else for a minute."

"No, it didn't. Thanks."

"You're welcome. Anyway, other reasons I was hoping you'd come in while I was working. I wanted to tell you I've sent a letter to your cousin Clarise Harper. If I don't hear back from her in a week, I'll do a follow-up. And I have several detailed family trees for you, the Harpers, your mother's family, your first husband's. I actually found an Amelia Ashby. No, leave that head right where it is," he said, tightening his grip when she started to sit up straight.

"She's not connected, as far as I can see, as she lived and died in Louisiana, and is too contemporary. I spent some time tracking her back, to see if I could find a link to your Amelia—a namesake sort of thing—but it's not happening. I have some e-mail correspondence from the great-granddaughter of the housekeeper who worked in Harper House from 1887 to 1912. She's a lawyer in Chicago, and is finding the family history interesting enough to put out feelers of her own. She could be a good source, at least on that one branch."

His hand stroked gently up and down her arm, relaxing her. "You've been busy."

"Most of that's just standard. But I've been thinking about the less ordinary portions of our project. When we made love—"

"What portion of the project does that come under?"

He laughed at her dry tone, and rubbed his cheek over her hair. "I put that in the extremely personal column and am hoping to fill a lot of pages in that file. But I've got a point. She manifested—that would be the word, right?"

"Can't think of a better."

"She blew open doors, slammed them shut, set the clocks off, and so on. Without question showed her feelings about what was going on between us, and has since we started that personal file."

"And so?"

"I'm not the first man you've been personal with in that house."

"No, you're not."

"But you haven't mentioned her having similar tantrums over you and John Ashby or you and Bryce Clerk—or anyone you might have had a relationship with otherwise."

"Because it never happened before."

"Okay. Okay." He got up, walking back and forth as he talked. "You lived in the house when you and John Ashby were dating, when you became engaged."

"Yes, of course. It's my home."

"And you lived here, primarily, after you were married, exclusively after your parents died."

She could see him working something out in his head. No, she corrected. It's already worked out, he was just going through the steps of it for her benefit.

"We stayed here often—my mother wasn't well, and my father couldn't cope with her half the time. When he died, we lived here, in an informal sort of way. When she died, we moved permanently into the house."

"And during all that time, Amelia never objected to him? To John."

"No. I stopped seeing her when I turned, oh, eleven, I'd say, and didn't see her again until after I was married. We hadn't been married long, but were already trying to have children. I thought I might be pregnant, and I couldn't sleep. I went outside, sat in the garden, and I saw her. I saw her and I knew I was carrying a child. I saw her at the onset of every pregnancy. Saw or heard her, of course, when the boys were little."

"Did your husband ever see her?"

"No." She frowned. "No, he didn't. Heard her, but never saw her. I saw her the night he died."

"You never told me that."

"I haven't told you each and every time I . . ." She trailed off, shook her head. "No, I'm sorry, I didn't tell you. I've never discussed it with anyone. It's very personal, and it's painful still."

"I don't know what it's like to love and lose someone the way you loved and lost your John. I know it must seem like prying, and it is. But it's all of a piece, Roz. I have to know, to do the job, I have to know this sort of thing."

"I didn't think you would, when I hired you. That you'd have to know personal things. Wait." She lifted a hand before he could speak. "I understand better now. How you work, I think, how you try to see things. People. The board in the library, the pictures on it so you *can* see who they were. All the little details you accumulate. It's more than I bargained for. I think I mean that in a good way."

"I need to be immersed."

"Like you were with a brilliant and twisted poet," she said with a nod. "I also believe you have to know, and that I'm able to tell you these things, because of what we're becoming to each other. Conversely, that may be why it's hard for me to tell you. It's not easy for me to feel close to someone, to a man. To trust, and to want."

"Do you want it easy?"

She shook her head. "How do you know me so well already? No, I don't want it easy. I suspect easy. I'm having a time with you inside myself, Mitchell. That's a compliment."

"Same goes."

She studied him, standing there, vital and alive, with the arbor and its sleeping roses behind him. With warmth and sun, the roses would wake. But John, her John, was gone.

"John was coming home from his office in Memphis. Coming home late from a meeting. The roads were slick. It had been raining and the roads were slick, and there was fog."

Her heart gave a little hitch as it did, always, when she remembered.

"There was an accident. Someone driving too fast, crossed the center line. I was up, waiting up, and dealing with the boys. Harper had a nightmare, and both Mason and Austin had colds. I'd just settled them down, and was going to bed, irritated a little that John wasn't home yet. And there she was, standing there in my room."

She gave a half laugh, brushed a hand over her face. "Gave me a hell of a jolt, thinking oh, hell, am I pregnant, because believe me, I wasn't in the mood for it right at the moment after dealing with three restless, unhappy children. But something in her eyes didn't look right. Too bright, and I want to say too mean. It scared me a little. Then the police came, and well, I wasn't thinking about her anymore."

Her voice had remained steady throughout. But her eyes, her long, lovely eyes, mirrored the grief.

"It's a hard, hard thing. I can't even imagine it."

"Your life stops right there. Just stops. And when it starts up again, it's different. It's never what it was before that moment. Never."

He didn't touch her, didn't comfort, didn't support. What was in her heart, for this moment, in this winter garden belonged to someone else.

"You had no one. No mother, no father, no sister, no brother."

"I had my sons. I had this house. I had myself." She looked away, and he could see her draw herself back, close that door to the past. "I understand where you're going with this, and I don't understand it. She never bothered to object before, not to John, or anyone I was with after, not to Bryce. She did, occasionally express some disapproval— I've told you that before. But nothing on the scale she has recently. Why would that be?"

"I've been trying to work that out. I have a couple of theories. Let's go inside first. The light's going and you're going to be chilled straight through. Not much meat on you. That wasn't a complaint," he added when she narrowed her eyes.

Deliberately she bumped up the southern in her voice. "I come from a line of women with delicate builds."

"Nothing delicate about you," he corrected and took her hand as they walked toward the house. "What you are is a long wild rose—a black rose with plenty of thorns."

"Black roses don't grow wild. They have to be cultivated. And no one's ever managed a true black."

"A black rose," he repeated and brought their joined hands to his lips. "Rare and exquisite."

"You keep talking like that, I'll have to invite you up to my private quarters."

"I thought you'd never ask."

thirteen

❧

"I thought I should tell you," Roz began as they walked toward the house, "that my . . . household is very interested in my more personal relationship with you."

"That's all right, so am I. Interested in my personal relationship with you."

She glanced down at their joined hands and thought what a lovely design it was that fingers could link so smoothly together. "Your hand's bigger than mine, considerably. Your palm's wider, your fingers longer. And see how your fingers are blunt at the tip where mine taper some?"

She lifted her arm so their hands were eye level. "But it makes such a nice fit."

With a soft laugh, he said her name. Said it tenderly. Rosalind. Then paused briefly to angle his head down and touch his lips to hers. "So does that."

"I was thinking the same. But I'd as soon keep those thoughts, and that personal interest, between you and me."

"Hard to do, since we have other people in our lives. My

son wanted to know where I came up with the brunette babe I was with at the Ole Miss game."

"And you told him?"

"That I'd finally managed to get Rosalind Harper to give me a second look."

"I gave you plenty of looks," she said, and sent him another as they started up the steps to her terrace. "But I've gotten into the habit of being selfish with my private life, and I don't see any reason we can't enjoy each other without filing regular bulletins on our sex life."

She reached for the terrace door. It blew open, barely missing striking her face. A blast of frigid wind gushed out of her room, knocking her back a full step before Mitch managed to grab her, then block her body with his.

"Good luck!" he shouted over the scream of air.

"I will not tolerate this." Furious, she shoved him aside and bulled her way through the door. "I will not tolerate this sort of thing in my house!"

Photographs flew off tables like missiles while lamps flashed on and off. A chair shot across the room, slamming into a chest of drawers with a force that had the vase of hothouse orchids spinning. When she saw the vanity mirror her sons had given her start to slide, she leaped forward to grab it.

"Stop this idiotic *bullshit* right now. I'm not going to put up with it."

There was pounding, monstrous fists of fury, on the walls, in the walls, and the floor trembled under her feet. A large Baccarat perfume bottle detonated, a crystal bomb that spewed jagged shards like shrapnel.

In the midst of the whirlwind, Roz stood, clutching the vanity mirror, and her shout over the explosions of shattering glass, the ferocious banging, was Arctic ice.

"I'll stop every attempt to find out who you are, to right whatever wrong was done to you. I'll do whatever it takes to remove you from this house. You won't be welcome here.

"This is *my* house," she called out as fire erupted in the hearth and the candlestick on the mantel spiraled up into the air. "And I will, by God, clear you out of it. I swear on my life, I will remove you."

The air died at once, and what had been spinning in it fell with thuds or crashes to the floor.

The door burst open instantly. David, Logan, and Stella pushed through it an instant before Harper barreled through the terrace doors.

"Mama." Harper lifted her right off her feet, his arms banded around her. "Are you all right?"

"I'm fine. I'm fine."

"We couldn't get in." Stella touched Roz's back with a trembling hand. "Couldn't get the doors open."

"It's all right now. Where are the children?"

"Hayley. Hayley's got them downstairs. When we heard—God, Roz, it sounded like a war."

"Go tell her everything's all right." She pressed her cheek to Harper's before she pulled back. "Go on now."

"What happened here?" David demanded. "Roz, what the hell happened?"

"We started to come in, and she objected . . . strongly."

"Your mother slapped her back for it," Mitch told Harper. "Let her know who runs this house."

"You're bleeding," Harper said dully.

"Oh, my God." Roz shoved the vanity mirror into Harper's hands and moved quickly to Mitch to touch the cut on his cheek.

"Some flying glass. Nothing major."

"Got some nicks on your hands, too." She lowered her own before they could shake. "Well, let's clean them up."

"I'll pick up in here," Stella offered.

"No, leave it be. Go down, make sure Hayley and the kids are okay. Logan, you ought to take them to your place."

"I'm not leaving you." Stella stood firm, shook her head. "That's not negotiable."

"I'll stay here." Logan draped an arm around Stella's shoulders. "If that's all right with you."

"That's fine." Letting out a breath, she took the mirror back from Harper. "She'd've gotten more than a tongue-lashing if she'd broken this." She set it back in place, then turned to give Harper's hand a squeeze. "It's all right, baby. I promise."

"She does anything to hurt you, I'm finding a way to get her out."

"Like mother, like son." She smiled at him. "I told her the same, and since she stopped when I did, she must know I mean what I say. Go down now. Hayley can't leave the children, and she must be frantic. Mitch, come on into the bathroom. I'll clean those cuts."

"I don't want her alone up here tonight," Harper said when his mother left the room.

"She won't be," Mitch assured him.

When he went into the bath, Roz was already damping a cloth with peroxide. "They're just scratches."

"Doesn't mean they shouldn't be seen to, and since I've never doctored cuts caused by some ghost's tantrum, I'm doing it my usual way. Sit down."

"Yes'm." He sat, studying her face. "Not a scratch on you."

"Hmm?" Distracted, she glanced at her own hands, then looked at her face in the mirror over the sink. "I guess you're right."

"I don't think she wanted to hurt you. Not that she won't, directly or inadvertently, being as she's more than a little crazy. But this was a warning. It's interesting."

"I admire a man who can get cut up by an angry bitch of a ghost and find it interesting."

"I admire a woman who goes toe-to-toe with an angry bitch of a ghost and wins."

"My house." Her voice gentled as she tipped up his chin. "Here now, this won't hurt."

"That's what they all say."

But she cleaned the cuts with a deft and easy hand while he continued to watch her face.

"Looking for something?" she asked him.

"I'm wondering if I found it."

"This one here barely missed your eye." Shaken more than she cared to admit, she bent down to brush her lips over the cut. "There." She stepped back. "You'll live."

"Thanks." He took both her hands, those sharp green eyes on hers. "I have some theories."

"And I'm anxious to hear them. But I want to clean up that mess in there first, then I want a glass of wine. A very big glass of wine."

"I'll give you a hand."

"No, I'd rather do it myself. In fact, I think I need to."

"You make it hard, always asking me to take a step back."

"I guess I do." She brushed a hand through his hair. "Maybe it'll help if I tell you it comforts me to know you're confident enough in yourself to take that step back when I need you to."

"Maybe that's something else that makes this a good fit."

"I think so. I'd appreciate it if you'd go down with the others, give me a half hour to put things back to rights. It'll settle me down a little."

"Okay." He got to his feet. "I'm staying the night. I'll take a page from Stella's book and tell you that part's not negotiable. But you can use the half hour to decide if I'm staying in there with you or in a guest room."

He left her frowning after him.

* * *

He found everyone in the kitchen. Like family, he thought, gathered together in the hub of the house with something simmering on the stove, a baby crawling on the floor, and two young boys pulling on jackets while their little dog jumped with excitement.

Every eye shifted to him, and after a beat of silence, Stella began speaking brightly to her sons. "Go ahead and let him run, but stay out of the flower beds. We're going to eat soon."

There was a lot of scrambling, barking, a scream of laughter from Lily, then dog and boys were gone with a slam of the back door.

Stella's hand slipped into Logan's. "How is she?"

"Steady, as usual. She wanted half an hour." Mitch looked at Harper. "I'm staying tonight."

"Good. I think that's good," Hayley said. "The more the better. It gets so you're used to having a ghost in the house, but it's different when she starts throwing things at you."

"You, specifically, from the look of it," Logan put in.

"Noticed that?" Mitch rubbed absently at his cut cheek. "Interesting, isn't it? There was a lot of rage up in that room, but nothing—nothing tangible—was directed at Rosalind. I'd say there was deliberate care not to do her physical harm."

"If there hadn't been, she'd be out." Harper scooped up Lily when she tried to climb up his leg. "And I'm not talking about my mother."

"No." Mitch nodded. "And Roz expressed just about the same sentiment."

"And she's alone up there," David chimed in, then glanced up from his work at the stove. "Because she means it. Everyone in this house, dead or alive, knows she means it."

"And we're all down here, leaving her be because she runs this show." Logan leaned back against the counter.

"That may be, but after this, she'll have to get used to giving up the wheel from time to time. Is that coffee fresh?" Mitch asked with a nod toward the pot.

UPSTAIRS, ROZ PICKED UP THE PIECES OF THE PERSONAL treasures she'd kept in her bedroom. Little mementos, little memories, shattered now.

Willful destruction, she thought, that was the worst of it. The waste of the precious through selfish temper.

"Like some spoiled child," she mumbled as she worked to put order back to her space. "I didn't tolerate that behavior from my own children, and I won't tolerate it from you. Whoever the hell you are."

She straightened furniture, then moved to the bed to remake it. "You best just keep that in mind, Amelia. You best just remember who's mistress of Harper House."

She felt better, amazingly better, taking action, putting her room to rights, saying her piece, even if it was to an empty room.

Steadier, she stepped into the bathroom. Her hair, short as it was, stood up in spikes from the wind that had blown through her bedroom. Not, Roz decided, a good look for her. She brushed it into order, then idly freshened her makeup. And thought about Mitch.

Fascinating man. She couldn't remember the last man who'd fascinated her. It was interesting, and telling, that he'd stated he was staying the night—no polite request, just a flat statement. Then left it to her where he would sleep.

Yes, it was a fascinating man who could be both dominating and obliging in the same sentence.

And she wanted him. It felt wonderful to want, to need, to have this good, healthy lust bubbling inside her.

Certainly she was beyond the stage where she had to deny herself a lover, and smart enough now to recognize when that lover was a man she could respect. Maybe trust.

Trust was just a little tougher than respect, and a whole lot tougher than lust.

So they'd start with what they had, she decided, and see where it went.

When she came out, she heard music, Memphis blues played low, from her sitting room. Her frown was back as she stepped over to the doorway.

Dinner for two was set on her gateleg table—slices of David's roast chicken, snowy mashed potatoes, spears of asparagus, golden biscuits.

How the boy managed to put together her favorite comfort foods was beyond her, but that was her David.

And there was Mitch standing in the candlelight, pouring her a glass of wine.

She felt a lurch—heart and belly—like a blow. Sucker punch, she thought dully, that was both rude and shocking. More than lust, when lust was all she wanted. But more was standing there, with cuts on his hands and face, whether she wanted it or not.

Then he looked over, and smiled at her.

Well, damn it! was all she could think.

"We thought you'd like a quiet meal," he said. "A little calm in the storm. And since I wanted to talk to you, I didn't give your front-line soldiers any argument."

"Soldiers. That's an interesting term."

"Apt enough. Harper would pick up the sword in a heartbeat for you—and I imagine your other sons are the same."

"I like to think I can fight my own battles."

"Which is only more reason they'd stand for you. Then there's David." He stepped over, held out the wine. "Your fourth son, I'd say, in everything but blood. He adores you."

"It's mutual."

"Then there's Logan. Though I'm not sure he'd appreciate the imagery, I see him as a knight to your queen."

She took a sip of wine. "I'm not sure I like the imagery, either."

"But there it is."

He picked up his water glass, toasted her. "You're no more just his employer than you are to Stella or Hayley. And those kids? You're an intimate and vital part of their lives now. When I went downstairs, walked into the kitchen, what I saw was a family. You're the core of that family. You *made* that family."

She stared at him, then let out a huff of breath. "Well. I don't know just what to say to that."

"You should be proud. Those are good people in your kitchen. By the way, does Harper know he's in love with Hayley?"

This time when she stared, she lowered herself into a chair. "You're more intuitive and more observant than I gave you credit for, and I gave you credit for quite a bit. No, I don't think he knows—at least not completely. Which may explain why she's completely oblivious to what he feels for her. She knows he loves Lily. I suppose that's all she sees, at the moment."

"How do you feel about it?"

"I want Harper to be happy, and to have what he wants most in life. We should eat before this gets cold."

A polite way, Mitch surmised, of telling him she'd discussed the intimacies of her family enough with him. The woman had lines, he thought, very defined lines. It would be challenging, and interesting, to pick and choose which to cross, and the when and how of it.

"How are you feeling?"

"I'm fine. Really. Just needed to calm myself down a little."

"You look more than fine. How is it, Rosalind, you can look so beautiful?"

"Candlelight flatters a woman. If we had our way, Edison would never have invented that damn lightbulb."

"You don't need candlelight."

She lifted her brows. "If you're thinking you need to seduce me over roast chicken so I won't scoot you off to one of the guest rooms after dinner, you don't need to worry. I want you in my bed."

"Regardless, I'm going to seduce you. But at the moment, I was just stating the facts. Aside from that, this is some terrific roast chicken."

"I like you. Thought I'd say that straight-out. I like the way you are. I don't feel there are a lot of pretenses about you, not a lot of show. That's a nice change for me, in this area."

"I don't lie. Gave it up along with the bottle. That's the one thing I can promise you, Roz. I won't lie to you."

"As promises go, that's the one I'd value most."

"Then keeping with that theme, there's something I'd like to ask you. What happened earlier, that . . . upheaval, we'll call it. That was new."

"Yes, and I'm hoping it was a first and last sort of thing."

"She never objected in any way to your engagement or your marriage to John Harper."

"No, as I told you before."

"Or to any relationship you had after, to Clerk."

She gave a little shrug. "Some irritation, we could say, off and on. Disapproval, annoyance, but no, not rage."

"Then I have a theory—one you may not like to hear. But in addition to not lying to you, I'm going to speak my mind, as I expect you'll speak yours."

"Should be interesting."

"She needs children in the house—that's what brings

her comfort, or gratification. You and John would bring children into the house, so she had no strong objection. He was a means to an end."

"That's a very cold theory."

"Yes, and it gets colder. Once there were children, there was no more need for him, so his death was, in my opinion, something she saw as right, even just."

Her color drained, leaving her face white and horrified. "If you're suggesting she somehow caused—"

"No." He reached out, laid his hand over hers. "No. Her limitations are this house, the grounds. I'm no expert in the paranormal, but that's what works. That's what makes sense. Whatever she is, or has, is centered here."

"Yes." Relaxing again, she nodded. "I've never experienced, or heard of anyone experiencing anything regarding her beyond the borders of my land. I would have. I'm certain I'd know, or have heard if there'd been anything."

"She's bound to this place, and maybe to this family. But I doubt the grief you and your sons felt when John died touched her. And she can be touched. We saw that with Stella last spring when she communicated with her as a mother. We saw it tonight, when you laid it on the line to her."

"All right." She nodded, reached for her wine. "All right, I'm following you, so far."

"When you began to socialize again, to see men, even to have lovers, she was only mildly annoyed. Disapproving, as you said. Because they didn't matter to you, not deeply. They weren't going to be a part of your life, of this house, not for the long run."

"You're saying she knew that?"

"She's connected to you, Roz. She knows what's inside you, at least enough to understand what you think and feel, things you might not say out loud."

"She gets inside my head," she said softly. "Yes, I've

felt that. I don't like it. But what happens to your theory when you add Bryce? I married him. He lived here. And though she acted up a few times, there was nothing extreme, nothing violent."

"You didn't love him."

"I married him."

"And divorced him. He wasn't a threat to her. It seems she knew that before you did. At least before you consciously knew it. He was . . . superfluous, let's say, to her. Maybe it was because he was weak, but for whatever reason, still, no threat to her. Not from her view."

"And you are."

"Clearly. We could suppose it has to do with my work, but that doesn't jibe. She wants us to find out who she was, what she was. She just wants us to work for it."

"You seem to know her very well, on short acquaintance."

"Short, but intense acquaintance," he pointed out. "And understanding the dead is part of my work. It's actually the part—the personalizing—that makes it the most compelling for me. She's angry that you've allowed me into your life, into your bed."

"Because you're not weak."

"I'm not," he agreed. "And also because I matter to you, or I will. I'm going to make sure of it. Because what we're moving toward, you and I, is important."

"Mitch, we're having an affair, and while I don't take that lightly, I—"

"Rosalind." He laid his hand over hers, kept his eyes on hers. "You know very well I'm falling in love with you. Have been since the minute I opened my apartment door and saw you standing there. Scares the hell out of me, but that doesn't change it."

"I didn't know." She drew back, and her hand pressed on her heart, ran up to her throat and back again. "I didn't, and that makes me as oblivious as Hayley. I thought we had a great deal of attraction for each other, and mutual respect along with . . . what are you grinning at?"

"You're nervous. I've never seen you nervous. How about that?"

"I'm not nervous." She stabbed at the last bite of her chicken. "I'm surprised, that's all."

"Scared's what you are."

"I'm certainly not." With some heat, she shoved back from the table. "I'm certainly not. All right, I am." She pushed to her feet when he laughed. "Yes, that should please you. Men love putting women into a state."

"Oh, bullshit."

There was a ring of steel, even through the humor. Intrigued by both, she turned back. "You're an awfully confident individual."

"You meant that as a compliment the first time you said it. This time you mean *arrogant*, and right back at you, honey."

With that, she laughed. Then pressed her fingers to her eyes. "Oh, God. God, Mitchell, I don't know if I've got it in me for another *important* relationship. They're so much damn work. Love can be, should be, so consuming, so demanding. I just don't know that I've got the stamina, or the heart, or the generosity."

"I have no doubt you've got plenty of all three, but we'll take it as it goes, and see."

He rose. "Can't say I mind making you a little nervous," he said as he walked to her. "Nothing much shakes you, at least not so it shows."

"You have no idea."

"Oh, I think I do." He slipped his arms around her, led her smoothly into a dance, swaying to the throb of the music. "One of the sexiest things about you is your unshakable capability."

"I'm capable." She tipped her head up. "I want my

accountant to be capable, but I sure as hell don't want to sleep with him."

"I find it devastatingly sexy."

"Is this the seduction part of the evening?"

"Just getting started. Do you mind?"

He thought her capable, she realized, and found that appealing. And he made her feel soft, and cherished. "You asked me that the first time you kissed me. I didn't mind then, either."

"I love that you're beautiful. Shallow of me, but there you go. A man's entitled to some flaws."

Amused, she trailed a finger up the back of his neck. "Perfection's boring—but, God, don't tell Stella I said so."

"Then I'll never bore you."

He touched his lips to hers lightly, once, twice, then slowly, slowly, sank into the kiss.

It spilled through her, the warmth, and the life, the thrill and the power. She moved with him, that sensuous dance, that sensuous kiss, and let herself glide. Like a woman glides over a path strewn with fragrant petals. Through moonbeams. And into love.

She heard a door shut quietly, and opened her eyes to see that he'd circled her into the bedroom.

"You're a clever dancer, Dr. Carnegie." Then laughed when he spun her out, and back. "Very clever."

He kissed her again, spinning until her back was pressed to the door, until the kiss took on a bite. Then he ran his hands down her arms, stepped back.

"Light the candles," he said. "I'll light the fire."

Shaken, right down to the soles of her feet, she leaned against the door. Her heart felt swollen and tender, and its beat was a throbbing ache in her breast. When she moved, she moved carefully, like a woman sliding through the fog of a dream. And she saw her own fingers tremble as she set flame to candlewick.

"I want you." Her voice was steady enough, and she was grateful. "And the want is stronger and different than any I've felt before. Maybe it's because I—"

"Don't question it. Not tonight anyway."

"All right." She turned, as he did, so they faced each other across the room. "We'll leave it that I want you, very much. That it presses on me, not entirely comfortably."

In the gilded light, he crossed to her, took both her hands. "Let me show you how I feel."

He lifted her hands, turning them palms up to press his lips to one, then the other. Then he cupped her face, stroking his thumbs over her cheeks as his fingers slid back into her hair.

"Let me take you," he said as his mouth cruised over hers. "Tonight, just let me take you."

He asked for surrender. And surrender was a great deal to ask. But she gave him her mouth, then her body as his hands stroked over her. And they were dancing again, circling and swaying as the dreamy pleasure he offered slipped into her like rich, red wine.

He slid her shirt aside, and was murmuring in her ear, about her skin, her scent. And the dance was like floating.

She was giving him what he'd asked. Surrender. Though it was slow, inch by inch, he could feel it, that gorgeous yielding of self. He undressed her as they danced, taking almost painful care, almost painful pleasure in removing each barrier that blocked his hands from her flesh.

It was incredibly erotic, dancing in the firelight, the candlelight, her naked body pressed to his while he was still fully clothed. To see that long, lean line of her in the mirror, the way the light played over her skin, to feel that skin shiver under his hands. To feel her pulses jump under his mouth.

When he slipped his hand between her thighs, he felt her body jerk, heard her breath catch.

She was hot, already hot and wet. And her nails dug into his shoulders as he began to play her, lazily. Little tortuous strokes that had her breath going short and harsh, and his own blood pumping.

Her body plunged, then melted against his when she came. Her head fell back even as he continued to arouse, and her eyes were glazed and stunned.

She was so pliant he could almost pour her onto the bed. They watched each other as he stood, undressed.

Then he skimmed his finger over her leg, lifted it, bent to it, and rubbed his lips along her calf. "So much more I want from you."

Yes, she thought. So much more. And surrendering to it, to him, gave him all he wanted.

His mouth found her, shot her up again, breathlessly, until she had to grip the spread or fly apart.

He exploited and explored, and took, took while the air went thick and sweet as syrup, and the deepest, darkest pleasures quivered inside her.

She could hear herself sobbing for him, even as he slid into her. His languorous pace never altered, only built arousal higher with a near brutal patience, a delicious, drugging friction. She had no choice, no control any longer, could only quiver, could only ache, could only enjoy as he nudged her closer and closer to the edge.

And when she fell that final time, it was like flying.

SHE WAS STILL TREMBLING. IT WAS RIDICULOUS, SHE told herself. It was foolish, but she couldn't seem to stop. She was warm, even overwarm, and only then realized both of them were slick with sweat.

She'd been thoroughly seduced, then thoroughly used. And she couldn't find a thing wrong with either.

"I'm trying to think of something appropriate to say."

His lips moved against her neck. "How about 'wow'?"

She managed to move her heavy arms enough to brush a hand through his hair. "That probably covers it. I came three times."

"Four."

"Four?" Her voice was as hazy as her vision. "I must've lost count."

"I didn't." And there was a wicked satisfaction in his tone, one that she saw reflected in his face as he rolled onto his back.

"Since I'm in such a blissful state, I'm going to admit that's the first time I've ever come four times."

He reached down, found her hand, linked fingers. "Stick with me, kid, and it won't be the last."

She laughed, a full-out bawdy roll of laughter, then shifted to prop herself up on his chest. "Pretty proud of yourself."

"Damn right."

"Me, too." She pillowed her head over his heart, shut her eyes. "I go running around six."

"Is that A.M.?"

"Yes, it is. Harper's got some spare clothes in the next bedroom, if you want to join me."

"'Kay."

She let herself drift, like a cat curled for a nap. "She left us alone."

"I know."

fourteen

❧

GARBED IN A SUIT AND TIE AND ARMED WITH A DOZEN yellow roses and a box of Godiva chocolates, Mitch rode the elevator to Clarise Harper's third-floor apartment in the retirement complex. His letter from her was in his brief-case, and the formal, lady of the South tone had given him a broad clue that this was a woman who would expect a suit—and a floral tribute—just as Roz had instructed.

She wasn't agreeing to a meeting, he thought, but was, very definitely, granting him an audience.

No mention of Rosalind, or any of the occupants of Harper House, had been made in their correspondence.

He rang the bell and prepared to be charming and per-suasive.

The woman who answered was young, hardly more than twenty, dressed in a simple and conservative black skirt, white blouse, and low-heeled practical shoes. Her brown hair was worn in what he supposed women still called a bun—a style that did nothing to flatter her young, thin face.

Mitch's first impression was of a quiet, well-behaved

puppy who would fetch the slippers without leaving a single tooth mark on the leather.

"Dr. Carnegie. Please come in, Miss Harper is expecting you."

Her voice suited the rest of her, quiet and well-bred.

"Thank you." He stepped inside, directly into the living room furnished with a hodgepodge of antiques. His collector's eye spotted a George III secretaire chest and a Louis XVI display cabinet among the various styles and eras.

The side chairs were probably Italian, the settee Victorian—and all looked miserably uncomfortable.

There was a great deal of statuary, heavy on the shepherdess and cat and swan themes, and vases decorated within an inch of their lives. All the china and porcelain and crystal sat on stiffly starched doilies or runners.

The walls were painted a candy pink, and the tweed beige wall-to-wall was buried under several floral area rugs.

The air smelled like the inside of a cedar chest that had been bathed in lavender water.

Everything gleamed. He imagined if an errant mote of dust dared invade such grandeur, the quiet puppy would chase it down and banish it instantly.

"Please, sit down. I'll inform Miss Harper that you're here."

"Thank you, Miss . . ."

"Paulson. Jane Paulson."

"Paulson?" He flipped through the family tree in his mental files. "A relative, then, on Miss Harper's father's side."

The faintest hint of color bloomed in her cheeks. "Yes. I'm Miss Harper's great-niece. Excuse me."

Poor baby, he thought when she slipped away. He maneuvered through the furniture and condemned himself to one of the side chairs.

Moments later he heard the click and step, and the woman herself appeared.

Though she was rail thin, he wouldn't have said frail, despite her age. More, he thought at first glance, a form that was tough and whittled down to the basics. She wore a dress of rich purple, and leaned on an ebony cane with an ivory handle.

Her hair was a pristine white helmet, and her face—as thin as her body—was a map of wrinkles under a dusting of powder and rouge. Her mouth, thin as a blade, was poppy red.

There were pearls at her ears and her throat, and her fingers were studded with rings, glinting as fiercely as brass knuckles.

The puppy trailed in her wake.

Knowing his role, Mitch got to his feet, even managed a slight bow. "Miss Harper, it's an honor to meet you."

He took the hand she extended, brought it to within an inch of his lips. "I'm very grateful you were able to find the time to see me." He offered the roses, the chocolates. "Small tokens of my appreciation."

She gave a nod, which might have been approval. "Thank you. Jane, put these lovely roses in the Minton. Please be seated, Dr. Carnegie. I was very intrigued by your letter," she continued as she took her seat on the settee and propped her cane on the arm. "You're not from the Memphis area originally."

"No, ma'am. Charlotte, where my parents and my sister still live. My son attends the university here, and I relocated in order to be close to him."

"Divorced from his mama, aren't you?"

She'd done her research, Mitch thought. Well, that was fine. So had he. "Yes, I am."

"I don't approve of divorce. Marriage isn't a flight of fancy."

"It certainly isn't. I confess my marital difficulties were primarily on my shoulders." He kept his eyes level with her piercing ones. "I'm an alcoholic, and though in recovery now for many years, I caused my former wife a great deal of distress and unhappiness during our marriage. I'm pleased to say she's remarried to a good man, and we have a cordial relationship."

Clarise pursed her bright red lips, nodded. "I respect a man who takes responsibility for his failings. If a man can't hold his drink, he shouldn't drink. That's all there is to it."

Old bat. "I'm proof of that."

She continued to sit, and despite nearly eight full decades of wear and tear, her back was straight as a spear. "You teach?"

"I have done. At the moment, I'm fully occupied with my research and writing of family histories and biographies. Our ancestry is our foundation."

"Certainly." Her gaze shifted when Jane came in with the flowers. "No, not there," she snapped. "There, and be careful. See to the refreshments now. Our guest can't be expected to sit here without being offered basic hospitality."

She turned her attention back to Mitch. "You're interested in the Harper family."

"Very much."

"Then you're aware that the Harpers are not only my foundation, but a vital part of the foundation of Shelby County, and indeed the state of Tennessee."

"I am, very keenly aware, and hope to do justice to their contributions. Which is why I've come to you, for your help, for your memories. And in the hope that you'll come to trust me with any letters or books, any written documentation that will help me to write a thorough and detailed account of the Harper family history."

He glanced up as Jane came out carrying a teapot and cups on a large tray. "Let me help you with that."

As he crossed to her, he saw the woman's eyes shoot over to her aunt. Obviously flustered, she allowed him to take the tray. "Thank you."

"Pour the tea, girl."

"Miss Paulson would be your great-niece on your father's side," Mitch began easily, and took his seat again. "It must be comforting to have some of your family so close."

Clarise angled her head, regally. "Duty to family is paramount. I would assume, then, you've done considerable research to date."

"I have. If you'll permit me." He opened his briefcase and took out the folder he'd prepared for her. "I thought you might enjoy having this. The genealogy—a family tree—I've done."

She accepted the folder, wagged her fingers in the air. On command, Jane produced a pair of reading glasses on a gold chain.

While she looked over the papers, Mitch did his best to swallow down the weak herbal tea.

"How much do you charge?"

"This is a gift, Miss Harper, as you've not requested my services. It's I who request your help in a project I'm very eager to explore."

"We'll be clear, Dr. Carnegie, that I won't tolerate being asked for funds down the road."

"Absolutely clear."

"I see you've gone back to the eighteenth century, when the first of my family immigrated from Ireland. Do you intend to go back further?"

"I do, though my plan is to focus more on the family here, in Tennessee, what they built after they came to America. The industry, the culture, their leading roles in both, as well as society. And most important, for my purposes, the family itself. The marriages, births, deaths."

Through the lenses of her reading glasses, her eyes were hawklike. Predatory. "Why are household staff and servants included here?"

He'd debated that one, but had gone with his instincts.

"Simply because they were part of the household, part of the texture. In fact, I'm in contact with a descendant of one of the housekeepers of Harper House—during your mother, Victoria Harper's, childhood. The day-to-day life, as well as the entertaining the Harpers have been known for are essential elements of my book."

"And the dirty linen?" She gave a regal sniff. "The sort servants are privy to?"

"I assure you, it's not my intention to write a roman à clef, but a detailed, factual, and thorough family history. A family such as yours, Miss Harper," he said, gesturing toward the file, "certainly has had its triumphs and tragedies, its virtues and its scandals. I can't and won't exclude any that my research uncovers. But I believe your family's history, and its legacy, certainly stands above any of its very human failings."

"And failings and scandal add spice—spice sells."

"I won't argue with that. But certainly, with your input, the book would have a stronger weight on the plus side, we could say."

"We could." She set the folder aside, sipped her tea. "By now you've certainly been in contact with Rosalind Harper."

"Yes."

"And . . . she's cooperating?"

"Ms. Harper has been very helpful. I've spent some time in Harper House. It's simply stunning. A tribute to what your family built since coming to Shelby County, and a tribute to charm and grace as well as continuity."

"It was my great-great-grandfather who built Harper House, and his son who preserved it during the War of Northern Aggression. My grandfather who expanded and modernized the house, while preserving its history and its traditions."

He waited a moment for her to continue, to speak of her

uncle's contribution to the estate. But when she stopped there, he only nodded. "Harper House is a testament to your family, and a treasure of Shelby County."

"It is the oldest home of its kind consistently lived in by one family in this country. The fact is, there is nothing to compare with it, to my mind, in Tennessee, or anywhere else. It is only a pity my cousin was unable to produce a son in order to carry the family name."

"Ms. Harper uses the family name."

"And runs a flower shop on the property." She dismissed this with another sniff and a flick of her ring-spangled fingers. "One hopes that her eldest son, when he inherits, will have more sense and dignity, though I see no indication of it."

"Your family has always been involved in commerce, in industry, in business."

"Not at home. I may decide to give you my cooperation, Dr. Carnegie, as my cousin Rosalind is hardly the best source for our family history. You may deduce we are not on terms."

"I'm sorry to hear that."

"It could hardly be otherwise. I'm told that even now she has outsiders, and one of them a Yankee, living in Harper House."

Mitch waited a beat, saw that he was expected to verify. "I believe there are houseguests, and one is also a distant relation, through Ms. Harper's first husband."

"With a baby out of wedlock." Those brightly painted lips folded thin. "Disgraceful."

"A . . . delicate situation, but one that happens, very often in any family history. As it happens, one of the legends I've heard regarding the house, the family, deals with a ghost, that of a young woman who may have found herself in this same delicate situation."

"Balderdash."

He nearly blinked. He didn't believe he'd ever heard anyone use that term in actual conversation.

"Ghosts. I would think a man with your education would be more sensible."

"Like scandal, Miss Harper, ghosts add spice. And the legend of the Harper Bride is common in the area. Certainly it has to be mentioned in any detailed family history. It would be more surprising if a house as old and rich in history as Harper House didn't have some whisper of hauntings. You must have grown up hearing the story."

"I know the story, and even as a child had more sense than to believe such nonsense. Some find such things romantic; I do not. If you're skilled or experienced at your work, you'll certainly find that there was no Harper bride who died in that house as a young woman—which this ghost is reputed to be. Not since the story began buzzing about."

"Which would have been?"

"In my grandfather's time, from all accounts. Your own papers here," she said as she tapped the folder, "debunk any such foolishness. My grandmother lived to a ripe age, as did my mother. My aunts were not young women when they passed. My great-grandmother, and all of her children who survived their first five years, lived well past their forties."

"I've heard theories that this ghost is a more distant relation, even a guest or a servant."

"Each nonsensical."

He fixed a pleasant smile on his face and nodded as if in agreement. "Still, it adds to the lore. So none of your family, to your knowledge, actually saw this legendary bride?"

"Certainly not."

"Pity, it would have made an interesting chapter in the history. I'd hoped to find someone who'd have a story to tell, or had written of it in a journal or diary. But as to journals or diaries, in a more earthbound sense. I'm hoping to add some to my research, to use them to personalize this family history. Do you have any that your mother or father, or other ancestors kept? Your grandmother's perhaps, your own mother's, aunts', cousins'?"

"No."

Out of the corner of his eye he saw Jane open her mouth as if to speak, then quickly close it again.

"I hope you'll allow me to interview you more in-depth, about specifics, and whatever anecdotes you'd care to share. And that you'd be willing to share any photographs, perhaps copy them at my expense for inclusion in the book."

"I'll consider it, very seriously, and contact you when I've made my decision."

"Thank you. I very much appreciate the time you've given me." He got to his feet, offered his hand. "Your family is of great interest to me, and it's been a pleasure to speak with you."

"Goodbye, Dr. Carnegie. Jane, show the man out."

At the door he offered his hand to Jane, smiled straight into her eyes. "It was nice to meet you, Miss Paulson."

He walked to the elevator, then rocked back and forth on his heels as he waited for the doors to open.

The old woman had something—something she didn't want to share. And the quiet little puppy knew it.

ROZ STROLLED HOME THROUGH HER WOODS IN THE best of all possible moods. It was nearly time for the major spring opening. Her season would begin with a bang, the work would be long, hard, and physical—and she'd love every minute.

The new potting soil was already beginning to move, and once the season got into swing, the twenty-five–pound bags were going to march out the door.

She just felt it.

The fact was, she admitted, she felt everything. The hum in the air that said spring, the streams of sunlight that spilled through the branches, the loose and limber swing of her own muscles.

Hardly a wonder they were loose and limber after last night, she thought. Four orgasms, for God's sake. And Mitch was a man of his word. Stick with me, he'd said, and it won't be the last time.

He'd proven just that in the middle of the night.

She'd had sex twice in one night, and that was certainly worth a red letter on her calendar.

With John . . . they'd been young and hadn't been able to get enough of each other. Even after the children had come, the sexual aspect of their marriage had been vital.

Then it had been a long, long time before she'd allowed another man to touch her. And to be honest, none ever had. Not really, not beyond the physical.

Bryce hadn't. But she'd thought, for a while at least, that it was her own fault, or her own nature. She hadn't loved him, not deep down. But she'd liked him, she'd enjoyed him, and had certainly been attracted to him.

Stupidly, but that wasn't the point now.

The sex had been adequate at best, and adequate had been enough for her. She'd wanted—needed—companionship, partnership.

Since the divorce, for a considerable time prior to it, if truth be told, she'd been celibate. Her own choice, and the right one for her.

Until Mitch.

Now he'd turned her inside out, and God, she was grateful. And relieved, if it came to that, to know her sex drive was in fine working condition.

He said he was falling in love with her, and that put a little knot in her belly. Love still meant specific things to her.

Marriage and family. And those were too enormous to take lightly.

She'd never take marriage lightly again, so she could hardly take love, what she considered its precursor, lightly.

But she could, and she would, enjoy him, and the way she felt on this spectacular evening.

She crossed her own lawn and saw that her earliest daffodils were blooming buttery yellow. Maybe she'd go in, get her sheers, and cut some for her bedroom.

As she approached the house, she saw Stella and Hayley on the veranda, and raised her hand in a wave.

"I smell spring," she said. "We're going to want to start moving . . ." She trailed off as she saw their faces. "Well, don't you two look solemn. Trouble?"

"Not exactly. Mrs. Haggerty was in today," Stella said.

"Is something wrong with her?"

"Not with her. She wondered how you were doing, though, if you were all right."

"Why wouldn't I be?"

"She was concerned the scene at the garden club meeting had upset you."

"Oh." Roz shrugged. "She should know better."

"Why didn't you tell us?" Stella demanded.

"Excuse me?"

"She said that bitch, that walking Barbie, insulted you right there in front of everybody," Hayley cut in. "That she was spreading lies and rumors and accused you of harassing that asshole she's hooked herself up with."

"You seem to have most of the facts. She should have added, if she didn't, that Mandy came off looking foolish and shrill, and was certainly more embarrassed by the whole thing than I was."

"You didn't tell us," Stella repeated.

"Why would I have?" The tone was aloof.

"Because whether or not she was more embarrassed, it

had to upset you. And while you're the boss, and blah, blah, blah—"

"Blah, blah, blah?"

"And a little bit scary," Stella added.

"A little?"

"The fear factor has diminished considerably over the past year."

"I'm not afraid of you," Hayley said, then hunched her shoulders when Roz turned cool eyes to hers. "Very much."

"Despite us being your employees, we're friends. Or we thought we were."

"Oh, for God's sake. Girls are so much more complicated than boys." On a long sigh, Roz plopped down on the porch swing. "Of course we're friends."

"Well, if we're friends, especially *girl* friends," Hayley continued, and sat beside Roz on the swing, "you're supposed to tell us when some skinny-assed bitch rags on you. How else are we going to know we hate her guts? How else are we going to know to think up nasty things to say about her? Like, here's one. Did you know that seventy-three percent of women whose name ends with the *i* sound are bimbos?"

Roz sat a moment. "Is that one of your factoids or did you just make it up?"

"Okay, I made that one up, but I bet it's true if they dot the *i* with a little heart—after the age of twelve. And I bet, I just bet she does. So. Bimbo."

"She's just a foolish girl who believes a very smooth liar."

"I stand by bimbo."

"She had no right to say those things, to your face or behind your back." Stella sat on Roz's other side.

"No, she didn't, and she came out the worse for it. And all right, it did upset me at the time. I don't like my personal business aired in public forums."

"We're not a forum," Hayley stated firmly. "Or the public."

Saying nothing for a moment, Roz laid a hand on each of their thighs and gave them a little rub.

"As I said, females are more complicated than men, and even being female, I probably understand men better. I certainly didn't mean to hurt your feelings by keeping something like this to myself."

"We just want you to know we're here for you, for the good stuff, and the bad stuff."

Hayley's words touched her. "Then you should know I've long since put Mandy out of my mind, as I do with unimportant people. And I'm in much too good a mood to think about her now. When a woman, especially a woman within spitting distance of fifty, has herself a lover who performs excellently twice in one night, so well in fact that she needs the fingers on both hands to count the number of orgasms experienced, the last thing on her mind is some silly girl with no manners."

She gave each of their thighs another pat, then rose. "There, that's some good stuff," she said and strolled into the house.

"Wow," Hayley said after she managed to close the mouth that had fallen open. "I mean, mega-wow. How many times do you think he got her off? At least six, right?"

"You know what I thought the first time I saw Roz?"

"Uh-uh."

"That I wanted to be her when I grew up. And boy, do I."

ROZ WALKED STRAIGHT BACK TO THE KITCHEN, AND straight to the coffeepot. Once she had a cup, she sidled over and gave David's cheek a kiss as he stood at the stove making his famed hot chocolate.

"Boys outside?"

"Running off some energy with Parker, and working up anticipation for hot chocolate. My other guest, as you see, has conked on me."

Stella grinned toward the highchair, where Lily snoozed in the tipped-back seat. "Isn't she a doll baby, and aren't you a sweetheart for minding three children so those girls could waylay me."

"We do what we can. And you should've mentioned what that silly bitch pulled."

"You ever known me not to be able to handle a silly bitch?"

"I've never known you not to be able to handle anything, but you should've mentioned it. How else am I going to know what shape to make the voodoo doll?"

"Don't worry, Bryce'll stick plenty of pins in her before he's done."

"Don't expect me to feel sorry for her."

"It's her cross to bear."

"Dinner in about an hour," he called as she started out of the room. "And you've got some phone messages. They were on your line so I didn't screen them."

"I'll get them upstairs."

She took her coffee with her, and toed off her shoes after she crossed the threshold to her room. Then she pushed the button on the answering machine.

"Roz, I didn't want to bother you at work."

"What a nice voice you have, Dr. Carnegie," she mused aloud, and sat on the side of the bed to enjoy it.

"It's my pizza night with Josh. I forgot to mention it. I like to think you'll miss me, and that I can make up for it by taking you out tomorrow. Whatever, wherever you'd like, just let me know. In addition, I did some work today, and I'd like to talk to you about that tomorrow. I should be over there by noon. If I don't see you, you can reach me on my cell. I'll be thinking of you."

"That's nice to know. That's very nice to know."

She was still daydreaming a little when the next message began.

"Ms. Harper, this is William Rolls from the Riverbend Country Club. I received your letter this morning, and am very sorry to hear that you're dissatisfied with our services and have resigned as a member. I must admit to being surprised, even stunned, by your list of complaints, and only wish you had been able to speak with me about them personally. We have valued your association with Riverbend for many years, and regret your decision to end it. If you'd care to discuss this matter, please feel free to contact me at any time at any of the following numbers. Again, I sincerely regret the circumstances."

She sat very still until the entire message played through. Then she shut her eyes.

"Fuck you, Bryce."

WITHIN AN HOUR SHE'D NOT ONLY SPOKEN WITH William Rolls, had assured him she wasn't dissatisfied, had no complaints and had not written any letter, but she had a faxed copy of the letter in question in her hand.

And a head of steam that threatened to blow like a geyser.

She was dragging her shoes back on when Hayley popped in, the baby on her hips. "David says dinner's . . . whoa, what's wrong?"

"What's wrong? You want to know what's wrong? I'll tell you what's wrong." She snatched the letter up from where she'd tossed it on the bed. "Here's what's wrong. That miserable, snake-spined son of a bitch has tried my patience once too often."

" 'The admittance of individuals of lower-class backgrounds and mixed ethnicity,' " Hayley read, holding the paper out of Lily's reach. "'Staff members of dubious character. Demeaning intimacy between staff and members, substandard service.'" Her eyes were huge as she shifted them back up to Roz's face. "You didn't write this."

"Of course I didn't. And I'm going to take that letter, find Bryce Clark, and stuff it down his lying throat."

"No." Hayley jumped to block the door, her move so fast it had Lily laughing and bouncing in anticipation of another ride.

"No? What do you mean *no*? I'm done taking this. Finished. And he's going to know it when I'm done with him."

"You can't. You're too mad to go anywhere." The fact was, she'd never seen Roz this angry, and Stella's term of a little bit scary was currently bumped up too many levels to count. "And I don't know much about this sort of thing, but I'd bet a month's pay this is just what he's hoping for. You need to sit down."

"I need to kick his balls blue."

"Well, yeah, that'd be great. Except he's probably expecting it, and he's probably got something worked out so you'll get arrested or something for assault. He's playing you, Roz."

"You think I don't know that?" She threw her arms out as she spun around, looking for something to kick, to hurl, to punch. "You think I don't *know* what that bastard's doing? I'm not going to *stand* here and take it anymore."

The shout, the fury in it had Lily's face crumpling, her little mouth trembling an instant before the wail.

"God, now I'm scaring babies. I'm sorry. I'm sorry. Here, let me have her."

Lily continued to sob as Roz took her out of Hayley's arms and cuddled her in her own. "There, sweetheart, I'm not mad at you, I'm not mad at your mama. I'm so sorry, baby girl." She crooned, and nuzzled while Lily clung to her. "I'm mad at this no-account, slimy-assed, cocksucking son of a bitch who's doing whatever he can to complicate my life."

"You said *cocksucking*," Hayley whispered. Awed.

"Sorry. She doesn't know what I'm saying, so it won't hurt her." Lily's tears were down to sniffles as she began to pull at the ends of Roz's hair. "I shouldn't have yelled like that in front of her. It's the tone that scares her, not the words."

"But you said *cocksucking*."

This time Roz laughed. "I'm so mad," she said, walking the baby, and calming them both. "Just so mad. And you're right, and that's just annoying. I can't go tearing out of here and going after him. It's just what he's looking for. It's all right, it'll be all right. He can't do anything that can't be fixed."

"I'm sorry Roz. I wish I could go kick his balls blue for you."

"Thanks, honey, that's a sweet thing to say. We'll just go down to dinner." She held Lily up, blew on her belly to make her laugh. "We'll just go down to dinner and forget all about the asshole, won't we, baby girl?"

"You're sure?"

"Absolutely."

"Okay. You know, I don't know as snakes have spines."

Roz blinked at her. "What?"

"You said *snake-spined*—before, when you were raving about Bryce. I'm not sure they have actual spines. Maybe just some sort of skeletal cartilage. Could be wrong, though. I don't much like snakes, so I haven't paid a lot of attention."

"You never fail, Hayley, just never fail to baffle me."

fifteen

❧

Roz put Mitch off for a day, then for two. She wanted her head clear, her temper calm, and it wasn't happening quickly. She needed a meeting with her lawyer, and felt obliged to schedule another with William Rolls at the club.

She hated, absolutely hated, being pulled away from her work, particularly at the very start of high season. She could thank God for Stella, as always for Harper, and for Hayley as well. She could be confident that her business was in the best of hands.

But those hands weren't hers, at least not while she was running around tidying up the mess Bryce had made for her.

With the hateful errands done, she trudged through a soaking rain toward the propagation house. For an hour or two, at least, she could dive into the final prep work for the spring season. And she could take her headache, and her sour mood, into a private spot and let the work do its magic.

When she was done for the day, she told herself, she was going to find Mitch. If he wasn't working in her library, she'd call him. She wanted his company—or hoped she would by that evening.

She wanted conversation, about something other than her problems. And wouldn't it be nice to relax with him, maybe up in her sitting room, by the fire—especially if the rain continued—and bask a little in the way he looked at her?

A woman could get very used to having a man look at her as if she were beautiful and desirable and the only one who mattered.

Get used enough to it, she might start to believe it. She'd like to believe it, Roz realized. What a difference it made, being drawn to a man you felt you could trust.

She opened the door to the propagation house.

And stepped into her own bedroom.

The fire was simmering low, the only light in the room. And it tossed flickers of gold, hints of red into the shadows. She heard them first, the quick breath, the low laughter, the rustle of clothing.

Then she saw them in the firelight, Bryce, her husband, and the woman who was a guest in her home. Embracing. No, more . . . grappling, hurrying to touch, to taste each other. She could feel the excitement from them, the snap of the illicit thrill. And knew, even in those few shocked seconds, this wasn't the first time. Hardly the first time.

She stood, with the sounds of the party dim behind her, and absorbed the betrayal, and the greasy slide of humiliation that was under it.

As she had before, she started to step back, to leave them there, but he turned his head, turned it toward her even as his hands cupped another woman's breasts.

And he smiled, bright and charming and sly. Laughed, low and pleased.

"Stupid bitch, I was never faithful. None of us are."

Even as he spoke, his face changed, light and shadow playing over it as it became Mitch's face.

"Why should we be? Women are meant to be used. Do you really think one of you matters more than another?" That lovely voice dripped derision as he fondled the woman in his arms. "We all lie, because we can."

Those shadows floated and the face became John's. Her husband, her love. The father of her sons. "Do you think I was true to you, you pathetic fool?"

"John." The pain nearly took her to her knees. So young, she thought. So alive. "Oh, God, John."

"Oh, God, John," he mimicked, as his hands made the woman he embraced moan. "Needed sons, didn't I? You were nothing more than a broodmare. If I'd been luckier, I'd have lived and left you. Taken what mattered, taken my sons, and left you."

"That's a lie."

"We all lie."

When he laughed, she had to press her hands over her ears. When he laughed, it was like fists pounding on her body, on her heart, until she did simply sink to her knees.

She heard herself weeping, raw, bitter sobs.

She didn't hear the door open behind her, or the startled exclamation. Arms came around her, hard and tight. And she smelled her son.

"Mama, what's wrong? Are you hurt? Mama."

"No. No." She clung to him, pressing her face into his shoulder and fighting to stop the tears. "I'm all right. Don't worry. I'm just—"

"You're not all right, and don't tell me not to worry. Tell me what it is. Tell me what happened."

"In a minute. Just a minute." She leaned against him, let him rock her there on the ground until his warmth seeped into her own icy bones. "Oh, Harper, when did you get to be so big and strong? My baby."

"You're shaking. You're not sick, you're scared."

"Not scared." She drew a deep breath. "A little traumatized, I guess."

"I'm taking you home. You can tell me about it there."

"I . . . yes, that's best." She drew back a little, wiped at her face. "I don't want to see anybody else just now. I sure as hell don't want anyone to see me. I'm a little bit of a wreck, Harper, and imagine I look like a major one."

"Don't worry. Want me to carry you?"

"Oh." Tears stung her eyes again, but warm ones. "My sweet boy. No, I can walk just fine. Tell me something first. Everything's the same in here, isn't it? Everything's as it should be in here?"

Because there was such tension in her voice, he looked around the greenhouse. "Everything's fine."

"Okay. Okay. Let's go home."

She let him lead her through the rain, around the buildings, and let out her first sigh of relief when she climbed into his car.

"Just relax," he ordered, and leaned over to fasten her seat belt himself. "We'll be home in a minute. You need to get warm."

"You'll make a good daddy."

"What?"

"You've got a nurturing bent—comes from being a gardener, maybe, but you don't just know how to take care, you take it. Christ, these have been a lousy couple of days."

"Did you have a fight with Mitch or something?"

"No." She kept her eyes closed as he drove, but her lips curved a little. "I don't get hysterical over a spat. I hope to God it takes more than that to bring me so low."

"I've never seen you cry like that, not since Daddy died."

"I don't guess I have." She felt the car turn, and opened her eyes so she could watch Harper House come into view. "Did you ever want me to give it up, this place?"

"No." His expression was utter shock as he looked over at her. "Of course not."

"Good. That's good to know for sure. I don't know if I could have, even for you."

"It's ours, and it's always going to be." He parked, and was out of the car and hurrying to her side before she could get out.

"I'm just a little shaky, Harper, not mortally wounded."

"You're going straight up, getting into some dry clothes. I'll bring you up some brandy."

"Harper, this is going to sound stupid, but I'm not quite ready to go upstairs."

"I'll get you some dry clothes. You can change in David's room."

"Thanks." He didn't even ask why, she thought. Didn't hesitate. What a man she'd raised.

"Go on back to David," he ordered. "Tell him I said you're to have some brandy, and some hot tea."

"Yes, sir."

Before she could move toward the stairs, Mitch came out of the library and started down the hall.

"I thought I heard the door—I've been keeping an ear . . ." He trailed off as he got closer, then lengthened his stride to reach her. "What is it? Are you sick, hurt?"

"No. Do I look sick?"

"You look pale as a sheet, and you've been crying. What is it?" He looked over her head into Harper's eyes. "What happened?"

"She doesn't really want to see anyone right now," Harper began.

"It's all right." She squeezed Harper's hand. "I did say that," she told Mitch, "but after I pull myself together a little more, I'd just as soon tell you both—all three of you, since I imagine David's in the kitchen—at once."

"She needs dry clothes," Harper stated. "If you'd take her back to David, get some brandy into her, I'll go fetch her some."

"For heaven's sake, this is what comes from being the little woman in a house full of big, strapping males. I don't have to be taken anywhere, and I can get brandy into myself."

"She's coming back." Harper nodded at Mitch. "You'll take care of her. I'll just be a minute."

"I've worried him now," Roz stated as Harper bounded up the steps. "I hate worrying him."

"Well, you're worrying me, too."

"I suppose it can't be helped. I wouldn't mind that brandy, though."

The minute they stepped into the kitchen, David rushed forward, concern tightening his face. Roz simply threw up a hand.

"I'm not hurt, I'm not sick, and there's no need to fuss. What I want is a shot of brandy, and the dry clothes Harper's bringing down. Mind if I change in your room?"

"No. Sit down." As he strode to a cabinet, he whipped the dishrag tucked into the waistband of his jeans, and used it to brush flour from his hands. "Who made her cry?"

Because the question was more of an accusation, tossed straight at Mitch, Mitch held up his hands for peace. "I've been here, remember? Harper just brought her in like this."

"I must point out, I'm sitting right here. And as I am, I can speak for myself. Thanks, baby." She lifted the snifter of brandy and took a quick, deep swallow. "Always hated this stuff, but it shoots straight to the spot."

She managed a smile as Harper came in with a sweatshirt, jeans, and thick socks. "My hero. Just give me a couple of minutes, and I'll try to explain what happened."

Harper waited until she'd gone into David's quarters, and the doors were closed.

"I found her sitting on the floor of the propagation house, crying. Just . . . sobbing. She hardly ever cries. Gets a little wet when something makes her really happy, or sentimental, but when she's sad or hurt—she doesn't let you see it."

"What's been going on the past few days?" Mitch demanded, and saw David and Harper exchange a look. "I knew there was something. She's been avoiding me."

"It's best if she tells you herself. David, she ought to have some tea, don't you think?"

"I'll put it on. Get that box of Nirvana caramels out of the fridge. Some chocolate will make her feel better. Mitch, why don't you light the fire there? I didn't bother with it today."

When Roz stepped back in, David was brewing tea, Harper was setting out fancy chocolates, and Mitch was babying a fire in the kitchen hearth.

"Makes me wonder why I haven't had some sort of jag long before this, if I get three good-looking men bustling around ready to wait on me. Before we sit down, Mitch, I should've told you before. I think you'll want your tape recorder."

"I'll get it."

It gave her a little more time, calming herself toward cool by the time they all sat together. She told them, was able to relay it matter-of-factly now. Though her hands went cold again, she simply warmed them on her teacup and finished describing her experience in the greenhouse.

"I always had a soft spot for the Bride," David began, "but now, I think she's just a stone bitch."

"Hard to argue." Roz picked up a piece of chocolate. "But it seems to me that she believes all this sincerely. Men are liars and cheats and no-good bastards. She wants me to believe it so I'm not used and hurt again."

"Mama." Harper stared hard into his own tea. "Do you believe Daddy wasn't faithful to you?"

"I don't believe anything of the kind. More than that, honey, I know he was faithful. Without a single doubt."

"She made you see him that way."

"She made me see him," Roz repeated. "And it broke my heart. To see him, just as he'd been. So young and vibrant and real. Just out of my reach. Out of my reach, when everything I felt for him came alive inside me again, just as vibrant and real. I knew it was a lie, even as it happened. And the cruel things she put into his mouth were never his. He was never cruel."

"She used your experience with Bryce, a painful incident," Mitch began. "And transferred that experience to the man who came before him. John. The man who came after him. Me. She'd rather hurt you, is compelled to hurt you, to save you from becoming involved with me."

"A bit late for that."

"Is it?"

"Do you think I'm so weak-minded, so spineless that I'd let her tricks influence me?"

"I think you're strong-minded, perilously close to a fault. I'm just not sure how much you disagree with her."

"I see. Well, well, well. I think I've told y'all what I can. I'm going to go on up, do some paperwork. Harper, it'd set my mind at ease if you'd go back to the nursery, just make sure everything's under control. David, the tea was just right, thanks."

She rose, strode out of the room without a second glance.

"Well, pissing her off brought the color back in her cheeks," David commented.

"Then she'll probably have a permanent healthy blush by the time I'm done. Excuse me."

"Brave, brave man," David stated as Mitch marched out.

"Or brick stupid," Harper said. "Either way, I think he's

in love with her. If he's stupid, she'll chew him up and spit him out, regardless. If he's brave, he might just make the cut. I hope he does."

ROZ HAD JUST REACHED HER BEDROOM WHEN MITCH caught up and walked right in behind her. She turned around, slow and deliberate.

"I don't believe I invited you in."

"I don't believe I asked for an invitation." Just as slow, just as deliberate, he closed the door. And to her shock, locked it.

"You're going to want to unlock that and step out again, or believe me, the wrath of this arguably psychotic ghost will be nothing compared to mine."

"You want a shot at me, take it. But I'll damn well know why first."

"I've just told you. I don't appreciate your invading my privacy this way, and presuming—"

"And that's bullshit. What led up to this? You've been brushing me off and evading me for days. The last time we were together, we were in that bed, and you were with me, Rosalind. I want to know what changed."

"Nothing. I've got my own life, just as you do." In a deliberate and, she could admit, petty move, she walked to the terrace doors, flung them open. "I had a lot to do."

He simply crossed over, slammed the doors shut. Locked them.

She wasn't sure she could get words past the fire of rage burning in her throat. "If you think for one minute I'll tolerate that—"

"Just be quiet." He snapped it out, and though blistering temper boiled inside her, she found herself measuring him in a new light.

"On second thought," he said before she could think of

a response, "answer one question. I told you I was falling in love with you. Was that a mistake?"

"Telling me? No. Falling, possibly. I'm a difficult woman."

"That's not a news flash."

"Mitchell, I'm tired, I'm angry, I'm emotionally . . . I don't know what the hell I am, but I don't want to fight with you now, because I'll fight dirty and regret it later. I don't want to talk to you. I don't want to be with you."

"I'm not leaving, because you're tired and you're angry, and in emotional turmoil. You don't want to talk or fight, fine. Lie down, take a nap. I'll wait until you're feeling stronger."

"God. God*damn* it." She whirled away, stormed toward the terrace doors, and unlocking them again, threw them open to the rain. "I need air. I just need some fucking air."

"Fine. Suck it in then, all you want. But this time, Rosalind, you're going to talk to me."

"What do you expect me to say? What do you want to hear?"

"The truth'll do."

"The truth, then. She *hurt* me." Emotion drenched her voice as she pressed a fisted hand to her heart. "She sliced me up and carved me out. Seeing John like that. I can't explain it, I don't have words for what it did to me."

She whirled back to him, and he saw her eyes were drenched, too. The tears didn't fall, and he could only imagine the vicious strength that held them back. But the golden brown swam with tears.

"She dropped me right down to the ground, and there was nothing I could do. How can I fight that? How can I fight something that doesn't really exist? Even knowing why she did it doesn't stop it from squeezing my heart into bloody pulp."

With an impatient gesture, she used the heels of her hands to swipe at any tear that escaped her control.

"He didn't deserve to be used that way. Do you see? He didn't deserve it. He was a good man, Mitchell. A good man, good husband, good father. I fell in love with him when I was fourteen. Fourteen years old, can you imagine? He made me a woman, and a mother, and God, a widow. I loved him, beyond measure."

"She can't touch what you feel for him. Nothing she can do can touch it. I didn't know him, but I'm looking at you, Rosalind, and I can see that. I can see him."

Her breath released on a shaky, painful sound. "You're right. You're right." She leaned against the doorjamb, stared out into the cool rain. "You didn't deserve to be used, either. You didn't—don't—deserve what she tried to make you in my mind. I didn't believe it of John, and I didn't believe it of you. But it hurt, nonetheless, it hurt."

She took another breath, a stronger one. "I don't equate you with Bryce. I hope you know that."

"I'd rather know what you feel instead of what you don't. Why haven't you wanted to see me, Roz?"

"Nothing to do with you, and everything to do with me. Don't you hate when people say that?"

"Enough that I'm having a hard time not grabbing you and shaking out the rest of it. You're not the only one with a healthy share of wrath."

"No, I believe I caught the leading edge of it just now. One of the things I like about you is you have a strong sense of control. I have such a vile temper, you've no idea. So I know all about control."

"Aren't we just two mature individuals."

"Oh, you're still mad at me." She let out a half laugh, then tried to give him what he'd asked for. The truth. "The last night I spent with you?"

She turned now, facing him fully with the open doors at her back. "It was beautiful, and meant so much in so many ways. The next day I thought of you, and when I came home from work, I was going to call you. There was a message from you on my machine."

"Roz, I have a standing date with Josh. My son—"

"I know. It wasn't that. God, don't start worrying I'm one of those needy females who craves a man's attention every minute of every day. It was the message after yours that set me off. It was about my membership at the country club, how I'd canceled it, and sent in some letter full of complaints and rude comments, and so on. Which, of course, I hadn't done."

"Clerk."

"Undoubtedly. Easy enough to straighten out, really— No." She shook her head. "Truth. It was irritating and embarrassing to straighten out. But either way it set me off. I was halfway out the bedroom door, blood in my eye, heading out to hunt him down like a sick dog when Hayley and the baby got in my way. She stopped me, for which I'm grateful. I don't know what I might've done with my temper up like that."

"I bet it would've been worth the price of a ticket."

"I'd probably have landed in jail for assault at the very least. I was raging so much I scared that baby, made her cry. And said a particularly foul word in front of her that dealt with Bryce's sexual activities should he have same with members of his own gender."

"Seeing Lily's not quite a year old, I don't imagine it made much of an impression."

"Regardless, I was nearly out of my mind with temper, and I got it under control, but it was simmering in there for a while. I wanted to cool down, all the way down. And I had to go meet with my lawyer, make a courtesy call at the club. Smooth everybody else's feathers."

"Next time it might occur to you that I'd like a chance to smooth yours."

"I'm mean when I'm mad."

"Bet you are."

She sank into a chair.

"Roz, you should go to the police with this."

"I did. One more embarrassment. And you don't need to tell me I've nothing to be embarrassed about. I feel it, so there it is. Nothing much they can do, of course, but I've documented all the things I know about. If and when it can be proved he's behind this, it's fraud, and it may be considered stalking. If I can burn his ass, Mitch, you can bet the bank I'll do just that."

He came over, crouched in front of her. "I'd like to help you light the match."

She laid a hand on his cheek. "I wasn't brushing you off. I was thinking of you, of finding you and seeing if you'd spend the evening with me. Right before I walked into that nasty little waking nightmare."

"Coincidentally, I've been thinking of you, and wondering if you'd spend the evening with me. Do you want to get out of the house for a few hours?"

"I don't. I really don't."

"Then we'll stay in."

"I'd like to ask you for something."

"Ask."

"There's a big, splashy affair coming up at the club. Formal dinner dance, the annual spring one. David was going to escort me. Even with what's happening with us, I'd planned to stick to that because I didn't like the idea of the talk and gossip that'll start if I was to show up with you. But screw that. I'd like you to go with me."

"Formal, as in tux?"

"I'm afraid so."

"I can manage it. We're all right, you and me?"

"We really seem to be, don't we?"

"You want to take a rest now?"

"No, I don't." Content, she leaned forward to kiss both

of his cheeks. "What I want is a long, hot bath. And I'd really like some company in the tub."

"That's a hell of an invitation." He got to his feet, drew her to hers. "Accepted. It may just be the perfect venue to tell you about my recent visit with Clarise Harper."

"Cousin Rissy? This I have to hear."

IT FELT LOVELY, IT FELT DECADENT, AND EXACTLY PERfect to soak in a bubble bath in the deep old tub, with her back resting against Mitch's chest.

Not even the end of the workday, and here she was having a sexy bath, with a man, music, and candles.

"Clarise gets meaner and leaner every blessed year," Roz commented. "I swear if she ever dies—because I'm not sure she'll agree to that eventuality—they won't even need a coffin. They'll just crack her in two like a twig and have done with it."

"I could tell she holds you in the same high regard."

"She despises me for many reasons, but the main is that I have this house, and she doesn't."

"I'd say that's high on the list."

"She's lying when she says she never saw or felt Amelia. I heard my grandmother talk about it. Clarise's memory is convenient and to suit herself. She doesn't tolerate any nonsense, you see, and ghosts fall into that category."

"She said 'balderdash.'"

Letting her head fall back, Roz laughed herself breathless. "Oh, she would. I can just hear it. Well, she can balderdash all she likes, but she's lying. And I know damn well she should have letters, maybe even journals, quite a number of photographs. There were things she took from the house when my father died. She'll deny it, but I know she helped herself here and there. We had one of our famous set-tos when I caught her taking a pair of candlesticks from the parlor, while my daddy was still being waked. Vicious old badger."

"I don't imagine she walked out with them."

"Not that time, anyway. I didn't care about the damn candlesticks—ugly things—but my daddy wasn't even in the *ground*. Still burns my ass. She claimed she'd given them to my father—which she certainly had not—and that she wanted them for sentimental reasons. Which was a load of stinking horseshit, as there isn't a sentimental cell in her dried-up body."

He rubbed his cheek over her hair as if to soothe, but she felt his body shaking with laughter.

"Oh, go ahead and let it out. I know how I sound."

"I love how you sound, but back to the subject. She might have taken other things, things you didn't see her with."

"I know she did, greedy vampire bat that she is. There was a picture of my grandfather as a boy, in a silver frame—Edwardian—a Waterford compote, two Dresden shepherdesses—oh, and other things that vanished after she paid calls."

"Hmm." He rested his chin on the top of her head, lazily soaped her arm. "What do you know about this Jane Paulson?"

"Not very much. I've met her at various weddings and funerals, that sort of thing, but I barely have a picture of her in my head. And when I do, I see this sweet-faced little girl. She's nearly twenty-five years younger than I am, if my math is right."

"Made me think of a puppy who's been kicked often enough to keep its tail between its legs."

"If she's living with Cousin Rissy, I can only imagine. Poor thing."

"She knows something, though."

Curious, Roz turned her head so she could see Mitch. "Why do you say?"

"Something went over her face when Clarise claimed not to have any journals, any diaries. As if she were going to be helpful and say: Oh, don't you remember the one . . . whatever. Then she caught herself, folded up. If I were a betting man, I'd wager heavy that Prissy Rissy has some information we could use."

"And if she doesn't want to share it, she'd burn it before she'd give it to you. She's that perverse."

"Can't if she doesn't know I know she's got it—and if we can persuade Jane to help us out."

"What are you going to do, seduce the poor girl?"

"Nope." He bent down to kiss Roz's wet shoulder. "You are. What I was thinking was that the girl could use a friend—maybe the prospect of another job. If you were able to contact her without Clarise knowing, give her some options . . ."

"And try to recruit her." Pursing her lips, Roz thought it through. "It's very sneaky, very deceptive. And I like it very much."

He slid his hands up, covered her breasts with them, and with frothy bubbles. "I was hoping you would."

"I don't mind playing dirty." With a wicked gleam in her eye, she squirmed around until she faced him. "Let's practice," she said, and dunked them both.

sixteen

❧

Under the humming chaos of spring season was a kind of simmering stress for the grower, especially if she happened to be the owner as well. Had she prepared enough flats, was she offering the right types and numbers of perennials?

Would the blooms be big enough, showy enough to attract the customers? Were the plants strong enough, healthy enough to maintain the reputation she'd built for quality?

Had they created enough baskets, pots, planters—or too many?

What about the shrubs and trees? Would the sidelines compliment the plants or detract from those sales?

Were the mulch colorants she'd decided to carry a mistake, or would her customer base enjoy the variety?

She left a great deal of this in Stella's hands; that's why she'd hired a manager. Roz wanted to compartmentalize many of the details—in someone else's compartment. But In the Garden was still her baby, and she experienced all the pride and worry a mother might over any growing child.

She could enjoy the crowds and confusion, the customers wheeling their wagons or flatbeds around the tables, over gravel and concrete to select just the right plants for their gardens or patio pots. She could and did enjoy consulting and recommending, and used that to balance out the little pang she experienced at the start of high season when she watched the plants she'd nurtured ride off to new homes.

At this time of year she often lectured herself about being sentimental over what she'd grown. But they weren't, and never could be, merely products to her. The weeks, months, often years spent nurturing specimens formed a connection for her that was very personal.

For the first few days of every spring season, she mourned the parting. Then she got down to business.

She was in the propagation house, taking a break from those crowds and calculating which plants to move into the retail area next when Cissy burst in.

"Roz, I'm desperate."

Roz pursed her lips. The usually meticulously groomed Cissy had more than one highlighted hair out of place, and a panicked gleam in her eyes. "I can see that. Your hairdresser retire? Your masseuse run off with a musician?"

"Oh, don't joke. I'm serious." She hustled down the tables to where Roz worked. "My in-laws are coming to visit."

"Oh."

"Just dropped that bomb on me this morning. And they're coming in two days. I *hate* when people just assume they're welcome."

"They are family."

"Which only makes it worse, if you ask me. You know she picks on me. She's picked on me for twenty-six years. If they hadn't moved to Tampa, I'd be a crazy woman by now, or in jail for murder. I need your help, Roz."

"I'm not going to kill your mother-in-law for you, Cissy. There are limits to friendship."

"I bet you could." Eyes narrowed, she took a long and calculating look around. "I bet there are all sorts of interesting poisons around here I could slip into her martini, and end this personal hell. I'll just hold that one in reserve. You know what she said to me?"

"No, but I guess I'm going to hear it."

"She said she supposed I hadn't replaced the carpet in the dining room yet, and how she'd just love to go out while she's here and find just the right thing. Not to worry about the time it took her, she had plenty now that she and Don have retired. And how I'd find that out for myself soon, since I'm reaching that age. I'm reaching *that age*. Can you imagine?"

"Seeing as you and I are about the same age, I might find some poison around here."

"Oh, and that's not the half of it. I'd be here all day if I got started, and I can't because I'm under the gun. She started snooting at me about the gardens and the lawn, and how she wondered I didn't do more than I did with mine, why I didn't take more pride in the home *her son* has provided me with."

"You have a lovely yard." Not that it reached its potential, but it was, in Roz's opinion, well kept and pretty enough.

"She just pushed my buttons—like she always does—and I just blurted out how I'd been slaving away, and put in new beds and whatnot. I just blathered, Roz, and now, unless you help me out, she's going to see I was lying through my teeth."

"If you want Logan, we can ask Stella what his schedule's like, but—"

"I hit her on the way back. He's booked—solid, she says—for the next two weeks." She clasped her hands together, as if in prayer. "I'm begging you, Roz. Begging you. Pull him off something and give him to me. Just two days."

"I can't yank him off another job—but wait," she said

when tears gathered in Cissy's eyes. "We'll figure this out. Two days." Roz blew out a breath. "It's gonna cost you."

"I don't care. Money's the least of it. My life's at stake here. If you don't help me, I'll just have to fly down to Tampa on the sly and murder her in her sleep tonight."

"Then let's get started saving your life, and hers."

She had a vision in mind, and cut a swath through her own nursery as she built on it. Cissy didn't blink when Roz accumulated plants, shrubs, ornamental trees, pots, and planters.

"Harper, I need you to go to the house, bring my pickup on around. We're going to load this up, and I'm going to steal you for a few hours. Stella, you tell Logan to come on by here when he finishes for the day. He's going to be putting in some overtime. He can pick up what I've earmarked, and bring it to this address."

She scrawled Cissy's address on a scrap of paper. "You come with him. I can use your hands, and your eye."

"Do you really think you can get all this done in less than two days?" Stella asked.

"I will get it done in less than two days because that's what I've got."

SHE LOVED A CHALLENGE. AND THERE WAS NOTHING like digging in the dirt to take her mind off any worries.

She measured, marked, tilled, dumped peat moss, and raked.

"Normally I'd want to take more time to prep the soil. Starting a new bed's an important event."

Cissy chewed on her lip, twisted the string of pearls she wore around her fingers. "But you can do it."

"Not much I can't do with dirt and plants. It's my gift." She nodded to where Harper was already setting in a decorative metal trellis. "And his. And you're going to learn something today. Put those gloves on, Cissy. You're going to do some slaving away, then you won't have lied."

"I don't give a red damn about the lie." But she tugged on the gloves.

Roz explained, in basic terms, that they'd do a four-season perennial garden. One that would impress, whatever time of year the in-laws visited. Iris and dianthus, campanula. Bleeding heart and columbine for instant bloom. With spring bulbs, craftily placed annuals, and the foliage from later bloomers filling in now.

And once the massive planters she'd chosen were done and exploding with flowers, the bed would be a showpiece even a persnickety mother-in-law would love.

She left Cissy setting in crested cockscomb and dusty miller and moved off to reorganize and fluff up the already established beds.

At the end of another hour, she realized they would use everything she'd brought with her, and then some.

"Harper?" She swiped at her sweaty forehead with the back of her hand. "You got your cell phone?"

He stopped working the vines onto the trellis long enough to pat at his pockets. "Somewhere. Truck maybe?"

Like mother like son, she thought, sent him a wave, and went around front to find it. She called Stella, rattled off another list of needs—having no doubt her manager would record them all, invoice, inventory, and deliver.

She planted cannas at the back fence, along with blue salvia and African daisies. Then sat back on her heels when Cissy walked to her with a tall glass.

"I made lemonade, from scratch. For my sins. My manicure is wrecked," she said as she handed Roz the glass. "And I'm already aching in places I forgot I owned. I don't know how you do this."

"I don't know how you play bridge every week."

"Well, to each his own, I suppose. I owe you a lot more than the check I wrote."

"Oh, you're going to be writing a couple more before it's over."

Cissy just closed her eyes. "Hank's going to kill me. He's going to take his nine iron and beat me bloody and dead."

"I don't think he will." Roz got to her feet, handed the empty glass back, then stretched her back. "I think he's going to be pleased and proud—and touched that you'd go to all this trouble—ruining a manicure on top of it—to make your home more beautiful for his mother's visit. To show her, and him, how much you value the home he's provided you with."

"Oh." A slow smile spread. "That's damn clever of you, Rosalind."

"Just because I don't have a husband doesn't mean I don't know how they work. I'm going to warn you, you don't take proper care of all this, I'll come over here and beat you senseless with Hank's nine iron myself."

Cissy looked around at the dirt, the half-planted beds, the shovels and rakes and bags of soil and additives. "It's going to look really nice when it's finished. Right?"

"Trust me."

"I am. Completely. And this is probably not the best time to tell you that son of yours is one handsome devil. I swear, my heart nearly shut right down when I handed him that lemonade and he flashed that grin at me. God almighty, he must have the girls at his feet, four layers deep."

"Never known him to have trouble finding one. Doesn't seem to keep them long, though."

"He's young yet."

* * *

IT WAS DARK WHEN SHE GOT HOME. DIRTY, A LITTLE achy, she poked her head in the library before heading upstairs. She'd seen Mitch's car out front.

"Working late?" she asked.

"Yeah. You, too?"

"I had an amazing day. Time of my life. I'm going to go up and scrape several inches of that day off me, then eat like a pig."

"Want company? I've got a couple of things to run by you."

"Sure, come on up."

"Been playing in the dirt?"

"Most of the day. Gardening emergency." She shot a grin over her shoulder as she started up the stairs. "A friend, an unexpected visit by in-laws, passive-aggressive tendencies, and a desire for one-upmanship. This resulted in a hell of a profit for my business and a terrific day for me."

She walked straight into her bathroom, stripped off her shirt. "Been a long time since I got seriously involved in the design and landscaping end of things. I'd nearly forgotten how much I love to get my hands into somebody's dirt and create something."

She undressed while she talked, in a practical sort of way, dumping her clothes in the hamper, leaning in to start the shower and test the water temperature, while he stood in the doorway, listening.

"A lot of the place was virgin ground—unrealized potential. I should feel guilty for charging her when it was such a good time for me—but I don't. We earned it."

"We."

"Had to call in the troops." She stepped into the shower. "Took Harper with me, then had Logan and Stella swing by as reserves later in the day. I put in the nicest four-season perennial garden. Looks sweet now, and in a few weeks the early daylillies will pop, and the wild indigo, then it'll move right into the spirea and ladybells, the meadow sage and fox-glove. Harper started this gorgeous purple clematis on a copper trellis and put in a trio of oakleaf hydrangeas. Then when Logan got there . . ."

She trailed off, stuck her head out, hair dripping. "I'm boring you senseless."

"Not at all. I may not know what you're talking about, but I'm not bored. You sound revved."

"I am. I'm going by tomorrow morning for some final touches and to present her with the final bill. She may faint, but she's going to wow her in-laws."

"You never did give me an answer about that plant for my apartment. You know, feng shui."

"No, I didn't."

He waited five seconds, heard nothing but water running. And laughed. "Guess that's answer enough. You know, I'm fairly intelligent and responsible. I could be taught how to care for a plant."

"Possibly, but your track record's ugly, Mitch. Just ugly. We may discuss a probationary period. I threatened to hurt Cissy if she didn't maintain what I did over there. I heard her talking to Logan about hiring him to come in twice a month to deal with it. And that's fine. We should all be self-aware enough to know our limitations."

"You water it. You put it in the sun. I can do that."

"As if that's all there is to it. You want to hand me a towel?"

She shut off the water, took the towel he handed her, and began to dry off. "We've been so busy at work I've barely been able to knock two thoughts together about anything else. Stella's wedding's right around the corner, too. And I know there are things that need my attention in this project."

He watched as she slathered on cream, as the scent of it mixed with the scent of her soap. "We'll manage it all."

"Winters fly by now that I've got the business. A lot more to do over the winter than people might think. And here we are, into another spring. I can hardly believe it's . . ."

Her eyebrows drew together, with that faint vertical line between them. Falling silent, she carefully replaced the top on her cream.

"Just hit you, didn't it?" he asked.

"What would that be?"

"The two of us, right now." He stayed where he was as she moved by him into the bedroom, as she opened a drawer for fresh clothes. "End of the workday, talking over the shower. It's all very married, isn't it?"

She slipped on cropped gray sweats, tugged a T-shirt over her head. "How do you feel about that?"

"Not entirely sure. A little nervous around the edges, I guess. Amazingly calm at the center. What about you?"

She rubbed the towel over her hair as she studied his face. "Getting married again wasn't just not on my radar, but top of my list of things to avoid. Such as poisonous snakes, frogs dropping out of the sky, ebola viruses, and such."

He smiled, leaned on the doorjamb. "I heard past tense."

"You have good ears. I fell in love once, very young. And when I fell in love, I married. It was very good, and I'll love John Ashby all of my life. I'll see him in the sons we made together, and know I wouldn't have them if we hadn't loved the way we did."

"People who can and have loved like that are fortunate."

"Yes, we are. At one time I was lonely. My boys were going their own way, and the house just seemed so empty, so quiet. I was sad, under the pride of seeing the young men I'd help create, I was so damn sad."

She walked back into the bathroom to hang the damp towel, then opened her daily moisturizer to smooth it over her face.

"I needed something to take that away, or thought I did. I wanted someone to share the rest of my life with. I picked someone who, on the surface, seemed right. That mistake cost me a great deal. Emotionally and financially."

"And because of that, you'll be very careful about another marriage."

"I will. But I'm in love with you, Mitchell." She saw the emotion rush into his eyes, and what a thrill it was to see it, to know it was there because of her.

She saw him start to step forward. And stop himself, because he knew she wanted him to wait. Another thrill, she thought, to be so well understood.

"I never expected to love again, not with the whole of my heart. That was the mistake I made with Bryce, you see. The basic mistake, in marrying someone I didn't love with the whole of my heart. Still, marriage is an enormous step. I hope you won't mind if I let you know when and if I'm ready to take it."

"I can work with that, because I love you, Rosalind. Mistakes I made before hurt people I loved. I won't make them again."

She walked to him. "We're bound to make new ones."

He leaned down, brushed his lips over hers. "That'll be all right."

"Yes, I think it might be all right. Why don't we go downstairs, see what David's got cooked up? Then you can tell me about your day instead of listening to me carry on about mine."

AS IT WAS LATE, THE CHILDREN HAD ALREADY EATEN and their parents were busy with bedtime rituals.

"Sometimes you can forget this house is full of people." Roz dug into spaghetti and meatballs. "Other times it's like being at the monkey house at the zoo."

"And you like it both ways."

"I do. I'm a contradictory soul. I need my solitude or I get mean. I get too much solitude, I get broody. I'm a pain in the ass to live with, you may want to factor that into the equation."

"I already have."

She paused, fork halfway to her mouth, then set it down as a long, rolling laugh spilled out of her. "Serves me right."

"I'm messy, often careless with details that don't interest me at that particular moment—and I don't have any intention of reforming. You can factor those in."

"Done. Now what did you want to talk over with me?"

"I never seem to run out of things I want to talk over with you."

"Men, in the first few weeks of love, talk more than they do or will for the following twenty years."

"See?" He gestured with his fork, then wound pasta around it. "Another advantage for finding each other a little later in life. We both know how it works. But what I wanted to discuss, primarily, was Clarise Harper."

"You're going to spoil my appetite, bringing her name up, and I do love meatballs and spaghetti."

"I paid another call on her this morning while, I assume, you were off digging gardens."

"Would you say you visited the third or fourth level of Hell?"

"Not that bad. She likes me, to a point. Finds me interesting, at least, and I'd say is amusing herself by feeding me what she likes and holding back what she doesn't want me to know."

He shoveled in spaghetti, then broke a hunk of garlic bread in half to split with her. "I have a tape, if you're interested. She told an entertaining story, she claimed her mother told her, about your grandfather when he was a boy—going off to sleep in a closet with a puppy he'd taken from a litter in the stables. He'd wanted it for a pet, and his mother had vetoed. No dogs in the house sort of thing. So he'd hidden it in his room for a week or so, keeping it in his closet, pilfering food out of the kitchen."

"How old was he?"

"About ten, she thinks. At least from what her mother told her. He was found out when he crawled into the closet with it, and fell asleep. Nobody could find him, turned the house upside down. Then one of the servants heard this whimpering and found the two of them in the back of his bedroom closet."

"Did he get to keep the dog?"

"He did. His father overruled his mother and let him keep it, though it was a mutt and apparently never learned any manners. He had it nearly eighteen years, so she remembers it herself, vaguely. He buried it behind the stables, put a little tree over the grave."

"Spot. My grandmother showed me the grave. There's even a little marker. She said he'd buried his beloved dog there, but must not have known the story about how he acquired it. She'd have told me."

"My impression is Clarise told me to illustrate that her mother's little brother was spoiled by his father."

"She would," Roz replied.

"I learned something else. Jane has every other Wednesday off. Or Wednesday afternoons. She likes to go to Davis-Kidd, have lunch in their café, then browse the stacks."

"Is that so?"

"Anyone who wanted to talk to her privately could run into her there. Tomorrow, in fact, as it's her Wednesday afternoon off."

"I haven't made time, recently, to go to the bookstore."

"Then I'd say you're due."

* * *

WITHOUT MITCH'S DESCRIPTION, ROZ DOUBTED SHE'D have recognized Jane Paulson. She saw the young woman— mouse-colored hair, drab clothes, solemn expression— come into the café and go straight to the counter.

She ordered quickly, like someone whose habits varied little, then took a table in a corner. She pulled a paperback book out of her purse.

Roz waited sixty seconds, then wandered over.

"Jane? Jane Paulson?" She said it brightly, with just a hint of puzzlement, and watched Jane jolt before her gaze flew up. "Well, isn't this something?"

Without waiting for an invitation, Roz took the second chair at the table. "It's been . . . well, I can't remember how long. It's Cousin Rosalind. Rosalind Harper."

"Yes, I . . . I know. Hello."

"Hello right back." Roz gave her hand a pat, then sat back to sip at her coffee. "How are you, how long are you in town? Just tell me every little thing."

"I . . . I'm fine. I live here now."

"No! Right here in Memphis? Isn't that something. Your family's well, I hope."

"Everyone's fine. Yes, everyone's just fine."

"That's good to hear. You give your mama and daddy my best when you talk to them next. What are you doing here in Memphis?"

"I, um . . ." She broke off as her cup of soup and half sandwich were served. "Thank you. Um, Cousin Rosalind, would you like something?"

"No, coffee's just fine." And she couldn't do it. She couldn't look at that miserable, distressed face any longer and lie.

"Jane, I'm going to be honest with you. I came here to-day to see you."

"I don't understand."

"I know you're living with Cousin Rissy, working for her."

"Yes. Yes, I . . . and I just remembered. I have errands to run for her. I don't know how I could've forgotten. I really should go and—"

"Honey." Roz laid a hand on hers, to hold her still, and hopefully to reassure. "I know just what she thinks of me, so you don't need to worry. I won't tell her we spoke. I don't want to do anything to get you in trouble with her. I promise you."

"What do you want?"

"First let me tell you that nothing you say will get back to her. You know how much she dislikes me, and the feeling couldn't be more mutual. We won't be talking about this, Clarise and I. So I'll ask you first, are you happy staying with her?"

"I needed a job. She gave me a job. I really should—"

"Mmm-hmm. And if you could get another job?"

"I . . . I can't afford a place of my own, right now." Jane stared into her soup as if it held the world, and the world wasn't a very friendly place. "And I don't have any skills. Any job skills."

"I find that hard to believe, but that can wait. If I could help you find a job you'd like, and an apartment you could afford, would you prefer that to working for and living with Clarise?"

Her face was very pale when she lifted her head. "Why would you do that?"

"Partially to spite her, and partially because I don't like to see family unhappy if the solution is a simple one. And one more partially. I'm hoping you can help me."

"What could I possibly do for you?"

"She has things from my home, from Harper House." Roz nodded as she saw the fear and knowledge flicker over Jane's face. "You know it, and I know it. I don't care—or have decided not to care—about the statuary, the things, we'll say. But I want the papers. The books, the letters, the journals. To be frank, Jane, I intended to bribe you to get them for me. I'd help you get yourself employed and established, give you a little seed money if you needed it, in exchange. But I'm going to do that for you anyway."

"Why?"

Roz leaned forward. "She would have beat me down, if she could. She'd have manipulated me, run my life, crushed my spirit. If she could. I didn't let her. I don't see why I should let her do the same to you."

"She didn't. I did it myself. I can't talk about it."

"Then we won't. I'm not going to browbeat you." She could, Roz knew, all too easily. And that's why she couldn't. "What I'm going to do is give you my numbers. Here's my home number, and my cell phone number, and my work number. You put these somewhere she won't find them. You must know she goes through your things when you're not there."

Jane nodded. "Doesn't matter. I don't have anything."

"Keep that attitude up, you'll never have anything. You think about what you want, and if you want me to help you get it. Then you call me."

"You'd help me even if I don't help you?"

"Yes. And I can help myself if and when I need to. She has what belongs to me, and I need it back. I'll get it. You want to get away from her, I'll help you. No strings."

Jane opened her mouth, closed it, then got quickly to her feet. "Cousin Rosalind. Could we . . . could we go somewhere else? She knows I come here, and she might . . ."

"Get reports? Yes, she might. All right, let's go somewhere else. My car's right out front."

SHE DROVE THEM TO A LITTLE DINER, OFF THE BEATEN path, where no one who knew them, or Clarise, was likely to dine. The place smelled of barbecue and good strong coffee.

She ordered both, for each of them, to give Jane time to settle her nerves.

"Did you have a job back home?"

"I, um, did some office work, at my father's company? You know he's got the flooring company."

"Do you like office work?"

"No. I don't like it, and I don't think I'm much good at it anyway."

"What do you like?"

"I thought I'd like to work in a bookstore, or a gallery? I like books and I like art. I even know a little about them."

"That's a good start." To encourage the girl to eat, instead of picking at the sesame seeds on her roll with restless fingers, Roz picked up half the enormous sandwich she'd already cut in two, and bit in. "Do you have any money of your own?"

"I've saved about two thousand."

"Another good start."

"I got pregnant," Jane blurted out.

"Oh, honey." Roz set the sandwich down, reached for Jane's hand. "You're pregnant."

"Not anymore." Tears began to slide down her cheeks. "Last year. It was last year. I . . . he was married. He said he loved me, and he was going to leave his wife. I'm such an idiot. I'm such a fool."

"Stop that." Voice brisk, Roz passed Jane a paper napkin. "You're no such thing."

"He was a married man, and I knew it. I just got swept away. It was so wonderful to have somebody want me, and it was so exciting to keep it all a secret. I believed everything he said, Cousin Rosalind."

"Just Roz. Of course you did. You were in love with him."

"But he didn't love me." Shaking her head, she began to tear the napkin into shreds. "I found out I was pregnant, and I told him. He was so cool, so, well not really angry, just annoyed. Like it was, I don't know, an inconvenience. He wanted me to have an abortion. I was so shocked. He'd said we were going to be married one day, and now he wanted me to have an abortion."

"That's very hard, Jane. I'm sorry."

"I said I would. I was awful sad about it, but I was going to. I didn't know what else I could do. But I kept putting it off, because I was afraid. Then one day I was with my mother, and I started bleeding, and cramping, right there in the restaurant where we were having dinner."

Tears spilled down her cheeks. Roz pulled a napkin from the metal dispenser and offered it.

"I had a miscarriage. I hadn't told her I was pregnant, and I had a miscarriage practically in front of her. She and Daddy were so upset. I was all dopey and feeling so strange, I told them who the father was. He was one of Daddy's golf partners."

This time she buried her face in the napkin and sobbed. When the waitress started over, Roz just shook her head, rose, and moved around the booth to slip in beside Jane, drape an arm over her shoulder.

"I'm sorry."

"Nothing of the kind. You go ahead and cry."

"It was an awful scene, an awful time. I embarrassed them, and disappointed them."

"I would think, under the circumstances, their minds and hearts should have been with you."

"I shamed them." She hiccupped, and mopped at her tears. "And all for a man who never loved me. I lost that baby, maybe because I wanted it not to be. I wished it would all just go away, and it did."

"You can't wish a baby away, honey. You can blame yourself some for conceiving it, 'cause that takes two. But you can't blame yourself for losing it."

"I never did anything in my life except what I've been told. But I did this, and that's what happened."

"I'm sorry it happened. We all make mistakes, Jane, and sometimes we pay a very stiff price for them. But you don't have to keep paying it."

She gave Jane's shoulders a last squeeze, then went back to her own side, so they'd be face-to-face. "Look at me now. Listen to me. The man who used you, he's out of your life?"

She nodded, dabbed at her eyes.

"Good. Now you can start deciding what you want to do. Build a life or keep sliding around on the wreck of the old one."

"You'd really help me get a job?"

"I'll help you get one. Keeping it would be up to you."

"She . . . she has a lot of old diaries. She keeps them in her room, locked in a drawer. But I know where the key is."

Roz smiled and sat back. "Aren't you something?"

seventeen

"She's not evil, right?" Hayley shifted Lily on her hip and watched Harper plug some portulaca into the bed outside the back door of his cottage. "I mean she's nasty and mean, but she's not evil."

"Obviously, you haven't heard Mama describe Cousin Rissy as the Uber-Bitch Demon from Hell."

"If she really is, then maybe she had something to do with Amelia. Maybe she's the one who killed her."

"She wasn't born—or spawned, as Mama would say—when Amelia died."

"Oh, yeah." But she wrinkled her forehead. "But that's only if we're right on the dates. If we're wrong, she could've done it."

"Assuming Amelia was murdered."

"Well, okay, assuming that. She has to have some reason for taking the diaries, and for keeping them. Don't you think?"

"Other than being a selfish, tight-assed old biddy?"

"Other than. All right, honey." As Lily squirmed, Hayley

put her down and began to walk her, holding her hands, up and down Harper's patio. "There could be things in the diaries that implicate her."

"Then why didn't she burn them?"

"Oh, I don't know," she snapped. "It's a theory. We've got to have a theory and a hypothesis so we can work to the solution, don't we?"

"If you say so, but my solution is Cousin Rissy's just a sticky-fingered, black-hearted, selfish witch. Look here, sweetie-pie." He plucked one of his moss roses, held it out at Lily's level. "Isn't that pretty? Wouldn't you like to have it?"

Grinning, she released her mother's hands, reached out.

"Uh-uh, you come on and get it," he told her.

And when he held it just beyond her fingertips, she took three toddling steps.

"Oh, my God. Oh, my God! Did you see? She walked. Did you see that?"

"Sure did." Harper steadied Lily when she closed her fist around the flower. "Look at you. Aren't you the one?"

"She took her first steps." Hayley sniffled, knuckled a tear away. "She walked right to you."

Always uneasy with tears, Harper looked up. "Sorry. I should've had you hold out the flower."

"No, no, that's not it. She took her first steps, Harper. My little girl. I saw her take her first steps. Oh, we have to show everybody." She did a quick dance, then scooped Lily up, making the baby laugh as she turned circles. "We've got to show everybody how smart you are."

Then she stopped, sighed. Leaning down, she brushed her lips over Harper's cheek. "She walked right to you," she repeated, then hurried toward the main house with the baby on her hip.

*   *   *

Roz loved having coffee on the patio with the awakening gardens spread out around her. She could hear Stella's boys playing with the dog, and the sounds turned back her memory clock to when those shouts would have been from her own sons.

It was pleasant to sit out like this in the early evening, with the light soft and blue and the smell of growing things quiet on the air. Pleasant, too, since she was in the mood to have company. She drank her coffee while Logan and Stella, David and Mitch talked around her.

She'd wanted Harper there, too, and Hayley. But Harper wasn't answering his phone—not a rare occurrence—and she hadn't been able to find Hayley or the baby.

"She said he was so happy with the way everything looked, he took her out so she could buy new patio furniture." Stella drained her glass of iced tea. "I've rarely seen a more satisfied customer—or a landscape design done and executed so quickly. Logan better keep his eye on you, Roz."

"Knew the yard, and the woman—and both well enough to be sure Cissy would love the changes. And hire Logan to keep it looking good."

"I'd hate to be that unhappy and intimidated by my mother-in-law." Stella smiled at Logan. "I'm getting a jewel."

"She feels the same, which is going to make my life a hell of a lot easier." He tipped his beer toward Stella. "Your days are numbered, Red."

"Two weeks, and counting. There's still so much to do. Every time I think I've got it all under control, something else pops into my head. Planning a small, simple wedding's full of complications."

"You say 'I do,' then you eat cake," Logan said, and earned a bland stare from his future bride.

"Jolene's been an enormous help," she went on. "So have Logan's mother and sister, by long-distance. And I just don't know what I'd do without you, David."

"Throw me the bouquet, and we're even."

"Speaking of your stepmama," Roz put in, "I spoke with Jolene today."

"You did?"

"If there's anyone who knows everybody in Shelby County, it's Jolene Dooley. And I recalled she had a friend who runs a nice little gallery and gift shop downtown. Jane's got a job interview next Wednesday afternoon."

"You work fast," Mitch said.

"That girl needed a break. Now we'll see what she does with it. Jolene also has a friend whose sister works at a rental management company. Turns out there's a one-bedroom apartment downtown, about six blocks from that gallery. Its current tenants are moving out in a couple weeks, and the lease fell through on the people who were going to move in."

"I should've said you work miracles."

"Oh, I just put in the request for them."

"Do you think she'll move on it?" Logan wondered. "Move out, and bring you the diaries? The way you described her, she didn't seem to have much spine."

"Some of us don't. And some of us find out we've got one, but misplaced it. She's young, and she doesn't have what you'd call a lot of spirit. And though I made it clear there were no strings, I'm fairly sure she'll feel obligated if she takes this job, and this apartment. Now whether she has the gumption to act on that obligation's another matter."

"If she doesn't?" Mitch asked.

"Then I expect Cousin Rissy and I are due for a come-to-Jesus talk. I have a few cards up my sleeve, and I'll play them if I have to."

David's eyes brightened as he leaned closer. "Dirt? Such as?"

"Family peccadilloes that she wouldn't care to have come to light, and that I'll assure her I will light up like Christmas unless she returns what belongs to Harper House." She tapped David on the chin. "But for now, they're my little secrets."

"Spoilsport."

She turned, as did everyone else, when Hayley shouted. Her face glowing, she rushed breathlessly to the table. "She walked. She walked right to Harper. Three steps!"

Nothing would do but that Lily demonstrate her new skill again. But she just buckled at the knees each time Hayley tried to nudge her into a step. And preferred crawling on the patio or trying to climb up Roz's chair.

"I swear she walked. You can ask Harper."

"I believe you." Roz hauled Lily up to nuzzle. "Teasing your mama, aren't you?" She pushed back, rose with Lily in her arms, then picked up a cracker, held it out to Hayley. "You might as well start early using one of the primary parenting tools. Bribery. Scoot down there, hold that cracker out."

As Hayley obeyed, Roz crouched, steadied Lily on her feet. "Harper held out a flower."

"That boy knows how to charm the girls. Go on, baby. Go get it."

To enthusiastic applause, Lily performed. Then she plopped down on her butt and ate the cracker.

When the others went inside, Roz sat with Mitch in the twilight.

"Would you be insulted if I said you make a beautiful honorary grandmother."

"The term *grandmother* is a bit of a jolt yet, but since I couldn't love that baby more if she were my own blood, no. She took her first steps to my boy. To Harper. It's hard for me not to focus on that, on the significance of it."

"She's not seeing anyone? Hayley?"

"Her life's centered on Lily right now. But she's young and full of passion. There'll be someone sooner or later. As for Harper, I can't keep up with the females who come and go. Still, he doesn't bring them home to meet me. There's significance in that, too."

"Well, speaking of sons, mine's seeing a new young lady. A local girl. And it happens her parents are members of your club. He'll be at the dinner dance tomorrow night. I'm looking forward to introducing you."

"I'd love to meet him. Who's the girl?"

"Her name's Shelby—after the county, I'm guessing. Shelby Forrester."

"It's a small and crowded world. Yes, I know Jan and Quill, Shelby's parents. I know her, too—and she's a lovely girl. Her parents and I are currently on . . . tenuous terms. Quill is doing business of some sort with Bryce, and it makes things a bit sticky between us. But that won't touch on anyone else."

"No one does complex connections and tenuous terms like the South."

"I suppose not, and I only mention it so that if you sense any awkwardness, you'll know why. But I'm prepared to be excruciatingly polite, so you needn't worry."

"I'm not, whether you decide to be polite or otherwise. Why don't we take a walk? That way I can hold your hand and find some shadowy and fragrant corner of the garden where I can kiss you."

"Sounds like a fine idea."

"You're doing a fine thing for Jane Paulson."

"Maybe, but my motivations are murky."

He laughed and brought her hand to his lips. "If your motivations were always pure, I doubt I'd find you as fascinating as I do."

"I do love astute flattery. Let's walk around to the stables. I'll show you Spot's marker."

"I'd like to see it. It might be a good place for me to broach another theory. One I've been chewing on for a while now."

As they walked down the path, she gauged the progress of her flowers and kept out an eagle eye for weeds.

"I'd as soon you spit it out as chew on it."

"I'm not entirely sure how you're going to feel about this one. I'm looking at dates, at events, at key moments and people, attempting to draw lines from those dates, events, moments, and people to Amelia."

"Mmm-hmm. I've always enjoyed having these stables here, leaving them be. As a kind of ruin."

Head cocked, hands fisted on hips now, she studied the crumbling stones, the weather-scarred wood. "I suppose I could have them restored. Maybe I will if I get those grandchildren and they develop an interest in horses. None of my boys did, particularly. It's girls, I think, who go through that equine adoration period."

She studied the building in the half light, the sagging roof and faded trim—and the vines, the climbers, the ornamental grasses she'd planted around it to give it a wild look.

"It looks like something you'd see in a movie, or more likely, in a storybook."

"That's what I like about it. My daddy's the one who let it go, or never did anything to preserve the building. I remember him talking about having it razed, but my grandmother asked him not to. She said it was part of the place, and she liked the look of it. The grave's around the back," she said. "I'm sorry, Mitch, I interrupted. Mind's wandering. Tell me your theory."

"I don't know how you're going to feel about it."

"Poison sumac," she said, nudging him away before he brushed up against a vine. "I'll have to get out here and get rid of that. Here we are." She crouched down, and with her ungloved hands plucked at weeds, brushed at dirt until she revealed the marker with the hand-chipped name in the stone.

"Sweet, isn't it, that he'd have buried his old dog here,

carved that stone for him. I think he must've been a sweet man. My grandmother wouldn't have loved him as much as she did if he hadn't been."

"And she did," Mitch agreed. "You can see the way she loved him in the pictures of them together."

"He looks sort of cool in most of the photographs we have of him. But he wasn't cool. I asked my grandmother once, and she said he hated having his picture taken. He was shy. Odd thinking of that, of my grandfather as a shy man who loved his dog."

"She was more outgoing?" Mitch prompted.

"Oh, much. She liked to socialize, nearly as much as she liked to garden. She loved hosting fancy lunches and teas, especially. She dressed up for them—hat, gloves, floaty dresses."

"I've seen pictures. She was elegant."

"Yet she could hitch on old trousers and dig in the dirt for hours."

"Like someone else we know." He skimmed a hand over her hair. "Your grandfather was born several years after the youngest of his sisters."

"Hmm. There were other pregnancies, I think. My grandmother had two miscarriages herself, and I recall, vaguely, her mentioning that her mother-in-law had suffered the same thing. Maybe a stillbirth as well."

"And then a son, born at the same time we've theorized Amelia lived—and died. Amelia, who haunts the house, but who we can't verify lived there—certainly not as a relation. Who sings to children, gives every appearance of being devoted to children—and distrusting, even despising men."

She cocked her head. Twilight was moving very quickly to dark, and with dark came a chill. "Yes, and?"

"What if the child that was born in 1892 was her child. Her son, Roz. Amelia's son, not Beatrice Harper's."

"That's a very extreme theory, Mitchell."

"Is it? Maybe. It's only a theory, in any case, and partially based on somewhat wild speculation. But it wouldn't be unprecedented."

"I would have heard. Surely there would have been some mention of it, some whisper passed along."

"How? Why? If the original players were careful to keep it quiet. The wealthy, the influential man craving a son—and paying for one. Hell, it still happens."

"But . . ." She pushed to her feet. "How could they hide that kind of deception? You're not talking about some legal adoption."

"No, I'm not. Just run with me on this a minute. What if Reginald hired a young woman, likely one of some breeding, some intelligence, who'd found herself in trouble. He pays the bills, gives her a safe haven, takes the child off her hands if it's a boy."

"And if it's a girl, he's wasted his time and money?"

"A gamble. Another angle might be he impregnated her himself."

"And his wife just accepted his bastard as her own, as the heir?"

"He held the purse strings, didn't he?"

She stood very still, rubbing her arms. "That's a very cold theory."

"It is. Maybe he was in love with Amelia, planned to divorce his wife, marry her. She might have died in childbirth. Or it could've been a straight business deal—or something else. But if that child, if Reginald Harper Jr. was Amelia's son, it explains some things."

"Such as?"

"She's never hurt you or anyone of your blood. Couldn't that be because you're her blood? Her descendant? Her great-grandchild?"

She paced away from the little grave. "Then why is she

in the house, on the property? Are you theorizing she birthed that baby here? In Harper House?"

"Possibly. Or that she visited here, spent time here. Maybe as the child's nurse, that's not unprecedented, either. That she died here, one way or the other."

"One way or—"

The grave was not small, and it had no marker. It gaped open dark and deep.

She stood over it, stood over that wide mouth in the earth. She looked down at death. The body in the tattered and filthy gown, the flesh that was melting away from bone. The smell of decay swarmed over her like fat, humming bees, stinging her eyes, her throat, her belly.

The ground was damp and slippery where she stood. Over it a thin, fetid fog crawled, smearing the black dirt, the wet grass with dirty tongues of gray.

She plunged the shovel through that fog, into the earth and grass, filled the blade. Then threw the earth into the grave.

The eyes of the dead opened, gleaming with madness and malice. Lifting a hand, bones piercing horribly through rotted flesh, it began to climb out of the earth.

Roz jolted, and slapped at the hands holding her.

"Easy, easy. Just breathe. Nice and slow."

"What happened?" She pushed at Mitch's hand again when she realized she was on the ground, cradled in his lap.

"You fainted."

"I certainly did not. I've never fainted in my life."

"Consider this your first. You went sheet white, your eyes rolled straight back in your head. I grabbed you when you started to go down. You were only out about a minute." Trembling a bit himself, he lowered his brow to hers. "Longest minute of my life, so far."

He took a long breath, then another. "If you're okay, would you mind if I just sat here a minute until I settle down?"

"Well, that's the damnedest thing."

"I didn't mean to upset you. We'll just table the theories. Let's get you inside."

"You don't think I passed out because you had me thinking my grandfather might've been born on the wrong side of the blanket? Christ. What do you take me for? I'm not some silly, spineless woman who questions her own identity because of the actions of her ancestors. I know who the hell I am."

Her color was back now, and those long-lidded eyes were ripe with irritation.

"Then you want to tell me why . . ." Now he went pale as polished glass. "God, Roz, are you pregnant?"

"Get a hold of yourself. A few minutes ago you're calling me a grandmother, now you're going into shock thinking I could be pregnant. I'm not going to present either one of us with a midlife baby, so relax. I had some sort of spell, I suppose."

"Care to elaborate?"

"One second we were talking, and the next I was standing—I don't know where, but I was standing over an open grave. She was in it. Amelia, and she was not looking her best."

She couldn't stop the shudder, and let her head rest against him. That good, strong shoulder. "More than dead, decomposing. I could see it, smell it. I suppose that's what took me down. It was, to put it mildly, very unpleasant. I was burying her, I think. Then she opened her eyes, started to climb out."

"If it's any consolation, if that had happened to me, I'd have fainted, too."

"I don't know if it was here, I mean this particular spot. It didn't seem like it, but I can't be sure. I've walked by here countless times. I planted that pachysandra, those sweet olives, and I never felt anything strange before."

"To risk another theory, you were never this close to finding out who she was before."

"I guess not. We'll have to dig." She pushed to her feet. "We'll have to dig and see if she's here."

THEY SET UP LIGHTS AND DUG BEYOND MIDNIGHT. The men, and Roz, with Stella and Hayley taking turns between shovels and remaining inside to mind the sleeping children.

They found nothing but the bones of a beloved dog.

"COULD BE METAPHORICAL."

Roz looked up at Harper as they walked the woods toward home the next day. She knew very well why he was with her, his arm slung casually around her shoulder, because Mitch had told him she'd fainted.

She'd barely had five minutes to herself since it happened. That was going to change, she thought, but she'd give him and the rest of her honorary family a day before she shooed them back.

"What could be metaphorical?"

"That, you know, vision thing you had. Standing over her grave, shoveling dirt on her." He winced. "I don't mean to wig you out."

"You're not. Who used to have nightmares after watching that Saturday morning show? What was it, *Land of the Lost*?"

"Jeez. The Sleestak." He shuddered, and only part of the movement was mocking. "I still get nightmares. But anyway, what I'm saying is you never stood over her grave, never buried her. She died a long time ago. But if we do the metaphor thing, we could say how you're trying to open her grave—but by missing something, not finding something, whatever, you're burying her."

"So, it's all in my mind."

"Maybe she's planting it there. I don't know, Mama."

She considered a moment. "Mitch has a theory. We were discussing it before I keeled over."

She told him, sliding her arm around his waist as she did. Together, they stopped at the edge of the woods, studying the house.

"Doesn't seem so far-fetched, all things considered," Harper said. "It always seemed like she was one of us."

"Seems to me it only opens up another box of questions, and doesn't really get us any closer to finding out who she was. But I know one thing. I want those diaries more than ever. If Jane doesn't come through, I'm going to take on Clarise."

"Want me to play ref?"

"I might just. If Amelia is part of the family, she deserves her due. That said, I don't feel the same about Clarise. She's always wanted more than her due, in my opinion. I don't know what it makes me to feel more sympathy for a dead woman, who may or may not be some blood kin, than I do for a live one who unquestionably is blood kin."

"She smacked me once."

Instantly Roz stiffened. "She did what?"

"Gave me a good swat one day, when she was visiting, and she caught me climbing on the kitchen counter going after the cookie jar. I was about six, I think. Gave me a swat, pulled me off and told me I was a greedy, disrespectful little brat."

"Why didn't you tell me? She had no right to touch you. I'd've skinned her for it."

"Then skinned me," he pointed out. "As you'd told me never to climb on the counter, and not to take any cookies without asking first. So I took my lumps and slunk off."

"Anybody was going to give you lumps it was going to be me. Nobody lays hands on my children, and in my court there is no statute of limitations on the crime. That bitch."

"There now." He gave her shoulders a squeeze. "Don't you feel better?"

"I believe I'll make her very sorry before I'm done." She walked with him toward the house. "You knew better than to put your hand in that cookie jar, Harper Jonathan Ashby."

"Yes'm."

She gave him a light elbow jab. "And don't you smirk at me."

"I wasn't, I was just thinking there are probably cookies in it now."

"I imagine so."

"Cookies and milk sound pretty good."

"I guess they do. Let's go harass David until we get some. But we have to do it now. I've got a date to get ready for."

ROZ KNEW THE STYLES AND COLORS THAT NOT ONLY flattered her, but suited her. She'd chosen the vintage Dior for its clean, flowing lines, and its pretty spun-gold color. The straight bodice, thin straps and rear drape left her back and shoulders bare.

But that back and those arms and shoulders were toned. She saw to it. So she saw no reason not to show them off. She wore her grandmother's diamonds—the drop earrings and tiered necklace that had come to her.

And knowing she'd regret it, slipped on the high, thin-heeled sandals that showcased the toenails she'd painted the same delicate gold as the dress.

She turned, to check the rear view in the mirror, and called out an absent "come in" at the knock on her door.

"Roz, I just wanted to . . ." Stella stopped dead. "Holy Mother Mary. You look spectacular."

With a nod in the mirror, Roz turned again. "I really do.

Sometimes you just want to knock them on their asses, know what I mean? I got an urge to do that tonight."

"Just—just stay there." She rushed out again, and Roz heard her calling for Hayley.

Amused, she picked up her purse—what had possessed her to pay so much for such a silly little thing—and began to slip what she considered necessary for the evening out inside it.

"You've got to get a load of this," Stella was saying, then pulled Hayley into the room.

Hayley blinked, then narrowed her eyes. "You've got to do a spin. Give us a little twirl."

Willing to oblige, Roz turned a circle, and Hayley crossed her arms over her chest and bowed her head.

"We are not worthy. Are those real diamonds? I know it's tacky to ask, but I can't help it. They're so . . . sparkly."

"They were my grandmother's, and particularly special to me. Which reminds me. I have something I thought you might like to wear for your wedding, Stella. It would cover the bases of something old, borrowed, and blue."

She'd already taken the box out of her safe, and now handed it to Stella.

"Oh, God."

"John gave them to me for my twenty-first birthday." She smiled down at the sapphire earrings. "I thought they might suit the dress you'd picked out, but if they don't I won't be offended."

"There's nothing they wouldn't suit." Gently Stella lifted one of the heart-shaped sapphire drops from the box. "They're exquisite, and more, I'm so . . ."

She broke off, waving a hand in front of her face as she sat on the side of the bed. "Sorry. I'm just so . . . that you'd lend them to me."

"If I had a sister, I'd like to think she'd enjoy wearing something of mine on her wedding day."

"I'm so touched, so honored. So . . . I'm going to have to sit here and cry for a couple minutes."

"That's all right, you go ahead."

"You know, the something old in that tradition's a symbol of the bride's link to her family." Hayley sniffed.

Roz patted her cheek. "Trust you to know. Y'all can sit here and have a nice cry together."

"What? Where are you going?" Hayley demanded.

"Downstairs. Mitch should be here shortly."

"But you can't." Biting her lip, and obviously torn between sitting with Stella or preventing a catastrophe, she waved her arms like a woman trying to stop a train. "You have to wait till he gets here, then you have to glide down the steps. That staircase is made for a woman to glide down. You've gotta make an entrance."

"No, I don't—and you sound like my mother, who made me do just that for my escort—thank God it was John so we could laugh about it after—at the debut she forced me into. Believe me, the world will not end if I greet him at the door."

She snapped her purse closed, took one last glance in the mirror. "Plus, there's another tradition I have to follow. If I don't go down, get David's approval on my dress, I'll hurt his feelings. There are tissues in the drawer beside the bed," she called out.

She'd barely finished modeling for David and getting his approval when Mitch was at the door.

Opening it, she had the pleasure of seeing his eyes widen and hearing the low whistle of his breath. "Just how did I get this lucky?" he asked her.

She laughed, held out her wrap. "The way you look in that tux, Doctor, you may get considerably luckier before the night's over."

eighteen

"I WAS TRYING TO REMEMBER THE LAST TIME I WORE A tux." Mitch slid behind the wheel of the car, giving himself the pleasure of another long look at Roz as he hitched on his seat belt. "Pretty sure it was a friend's wedding. His oldest kid graduates high school this year."

"Now, that's a shame, since you wear one so well."

"Lean over here once." When she did, he brushed his lips over hers. "Yeah, tastes as good as it looks."

"It certainly does."

Starting the engine, he pulled away from the house. "We could skip this business tonight and run off and get married. We're dressed for it."

She sent him a sidelong glance as he turned onto the main road. "Be careful how you bat those marriage proposals around, Dr. Carnegie. I've already shagged two in my time."

"Let me know if you want to try for three."

It felt spectacular, she realized, to be all dressed up and flirting with a handsome man. "You getting serious on me?"

"It's looking that way. You need to consider I'm a rent-the-tux kind of guy, but I'd spring for one when you decide to take the jump. Least I can do."

"Of course, that is a deciding factor."

He laid his hand briefly over hers. "I make a good living, and your money isn't an issue one way or the other with me. What baggage I've got, I've pretty well packed up. For the past many years, my son's been the singular essential element in my life. He's a man now, and while he'll always be my great love, I'm ready for other loves, other essentials."

"And when he moves to Boston?"

"It's going to cut me off at the knees."

This time she laid her hand on his. "I know just how it feels."

"You can't follow them everywhere. And I've been thinking it's easy enough to visit Boston now and again, or take a trip here and there when he's got a game somewhere appealing."

"I'm looking forward to meeting him."

"I'm looking forward to that, too. I'm hoping you're not going to be too uncomfortable with whatever friction there is between you and his date's parents."

"I won't be. Jan will. Being a spineless sort of woman who's decided to be embarrassed by her friendship, such as it was, with me. It's foolishness, but she's a foolish sort. I, on the other hand, will enjoy making her feel awkward."

She stretched back and spoke with satisfaction. "But then, I have a mean streak."

"I always liked that about you."

"Good thing," she said as they turned toward the club. "Because it's likely to come out tonight."

IT WAS FASCINATING, TO MITCH'S MIND, TO SEE HOW this set worked. The fancy dress, the fancy manners were a kind of glossy coat over what he thought of as basic high school clique syndrome. People formed small packs, at tables, in corners, or at strategic points where they could watch other packs. There were a few butterflies who flitted from group to group, flashing their wings, dipping into some of the nectar of gossip, then fluttering off to the next.

Fashion was one of the hot topics. He lost count of the times he overheard a murmured variation of: Bless her heart, she must've been drinking when she bought that dress.

He'd had a taste of it at Roz's holiday party, but this time out he was her escort, and he noted that changed the dynamics considerably.

And he was the new kid in class.

He was given the once-over countless times, asked who he was, what he was, who his people were. Though the manner of interrogation was always charming, he began to feel as if he should have a résumé typed up and ready to hand out.

Ages ran from those who'd certainly danced to the swing music the band played when it was new, to those who'd consider the music retro and hip.

All in all, he decided as he discreetly avoided discussing the more salient details of his work on the Harper family with a curious couple named—he thought—Bing and Babs, it was an interesting change of pace for a guy in a rented tux.

Spotting Josh, he used his son as an excuse to cut the inquisition short. "Excuse me, my son's just come in. I need to speak with him."

Mitch made a beeline through the tuxedos and gowns. "Hey, you clean up good." He gave Josh a one-armed hug around the shoulders, then smiled at the little brunette. "You must be Shelby."

"Yes, sir. You have to be Josh's daddy. He looks just like you."

"That takes care of the intros. Wow." Josh scanned the room. "Some hot-dog stand."

The ballroom was draped with twinkling lights, festooned with spring flowers. Wait staff manned one of three bars or roamed the room with trays of drinks and canapés. Diamonds glittered, emeralds flashed as couples took the dance floor to a hot rendition of Goodman's "Sing, Sing, Sing."

"Yeah, a little *Philadelphia Story*."

"What?"

Mitch sent Josh a pitying glance. "There were movies made before *The Terminator*."

"So you say, Pops. Where's your date?" Josh asked.

"She got swept away. I've been . . . oh, here she comes."

"Sorry, got myself cornered. Hello, Shelby. Don't you look pretty."

"Thanks, Ms. Harper. That's an awesome dress. Josh said you were coming with his father."

"It's nice to meet you at last, Josh. Your father's full of talk about you."

"Same goes. We'll have to find a quiet corner and compare notes."

"I'd love to."

"I see my parents over there." Shelby nodded toward a table. "I'd like to introduce you, Josh, and your daddy. Then I'll have done my duty, and you can dance with me."

"Sounds like a plan. Dad says you're into plants, Ms. Harper."

"Roz, and yes, I am."

"He kills them, you know," he added as they worked their way around the room.

"So I've seen."

"Mostly when they see him they just commit suicide and get it over with."

"Shut up, Josh."

"Just don't want you to pull a fast one on her." He gave his father a lightning grin. "Shelby says you live in that amazing house we passed on the way here."

"Yes, it's been in my family a long time."

"It's totally huge, and great looking." He angled his head enough to send his father a quick, and not-so-private, leer. "Dad's been spending a lot of time there."

"Working." Mitch managed, through years of practice, to give his son a light elbow jab in the ribs.

"I hope you'll come spend some time there yourself, very soon."

Roz paused by the table where Jan and Quill sat talking to other friends. "Hello, everyone." As Roz had expected, Jan stiffened, went a little pale. Deliberately, Roz leaned down, air-kissed Jan's cheek. "Don't y'all look wonderful."

"Mama, Daddy." Shelby angled herself around to make introductions. "This is Joshua Carnegie, and his father Dr. Mitchell Carnegie. My parents, Jan and Quill Forrester, and Mr. and Mrs. Renthow."

Quill, a solidly built man with a glad hand and subtle comb-over, pushed himself to his feet to pump Mitch's, then Josh's hand, then inclined his head to Roz. "Rosalind, how are you doing?"

"I'm doing just fine, Quill. How's business?"

He pokered up, but nodded. "Bumping right along."

"That's good to hear. Jan, I swear, Shelby's grown up to be an absolute beauty. You must be so proud."

"Of course. I don't think I understood you were acquainted with Shelby's escort."

"His father and I are great friends." Beaming, she slid her arm through Mitch's. "In fact, Mitch is researching the Harper family history. He's finding all sorts of secrets and scandals." Playing it up, she gave a little head toss, a little laugh. "We just love our scandals here in Shelby County, don't we?"

"That's where I've heard the name," Renthow spoke up. "I've read one of your books. I'm a bit of an amateur genealogist myself. Fascinating business."

"I think so. In any case, the Harper ancestors led me to Roz." In a smooth move, Mitch lifted her hand, kissed it. "I'll always be grateful."

"You know," Renthow put in, "I've traced my ancestry back to the Fifes in Scotland."

"Really?" Mitch perked up. "A connection to Duncan Phyfe, before he changed the spelling?"

"Yes, exactly." Obviously pleased, Renthow shifted in his chair to angle toward Mitch. "I'd like to put something more detailed together. Maybe you can give me some tips."

"Happy to."

"Why don't we all sit down for a few minutes?" Shelby began. "Then y'all can get acquainted while—"

"We're expecting friends," Jan interrupted. "Our table's full. I'm sure Rosalind and Dr. Carnegie can find another table. And we'll all be more comfortable."

"Mama," the word was a shocked whisper that Roz overrode with an easy smile. "We already have one, thanks. In fact, we're going to steal this handsome young couple here. Shelby, why don't I show you where we're sitting, and Josh and Mitch can get us both a drink?"

Hooking her arm through the girl's, Roz led her away.

"Ms. Harper, I . . . I'm sorry, Ms. Harper, I don't know what's the matter."

"Don't you worry about it. Here we are right here. Let's sit down, and you can tell me how you met that gorgeous young man before they get back. And you call me Roz, now. Why, we're practically on a double date here."

She put the girl at ease, chattering away until their dates returned with drinks and canapés. Only when Josh took Shelby to the dance floor did Roz show any fire.

"She didn't have to embarrass that child the way she

did. If she had a brain in that spiteful head of hers, she'd have known I wouldn't have sat with them. That's a sweet girl. I can only conclude she does not come by it naturally."

"You smoothed it over. One of the reasons I eased out of academia was to rid my life of these little snarling matches and petty grudges. But wherever you go, life's just pocked with them, isn't it?"

"I suppose. I mostly stay out of this arena, too. I have no patience for it. But I feel obliged to make an appearance now and then."

"You're not the only one," he said, and linked his fingers with hers on the table. "How much is it going to upset you to know Bryce Clerk just came in, with that same blonde he was with when he tried to crash your party?"

Her hand stiffened in his, then slowly relaxed. "I had a feeling he'd show. Well, that's all right. I'm just going to slip off to the rest room for a minute, give myself a little talking to, and freshen up. I don't intend to have another public scene, I promise you."

"Wouldn't bother me."

"That's nice to know, in case the talking to doesn't work."

She rose, walked out of the room, and turned down the corridor toward the lounges.

Inside, she freshened her lipstick and began to lecture herself on proper decorum.

You will not lower yourself to his level, no matter what the provocation.

You will not allow that silly girl to draw you into a catfight, even though you'd leave her bleeding on the floor without chipping a nail.

You will not—

Roz broke off the self-lecture when Cissy slipped in.

"I had to use a chainsaw to sever myself from Justine Lukes. Bless her heart, that woman can talk you deaf, dumb, and blind without having a single interesting thing come out of her mouth. I wanted to get over to your table. I swear, Roz, could you look any more glamorous?"

"I think I've reached the top of my game. How'd the visit with the in-laws go?"

"If I'd've cold-cocked her with a cast-iron skillet, she wouldn't have been any more stunned. I tell you, honey, even she couldn't find anything to pick at, though I did have to spill wine on my new shirt as a distraction when she asked me about one of the shrubs. The one with the arching branches and all those white flowers? Smells delicious."

"The drooping leucothoe."

"I suppose. Anyway, I owe you my very life on this one. Isn't that Jan's girl you're with?" Cissy sidled up to the mirror to fuss with her hair.

"Yes, she's with my date's son, as it happens."

"Both of whom I'm just dying to meet. I do love adding to my quota of handsome men. I suppose you saw Bryce slither in."

She shifted her gaze from her own face in the mirror to Roz's. "I broke away from Justine so I wouldn't have to pretend to be civil to him. I don't know if you've heard the latest, but—"

She broke off, zipping her lip when Jan came in with Mandy.

Both women stopped, but while Jan looked ready to move by quickly, Mandy marched forward and jabbed a finger at Roz.

"If you don't stop your harassment, I'm going to get a court order and have you arrested."

Entertained, Roz pulled out her compact. "I don't believe attending a country club event could be considered harassment, but I'll have my lawyer look into it in the morning."

"You know damn well what I mean. You called my spa

pretending to be me and canceled all my treatments. You're calling me day and night and hanging up when I answer."

Casually Roz dusted her nose. "Now why would I do any of those things?"

"You can't stand the fact that I'm going to marry Bryce."

"Has it come to that?" Roz closed her compact again. Part of her—that mean streak—did a little dance of joy. If Bryce had a rich one hooked, he was bound to leave her, and her family, alone. "Well, despite your rude behavior, you have all my sympathy."

"I know what you've been doing to Bryce, too, and to Jan because she's standing as my friend."

"I haven't done anything to any of you." She looked over at Jan. "And couldn't be less interested."

"Someone called one of Quill's top clients, pretending to be me," Jan said stiffly. "A drunken, vicious phone call that cost Quill an important account."

"I'm sorry to hear that, Jan. If you honestly believe I'd do something like that, I won't waste my time, or yours, telling you different. Excuse me."

She heard Cissy's exasperated, "Jan, how can you be so slow-witted" as the door shut behind her.

She started down the corridor only to come up short when she saw Bryce leaning against the wall. In hopes of avoiding a scene, she turned and started in the opposite direction.

"Retreating?" There was a laugh in his voice as he caught up with her. "You surprise me."

She stopped. She hadn't finished that talking to, she thought. In her current mood, it would've been a waste of time. "You never surprise me."

"Oh, I think I do and will again. I wasn't sure you'd be here tonight." His expression turned sly, and smug. "I heard somewhere that you'd dropped your membership."

"That's the thing about rumors, they're so often lies. Tell me, Bryce, what are you getting out of all this effort? Writing letters, making phone calls, risking criminal charges by falsifying credit cards."

"I don't know what you're talking about."

"Nobody here for the moment but you and me." She gestured up and down the empty corridor. "So let's move straight to the bottom line. What do you want?"

"Everything I can get. You'll never prove I made any calls, wrote any letters, used any credit cards. I'm very careful, and very smart."

"Just how long do you think you can keep it up?"

"Until I'm bored. I had a lot of time and effort invested in you, Roz, and you flicked me off. I don't like being flicked off. Now I'm back, and you won't get through a day without remembering that. Of course, if you were to make me a private, monetary offer—"

"That's never going to happen."

"Your choice." He gave a shrug. "There are things I can do to keep chipping away at you. I think you'll come around. I know just how important your reputation, your standing in Shelby County is to you."

"I don't think you do." She kept her eyes on his even when the lounge door opened several feet behind them. "You can't touch me, either, where it counts, no matter how many lies you spread, how many people you convince to believe them. Quill isn't a complete fool, and it won't take long for him to realize you're taking him for a ride. A costly one."

"You give him too much credit. What he is, is greedy. I know how to play on greed."

"You would, having so much of it yourself. Tell me, how much have you taken poor Mandy for so far?"

"Nothing she can't afford to lose. I never took what you couldn't afford, Roz." He skimmed his fingers over her cheek, and she let him. "And I gave you good value for your money. If you hadn't been so narrow-minded, we'd still be together."

"If you hadn't stolen from me, cheated on me with another woman in my own home, we might be—so I'll have to thank you for that. Tell me, Bryce, what is it about Mandy that appeals to you?"

"She's rich, but then so were you. After that, she's young and you weren't, and she's remarkably stupid. You weren't that, either. A little slow, but never stupid."

"Are you really going to marry her?"

"She thinks so." He took out a gold lighter, idly flicking the lid open and closed. "And who knows? Money, youth, malleability. She may just be the perfect wife for me."

"It does seem small of you to be going around, making prank calls, complicating her life—oh, and screwing with Quill and Jan, losing Quill clients. I think you need more constructive work."

"Two birds, one stone. It keeps them sympathetic to me and chips away at you."

"And what do you think will happen when they find out the truth?"

"They won't. As I said before, I'm careful. You'll never prove it."

"I don't think I'll have to. You always did like to boast and brag, Bryce." This time she patted him on the cheek, and thought of it as her kill shot. "Only one of your many failings." She gestured behind him to where Jan and Mandy stood, faces shocked, bodies still as statues.

Beside them, Cissy began to applaud lightly. Roz took a small bow, then walked away.

It was her turn to be surprised when she saw Mitch at the end of the corridor.

"Caught the show," he said casually, and slipped his hand over hers. "I thought the female lead was exceptional."

"Thank you."

"You okay?"

"Probably, but I wouldn't mind some air."

He led her out on the terrace. "Very slick," he said.

"Very impromptu," she corrected, and now, after it was done, her stomach began to jump. "But there he was, just dying to nip at me and posture around, and there they were, those pitiful, annoying women. The bonus being Cissy's presence, too. That little play will be making the rounds, word-for-word, in a New-York minute."

On cue, there was the sound of raised female voices from inside the ballroom, an abrupt crash, hysterical sobbing.

"Want to go in for the second act?"

"No, I don't. I think you should ask me to dance, right here."

"Then I will." He slipped his arms around her. "Beautiful night," he said while the scene played out through the open doors behind them.

"It really is." With a long sigh, she laid her head on his shoulder and felt all those sharp edges smooth out. "Just smell that wisteria. I want to thank you for not riding to my rescue back there."

"I nearly did." He brushed his lips over her hair. "But then, I thought you had it so completely under control, and I was enjoying my front-row seat."

"Lord, listen to that woman wail. Doesn't she have any pride? I'm afraid Bryce had one thing right. She is stupid, bless her heart. Dim as an underground cave on a moonless night."

"Dad!" Josh charged through the doorway. "You've *got* to come see this."

Mitch just continued to circle Roz on the terrace, though the music had long stopped, giving way to shouts and scuffling feet.

"Busy here," he replied.

"But Shelby's dad just clocked this guy. Punched him *out*. And this woman ripped into him—the other guy, not Shelby's dad. It's all about teeth and nails. You're missing it."

"Go on back, you can give us the play-by-play later. I'm going to be busy kissing Roz for a while."

"Man. I've got to come to country clubs more often." With that, Josh rushed back inside.

And Mitch lowered his mouth to Roz's.

SHE NEEDED TO RELAX. SHE'D HANDLED HERSELF, ROZ thought as she replaced her jewelry in its case, and she believed that what she'd been able to do had finally pried the monkey of a vindictive ex-husband off her back.

But the cost had been yet another public scene.

She was tired of them, tired of having her dirty linen flapped around for avid eyes to see. And she'd have to get over it.

She undressed, slipped into her warm flannel robe.

She was glad they'd been able to leave the club early. Hardly any reason to stay, she thought with a sharp smile. The place had been a glorious mess of overturned tables, spilled food and drink, horrified guests, and scrambling security.

And would be the talk of the gossip circuit for weeks, as she would be.

That was fine, that was expected, she told herself as she ran a warm bath. She'd ride it out, then things would get back to as close to normal as they ever did.

She poured in an extra dose of bubble bath, a lovely indulgence for a midnight soak. When she was done, all relaxed and pink and fragrant, she might just wander down to the library and crook a finger at Mitch.

Bless him for understanding she needed a little alone time. With a sigh, she slid into the tub, right down to the tips of her ears. A man who recognized a woman's moods, and accepted them, was a rare find.

John had, she remembered. Most of the time. They'd been so beautifully in tune, moving in tandem to build a family, enjoying their present and planning their future. Losing him had been like losing an arm.

Still, she'd coped, and damn well if she said so herself. She'd raised sons she, and John, could be proud of, kept a secure home, honored her traditions, built her own business. Not bad for a widow woman.

She could laugh at that, but the tension gathered at the base of her neck as she moved to the next phase. Bryce. A foolish, impulsive mistake. And that was all right, everyone was entitled to a few. But this one had done such damage, caused such upheaval. And public speculation and gossip, which in some ways was a bigger score to her pride.

He'd made her doubt herself so often during their marriage, where she'd always been so confident, so sure. But he had an eroding way about him, slick and sly with all those insistent little rubs under the charm.

It was a lowering thing to admit she'd been stupid—and over a man.

But she'd cooked him good and proper tonight, and that made up for a lot of irritation, embarrassment, and pain. He'd served himself up on a goddamn platter, she thought, and she'd stuck the fork in. He was done.

So good for her. Woo-hoo.

Now maybe it was time for yet another phase in the Life of Rosalind. Was she ready for that? Ready to take that big, scary step toward a man who loved her just as she was? Nearly fifty, and thinking about love and marriage—for the *third* time. Was that just insane?

Idly she played her toes through the trickle of hot water she'd left running to keep the bath warm.

Or was it a gift, already wrapped in pretty paper, tied with a big fat bow, and tossed in her lap?

She was in love, she thought, her lips curving as she let the tension drain away, closed her eyes. In love with an interesting, attractive, considerate man. A good man. With enough flaws and quirks to keep him from being boring.

She sighed, as contentment began to settle over her. And a thin gray mist crawled along the tiles.

And the sex? Oh, thank God for the sex, she thought with a lithe stretch and a purr in her throat. Hot and sweet, tender and exciting. Stimulating. Lord, that man was stimulating. Her body felt *juiced* again.

Maybe, just maybe they could have a life together. Maybe love didn't have to come at convenient and sensible times. And maybe the third time was the charm. It was something worth considering, very, very seriously.

Marriage. She drifted, drowsy now, trailing her fingers through the frothy water while the mist thickened, rising off the floor like a flood.

It came down to making an intimate promise to someone you not only loved, but trusted. She could trust Mitch. She could believe in him.

Would her sons think she'd lost her mind? They might, but it was her life, after all.

She'd enjoy being married—probably. Having someone else's clothes in the closet, someone else's books on the shelf. The man wasn't what you'd call tidy, but she could deal with that if . . .

The foamy water went ice cold. On a gasp, Roz shoved up from her lounging position, instinctively clutching her arms. Her eyes popped wide when she saw the room was full of fog, so dense she couldn't see the walls, the door.

Not steam, she realized, but a kind of ugly gray mist, as cold as the water and thick as iced soup.

Even as she started to stand, to climb out, she was dragged under.

With a leap in the belly, shock came first, before the fear. The utter shock of the frigid water, the sensation of being yanked down, held under, froze her before she began to fight. Choking, kicking, she strained to surface as the cold stiffened her limbs. She could *feel* hands clamped on her head, then nails digging into her shoulders, but through the film of the water, she saw nothing but floating bubbles and swirling mists.

Stop! Her mind screamed it. Using all her strength, she braced hands and feet and pushed up in one desperate lunge. Her head came up, broke through into the icy fog. She took one frantic gulp of air before the steely pressure on her shoulders shoved her under again.

Water sloshed over the rim of the tub as she struggled, burned her eyes and throat. She could hear her own muffled screams, as she flailed against what she couldn't see. Her elbow slammed against the side of the tub, shooting pain through terror.

For your own good. For your own good. You have to learn!

The voice was a hiss in her ear, a hiss that cut through the frantic beat of blood. Now she saw it, the face swimming above her, over the churning water, its lips peeled back on a grimace of fury. She saw the madness in Amelia's eyes.

He's no different. They all lie! Didn't I tell you? Why don't you listen? Make you listen, make you stop. Tainted blood. His blood's in you. Ruined you after all.

She was dying. Her lungs were screaming, her heart galloping as she fought wildly to find purchase, to find *air*. Something was going to burst inside her, and she'd die in the cold, scented water. But not willingly, not easily. She pounded out, with her hands, her feet. And with her mind.

Let go of me. Let go! I can't listen if I'm dead. You're killing me. If I die, you'll stay lost. If I die, you'll stay trapped. Murderer. Trapped in Hell.

She gathered herself again, fueled her straining muscles with the strength of survival, and rocketed up.

Water fumed, sliced through the mists to splash walls and floor in a small, violent tidal wave. Gripping the edge of the tub, she leaned over, choking, coughing out what she'd swallowed. Her stomach heaved, but she locked her arms around the rim. She wouldn't be pulled under again.

"Keep your hands off me, you bitch."

Wheezing, she crawled out of the tub and dropped weakly onto the soaked mat. As shudders racked her, she curled into a ball until she could find her breath. Her ears rang, and her heart thudded so brutally she wondered if she'd have bruised ribs to add to the rest.

She heard weeping.

"Your tears don't mean a lot to me at the moment." Not trusting herself to stand, she scooted over the floor until she could reach for a towel with a shaking hand, and pull it around her for warmth.

"I've lived with you all my life. I've tried to help you. And you try to drown me? In my own tub? I warned you I'd find a way to remove you from this house."

The words didn't come out nearly as strong or angry as she wanted. It was hard to sound in charge when her teeth were chattering, as much with fear as cold.

She jolted when the robe she'd hung on the back of the door drifted down and settled over her shoulders. "Why, thank you," Roz said, and did manage sarcasm well enough. "How considerate of you, after trying to kill me, to see that I don't catch cold. I've had about enough."

She shoved her arms in the robe and drew it close as she got shakily to her feet.

Then she saw Amelia, through the thinning mists. Not

the madwoman with crazed eyes and wild hair who'd loomed over her while she'd fought for her life, but a shattered woman with tears on her cheeks, and her hands clasped as if in prayer.

As she faded away, as the mists melted, another message appeared on the mirror. It said simply:

Forgive me.

"YOU COULD'VE BEEN KILLED."

Mitch paced the bedroom, anger all but sparking off his fingertips.

She'd gone down to make a pot of hot coffee, and to ask him to come upstairs. She'd wanted to be assured they weren't overheard when she told him.

"I wasn't. Happily." The coffee was helping, but she was still chilled, and willing to bundle under a thick cashmere throw.

"You might've died, while I was downstairs putzing around with books and files. You were up here, fighting for your life, and I—"

"Stop." But she said it gently. A woman who'd lived with men, raised sons, understood ego. "What happened, could have happened, didn't happen—none of it was your fault. Or mine, for that matter. The fault lies in what is no doubt an emotionally disturbed ghost. And I don't care how ridiculous that sounds."

"Rosalind." He stopped in front of her, knelt down, rubbed his hands over hers. They felt strong on hers, and warm. They felt solid. "I know how you feel about this house, but—"

"You're going to say I should move out, temporarily. And there's some good, solid sense in that, Mitch. But I won't. You can say it's because I'm stubborn, because I'm too damn hardheaded."

"And I will."

"But," she said, "besides that, and the fact I won't be chased away from what's mine, the problem won't be solved by moving out. My son lives on this property, as do others I care about very much. My business is on this property. Do I tell everyone to find other accommodations? Do I shut down my business, risk losing everything? Or do I stick it out, and work to find the answers?"

"She's escalating. Roz, for years she did little more than sing to children, an odd but relatively charming addition to the household. A little mischief now and then, but nothing dangerous. In the past year she's become increasingly unstable, increasingly violent."

"Yes, she has." Her fingers linked with his, held firm. "And you know what that tells me? It tells me we must be getting close to something. That maybe because we are, she's more impatient, more erratic. Less controlled. What we're doing matters to her. Just as what I think and feel matters, whether she approves or not."

"Meaning?"

He probably wouldn't take it well, she considered. But it had to be said. She'd promised him honesty, and took promises seriously. "I was thinking of you. Of us. When I finished sulking about tonight, and started to relax, I was thinking of the way I feel about you, and the way you feel about me."

"She tried to kill you because we love each other." His face stone hard when he pushed to his feet. "I'm the one who needs to leave, to stay away from here, and you, until we finish this."

"Is that how you deal with bullies? You give them their way?"

He'd started to pace again, but whipped around now, fury ripe in his eyes. "We're not talking about some asshole trying to steal lunch money on the playground. We're talking about your safety. Your goddamn life!"

"I won't give in to her. That's how I stay alive. That's how I stay in charge. You think I'm not furious, not frightened? You're wrong."

"I notice fury comes first."

"Because it's positive—at least I've always felt a good, healthy mad's more constructive than fear. That's what I saw in her, Mitch, at the end."

Roz tossed the throw aside and rose to go to him. "She was afraid, shocked and afraid and sorry—pitifully. You said once she didn't want to hurt me, and I think it's true."

"I also said she could, and I've been proven right." He took her face in his hands, then slid them down to her shoulders. "I don't know how to protect you. But I know I can't lose you."

"I'll be less afraid if you're with me."

He cocked his head, very nearly smiled. "That's very tricky."

"It is, isn't it?" She wrapped her arms around him, settled in when his came around her. "It also happens to be true. She asked me to forgive her. I don't know that I can, or will, but I need the answers. I need you to help me find them. And damn it, Mitch, I just need you—and that's hard for me to say."

"I hope it gets easier, because I like hearing it. We'll keep things as they are for now."

"Thank you. When I got out of there." She shifted her gaze toward the bathroom. "When I got out and pulled it together enough to think, I was so relieved you were downstairs. That I could tell you. That I wouldn't be alone tonight."

"Alone isn't even an option. Now." He scooped her off her feet. "You're getting into bed, bundling up."

"And you'll be . . ."

"Taking a closer look at the scene of the crime before I mop it up."

"I can take care of that, the mopping up."

"No." He tucked her in, firmly. "Give a little, get a little, Roz. Do what you're told, and stay in bed like a good girl. You've had a long and interesting day."

"Haven't I just?" And it felt wonderful to snuggle in the bed, knowing there was someone to look after some of the details. "I'm not sure what I'll have to give, but I'm going to ask you for a little something more."

"You want some soup? Something hot? Tea? Tea'd be better than coffee."

Look at you, she thought, Dr. Studly, with your black tie loose, and your tux shirt rolled up to the elbows, offering to make me soup. She reached for his hand as he sat on the side of the bed.

"No, but thanks. I'm going to ask you to keep what happened here between us for now."

"Roz, how does your mind work?" Frustration was so clear in his voice, on his face, she nearly smiled. "You were almost drowned in the tub by our resident ghost, and you don't want to mention it?"

"It's not that. We'll mention it, document it, go into great detail and discussion if need be. I just want to wait until after Stella's wedding. I just want a little calm. When Harper hears about this . . . Well, he's not going to take it well."

"Let me just say a big fat: Duh."

She laughed. "Everyone'll be upset, distracted, worried. And what good will it do? It happened, it's over. There are so many other things to deal with right now. I'm already going to be dealing with the fallout from what happened at the club. I can promise you word will be out, and it'll be a topic at my breakfast table tomorrow."

"And that bothers you."

"Actually, I think I'll enjoy it. I'm just small enough to bask in it. So let's leave this between us, until Stella's had her wedding. After that, we'll tell everyone, and deal with the fallout. But for the time being, we could use some undiluted happiness around here."

"Okay. I don't see that it'll matter."

"I appreciate it. I'm not so mad and scared now," she added, and slid down on the pillow. "I stopped her. I fought her off. I could do it again. That has to count for something."

Mitch leaned over to press his lips to her cheek. "Counts for a hell of a lot with me."

NINETEEN

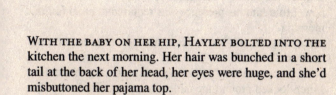

WITH THE BABY ON HER HIP, HAYLEY BOLTED INTO THE kitchen the next morning. Her hair was bunched in a short tail at the back of her head, her eyes were huge, and she'd misbuttoned her pajama top.

"I just talked to Lily's sitter," she announced to the room at large, "and her aunt belongs to the country club. She says Roz was in a fight last night."

"I certainly was not." Life could be heartwarmingly predictable, Roz thought and continued to spread jam thinly on a triangle of toast.

"What kinda fight?" Gavin wanted to know. "A punching fight?"

"I was not in a punching fight." Roz handed him the toast. "People exaggerate things, little man. It's the way of the world."

"Did you kick somebody in the face?"

Roz raised her eyebrows at Luke. "Of course not. You might say, metaphorically, I kicked somebody in the ass."

"What's met . . ."

"A metaphor's a fancy way of saying something's like something else. I could say I'm a cat full of canary this morning." She winked at Luke. "And that would mean I'm feeling very satisfied and smug. But I never laid a hand on him."

"Who?" Stella demanded.

"Bryce Clerk." The answer came from David as he poured more coffee. "My intelligence network is far-flung and faster than the speed of light. I heard about it last night, before eleven o'clock, Central Standard Time."

"And didn't tell anybody?" Hayley glowered at him as she strapped Lily in her high chair.

"Actually, I was waiting for all to be present and accounted for before I brought it up. Ah, here comes Harper now. I told him his presence was required at breakfast this morning."

"Really, David, it's no big deal, and I need to get ready for work."

"On the contrary." Shaking his head over his coffee, Mitch looked around the table. "It was extraordinary. The woman," he said with a long look at Roz, "is extraordinary."

Under the table she took his hand, gave it a warm squeeze. A silent thanks for letting this play out without any of last night's horror marring the mood.

"What's up?" Harper demanded. "We're having omelettes? How come we're having omelettes?"

"Because your mama likes them, and she needs to recharge her energies after hauling out her can of Whoop Ass last night."

"Don't be ridiculous," Roz replied, even as a chuckle tickled the back of her throat.

"What about last night? What Whoop Ass?"

"See what you miss when you don't go to the club?" David told Harper.

"If somebody doesn't fill in the blanks soon, I'm going

to go crazy." Hayley gave Lily a sip-cup of juice and plopped down. "Spill, every deet."

"There's not that much to tell," Roz began.

"I'll tell it." Mitch returned Roz's bland look equably. "She'll leave stuff out. Now, some of this I pried out of her, because I wasn't there at the time, and some of the other I got from my son. But I'll tell it all in one piece—more impact."

He started with the brief stop by the Forresters' table, then moved to the bathroom scene, then dramatized the altercation between Roz and Bryce outside the lounge area.

"Oh, my God, they walked out while you were talking to that . . ." Hayley cleared her throat, amended her first thought as she remembered the children. "Man."

"His back was to them," Mitch filled in. "It was perfectly staged."

Hayley fed Lily bits of egg and gaped at Roz. "It's so cool. Like, I don't know, a sting."

"The timing was exquisite," Mitch agreed. "You should've seen your mother, Harper, cool and slick as an iceberg, and just as dangerous."

"This kitchen is full of metaphors this morning," Roz commented. "Isn't anyone going to work?"

"Seen her like that." Harper scooped up some omelette. "Scary."

"It happened I was in a position to see the reaction of the ladies behind them," Mitch said, "and it was beautiful. He's mouthing off, bragging about how he can keep screwing around, the phone calls, the credit cards, and so on, and nobody'll pin him. He's insulting Quill, calling Mandy stupid. Utterly full of himself, and Roz just stands there—he doesn't even know she's just brought the ax down on his neck. She doesn't flick an eyelash, just keeps prompting him to say more and more until the son of a . . ." He remembered the kids. ". . . gun is buried in his own words.

Then, then, when it's done, she just waves a hand, so he turns and sees they're behind him. And she strolls away. It was beautiful."

"I hope they fell on him like dogs," Stella said under her breath.

"Close enough. Apparently, he tried to talk his way out of it, convince them that it was all a mistake, but the blonde, she's hysterical. Screaming, crying, slapping at him. The other goes straight to her husband, fills him in, so he knows it was Bryce's vindictiveness that lost him one of his top clients. He loses it—according to my son—and bulls his way to Bryce and punches him. People are jumping up, glasses are crashing, the blonde jumps on Clerk and starts biting and scratching."

"Holy cow," Gavin whispered, awed.

"They had to drag her off, and while they were, Quill took another shot, and they had to drag *him* off."

"I wish I'd seen that." Harper rose to get his choice of morning caffeine and came back to the table with a can of Coke. "I really do."

"People were running for cover, or pushing to get closer to the action," Mitch continued. "Slipping on olives from martinis, sliding around in salmon mousse or whatever, knocking over tables. They were at the point of calling the cops when in-house security broke it up."

"Where were you?" Hayley wondered.

"I was on the terrace making out with Roz. Dancing with Roz," he corrected with a wink. "We had a decent view through the doors and windows."

"It'll be the talk of the town for some time," Roz concluded. "As far as I'm concerned, all of them got just what they deserved. A bellyful of embarrassment. Now, I don't know about the rest of you, but I've got to get to work."

"Wait, wait, what about Bryce?" Hayley forked up some eggs for herself. "You can't leave us hanging."

"I couldn't say, but I suspect he'll scamper out of Shelby County with his tail between his legs. I don't think he'll be around anymore."

"That's it?" Hayley wondered. "You're not going to—" She broke off, wiped Lily's face. "That's good. It's good he's gone."

Roz ruffled both boys' hair, then got up to lay a kiss on the top of Lily's head. "I'll be giving the police my statement regarding possible charges for fraud this afternoon, as will Mitch, who heard everything Bryce said. I imagine they'll speak with the others who heard him flapping. Then we'll see what happens next."

"Even better," Hayley said with a smile. "Even much better."

"I don't punch or kick people in the face, at least not to date. But I don't get pushed around for long, either."

She walked out, pleased, even comforted, that the day had begun with laughter instead of worry.

ROZ STOOD ON THE LITTLE SLOPE AT THE EDGE OF HER woods and studied the spread and form of In the Garden. There were wonderful blocks of color, tender spring green, bold pinks, exotic blues, cheery yellows, and hot, hot reds.

The old, time-faded brown tables were full of those colors, displaying bedding plants in flats and pots. The ground itself erupted with it, blooming in an enthusiastic celebration of the season. The buildings looked fresh and welcoming, the greenhouses industrious. There were planters exploding with color and shape, hanging baskets dripping with them.

From this vantage she could see slices of the shrub area, and the ornamental trees, and all the way back to the field-grown, with its ruler-straight rows and muscular machines.

Everywhere she looked there were people, customers

and staff, bustling or browsing. Red wagons chugged along like little trains carrying their hopeful cargo. Flatbeds bumped over the gravel paths, and out to the parking area where their loads could be transferred into cars and trucks.

She could see the mountains of mulch, loose and bagged, the towers of pavers, the rails of landscape timbers.

Busy, busy, she thought, but with the charm she'd always envisioned in homey touches. The arbor already twined with morning glory vines, the curved bench strategically placed by a bubbling garden fountain, the flashy red of a hummingbird feeder dangling from a branch, the music of a wind chime circling gently in the breeze.

She should be down there, of course, doing some bustling herself, babying her stock, calculating inventory. Having a manager—even an exceptional one like Stella— didn't mean she shouldn't have her finger on every pulse.

But she'd wanted the air, the movement of it around her after hours in the denseness of the propagation house. And she wanted this view of what she'd built. What she'd worked for, gambled on.

Today, under a sky so freshly blue it might have been painted on glass, it was beautiful. And every hour she'd spent over all these years sweating, worrying, calculating, struggling was worth it.

It was solid and successful, and very much the sprawling garden she'd wanted to create. A business, yes, a business first and foremost, but a lovely one. One that reflected her style, her vision, her legacy.

If some insisted on seeing it as her hobby, let them. If some, even most, thought of her as the woman who'd glided around the country club in a gold gown and diamonds, that was fine. She didn't mind slipping on the glamour now and again. In fact, she could enjoy it.

But the truth of her, the core of her, was standing here,

wearing ancient jeans and a faded sweatshirt, a ballcap over her hair and scarred boots on her feet.

The truth of her was a working woman with bills to pay, a business to run, and a home to maintain. It was that woman she was proud of when she took the time to be proud. The Rosalind Harper of the country club and society set was a duty to her name. This, all the rest, was life.

She took a breath, braced herself, and deliberately pushed her mind in a specific direction. She would see what happened, and how both she and Amelia would deal with it.

So she thought: If this was life, hers to live, why couldn't she gamble yet again? Expand that life by taking into it, fully, the man who excited and comforted her, who intrigued and amused her?

The man who had somehow strolled through the maze that grief and work and duty and pride had built around her heart.

The man she loved.

She could live her life alone if need be, but what did it prove? That she was self-sufficient, independent, strong, and able. She knew those things, had been those things—and would always be those things.

And she could be courageous, too.

Didn't it take courage, wasn't it harder to blend one life with another, to share and to cope, to compromise than to live that life alone? It was work to live with a man, to wake up every day prepared to deal with routine, and to be open to surprises.

She'd never shied away from work.

Marriage was a different kettle at this stage of life. There would be no babies made between them. But they could share grandchildren one day. They wouldn't grow up together, but could grow old together.

They could be happy.

They always lie. They're never true.

Roz stood in the same spot, on a gentle rise at the edge of the woods. But In the Garden was gone. There were fields, stark with winter, barren trees, and the feel of ice on the air.

"Not all men," Roz said quietly. "Not always."

I've known more than you.

She walked across the fields, insubstantial as the mist that began to spread, a shallow sea, over the bare, black ground. Her white gown was filthy, as were her naked feet. Her hair was a tangle of oily gold around a face bright with madness.

Fear blew through Roz like a sudden, vicious storm. But she planted her feet. She'd ride it out.

The light had gone out of the day. Heavy clouds rolled over the sky, smothering the blue with black, a black tinged with violent green.

"I've lived longer than you," Roz said, and though she couldn't stop the shudder as Amelia approached, she stood her ground.

And learned so little. You have all you need. A home, children, work that satisfies you. What do you need with a man?

"Love matters."

There was a laugh, a wet chortle that screamed across Roz's nerves. *Love is the biggest lie. He will fuck you, and use you, and cheat and lie. He will give you pain until you are hollow and empty, until you are dried up and ugly. And dead.*

Pity stirred under the fear. "Who betrayed you? Who brought you to this?"

All. They're all the same. They're the whores, though they label us so. Didn't they come to me, ram their cocks into me, while their wives slept alone in their saintly beds?

"Did they force you? Did—"

Then they take what's yours. What was mine!

She slammed both fists into her belly, and the force of the rage, the grief, and the fury knocked Roz back two full steps.

Here was the storm, spewing out of the sky, bursting out of the ground, swirling though the fog and into the filthy air. It clogged Roz's lungs as if she were breathing mud.

She heard the crazed screams through it.

Kill them all! Kill them all in their sleep. Hack them to bits, bathe in their blood. Take back what's mine. Damn them, damn them all to hell!

"They're gone. They're dust." Roz tried to shout, but could barely choke out the words. "Am I what's left?"

The storm stopped as abruptly as it began, and the Amelia who stood in the calm was one who sang lullabies to children. Sad and pale in her gray dress.

You're mine. My blood. She held out a hand, and red welled in the palm. *My bone. Out of my womb, out of my heart. Stolen, ripped away. Find me. I'm so lost.*

Then Roz was alone, standing on the springy grass at the edge of the woods with what she'd built spread out below her.

SHE WENT BACK TO WORK BECAUSE WORK STEADIED her. The only way she could wrap her mind around what happened at the edge of the woods was to do something familiar, something that kept her hands occupied while her brain sorted through the wonder of it.

She kept to herself because solitude soothed her.

Through the afternoon she divided more stock plants, rooted cuttings. Watered, fed, labeled.

When she was done, she walked home through the woods and raided her personal greenhouse. She planted cannas in a spot she wanted to dramatize, larkspur and primroses where she wanted more charm. In the shade, she added some ladybells and cranesbill for serenity.

Her serenity, she thought, could always be found here, in the gardens, in the soil, in the shadow of Harper House. Under that fresh blue sky she knelt on the ground, and studied what was hers.

So lovely with its soft yellow stone, its sparkling glass, its bridal white trim.

What secrets were trapped in those rooms, in those walls? What was buried in this soil she worked, season after season, with her own hands?

She had grown up here, as her father had, and his father, and those who'd come before. Generation after generation of shared blood and history. She had raised her children here, and had worked to preserve this legacy so that the children of her children would call this home.

Whatever had been done to pass all of this to her, she would have to know. And then accept.

Settled again, she replaced her tools, then went into the house to shower off the day.

She found Mitch working in the library.

"Sorry to interrupt. There's something I need to talk to you about."

"Good, I need to talk to you, too." He swiveled away from his laptop, found a file in the piles on the desk.

"You go first," she told him.

"Hmm? Oh, fine." He scooped a hand through his hair, took off his glasses. Gestures she knew now meant he was organizing his thoughts.

"I've done just about all I can do here," he began. "I could spend months more on your family history, filling in details, moving back generations. In fact, I plan to do just that. But regarding the purpose for which you hired me, I'm at an impasse. She wasn't family, Roz. Not a Harper," he amended. "Not by birth, not through marriage. Absolutely

none of the data—names, dates, births, marriages, deaths—
nothing I have places a woman named Amelia in this
house, or in the Harper family. No woman of her approximate age died in this house during the time period we've
pinpointed."

"I see." She sat, wishing vaguely she'd thought to get
coffee.

"Now, if Stella is mistaken regarding the name—"

"She isn't." Roz shook her head. "It's Amelia."

"I agree. But there's no Amelia Harper, by birth, by
marriage, in any record. Oddly enough, considering the
length of time this house has stood here, there's no record
of any female in her twenties or thirties who died here. In
the house. Older or younger, yes, a few."

He set the file on top of a pile. "Ah, one of the most entertaining deaths to occur here was back in 1859, one of
your male ancestors, a Beauregard Harper, who broke his
neck, and several other bones, falling off the second floor
terrace. From the letters I've read describing the event,
Beau was up there with a woman not his wife engaged in a
sexual romp that got a little overenthusiastic. He went over
the rail, taking his date with him. He was dead when members of the household reached him, but being a portly fel-
low, he broke the fall of the female houseguest, who landed
on top of him and only suffered a broken leg."

"And terminal embarrassment, I imagine."

"Must have. I have the names of the women, the Harper
women, who died here listed for you. I have some records
on female servants who died here, but none fit the parame-
ters. I got some information from the Chicago lawyer I told
you about."

He began to dig for another file. "The descendant of
the housekeeper during Reginald Harper's time. She actually discovered she had three ancestors who worked
here—the housekeeper, the housekeeper's uncle who was

a groundsman, and a young cousin who served as a kitchen maid. From this, I've been able to get you a detailed history of that family as well. While none of it applies, I thought you'd like to have it."

"Yes, I would."

"The lawyer's still looking for data when she has time, she's entrenched now. We could get lucky."

"You've done considerable work."

"You'll be able to look at the charts and locate your great-great-uncle's second cousin on his mother's side, and get a good sense of his life. But that doesn't help you."

"You're wrong." She studied the mountain of files, and the board, crowded with papers and photos and handwritten charts behind Mitch. "It does help me. It's something I should have seen to a long time ago. I should have known about the unfortunate and adulterous Beau, and the saloon-owning Lucybelle, and all the others you've brought to life for me."

She rose to go to the board and study the faces, the names. Some were as familiar as her own, and others had been virtual strangers to her.

"My father, I see now, was more interested in the present than the past. And my grandfather died while I was so young, I don't remember having him tell me family stories. Most of what I got was from my grandmother, who wasn't a Harper by birth, or from older cousins. I'd go through the old papers now and again, always meaning to make time to do more, read more. But I didn't."

She stepped back from the board. "Family history, everyone who came before matters, and until recently I haven't given them enough respect."

"I agree with the first part, but not the second. This house shows the great respect you have for your family. Essentially, what I'm telling you is I can't find her for you. I believe, from what I've observed, what I feel, Amelia is your ancestor. But she's not your family. I won't find her name in family documents. And I don't believe she was a servant here."

"You don't."

"Consider the time, the era, the societal mores. As a servant, it's certainly possible that she was impregnated by a member of the family, but it's doubtful she would have been permitted to remain on staff, to remain in the house during her pregnancy. She would've been sent away, given monetary compensation—maybe. But it doesn't hold for me."

After one last glance at the board, she walked back to her chair and sat. "Why not?"

"Reginald was head of the house. All the information I have on him indicates he was excessively proud, very aware of what we could say was his lofty standing in this area. Politics, business, society. To be frank, Roz, I don't see him banging the parlor maid. He'd have been more selective. Certainly, said banging could have been done by a relative, an uncle, a brother-in-law, a cousin. But my gut tells me the connection with Amelia's tighter than that."

"Which leaves?"

"A lover. A woman not his wife, but who suited his needs. A mistress."

She was silent for a long moment. "You know what I find interesting, Mitchell? That we've come, from different directions, to the same point. You've gone through so many reams of documents that it gives me a headache just to think of them. Phone calls, computer searches, courthouse searches. Graphs and charts and Christ only knows. And by doing all that you've not only given me a picture of my family I've never looked at, people whose names I didn't know, but who are, in a very real sense, responsible for my life. But you've eliminated dozens of possibilities, dozens of perhaps as to who this poor woman was, so that we can whittle it down to the right answer. Do you think, when we do, she'll have peace?"

"I don't know the answer to that. Why are you so sad? It rips me to see you so sad."

"I'm not entirely sure. This is what happened today," she said, and told him.

"I was so afraid." She took a long breath. "I was afraid the night she locked us out of the children's room, and when you and I came in from the terrace and she had that fit of temper, tossing things around. I was afraid that night in the tub, when she held me under. I thought I wouldn't be that afraid again. But today, today when I stood there watching her walk toward me over the field, through the fog, I was petrified. I saw her face, the madness in it, a kind of insane purpose. The sort, I think now, that overcomes even death."

She gave herself a little shake. "I know how that sounds, but I think that's what she's done, somehow. She's overcome death with madness, and she can't break free."

"She didn't touch you this time. She didn't hurt you?"

Roz shook her head. "Not even at the peak of her rage. I couldn't breathe—felt like I was drawing in dirt, but part of that might've been sheer panic on my part. She spoke of killing, bathing in blood. There's never been any talk of murder in this house, but I wonder—oh, God, could they have killed her? One of my family?"

"She was the one talking of doing murder," he reminded her, "not of being murdered."

"True, but you can't trust a crazy woman to have all the facts straight. She said I was her blood. Whether it's true or not, she believes it." She took a deep breath. "So do you."

He got up from the desk to come around to her. Taking her hands, he drew her out of the chair and into his arms. "What do you believe?"

Comfort, she thought as she rested her head on his shoulder. There could be such comfort in a man if you allowed yourself to take it. "She has my father's eyes. I saw it at the end today. I've never seen it before, maybe never let myself. Did he take her child, Mitch, my great-grandfather? Could he have been so cold?"

"If all this is fact, she could have given the baby up. They might have had an arrangement, and she came to regret it. There are still a lot of possibilities."

"I want to know the truth now. Have to know it, whatever it takes."

She drew back, managed a smile. "Just how the hell do we go about finding a woman who may have been my great-grandfather's lover?"

"We have a first name, an approximate age, and we assume she lived in the Memphis area. We start with that."

"Is that natural optimism, or are you trying to smooth my feathers?"

"Some of both."

"All right, then. I'm going to go pour myself a glass of wine. Do you want anything?"

"I could use about a gallon of water to offset the five gallons of coffee I'd downed today. I'll come with you." He draped an arm around her shoulders as they walked to the kitchen.

"I might have to put this aside until after Stella and Logan's wedding. It's snuck right up on me. Seems to me, however demanding the dead may be, the living ought to have priority." She got out a bottle of water and a fresh lemon. "I can't believe those boys aren't going to be part of the household in a few more days."

She poured and sliced, then offered him the glass.

"Thanks. I think they'll be around enough you'll feel like they are."

"I like to think." She poured her wine, but the phone rang before she took the first sip. "Where is David anyway?" she asked, and answered herself.

She listened for a moment, then smiled slowly at Mitch. "Hello, Jane," she said and lifted her wine in a toast.

"THIS IS SO EXCITING. IT'S LIKE A SPY THRILLER OR something." Hayley bounced on her toes as she, Roz, and Stella rode the elevator up to Clarise Harper's apartment. "I mean, we spend the morning getting manicures and pedicures, and the afternoon sneaking around to hunt up secret documents. It's totally glamorous."

"Say that later if we're arrested and spending the night in jail with Big Bertha," Stella suggested. "If Logan has to marry me through jailhouse bars tomorrow, I'm going to be royally pissed."

"I told you not to come," Roz reminded her.

"And miss this?" After a bracing breath, Stella stepped off the elevator. "I may be fussy, but I'm no coward. Besides, Hayley has a point. It is exciting."

"Going into a crabby old woman's overfurnished apartment and taking away what's rightfully mine—along with a scared little rabbit—doesn't strike me as exciting. Jane could have gotten them out herself, saved us the trip. There's enough to do with the wedding tomorrow."

"I know, and I appreciate, so much, you giving us the day off so we could primp." On impulse, Stella kissed Roz's cheek. "We'll work twice as hard after the wedding to make up for it."

"You might just have to. Now just pray the old ghoul is out getting her hair permed, as advertised, or this will be ugly."

"Don't you sort of hope it is?" Hayley began, but the door creaked open. Jane peeked out through the crack.

"I . . . I didn't expect anyone but you, Cousin Rosalind. I don't know if we should—"

"They work for me. They're friends." With no patience

for dithering or ado, Roz nudged the door open, stepped inside. "Jane, this is Stella and Hayley. Jane, did you pack all your things?"

"Yes, there isn't much. But I've been thinking, she's going to be so upset when she gets home and finds me gone. I don't know if I should—"

"This place is as horrible as ever," Roz observed. "Positively reeks of lavender. How do you stand it? That's one of our Dresden shepherdesses there, and that Meissan cat, and . . . screw it. Where are the diaries?"

"I didn't get them out. I didn't feel right—"

"Fine. Give me the key, show me where, and I'll get them. Let's not waste time, Jane," Roz added when the girl simply stood biting her bottom lip. "You have a new apartment waiting, a new job starting bright and early Monday morning. You can take them or leave them, your choice. But I'm not leaving this lavender-stinking apartment without what's mine by right. So you can give me the key, or I'll just start tossing things around until I find what I'm after."

"Oh, God. I feel sick." Jane dug into her pocket, pulled out an ornate brass key. "The desk in her room, top drawer." Pale as glass, she gestured vaguely. "I'm dizzy."

"Snap out of it," Roz suggested. "Stella, why don't you help Jane get her things?"

"Sure. Come on, Jane."

Trusting Stella to deal with the situation, Roz turned to Hayley. "Watch the door," she ordered.

"Oh, boy, hot damn. Lookout man."

Despite herself, Roz chuckled all the way into Clarise's bedroom. There was more lavender here, with an undertone of violets. The bed had a padded headboard of gold tufted silk, with an antique quilt Roz knew damn well had come out of Harper House. As had the occasional table by the window, and the art nouveau lamp.

"Pilfering old bitch," Roz grumbled and went directly to the desk. She turned the key, and couldn't quite hold back the gasp when she saw the stacks of old leather-bound journals.

"This is going to be a kick right in your bony ass," she decided and, opening the satchel she carried over her shoulder, carefully slid the books inside.

To make certain she had them all, she opened the rest of the drawers, riffled without qualm through the nightstands, the bureau, the chest of drawers.

Though she felt silly, she wiped off everything she'd touched. She wouldn't put it past Clarise to call the cops and claim burglary. Then she left the key, plainly in sight, on top of the desk.

"Stella took her down," Hayley announced when Roz stepped out. "She was shaking so hard we thought she might have like a seizure unless she got out of here. Roz, the poor thing only had one suitcase. She got everything she owned into one suitcase."

"She's young. She'll have plenty of time to get more. Did you touch anything in here?"

"No. I thought, you know, fingerprints."

"Smart girl. Let's go."

"You got them?"

Roz patted the satchel. "Easy as taking candy from a baby, which Clarise has been known to do."

It wasn't until they'd settled Jane into her apartment and were well on the way home that Roz noticed Hayley was uncharacteristically silent.

"Don't tell me you're having second thoughts, guilty qualms, whatever."

"What? Oh, no. No. Those journals are yours. If it'd been me, I'd have taken the other things that belonged to Harper House, too. I was thinking about Jane. I know she's younger than me, but not all that much. And she seems so,

I don't know, fragile and scared about everything. Still, she did a brave thing, I guess."

"She didn't have what you had," Roz said. "Your gumption, for one, and a lot of that's just the luck of the draw. But she didn't have a father like yours. One who loved her and taught her, and gave her a secure and happy home. She doesn't feel strong and attractive, and you know you are."

"She needs a good haircut, and better clothes. Hey, Stella, wouldn't it be fun to make her over?"

"Down, girl."

"No, really. Later when we've got the time. But I was thinking, too, how she looked when she walked into that little apartment. How grateful and surprised she was that you'd sent some things over, Roz. Just basic things like a couch and bed, and food for the kitchen. I don't guess anyone's ever done anything for her, just to be decent. I felt so sorry for her, and happy for her at the same time, the way she looked around, all dazzled and weepy."

"Let's see what she does with it."

"You gave her the chance to do something. Just like you did with me, and Stella, too."

"Oh, don't start."

"I will. We all came to this corner, and you're the one who gave us a hand to get around it and start down the road. Now Jane's got a place of her own, and a new job. I've got a beautiful baby and a wonderful home for her. And Stella's getting married tomorrow."

She began to sniffle, and Roz rolled her eyes toward the rearview mirror. "I *really* mean don't start."

"I can't help it. I'm so happy. Stella's getting married tomorrow. And y'all are my best friends in the whole, wide world."

Stella passed tissues over the seat, and kept one out for herself.

* * *

THERE WERE SIXTEEN JOURNALS IN ALL, FIVE OF HER grandmother Elizabeth Harper's, and nine written by her great-grandmother Beatrice. And each was filled, first page to last.

There were some sketches as well, Roz noted on a quick flip-through—her grandmother's work. It made her feel warm to look at them.

But she didn't need Mitch to tell her that even though they had the books, the job of reading them and finding anything pertaining to Amelia was daunting.

"They're not dated." Rubbing her eyes, Stella leaned back on the sofa in the parlor. "From what I can tell at a quick glance, Beatrice Harper didn't use a journal per year, but simply filled each, however much time that involved, and moved to the next."

"So we'll sort them as best we can," Mitch said, "divide them up, and read each through."

"I hope I get a juicy one." Due to the circumstances, David had put together an elaborate high tea, and now helped himself to a scone.

"I'll want them all accounted for, at all times. But we have a wedding tomorrow. Stella, I don't want you to overdo it. I'm not going to be responsible for you getting married with circles under your eyes. Who could that be?" Roz said when the doorbell rang. "Everyone's here. No, sit, David. I'll get it."

She walked out with Parker prancing at her heels, barking as if to let her know he was on the job. When she opened the door, Roz's eyebrows winged up. And her smile was sharp as a blade.

"Why, Cousin Rissy, what an unpleasant surprise."

"Where is that useless girl, and my property?"

"I haven't the vaguest idea what you're talking about, and

care even less." She noted her aunt had hired a sedan, and driver, for the trip from the city. "I suppose good manners dictate I ask you in, but I warn you, I'm not above arranging a strip search before you go—which would be traumatic for all parties—so don't even think about taking anything."

"You are, and always have been, a rude and dislikable creature."

"Isn't that funny?" Roz stepped back so Clarise could march into the foyer with her cane. "I was thinking the same thing about you. We're in the parlor, having tea." Roz stepped to the doorway. "Cousin Rissy is paying a call. Isn't that unfortunate? You may remember my son, Harper. You always enjoyed complaining about him incessantly on your other visits. And David, Harper's childhood friend who tends Harper House, and would have counted the silverware."

"I'm not interested in your sass."

"I have so little else to offer you. I believe you've also made the acquaintance of Dr. Carnegie."

"I have, and will be speaking to my lawyer about him."

He smiled broadly. "It's Mitchell Carnegie. Two els."

"This is Logan Kitridge, friend, neighbor, and employee, who is the fiancé of Ms. Stella Rothchild, who manages my garden center."

"I have no interest in your motley arrangement of employees, or your questionable habit of crowding them into Harper House."

"These are her children, Gavin and Luke, and their dog, Parker," Roz continued as if Clarise hadn't spoken. "And a young cousin of mine, on the Ashby side, also an employee, Hayley Phillips, and her beautiful daughter, Lily. I believe that covers everyone. David, I suppose you'd better pour Clarise a cup of tea."

"I don't want tea, particularly any prepared and poured by a homosexual."

"It's not catching," David offered, unfazed.

"Why, David, you're a homosexual?" Roz feigned surprise. "How amazing."

"I try to be subtle about it."

"Where is Jane?" Clarise demanded. "I insist on speaking to her this instant."

Roz picked up a tiny cookie and gave it to a delighted Lily. "And Jane would be?"

"You know very well. Jane Paulson."

"Oh, of course, Cousin Jane. I'm afraid she's not here."

"I won't tolerate your lies." At her tone, Parker sent up a warning growl. "And keep that horrible little dog away from me."

"He's *not* horrible." Gavin sprang up, and was immediately grabbed by his mother. "You're horrible."

"And if you're mean," Luke piped up, "he'll bite you, because he's a good dog."

"Gavin, you and Luke take Parker outside. Go on, now." Stella gave Gavin a little squeeze.

"Get the Frisbee," Logan suggested, with a wink for the boys. "I'll come out in a few minutes."

Gavin picked up the dog, scowling on the way out, and Luke stopped at the door. "We don't like you," he said and strode on his sturdy little legs behind his brother.

"I see your employees are no better equipped to raise well-mannered children than you, Rosalind."

"Apparently not. I'm so proud. Well, since you won't have tea, and I can't help you regarding Jane, you must want to be on your way."

"Where are the journals?"

"Journals? Do you mean the journals written by my grandmother and my great-grandmother that were taken out of this house without my permission?"

"Your permission was not required. I'm the oldest living Harper, and those journals are mine by right."

"We certainly disagree on that, but I can help you as to their location. They're back where they belong—morally, legally, and ethically."

"I'll have you arrested."

"Oh, please, try. Won't that be fun?" The dangerous iceberg was back as she sat on the arm of a chair, crossed her legs casually. "Won't you just relish having your name, the Harper family name, smeared all over the press, talked about all over the county?" Her eyes went hot, in direct contrast to the chill of her voice. "Because I'll see that it is. I'll grant every interview and discuss the whole unseemly mess over cocktails at every opportunity. Such things don't concern me."

She paused, leaning down to take the cookie Lily was holding up to her. "Why, thank you, sugar-pie. But you?" she said to Clarise. "I don't think you'll enjoy being the butt of gossip and innuendo and jokes. Particularly when it'll come to nothing. I have possession of what is my legal property."

She picked Lily up, set her on her knee, and gave the cookie back while the room remained silent but for Clarise's outraged breaths. Roz decided it was one of the rare times she could actually, and accurately, describe a scene with the phrase *her bosom heaved.*

It was glorious.

"If you want to have the police question how I came to regain possession, I'll be happy to tell them. And I hope you enjoy explaining to them how you had what belongs to Harper House, and therefore me, locked away in your desk. Along with several other expensive pieces that are catalogued as Harper House property."

"You'll dirty the family name!" Her face dark with rage, Clarise stepped forward. "You have no right. You have no business digging into what is best left buried."

Calmly Roz passed the baby to Mitch, where Lily

babbled and generously offered to share her mangled cookie. She heard Mitch's murmured "Take her down, honey" as she got to her feet. "What are you afraid of? What did they do to her? Who was Amelia?"

"Nothing but a tramp, a low-class whore who got no more than she deserved. I knew, the minute you were born, that blood would tell in you. I see it has."

"So I am from her," Roz said quietly.

"I'll speak no more about it. It's a crime and a sin that a woman like you is mistress of this house. You have no right here, and never did. You're no-account, grasping, nothing but a blight on the family name. My grandmother would've set the dogs on you before she let your kind cross the threshold of Harper House."

"Okay, that's about enough." Before Roz could speak—and she had plenty to say—Harper was up and across the room. "You're leaving, and you're never coming through that door again."

"Don't you back-talk me, boy."

"I'm not eight anymore, and you're not welcome here. You think you can stand here and insult my mother? A woman with more class in one eyelash than you could cobble together out of every dried-up bone in your body? Now, I can show you the way out, or I can kick you out. Your choice."

"You're just like her."

"That's the first genuine thing you've said since you came in. This way, *Cousin* Rissy."

He took her arm and, though she tried to swat him away, led her out of the room.

There was a beat of silence, then Hayley's low whistle. "Go, Harper."

twenty

Upstairs in the sitting room, Mitch lifted Roz's feet into his lap, and began to rub. "Long day for you."

"Wasn't it just."

"You got in some mighty swings, Slugger."

"I did, but Harper sure did bat clean-up and knock it out of the park."

"I know I'm in love when my girl can talk in baseball analogies." He lifted her foot higher to kiss her ankle. "I'll take my share of the journals with me. I should be able to get a start on them tonight."

"You've had a long day yourself. After the wedding's soon enough." She tipped her head back, closed her eyes as his thumb pressed into her arch. "Besides, if you go, you'll stop rubbing my feet."

"I was hoping this would be a suitable bribe."

"You don't need a bribe. I was hoping you'd stay."

"It so happens I have my suit for the wedding out in the car."

Her eyes stayed closed; her lips curved. "I like a man who thinks ahead."

"I wasn't sure there'd be a place for a man in the house tonight. Wedding eve, female rituals."

"We started our rituals at the salon this morning, and we'll pick them up tomorrow. They're going to make a lovely family, aren't they?"

"They already do. I enjoyed watching those boys stand up to the old woman, and your elegantly executed shots. Followed by Harper's base-clearing run."

"We were all wonderfully rude, weren't we? Of course, she won't speak to you again. Won't help you with your book."

"I'm not worried about it. And—we'll call it postseason play—she's unlikely to be entertained by what I write about her."

"I will be. She knows. She knows who Amelia is, what happened to her. I suppose she always has. There's a possibility she destroyed any journals with a mention of her—a small one, as anything pertaining to Harper House is sacrosanct to her. But it's something we should be prepared for."

"We just need a few seeds. I can propagate from there."

She opened her eyes. "Aren't you clever? I know I'm in love when my guy can talk in gardening terms."

"You haven't seen anything yet. Rosalind, I'm seduced by your feet."

"My feet?"

"Crazy about them. I just never know . . ." Slowly he drew off one of her thick socks. "What I'll find. Ah." He brushed a finger over her toenails, painted pale shell pink, with just a hint of glitter. "Surprise, surprise."

"They're often one of my little secrets."

He lifted her feet, traced his lips down her arch. "I love secrets."

There was something powerful about pleasuring a strong woman, watching her, feeling her surrender to sensation. A tiny quiver, a quiet sigh was unspeakably erotic when you knew the woman yeilded to no one.

From attraction to passion, from passion to love. It was a journey he'd never planned to make again. Yet here he was. When he touched her, he knew she was the woman, the only woman he wanted to spend his life with. He wondered how he'd reached this point in his life without knowing, and needing, her scent, the sound of her voice, the fascinating textures of her skin.

When she rose up, locking her arms around him, fixing her mouth warmly on his, his heart nearly burst.

"I can see you in the dark," he told her. "I can hear you when you're miles away."

The small sound she made was pure emotion as she sank into him.

She held tight, tight a moment with her head on his shoulder, her heart knocking against his. How love could be so many different things at so many different times, she'd never understand. She could only be grateful for it, grateful to have found this love at this time.

She would cherish it. Cherish him.

She eased back to take his face in her hands, so their eyes met. "It's harder when you come into something like this, knowing more, having more behind you. But at the same time, it's more itself. Fuller, richer. I want you to know that's how I feel with you. Full and rich."

"I don't think I can do without you, Rosalind."

"Good." She touched her lips to his. "Good," she repeated and slid slow and deep into the kiss.

She curled around him, breathing him in. His hair, his skin. Here, unbearable tenderness, and there, a simmering excitement. While her mouth clung to his, her fingers flipped open the buttons of his shirt, lifted her arms so he could draw her away and they could press together, warm flesh to warm flesh.

He pressed her back onto the couch, let his hands and lips roam over her. Breasts and shoulders and throat, down to that impossibly narrow torso.

There were signs of the children she'd borne, the men she'd made. For a moment he lay his cheek on her belly, amazed he'd been given the gift of a woman so vital, so potent.

She stroked his back, gliding on the shimmer that coated her senses, lazily working her hands between them to unbutton his jeans. She found him hard and hot, and felt her own muscles bunch and quiver in anticipation.

Now they tugged at clothes, and once again she rose up. This time she straddled him, staring into those bottle-green eyes as she slowly, slowly took him inside her.

"Ah. God." She gripped the back of the couch, her fingers digging in.

With a brutal hold on control, she rode, hips moving in a tortuously gentle rhythm, strong thighs caging him as she set the pace.

She could feel his hands on her, a desperate grip on her hips as he struggled to let her lead. Then a smooth caress up her back, a slick stroke to cup her breasts.

She tightened around him, pressing her mouth to his when she came so he could taste her moan. He was buried in her, their arms locked around each other, when she threw her head back. When her eyes, glassy with arousal, finally closed.

And she whipped him, joyfully, to the finish.

ROZ WOKE AT FOUR, TOO EARLY TO JOG, TOO LATE TO talk herself back to sleep. She lay awhile, in the quiet dark. It amazed her how quickly she'd gotten used to having

Mitch in her bed. She didn't feel crowded, or even surprised to have him sleeping beside her.

It felt more natural than she'd expected—not something
she had to adjust to, but something she'd discovered she no
longer wanted to do without.

She wondered why it didn't feel odd to wake with him,
to start the daily routine with another person in her space.
The bathroom shuffle, the conversation—or the silence—
while they dressed.

Not odd or strange, she decided, maybe because some
part of her had been waiting to make this unit again. She
hadn't looked for it, or sought it, hadn't pined without it.
In some ways, the years alone had helped make her the
woman she was. And that woman was ready to share the
rest of her life, her home, her family, with this man.

She slipped out of bed, moving quietly. Another change,
she realized. It had been a long time since she'd had to
worry about disturbing a sleeping mate.

She moved to her sitting room to choose one of the
journals. She ran her hand gently over one of her grandmother's. Those she would save for later, those she would
read for pleasure and for sentiment.

What she did now, she did for duty.

It took her less than fifteen minutes to conclude she and
her great-grandmother wouldn't have understood each other.

*Weather remains fine. Reginald's business keeps him
in New Orleans. I was unable to find the shade of
blue silk I'm seeking. The shops here are simply not
au courant. I believe we must arrange a trip to Paris.
Though it's imperative we engage another governess
for the girls before we do. This current woman is
entirely too independent. When I think of the money
spent on her salary, her room and board, I find
myself most dissatisfied by her service. Recently*

*I gave her a very nice day dress, which didn't suit me,
and which she accepted without a qualm. However,
when I ask for some small favor, she behaves very
grudgingly. Surely she has time to run a few simple
errands when there's nothing else on her plate but
minding the girls and teaching a few lessons.*

*I have the impression she considers herself above
her station.*

Roz stretched out her legs, flipped through pages. Most
of the entries were more of the same. Complaints, tidbits
about shopping, plans for parties, rehashes of parties attended. There was very little dealing with the children.

She set that one aside for later, picked up another. Skimming, she found an entry on dismissing a maid for giggling
in the hallway, another on a lavish ball. Then stopped, and
read more carefully when an entry caught her eye.

*I've miscarried again. Why is it as painful to lose a
child as to birth one? I'm exhausted. I wonder how
I can suffer through this process yet again in the
attempt to give Reginald the heir he so desperately
wants. He will want to lie with me again as soon as
I am able, and that ordeal will continue, I suspect,
until I conceive once more.*

*I can find no pleasure in it, nor in the girls who are
a daily reminder of what I have yet to accomplish.*

*At least, once I conceive yet again, I will be left
to myself for the months of waiting. It is my duty to
bear sons. I will not shirk my duty, and yet it seems
I am unable to bring forth anything but chattering
girls.*

*I want only to sleep and forget that I have failed,
once again, to provide my husband and this house
with the heir they both demand.*

Children as duty only, Roz thought. How sad. How must those little girls have felt, being failures because of their sex? Had there been any joy in this house during Beatrice's reign as its mistress, or had it all been duty and show?

Depressed, she considered switching to one of her grandmother's journals, but ordered herself to glance through one more.

> *I'm sick to death of that busybody Mary Louise Berker. You would think because she's managed to birth four sons, and is once again fat as a cow with yet another child, she knows all there is to know about conception and child-rearing. This is hardly the case. Her sons run around like wild Indians, and think nothing of putting their grubby little hands on the furniture in her parlor. And she just laughs and says* boys will be boys *when they and their scruffy dogs—three of them!—come romping in.*
>
> *She had the nerve to suggest I might see her doctor, and some* voodoo *woman. She swears she'll have the girl she pines for this time because she went to this hideous person and bought a charm to hang over her bed.*
>
> *It's bad enough she dotes on those ruffians in a most unseemly way, and often in public, but it's beyond belief that she would speak to me about such matters, all under the guise of friendship and concern.*
>
> *I could not take my leave soon enough.*

Roz decided she'd have liked Mary Louise. And wondered if the Bobby Lee Berker she'd gone to high school with was a descendant.

Then she saw it, and her heart took a hard jump into her throat.

*I have locked myself in my room. I will speak to
no one. The humiliation I have been dealt is beyond
bearing. For all these years I have been a dutiful
wife, an exceptional hostess, I have overseen the
staff of this house without complaint, and worked
tirelessly to present the proper image for our societal
equals and Reginald's business associates.*

*I have, as wives must, overlooked his private
affairs, satisfied that he was always discreet.*

Now this.

*He arrived home this evening and requested that
I come to the library so he could speak to me
privately. He told me he had impregnated one of his
mistresses. This is not a conversation that should
take place between husband and wife, and when this
was my response, he brushed it aside as if it was no
matter.*

As if I am no matter.

*I am told that I will be required to create the
illusion that I am expecting. I am told that if this
creature delivers a son, it will be brought into our
home, it will be given the Harper name and raised
here. As his son. As my son.*

*If it is a girl, it will be of no matter. I will have
another "miscarriage" and that will be that.*

*I refused. Of course I refused. To take a whore's
child into my home.*

*Then he gave me this choice. Accept his decision,
or he would divorce me. One way or the other, he will
have a son. He prefers that I remain his wife, that
neither of us are exposed to the scandal of divorce,
and he will compensate me well for this one thing. If I
refuse, it will be divorce and shame, and I will be sent
away from the home I have cared for, the life I have
made.*

So there is no choice.

I pray that this slatern delivers a girl child. I pray it dies. That she dies. That they all burn in Hell.

Roz's hands shook. Though she wanted to read on, she stood first, walked to the terrace doors. She needed air. With the book in her hand, she stood outside, breathing in the early morning.

What kind of man had this been? To have forced his illegitimate son on his wife. Even if he hadn't loved her, he should have respected her.

And what love could he have had for the child, to have subjected him to a woman who would never, could never, care for him as a mother? Who would always resent him? Even despise him?

And all to carry on the Harper name.

"Roz?"

She didn't turn when she heard Mitch's voice behind her. "I woke you. I thought I was quiet."

"You were. You just weren't there."

"I found something. I started reading through some of the journals. I found something."

"Whatever it is, it's upset you."

"I'm sad, and I'm angry. And I'm surprised that I'm not surprised. I found an entry . . . No, you should read it for yourself." She turned now, held the book out, open to where she'd stopped. "Take it into the sitting room. I just need another minute here."

"All right." He took the book, then, because there was something in her eyes that pulled at his heart, he cupped her chin in his free hand and kissed her softly.

She turned back to the view, to the grounds and the gardens going silver with oncoming dawn. The home that had been her family's for generations. Had it been worth it? she wondered. Had the pain and humiliation one man had caused been worth holding this ground under one name?

She walked back in, sat across from Mitch. "Is this where you stopped?" he asked her.

"I needed to absorb it, I guess. How cruel he was to her. She wasn't an admirable woman, not from what I've read in her own diaries. Selfish, self-absorbed, petty. But she deserved better than this. You haven't given me a son, so I'll get one elsewhere. Accept it, or leave. She accepted."

"You don't know that yet."

"We know." She shook her head. "We'll read the rest, but we know."

"I can go through this, and the others, later. Myself."

"No, let's do it now. It's my legacy, after all. See what you can find, will you? I'm going down to make coffee."

When she came back, she noted he'd gotten his reading glasses. He looked like a rumpled scholar, she thought, pulling an all-nighter. Shirtless, jeans unbuttoned, hair mussed.

That same tenderness floated over her, like a balm over the ache in her heart.

"I'm glad you were here when I found this." She set the tray down, then leaned over, kissed the top of his head. "I'm glad you're here."

"There's more." He reached up for her hands. "Do you want me to summarize?"

"No, read her words. I want to hear her words."

"There's snippets here and there, her thoughts on this worked into daily entries. Her humiliation and the rage under it. She made him pay in the only way she knew, by spending his money lavishly, by shutting him out of her bed, taking trips."

"A stronger woman would have thumbed her nose," she said, pouring coffee, "taken her children and left him. But she didn't."

"No, she didn't. Times were different for women then."

"The times may have been different, but right's still right."

She set down his coffee, and this time sat beside him. "Read it, Mitch. I want to know."

"He brought the bastard home, with some trollop of a wet nurse he brought in from one of his country holdings. Not the mother, he says, who remains in the house in town where he keeps her. He has his son at last, a squalling thing wrapped in a blanket. I did not look at it, and will not. I know only that he has paid the doctor to keep him quiet, and that I am required to continue to remain in the house, receiving no callers for another few days.

"He has brought this thing home in the dead of night, so the servants will believe I delivered it. Or will pretend to believe it. He has named it. Reginald Edward Harper, Jr."

"My grandfather," Roz murmured. "Poor little boy. He grew to be a fine man. A kind of miracle, I suppose, given his beginnings. Is there anything on his mother?"

"Not in this book, though I'll go through it more carefully."

"There will be more, in one of the other journals. She died here, Amelia did. At some point Beatrice must have seen or spoken with her, or dealt with her in some way."

"I'll start looking now."

"No." Tired, she rubbed at her eyes. "No, there's a wedding today. Today is for joy and fresh starts, not for grief and old secrets. We know enough for today."

"Rosalind, this in no way changes who you are."

"No, it doesn't. Of course it doesn't. But it makes me think, that for people like this . . . for people like Reginald and Beatrice, marriage was a practicality. Social standing, breeding, family backgrounds. Maybe there was some affection, or some attraction, but at its core, it was business. The business of maintaining families at a certain level. And children were just tools to accomplish that. How sad for them, and how tragic for the children. But today . . ."

She drew a deep breath. "Today we're seeing it shouldn't be that way. We're going to watch two people who love each other make promises, make a marriage, cement a family. I'm glad you're here, Mitch, and I'm glad we found this today. Because this wedding is just what I need now."

IT WAS THE PERFECT DAY FOR IT, TAILOR-MADE WITH candy-blue skies and balmy air scented with flowers. The gardens Logan and Stella had made bloomed in a lovely array of color and shape.

There were chairs set up on the lawn, covered with pale peach drapes and forming an aisle where Stella would walk on her father's arm, toward Logan and her sons.

Roz turned from the window to watch Jolene fuss with the flowers in Stella's hair.

"You make a picture," she said. "Both of you."

"I'm going to start crying again." Jolene waved a hand in front of her face. "I can't count how many times I've repaired my makeup. I'm going to run out just for a minute, honey, check on your daddy."

"Okay." Stella waited until Jolene scurried out. "I was going to be mad and upset that my mother refused to come. Too much trouble to make the trip—not like it's my first time—and she wasn't going to sit around in the same space as *that* woman, which she continues to call Jolene even after all these years."

"Her loss, isn't it?"

"It is—and my gain, really. It's Jolene I want today

anyway. And you, and Hayley." Stella lifted her hand to touch the sapphires in her ears. "They're so perfect."

"They do the trick. Look at you." Feeling a little misty herself, Roz stepped closer to study her friend.

The dress was simple, a pale, pale blue with narrow straps, a straight bodice and a long skirt with a slight bell. There were two dahlias pinned in her curling red hair. One white, one blue. And her face was luminous, as a bride's was meant to be.

"I feel absolutely beautiful."

"You should. You are. I'm so happy for you."

"I'm not nervous anymore, not even a little jump in the belly." Stella pressed a hand to it as she blinked tears back. "I think about Kevin, my first wedding, the years we had together, the children we made together. And I know, in my heart, I know he's okay with this. Logan's a good man."

"A very good man."

"I made him wait almost a year." She let out a laughing breath. "Time's up. Roz, thank you for all you've done."

"You're welcome. Ready to get married?"

"I'm absolutely ready."

It was sweet, Roz thought, and it was lovely. The man and woman, the young boys, coming together in the gardens of the home they'd share. Logan, big and strong and handsome in his suit, Stella, bright and beautiful in her bride dress, and the children grinning even when Logan kissed the bride.

The guests broke into spontaneous applause as Logan swept Stella off her feet and spun her in a circle. And Harper topped off the moment by popping the first bottle of champagne.

"I don't know when I've seen a happier couple," Mitch commented, and tapped his glass to Roz's. "Or a prettier family. You do good work."

"I didn't do anything."

"It's like a family tree. These two come from one of

your branches. May not be blood, but it comes to the same. It's their connection to you that brought them together. They did the rest, but the connection started it."

"That's a nice thought. I'll take it." She lifted her glass, sipped. "There's something I want to talk to you about a little later. I wanted to wait to bring it up until after Stella had her day. A wedding day, by rights, belongs to the bride."

"What's it about?"

"I guess you could say it's about connections." She rose on her toes to kiss him. "We'll talk about it after we go home. Fact is, I've got to run back real quick. With all this commotion I forgot the special bottle of champagne I have back home for the bride and groom and their wedding night."

"I can run get it."

"No, it'll be quicker if I do. I'll be back in fifteen minutes."

As she got to the car, she stopped as Hayley called her.

"Roz! Hold up. Is it okay if we ride with you?" A little breathless, she stopped at the car with a crying Lily in her arms. "I've got a cranky girl here, needs a little nap. But she won't go down. Car ride'll do the trick. We can take mine, it has the car seat."

"Sure. It's going to be a quick run, though."

"That's all right." She walked to her own car, battled an objecting Lily into the seat. "Rides always calm her down, and if she goes to sleep, I can just sit out here with her until she wakes up. Then we'll both have a better time at the party."

As advertised, the crying stopped, and Lily's head began to droop before they were down the lane to the main road.

"Works like a charm," Hayley said.

"Always did with mine, too. She looks so sweet in her pink party dress."

"Everything looked so beautiful. If I ever get married,

I want it to be just like that. Springtime, flowers, friends, shiny faces. I always thought I wanted a big church extravaganza, but this was so romantic."

"Just right for them. It's nice to— Slow down. Stop the car!"

"What? What's the . . . oh, my God."

They looked over at In the Garden. Roz had closed for the day so everyone could enjoy the wedding. But someone, she could see, had been there. Someone, she thought, still was.

Several of her outdoor displays were overturned, and a car was parked sideways, crushing one of her beds.

"Call the police," Roz snapped and was already out of the car. "You and the baby get out of here now. Go back to Logan's right now."

"Don't. Don't go in there now."

"This is my place." And she was already running.

Her flowers, she thought. Plants she'd started from seed or cutting, babied along, nurtured and loved. Destroyed, beaten down, ripped to pieces.

Innocent, she thought as she took only a moment to grieve for the loss and waste. Innocent beauty crushed to nothing.

There would be payment made.

She heard glass shatter, and charged around the back of the main building. She saw Bryce, swinging a baseball bat at another window.

"You son of a bitch."

He whirled. She saw the shock first, then the rage. "Thought you were busy today. Figured I'd be done before you came by."

"You figured wrong."

"Doesn't matter a damn." He slammed the bat into the next window. "Time you learned a lesson. You think you can humiliate me in public? Set the cops on me?"

"You humiliated yourself, and if you don't put that down and get the hell off my property, I'm going to do more than set the cops on you."

"Such as? Just you and me now, isn't it?" He slapped the bat against his palm, took a step toward her. "Do you know what you cost me?"

"I've got a general idea, and it's going to be more. Trespassing, destruction of property."

He didn't use the bat, though she saw in his eyes, just for an instant, that he considered it. But he swung out with his hand, cracking her across the cheekbone and sending her sprawling.

That was all it took. She was up like a flash and launching herself at him. She didn't use nails and teeth as Mandy had. She used her fists, and took him so by surprise, he fell to his knees before he managed to block her, and strike out at her again.

But the blow didn't land.

The wind came up so fast, so cold, so furious, that it flung Roz back against the building. Her head rapped sharply against wood so she had to shake it clear.

When she did, she saw Amelia sweeping across the ground, dirty white gown flying, hands curled like lethal claws. Murder in her eye.

And so did Bryce.

He screamed, a single high-pitched shriek of terror before he began to claw at his throat and gasp for air.

"Don't. For God's sake." Roz tried to push forward, but was slapped back by the pressure of the wind. "Don't kill him. It's enough, it's enough! He can't hurt me. He won't hurt me."

Gravel spat and spun, and the figure in white circled, vulturelike, over the man collapsed on the ground raking his own throat bloody.

"Stop. Amelia, stop. Great-grandmama."

Amelia's head lifted, turned, and her eyes met Roz's.

"I know. I know I come from you. I know you're trying to protect me. It's all right. He won't hurt me now. Please." She pushed forward again, managed two steps with an effort that sucked her breath out of her lungs. "He's nothing!" she shouted. "A bug. But he taught me some important lessons. And I'm going to teach him some hard ones. I want him to live so he pays."

She fought forward another step, holding her hands out, palms up. "There will be payment, I swear to you. For me, and on the blood we share, I swear there'll be payment for you."

He was breathing again, Roz noted, short, harsh breaths, but air was wheezing in and out of Bryce's white, white lips. She crouched down, spoke calmly. "Looks like it wasn't just you and me after all."

The wind began to die, and through it she heard shouts and running feet. When she straightened, Amelia was gone.

She staggered back on rubbery legs as Harper flew around the side of the building two strides ahead of Mitch.

"I'm all right. I'm fine." Though she felt her head circle like a carousel. "But this one might need a little medical attention."

"Fuck him. Mama." Harper grabbed her, feathered his hands over her face. "Jesus Christ. Jesus, he hit you?"

"Sucker punched me, but I got him back, believe me. Got him worse. And Amelia finished him off. I'm all right, baby, I promise you."

"Cops are on their way." She looked over at the tremble in Mitch's voice, and saw from his face it was partly from fear, partly from rage. "Hayley called them on her cell on the way back to get us."

"Good. Good." She was *not* going to faint again. No matter what. "Well, we're just going to press all sorts of charges." She brushed at her hair, then her dress, and noticed a tear on the skirt. "Goddamn it, I bought this especially for today. All *sorts* of charges."

She drew in a breath, struggling with temper and giddiness. "Harper, honey, will you do me a favor and take this worthless piece of trash around front, you and Mitch wait for the police. I don't want to see him for a minute or two. I might finish what Amelia started."

"Let me haul him up first." Mitch bent down, yanked Bryce up on his buckling legs. Then with eyes burning green, he glanced toward Roz.

"Sorry," he said before he plowed his fist into Bryce's face and sent him sprawling again. "Hope you don't mind."

"Not a bit," Roz told him, and despite the churning in her belly found her lips spreading into a wide, wide grin. "Not a damn bit. Harper, you mind taking it from here? I'd like a word with Mitch."

"Happy to." He dragged Bryce off, and shot a look over his shoulder. "Mama, you sure can kick ass."

"Yeah." She drew in a breath, let it out. "If it's all the same to you," she said to Mitch, "I'm just going to sit down right here until I get my feet back under me. That asskicking took something out of me."

"Wait." He peeled off his jacket, spread it on the ground. "No point in messing up that dress any more than it is."

She sat down, then tipped her head onto his shoulder when he joined her. "My hero," she declared.

epilogue

SHE SAT QUIETLY UNTIL HER HEART RATE SLOWED TO normal, until the tangle of nerves, of rage, of reaction in her belly eased a little.

Broken glass glittered in the sunlight. Glass could be replaced, she reminded herself. She'd mourn her flowers, but she'd save some of the wounded, and she'd grow more.

She'd grow an abundance of more.

"How's your hand?" she asked Mitch.

"Fine. Good." He all but spat it out. "He's got a chin like a marshmallow."

"Big strong man." She turned to wrap her arms around him, and didn't mention Mitch's raw, scraped knuckles.

"He must've gone crazy to think he could get away with this."

"A little, I guess. I imagine he planned to be done wrecking my place before the reception was over. He'd figure we'd blame it on kids—or the police would. And all I'd have was a mess on my hands. A man like that doesn't have any respect for women, doesn't believe one can best him."

"One did."

"Well, two. One live one, one dead one."

Since the faintness had passed, she got to her feet, held out a hand for his. "She was like fury, Mitch. Flying over the ground, through tables, and so fast. Wicked, wicked fast," she stated. "He saw her, Bryce saw her coming at him, and he screamed. Then she was choking him. Or, I think, making him believe he was choking. Her hands weren't on him, but she was strangling him."

She rubbed her arms, then clutched gratefully at the lapels of his jacket, drawing them tight when he draped it over her shoulders. She didn't know if her bones would ever be warm again.

"I can't describe it. I can hardly believe it happened. Everything so fast and wild."

"We could hear you shouting," he explained. "You cost both me and your son several years of our lives. I'm going to say this once."

He turned, took the lapels himself to hold her still and facing him. "And you're going to hear it. I respect and admire your steely will, Rosalind, and appreciate your temper and your capability. But the next time you so much as think about taking on some lunatic with a bat on your own, *I'm* doing some ass-kicking. And it's going to be your ass with the bull's-eye painted on it."

She angled her head, studied his face, and saw he meant exactly what he said. Son of a gun.

"You know, if I hadn't already decided on this thing I'm about to ask you, that would've done it. How could I resist a man who lets me fight my own battles, then when the moment's right, steps in and cleans house? After the dust is clear he gives me a good piece of his mind for being an idiot. Which I was, no question, no argument."

"Glad we agree on that."

She took the last step toward him, lifted her arms, and hooked them around his neck. "I really love you."

"I really love you back."

"Then you won't have a problem marrying me."

She felt his body jerk, just a little, just once, then it settled in against her, warm and true. "I don't see a problem with that. You're sure?"

"Couldn't be more sure. I want to go to bed with you at night, wake up with you in the morning. I want to sit and have coffee with you whenever I please. Know you're there for me, and I'm there for you. I want you, Mitch, for the rest of my life."

"I'm ready to get started on that." He kissed her bruised cheek, her uninjured one, her brow, her lips. "I'm going to learn how to tend at least one flower. A rose. My black rose."

She leaned on him. She could lean on him—and trust him to step back when she needed to stand on her own.

Everything inside her calmed, even when she looked at the destruction of what was hers. She would fix it, save what could be saved, accept what couldn't.

She would live her life, and plant her gardens—and walking hand-in-hand with the man she loved, watch both bloom.

And in the gardens of Harper House, someone walked, and raged, and grieved. With mad eyes burning into the candy-blue sky.

Turn the page for a look at

RED LILY

the final book in the
IN THE GARDEN TRILOGY.
Coming in December from Jove Books.

ONE

July, 2005
Harper House

TIRED DOWN THROUGH THE MARROW, HAYLEY YAWNED until her jaw cracked. Lily's head was heavy on her shoulder, but every time she stopped rocking, the baby would squirm and whimper, and those little fingers would clutch at the cotton tank Hayley was sleeping in.

Trying to sleep in, Hayley corrected and murmured hushing noises as she sent the rocker creaking again.

She knew it was somewhere in the vicinity of four in the morning, and she'd already been up twice before to rock and soothe her fretful daughter.

She'd tried—at about the two A.M. mark—to snuggle the baby into bed with her so they'd both get some sleep. But Lily would have nothing but the rocker.

So Hayley rocked and dozed, rocked and yawned, and wondered if she'd ever get eight straight again in this lifetime.

She didn't know how people did it. Especially single mothers. How did they cope? How did they stand up under all the demands on heart, mind, body—wallet?

How would she have managed it all if she'd been completely on her own with Lily? What kind of life would they have had if she had no one to help with the worry, the sheer drudgery, the fun and the foolishness? It was terrifying to think of it.

She'd been so ridiculously optimistic and confident, and *stupid*, she thought now.

Sailing along, she remembered, at nearly six months pregnant, quitting her job, selling most of her things, and packing up that rattletrap car to head out.

God, if she'd known then what she knew now, she'd never have done it.

So maybe it was good she hadn't known. Because she wasn't alone. Closing her eyes, she rested her cheek on Lily's soft, dark hair. She had friends—no, family—people who cared about her and Lily and were willing to help.

They didn't just have a roof over their heads, but the gorgeous roof of Harper House. She had Roz, distant cousin and then only through marriage, who'd offered her a home, a job, a chance. She had Stella, her best friend in the world to talk to, to bitch to, to learn from.

Both Roz and Stella had been single parents—and they'd coped, she reminded herself. They'd better than coped, and Stella had had two young boys to raise alone. Roz *three*.

And here she was wondering how she'd ever manage one, even with all the help only a request away.

There was David, running the house, cooking the meals, and just being wonderfully David. What if she had to cook every night after work? What if she had to do all the shopping, the cleaning, the hauling, the *everything* in addition to holding up her end at her job and caring for a fourteen-month-old baby?

Thank God she didn't have to find out.

There was Logan, Stella's gorgeous new husband, who

was willing to tinker around with her car when it acted up. And Stella's little guys, Gavin and Luke, who not only liked to play with Lily but were giving Hayley a hint of the sort of things she had coming in the next few years.

There was Mitch, so smart and sweet, and he liked to scoop Lily up and cart her around on his shoulders while she laughed. He'd be officially here all the time now, she thought, once he and Roz got back from their honeymoon.

It had been so nice, so much fun, to watch both Stella and Roz fall in love. She'd felt a part of it all—the excitement, the changes, the expansion of her new family circle.

Of course, Roz's marriage meant she'd have to stop dragging her feet on finding a place of her own. Newlyweds were entitled to privacy.

She wished there was a place close by. Even on the estate. Like the carriage house. Harper's house. She sighed a little as she rubbed a hand over Lily's back.

Harper Ashby. Rosalind Harper Ashby's firstborn, and one delicious piece of eye candy. Of course she didn't think about him that way. Much. He was a friend, a co-worker, and her baby girl's first crush. By all appearances, that love affair was mutual.

She yawned again, as lulled as the baby by the rhythm of the rocking and the early morning quiet.

Harper was, well, just flat-out amazing with Lily. Patient and funny, easy and loving. Secretly she thought of him as Lily's surrogate father—without the benefits of smoochies with Lily's mother.

Sometimes she played pretend—and what was the harm in that?—and the surrogate part of surrogate father didn't apply. The smoochies did. After all, what red-blooded American girl—currently very sex-deprived girl—wouldn't fantasize now and again about the tall, dark, and ridiculously handsome type, especially when he came along with a killer grin, heart-melting brown eyes, and a pinchable butt?

Not that she'd ever pinched it. But in theory.

Plus he was completely smart. He knew everything there was to know about plants and flowers. She loved to watch him working in the grafting house at In the Garden—the way his hands held a knife or tied raffia.

He was teaching her, and she appreciated it. Appreciated it too much to indulge herself and take a nice hungry bite out of him.

But imagining doing it didn't hurt a thing.

She eased the rocker to a stop, held her breath, and waited. Lily's back continued to rise and fall steadily under her hand.

Thank God.

She got up slowly, moving toward the crib with the stealth and purpose of a woman making a prison break. With her arms aching, her head musty with fatigue, she leaned over the crib and gently, inch by inch, laid Lily on the mattress.

Even as she draped the blanket over her, Lily began to stir. Her head popped up and she began wailing.

"Oh, Lily, please, come on, baby." Hayley patted, rubbed, swaying on her feet. "Ssh, now, come on. Give your mama a little break."

The patting seemed to work—as long as she kept her hand on Lily's back, the little head stayed down. So Hayley sank to the floor and stuck her arm through the crib slats. And patted. And patted.

And drifted off to sleep.

IT WAS THE SINGING THAT WOKE HER. HER ARM was asleep, and stayed that way when her eyes opened. The room was cold; the section of the floor where she sat beside the crib a square of ice. Her arm prickled from shoulder to fingertip as she shifted, keeping a protective hand on Lily's back.

The figure in the gray dress sat in the rocker, softly singing the old-fashioned lullaby. Her eyes met Hayley's, but she continued to sing, continued to rock.

The jolt of shock cleared the mustiness from Hayley's head and had her heart taking one hard leap into her throat.

Just what did you say to a ghost you hadn't seen for several weeks? she wondered. Hey, how are you? Welcome home? Just what was the proper response, especially when the ghost in question was totally whacked.

Her skin was slicked with cold when Hayley pushed slowly to her feet so she could stand between the rocker and the crib. Just in case. Because it felt as if a few thousand needles were lodged in her arm, she cradled it against her body, rubbing it briskly.

Note all the details, she reminded herself. Mitch would want all the details.

She looked pretty calm for a psychotic ghost, Hayley decided. Calm and sad, the way she had the first time Hayley had seen her. But she'd also seen her with crazed, bulging eyes.

"Um. She had to get some shots yesterday. Inoculations. She's always fussy the night after she gets them. But I think she's settled down now. In time to get up again in a couple of hours, so she'll probably be cranky for the babysitter until she gets her nap. But . . . but she should sleep now, so you could go."

The figure faded away seconds before the singing did.

DAVID FIXED HER BLUEBERRY PANCAKES FOR BREAK-fast. She'd told him not to cook for her or Lily while Roz and Mitch were gone, but he always did. Since he looked so cute fussing in the kitchen, she didn't try very hard to discourage him.

Besides, the pancakes were awesome.

"You've been looking a little peaky." David gave her cheek a pinch, then repeated the gesture on Lily to make her giggle.

"Haven't been sleeping much lately. Had a visitor last night." She shook her head when his eyebrows rose and his mouth curved into a leer. "Not a man—too sad for my bad luck. Amelia."

Amusement faded immediately, to be replaced by concern as he slid into the breakfast nook across from her. "Was there trouble? Are you all right?"

"She was just sitting in the rocker, singing. And when I told her Lily was fine, that she could go, she did. It was completely benign."

"Maybe she's settled down again. We can hope. Have you been worried about that?" He took a careful study of her face, noted the smudges under the soft blue eyes, the pallor beneath the carefully applied blush on her cheeks. "Is that why you haven't been sleeping?"

"Some, I guess. Things were pretty wild around here for a few months. Our gooses were constantly getting bumped. Now this lull. It's almost creepier."

"You've got Daddy David right down here." He reached over to pat her hand, his long, concert-pianist's fingers giving it a little extra rub. "And Roz and Mitch will be back today. The house won't feel so big and empty."

She let out a long breath, relieved. "You felt that way, too. I didn't want to say, didn't want you to feel like you weren't enough company or something. 'Cause you are."

"You, too, my treasure. But we've gotten spoiled, haven't we? Had a houseful for a year around here." He glanced toward the empty seats at the table. "I miss those kids."

"Aw, you softie. We still see them, everybody, all the time, but it's weird, having everything so quiet."

As if she understood, Lily launched her sip-cup so that it slapped the center island and thudded on the floor.

"Atta girl," David told her.

"And you know what else?" Hayley rose to retrieve the cup. She was tall and lanky, and much to her disappointment, her breasts had reverted to their pre-pregnancy size. She thought of them as an A-minus cup. "I think I'm getting in some sort of mood. I don't mean rut, exactly, because I love working at the nursery, and I was just thinking last night—when Lily woke up for the millionth time—how lucky I am to be here, to be able to have all these people in our lives." She spread her arms, let them fall. "But, I don't know, David, I feel sort of . . . blah."

"Need shopping therapy."

She grinned and got a washcloth to wipe Lily's syrupy face. "It is the number-one cure for almost everything. But I think I want a change. Something bigger than new shoes."

Deliberately, he widened his eyes, let his jaw go slack. "There's something bigger?"

"I think I'm going to cut my hair. Do you think I should cut my hair?"

"Hmm." He cocked his head, studied her with his handsome blue eyes. "It's gorgeous hair, that glossy true black. But I absolutely loved it the way you wore it when you first moved here."

"Really?"

"All those different lengths. Tousled, casual, kicky. Sexy."

"Well . . ." She ran her hand down it. She'd grown it out, nearly to her shoulders. An easy length to pull back for work or motherhood. And maybe that was just the problem. She'd started taking the easy way because she'd stopped finding the time or making the effort to worry about how she looked. She wiped Lily off and freed her from the high chair so she could wander around the kitchen. "Maybe I will then. Maybe."

"And toss in the new shoes, sweetie. They never fail."

IN HIGH SUMMER BUSINESS SLOWED AT THE GARDEN center. It never trickled down too far at In the Garden, but in July the heady late-winter-through-spring rush was long over. Wet heat smothered west Tennessee, and only the most avid of gardeners would suffer through it to pump new life into their beds.

Taking advantage of the lull, and her mood, Hayley wheedled a salon appointment, and an extra hour off from Stella.

When she drove back to work after her extended lunch break, it was with a new 'do, *two* new pair of shoes, and a much happier attitude.

Trust David, she decided.

She loved In the Garden. Most days she didn't feel as if she was going to work at all. There couldn't be a better quality in a job than that, in her opinion.

She enjoyed just looking at the pretty white building that looked more like someone's well-tended home than a business, with the seasonal beds spreading out from its porch and the pots full of colorful blooms by its door.

She liked the industry across the wide gravel lot—the stacks of peat and mulch, the pavers and landscape timbers. The greenhouses that were full of plants and promises, the storage buildings.

When it was busy with customers, winding along the paths, pulling wagons or flatbeds full of plants and pots—everyone full of news or plans—it was more like a small village than a retail space.

And she was a part of it all.

She stepped in and did a turn for Ruby, the white-headed clerk who manned the counter.

"Don't you look sassy," Ruby commented.

"I feel sassy." She ran her fingers through her short shaggy hair, then let it fall again. "I haven't done anything new with my hair in a *year*. More. I almost forgot what it was like to sit in a beauty parlor and have somebody do me."

"Things do slide with a new baby. How's our best girl doing?"

"Fussy last night after her shots. But she bounced back this morning. My butt was dragging. Pumped now though." To prove it, she flexed her arms to show little bumps of biceps.

"Good thing. Stella wants everything watered, and I do mean everything. And we're waiting on a big delivery of new planters. They'll need to be stickered and shelved once they come in."

"I'm your girl."

She started outside in the thick, drowsy heat, soaking the bedding plants, the annuals and perennials who'd yet to find a home. They made her think of those awkward kids in school who never got picked for the team. As a result, she had a soft spot for them and wished she had a place where she could dig them into the soil, let them bloom, let them find their potential.

One day she would have a place. She'd plant gardens, take what she'd learned here and put it to use. Make something beautiful, something special. There would have to be lilies, naturally. Red lilies, like the ones Harper brought to her when she was in labor with Lily. A big, splashy pool of red lilies, bold and fragrant, that would come back year after year and remind her how lucky she was.

Sweat trickled down the back of her neck, and water dampened her canvas skids. The gentle spray annoyed the gang of bees covering the sedum. So, come back when I'm finished, she thought as they flew off with an annoyed buzz. We're all after the same thing here.

She moved slowly, half dreaming, down the tables holding the picked-over stock.

And if one day she had a garden, there would be Lily playing on the grass. With a puppy, she decided. There should be a puppy, all fat and soft and frisky. If she was able to have all that, couldn't she add a man? Someone who loved her and Lily, someone funny and smart who made her heart beat just a little faster when he looked at her?

He could be handsome. What was the point of a fantasy if the guy wasn't great-looking? Tall—he could be tall—with good shoulders and long legs. Brown eyes, deep delicious brown, and lots of thick dark hair she could get her hands into. Good cheekbones, the kind you just wanted to nibble your way along until you got to that strong, sexy mouth. And then—

"Jesus, Hayley, you're drowning that coreopsis."

She jerked, whipping the sprayer, then with a little yip of distress whipped it back again. But not before the water hit Harper dead on.

Gut shot, she thought, torn between embarrassment and inappropriate giggles. He looked down at his soaked shirt and jeans with a kind of grim resignation.

"Got a license for that thing?"

"I'm sorry! I'm so sorry. But you shouldn't sneak up behind me that way."

"I didn't sneak anywhere. I walked."

His voice was aggravated, but so Memphian, she thought, where she knew hers hit twang when she was excited or upset. "Well, walk louder next time. I really am sorry though. I guess my mind was wandering."

"This kind of heat, it's easy for the mind to wander then

lie down to take a nap." He pulled the wet shirt away from his belly. His eyes crinkled at the corners when he narrowed them. "What did you do to your hair?"

"What?" Instinctively she reached up, pulled her fingers through it. "I had it cut. Don't you like it?"

"Yeah, sure. It's fine."

Her finger itched on the trigger of the sprayer. "Please, stop. That kind of flattery'll just go to my head."

He smiled at her. He had such a great smile—sort of slow, so that it shifted the angles of his face and lit up in those deep, dark brown eyes—she nearly forgave him.

"I'm heading home, for a bit anyway. Mama's back."

"They're back? How are they? Did they have a good time? And you don't know yet because you haven't been home. Tell them I can't wait to see them, and that everything's fine over here, and Roz shouldn't worry and come over and start in working when she's barely walked in the door. And—"

He cocked his hip, hooked a thumb in the front pocket of his ancient jeans. "Should I be writing any of this down?"

"Oh, go on then." But she laughed as she waved him away. "I'll tell them myself."

"See you later."

He walked off, the man of her daydreams, dripping a little.

She really had to get her mind off Harper, she warned herself. Get it off and keep it off. He wasn't for her, and she knew it. She walked over to give the potted shrubs and climbers a good soak.

She wasn't even sure she wanted anybody to be for her—right yet, anyway. Lily was her number-one priority, and after Lily came her job. She wanted her baby happy, healthy, and secure. And she wanted to learn more, do more at the nursery. The more she learned, the less it would be a job, and the more it would be a career.

Pulling her weight was fine, but she wanted to do more.

After Lily, her work, and the family she'd made here, came the fascinating and spooky task of identifying Amelia, the Harper Bride—and laying her to rest.

Most of that fell to Mitch. He was the genealogist, and along with Stella the most organized mind of the bunch. And wasn't it cool that he and Roz had found each other, fallen in love, because Roz had hired him to research the family tree to try to find where Amelia fit in? Not that Amelia had cared for the falling in love part. Boy, she'd been a stone bitch about it.

She might get mean again, too, Hayley thought. Now that Roz and Mitch were married and Mitch was living at Harper House. She'd been quiet for awhile, but it didn't mean she'd stay quiet.

If and when the whirlwind resumed, Hayley intended to be ready for it.